GW01236558

ROCK CRUSH AND ROLL

HUNTER SNOW

Rock Crush and Roll
Copyright © 2023 by Hunter Snow

All rights reserved. No part of this publication may be reproduced, distributed, or transmitted in any form or by any means, including photocopying, recording, or other electronic or mechanical methods, without the prior written permission of the author, except in the case of brief quotations embodied in critical reviews and certain other non-commercial uses permitted by copyright law.

Tellwell Talent
www.tellwell.ca

ISBN
978-1-7390476-0-3 (Paperback)
978-1-7390476-2-7 (eBook)

TABLE OF CONTENTS

For CRT without explanation.

CHAPTER 1

Tyler's phone vibrated early on Sunday morning but she was already awake, worrying about the bands she managed and, really, life in general. The music industry was more competitive than college basketball during the month of March. It was also never-ending and without a champion.

"What's wrong?" she asked, as there was clearly a problem. Kim wouldn't be calling at this hour to shoot the shit about the weather.

"Sorry, dude." The tour manager called everyone "dude" as a matter of principle.

She groaned. "Let me guess . . ."

"Josh forgot his passport." Kim's voice showed no sign of surprise. It was commonplace for musicians—at least the ones they worked with—to forget something.

"Drummers." Tyler rubbed her eyes, not ready to start her day and definitely not with this news. "They're the worst." She meant men in general, but she didn't need to explain that to her best friend. They'd both been single for eons.

"Yeah. I know, right?" Kim slurped some sort of beverage. "But it's my fault. It's my responsibility to check."

"He's an adult, isn't he? I mean, in theory." She threw back the covers with purpose and kicked herself onto the hardwood floor. "Hold on, I'm putting you on speaker while I get dressed."

"Josh doesn't even have a driver's license, or he could've used it to board the plane."

"That's probably a good thing."

"At least you're only handling their day-to-day . . ." Kim's voice trailed off into the ether. "Shit. These earbud thingies keep slipping. Dude, I can't believe Sebastien agreed to sign these fucking hellions."

The sound of her boss's name before coffee was almost too much to bear. She yanked the elastic band from her topknot and held a wreath full of hair. "Fucker pawned them off on me, didn't he? I'm sure he didn't tell the Westgrays they'd be dealing with me. I'd never willingly manage them."

"What's that stupid thing he's always saying?"

"More pucks on the net."

"Yeah. Sebastien's a fucking idiot." An airport announcement blared over the speakers. "So is Josh, for that matter. I'm looking right at him. *Unbelievable.* He's sprawled across a whole row of seats while people are standing. I'd make him go home but our flight leaves in, like, two hours."

"Where are his roommates?"

"He's tried calling, texting, but they're probably sleeping."

More like passed out. Josh's roommates were party animals— not that she'd seen animals partying outside of a zoo or a dog park.

"Fucking hell," Tyler said after a beat.

"Sorry." Kim had obviously screwed up so she didn't need to rub it in. "I've been too easy on them. No more Mr. Nice Guy."

"That's a great song. I love Alice Cooper. Hey, who knew all that babysitting I did as a teenager was practice for coddling musicians. But seriously, don't worry about it. I'm more annoyed than anything. Does he at least know where his passport is?"

"He thinks it's in the kitchen. Oh, and the side door's open— more like broken—but text if you can't find it."

"Will do. I'll let you know when I'm five minutes out."

Tyler twisted her hair back into a topknot and checked the time. She glanced at her Shih Tzu rescue as he slept at the foot of her bed. Sneaking out of her room wasn't an option since Rory's hearing was almost god-like. Plus he clung to her like plastic wrap because his previous family had surrendered him to a local shelter, simply because he didn't bark. It hardly made him defective. She wanted a little buddy, not a guard dog to protect her.

"Hi Ror!" Did everyone give their dog a nickname? Rory Bear, Rorster, and Ror-Ror were her favorite things to call him.

With a jerk the dog lifted his head, metal tags clinking from his collar. Rory looked at her as if to say, *What the hell, Mommy?*

"Time to get up!"

With no time to spare she buckled Rory into the passenger seat of her rusted-out SUV. The truck's manufacturer had named it "Radiant Red," but now "Lackluster Red" seemed more appropriate.

Droplets of water speckled the windshield so she turned on the wipers. People called it "Rain City" for a reason. It fucking poured here. But the worst was yet to come since it was only the end of September. Tyler had lived in Vancouver for over a decade but her home was still in Winnipeg.

As the saying went, you could take the girl out of Manitoba . . .

But no one had ever said that.

Tyler zipped along Commercial Drive, pretending that she was a Formula 1 driver. She'd binged *Drive to Survive* on Netflix last summer, and now she was obsessed with all the teams, but she only cheered for Mercedes. Lewis Hamilton was her number one, and whenever he had pole position she thought of something sexual.

She parked in the driveway of Josh's house and left the engine running. Having a shoddy alternator, she couldn't run the risk of her truck not starting.

The *Stranger Things* music played in her head as she inched the door open and stepped into the kitchen. *Gross.* The stench of wet cigarettes permeated the air and beer splatter covered the walls. Pinching her nose, she searched for the drummer's passport.

How do people live like this? She stepped over a graveyard of empty beer cans. *Ah-ha!* The evidence of beer pong was left on display. They'd lined up red Solo cups like bowling pins on both ends of the kitchen table.

She spied a dark blue booklet with a gold emblem under the mess, and with a tug she unstuck Josh's passport from the table and held it like Rory's poop bag.

Twenty minutes later Tyler drove up the ramp to the airport's Departures. *Thank god.* Kim was already at the drop-off marker, her bright pink hair standing out like a flamingo.

Tyler lowered the passenger-side window as she approached the curb.

"Dude, their flight just got delayed an hour." Kim reached for Josh's passport and smiled at Rory, asleep in the shape of a neck pillow. He looked like a miniature panda with his black and white markings.

"Of course it did." It was a running joke around the office that Air Canada wasn't happy unless you were unhappy. "Rory, wake up. It's Kim!"

"Hey, buddy," Kim whispered, and the dog thumped his tail against the seat. Rory liked everyone but he played favorites with his mom's bestie. "Any plans for today?"

Tyler checked her watch. "Just working from home."

Kim rolled back the rim of her coffee cup. "You're supposed to be working *for* the weekend, not on it."

"Says the person going on tour."

"Slim pickings out there." Kim made a pouty face and chucked her cup into the recycling can. "Believe me, the Westgrays aren't on my top-ten list."

"I miss Letterman." She picked at the worn vinyl on her steering wheel. "The Westgrays are super high maintenance. You're going to have to burp and feed them."

"I draw the line at bathing them." Kim's dark brown eyes seemed to lighten when she laughed. "Anyway, enough about them. Dude, if you ever want to meet someone you'll have to put yourself back out there."

Online dating was simply out of the question. Last year, while she was standing in line at a coffee shop, she'd watched in amazement as a guy who was barely a five swiped left on girls who were tens. What hope did any woman have if anything less than perfection was the standard.

Tyler grinned. "I know for a fact you haven't had a date this year."

Kim covered a yawn with the back of her hand. "True, but I don't want a baby—or a husband."

"You're twenty-seven. There's lots of time."

"Try telling that to my mother." Mrs. Tanaka didn't approve of her daughter's line of work or her pink hair. Kim had often complained about being a child of hardworking immigrants. Her parents had expected her to be married with children by now, not telling bands what time they had to meet in the hotel lobby.

Tyler tapped her lips. "You know, I'm thinking about having a kid on my own."

"Like, with a sperm donor or sex with a stranger?"

"Shh!" She held her index finger to her mouth and whispered, "I'm thinking about freezing my eggs, but it's ten grand."

"Fuck it." Kim shrugged one shoulder. "Just go to the Roxy."

"Hard pass." She gave Rory a boop on his nose. "Even the bartenders are musicians there. No fucking thanks." The Roxy Cabaret was famous for last-call hookups and morning regrets. It was no secret that hockey teams and touring artists always made a stop there. "Shit! I forgot to tell you . . . my indie band got that opening slot."

5

"I heard! Those guys are all over Insta. I love that name—Yestown." Kim tapped Josh's passport against the truck's windowsill. "Any last words of wisdom for these knuckleheads?"

Tyler shook her head once. "I don't have that kind of time." She sat upright and gripped the steering wheel like she was driving through a whiteout. "Tell Josh not to ask for any favors. He's on my shit list."

Kim nodded, stepping back from the curb. "I'll tell him to send you flowers."

"He shouldn't waste his money. I saw his house." She honked twice and Rory shook his head, ears flapping. "Have a safe trip. And text when you land."

Her babysitting job was a permanent position . . . but without benefits.

Driving home from the airport Tyler sucked in a breath of air. *Shit, the invoices!* The office had been busier than usual during the week and it had fallen off her list of priorities. With it being month-end, she needed to check it off her to-do list before the morning.

"A quick detour then home," she told Rory, scratching him behind the ears. "Who wants to go to the office?"

Rory wagged his tail.

The Sebastien Dumas Management office was in the sketchiest part of town. Last month several random stabbings had taken place in the Downtown Eastside, putting everyone's safety in jeopardy.

Tyler parked in the office's secured garage and climbed two flights of stairs. She unclenched the keys from her knuckles and unlocked the door, punching in the alarm code: 2-1-1-2. Once inside, Rory sniffed around in search of his colleagues but the office was as empty as Rogers Arena during the playoffs.

Tyler needed a coffee fix so she dropped off her shit in her office. It would take a cup the size of her head to get her brain working properly.

She headed toward the kitchen, Rory's collar jangling as he trotted along beside her.

"Come on, buddy." She ran ahead of him but he blasted off in a full sprint.

Fast fucker.

Rory waited in the kitchen—the "cookie room." He demanded one for finishing first in the race to the kitchen.

Once cookie time was over she scooped five tablespoons of generic coffee into a paper filter and poured tap water into the dispenser. Sebastien cheaped out on everything and proudly called himself a miser. The letterhead read "SDM," because it used less ink than "Sebastien Dumas Management."

She poured a cup of coffee while singing Dolly Parton's "9 to 5" poorly, opened the fridge, and searched for a container of soy milk with her name on it. She'd bought it herself since SDM didn't provide employees with "extras."

But there it sat in the blue bin: empty, crumpled, and disregarded.

Fucking interns. At least they'd recycled it.

Back at her desk with a cup of bitter black coffee, Tyler powered on her computer with confidence. As a rule she returned her messages within the hour, but any longer posed a problem. There were only two reasons for her being unresponsive: the location didn't have Wi-Fi or she was dead in a ditch.

You shouldn't be texting while driving.

"Where to start?" She smiled at Rory but he couldn't help even if he'd wanted to. She could barely help herself since math wasn't her strong suit.

Last year, when their receptionist quit without notice, the administrative duties fell into Tyler's portfolio. Sebastien had told her that she'd learn from the experience, but it was just a lame excuse for more free labor. She'd already been there for fourteen years and was ready to move on, but her boss had threatened to ruin her career, and he kept promises if it meant hurting people.

Of course, her dad had warned her about Sebastien's antics before she'd started her internship at SDM. Tyler's dad, Paul "Bert" Robertson, had known Sebastien since the early Winnipeg club years. Back in the day they were competitors of sorts, although the best bands hired her dad to play lead guitar while her boss took rhythm guitar gigs with the duds. And now that Sebastien had the upper hand by employing his former rival's daughter, he was loving every minute of it. Plus it put Bert in his debt for hiring her after the internship was over, and favors were his currency. Sebastien wasn't "good prairie folk" like the Robertsons. He was a Francophone from Quebec City, and problems came with the territory.

An hour later Rory perked up from his dog bed, alerting Tyler that he'd heard something. A burglar would have been preferable to Sebastien since the thief was sure to be quiet, unlike her boss, her nemesis.

A groan rumbled from the back of her throat as she rolled her chair out of the way and followed her furry friend down the hallway. She laughed at how Rory's bum wiggled when his little legs hit the carpet.

"Can I help you?" she asked, approaching the reception area.

"Hi," a cute guy said with a smile. He came up to Tyler's eye level and wore an oversized black beanie and dark-rimmed glasses. "It's me. Cary."

I'm an idiot.

She hadn't recognized Cary Kingston, the most famous rock star on the planet. Of course, he wasn't always famous; Sebastien had discovered him at a dive bar in Winnipeg more than twenty years earlier. Her boss had mortgaged his house, rolling the dice on the eighteen-year-old guitar virtuoso, beating the house with consecutive gold records.

"I'm sorry. The glasses threw me." She hugged him and it kicked her olfactory memory into gear. While she was interning she'd met Cary, her high school crush, backstage at one of his concerts, and the lingering scent of Calvin Klein's Obsession had stayed with her for days afterwards. The person who came up with the name of the fragrance: a genius.

"No worries," he said, laughing it off like it wasn't a big deal. His deep, raspy voice was one in a million, maybe a billion. "I wear them on purpose."

"What are you doing here?" She twisted her mouth to the side. "Aren't you supposed to be in Chicago or something?"

He shrugged. "I had a day off, so I came here to sort out some business."

Cary lived in Los Angeles—more specifically, Malibu—but he kept a place in Vancouver because he was Canadian by birth. His hometown, Brandon, Manitoba, was two-and-a-half hours west of Winnipeg. They call Brandon the "Wheat City," and everyone eats gluten there.

A sneeze drew their attention to the floor, where Rory lay on his back like a sun-tanner in Ibiza.

"Rory!" Cary dropped to his knees and scratched the dog's belly. "Who's a good boy?"

"You're embarrassing me, Rory." Tyler rested her hands on her hips, aware that millions of women would have gladly traded places with her dog, including herself. "Don't you have any shame?"

"No, Mom," Cary answered for him. "Hold on." He grabbed his phone. "I want to take his picture. He looks like a centerfold model."

"My angel the centerfold."

"I'm surprised you know that song."

"I know a lot of old songs, including yours."

"Funny." He winked at her and she tried not to die. Was he still dating Emma what's-her-name? It didn't matter. It's not like he was going to marry her. Cary had been on the Most Eligible Bachelors list for twenty years and counting.

"Is there any mail for me?" he joked.

It wasn't a serious question. Obviously his fans loved sending him things. Some of the letters and gifts were weird, others obscene. After the unwanted items didn't sell on eBay, Sebastien donated them to charity for the tax receipt.

"Knock yourself out." She gestured to the Mount Everest of fan mail. "There's coffee in the kitchen. Help yourself."

"I've had the office coffee," he complained. "How about going to Artigiano?"

"Excuse me? Our coffee isn't good enough for you?"

"No." He pulled down his beanie. "It's fine."

She laughed, tightening her topknot, looking for any reason to leave. "It tastes like shit. Let's get out of here."

After Tyler set the office alarm she locked the door, checking it behind them. If only she'd worn something other than her Skull Skates hoodie and black leggings, but who the fuck knew she'd be running into Cary Kingston?

The clouds were threatening, gray and low to the ground, as Tyler, Cary and Rory walked down the street toward the coffee shop. He pointed to the pastel-colored building on the northwest corner of Hastings and Cambie.

"I love the Dominion Building. Look at the ornamental detail and arched windows." He raised his phone and snapped a picture. "Pretty impressive for the early nineteen-hundreds."

"I suppose." Her voice came out unsure. "I've never noticed it."

"How's that possible?" His gaze bounced to the roof. "It used to be the tallest building in the British Empire."

"I don't know." She shrugged, thinning her lips until they disappeared. "I guess I forget to look up."

When they arrived at the coffee shop only a sliver of light shone onto the patio, so no one was sitting outside. Vancouverites didn't do well in cold weather, unless it was in Whistler.

"Let's grab a table out here," Tyler suggested. Being seen in public with Cary wasn't her idea of a quiet Sunday morning.

"I'll go in," he offered as his lenses darkened over his bright hazel eyes.

She only agreed to let him go inside because she couldn't leave Rory on his own. He'd go anywhere with anyone at any time.

"Thanks." She handed him a ten-dollar bill. "I'll have a latte, please, with soy milk."

"I've got it." He laughed, waving at her money like it was worthless. But she handed it to him again and he took it begrudgingly.

Tyler found a table against the building for a little more privacy. Rory plopped himself on his butt under it, facing the door as if waiting for Cary. While she and Rory waited for the man they were both a bit obsessed with, Tyler opened her phone to see if she had any messages.

Ten minutes later she glanced at her watch. Rory was now lying with his head propped between his paws, looking longingly at the door. Being the best coffee shop in Vancouver, Artigiano was always busy, but the wait seemed to be longer than usual so she peeked inside.

Cary was signing autographs. How could she have thought otherwise?

Busted.

He caught her staring at him and she smiled shyly. Nodding once, she flashed a thumbs-up.

A few moments later Cary appeared holding two large ceramic cups. Rory popped up on all fours, entire body wagging in excitement.

"Sorry about that." He handed her the latte and bent to ruffle Rory's fur in the process.

Lucky dog.

She tried not to be jealous as Cary showered him with affection.

"Thanks." She cradled the cup using lotus hands. "No worries." She frowned at a gaggle of women who'd brazenly sat at the table next to them. "You're good with your fans. The Kingers."

He shrugged, ducking almost bashfully as he lowered into the chair. "It's my job," he said. "No fans, no career."

"Doesn't it bother you?" She scrunched her nose in revulsion. "Being famous, I mean."

"Bother me?" He shook his head. "Absolutely not. Fame just means more people know me."

"Being famous is my worst nightmare." She paused and raised a finger, thinking of something worse. "Along with Burning Man. Too many hippies."

"There's a reason I'm on the road a hundred days a year."

She nodded. "Sebastien's always saying, 'As long as Cary's on tour we're keeping the lights on around here.'"

His gaze steadied on her face. "I tour for my fans, not Sebastien."

Yeah. Fuck Sebastien.

"Hi, Cary!" The gaggle shouted in unison. He twisted around and gave them a royal wave, and Tyler glared in their direction.

"So, what's going on at the office?" he asked, not letting on that people were taking his picture.

"Oh, the usual." Like Sebastien yelling at the interns and anyone else within earshot on the regular. Everyone in the music industry called him "Sebastard," but he couldn't have cared less about his bad reputation. As an afterthought she said, "Nothing much new around here."

"Have you heard anything good lately?"

"The new Billie Eilish is pretty dope."

Did I just say dope?

"I mean, any new bands?"

"Oh my god, there's this band from Toronto I'm in love with!" She played one of their songs in her head. Tyler had inherited an incredible ear for music but not the talent to play it.

Cary smiled at the gaggle as they took selfies like Kardashians. "Are we signing them?"

She rolled her eyes. "It's a girl band."

"And?" He took off his glasses and rubbed his eyes with his wrists.

"When was the last time Sebastien managed a female artist?" On top of everything her boss was a proper misogynist. "Like, never."

Cary counted on his fingers. "Yeah, I guess you're right." He blew on his coffee before taking a sip. "Anything else you're listening to?"

"There's this indie band I'm managing myself, but Sebastien doesn't think they're any good." At first she was pissed off that her boss didn't believe in Yestown's music, but after some thought she decided that she was better off without his interference. As the band's manager of record she was going to break them—with or without him. "I'd take on that girl band too, but I haven't seen them play yet."

"What kind of music are you looking for?" he asked.

"Anything, as long as it's good."

"I listen to everything." He adjusted his glasses. "Well, just about."

"Polka?" She laughed.

"I *wish* my album covers looked that cool."

She nearly spit out her coffee. Polka album covers were always cheesy, almost to the point of being good. "It's all about the song, don't you think?"

"Absolutely. What's your favorite record?"

"I couldn't pick just one. It's like choosing your favorite kid. I mean, I'd imagine." She leaned forward, drawing her eyebrows together. "Do you have a favorite?"

"Anything by the Humbler."

As they continued chatting the coffee shop patrons closed in on them like zombies in Michael Jackson's *Thriller* video.

"It's getting crowded," she said, her annoyance with the noisy intrusions growing.

Cary turned his head to the fans and back again. "Want to get out of here?"

"Yes!" She jumped out of her seat. "We can head back to the office and load your mail into my truck, and I'll drive you home."

Regret washed over Tyler as soon as the words left her mouth. He didn't need a ride from her. He drove around in limos, not old jalopies. She'd let him off the hook from feeling obligated to ride in her truck once they got back to the office.

After Tyler grabbed the mail from the office they walked down the stairs to SDM's parking garage. She pointed to the car parked beside hers. "My next one's going to be electric." Right now she couldn't afford to buy anything newer. "Something quieter. Are you sure you don't want to call for a car?" While they'd collected the mail she'd ruefully revealed that her truck was a little beat up and suggested maybe he'd want to call for a car to take him and his mail back to his house, but he'd firmly declined.

Cary heaved the mailbags into the trunk and climbed into the passenger seat. "Nope. This is great. Need a hand?" he asked, noticing her wrestling with the dog.

"I'm good." But she wasn't good at all. Rory was squirming around like a worm on a fishing hook, and she had nothing to bait him with. As she tried to buckle him into the back seat, his harness slipped through her fingers and he hurdled the console, jumping into Cary's lap and licking his face. "Rory Robertson! Get down!"

"It's fine." Cary held the miniature panda on his lap.

Rory loved riding shotgun.

Thankfully her truck started after one turn of the key, so she headed south toward Yaletown on Richard's Street, driving slower than the speed limit because her two-million-dollar insurance policy wasn't enough coverage with Cary sitting next to her.

He pointed to the window. "I live just around the corner."

She tapped on the steering wheel. "Hey, have you heard the new Arkells song?"

Cary turned his head. "Who?"

"Arkells." She annunciated clearly. "Their new song."

"Arkells?"

"Oh my god, Cary!" She took her eyes off the road for a split second. "They're my favorite band. Banger after banger."

"I'll check it out. You can turn at the next left."

"I know where you live. I have keys to your penthouse."

"You do, do you?" He pushed back his beanie and smirked.

She had to admit that it sounded a little creepy. "I mean, the office—the office has keys to your penthouse. For emergencies." She'd left his deliveries with the building's concierge so there was no reason for her to be up there.

"Relax." He gave her shoulder a squeeze. "I was joking."

I'm never washing this hoodie.

When they arrived at their destination she hung her head and breathed audibly in relief. Sebastien would have murdered her in cold blood if anything had happened to him.

Cary stepped out of the truck and buckled Rory into the passenger seat. "There you go, little buddy."

She gave her dog a cool stare before cranking her neck toward the rear. "Do you need any help back there?"

"I've got it, thanks." He hoisted the bags out of the SUV with little effort. "I'm buried with paperwork today and I might do some writing later." He walked around the vehicle to the driver's side window and gave her a charming smile filled with a little heat. "How about meeting me for a drink later? Around ten? I have some checks for Sebastien." He pointed. "There's a place across the street we can meet at."

"Sure." She gulped down the air bubble lodged in her throat. "Sounds good."

Cary flashed his famous smile. "Thanks for the ride. Looking forward to tonight."

What did I get myself into?

CARY

"Wow," Cary said as the SUV drove away. The moment he'd met Tyler all those years earlier he'd liked her immediately. Unfortunately, every time he ran into her she was all business, not impressed with him in the least.

He shouldn't have said anything about the checks for Sebastien because that made it sound like a business meeting. But it was awkward to ask someone you work with on a date. Hell, it could even be considered harassment nowadays.

Tonight he'd pull out all the stops and reserve the entire restaurant. She'd seemed a little annoyed with the fans at the coffee shop, and it was the only way to get to know her better without constantly being interrupted.

Cary's phone vibrated and he answered in a jovial tone, "Hey, Vegas!"

"The coast is clear," Vegas said, not big on salutations or small talk. His tour manager was a man of few words but Cary knew exactly what he meant. Emma had been on her way to Chicago to surprise him when he booked—or had asked Vegas to book—a flight to Vancouver, avoiding the drama that accompanied her visits. Emma Turner, a B-list actress, was an insufferable diva. They'd been on and off for years, but mostly off, depending on who you were talking to.

"Thanks for taking care of that." Cary dropped the mailbags by his feet and ripped off his beanie in frustration. "I've told her a million times, we're not getting back together."

A brief pause followed.

"You good?" Vegas asked.

"I'm great." The building's concierge opened the door for Cary. "I'll see you tomorrow."

"See you, man."

Had Cary been stupid to think that Emma was different than the other women he'd dated? Absolutely. Emma was an angel at first, but that's how all demons started out. Their relationship had been one of convenience, mostly on her end. The more tabloids she was in, the more she worked. It wasn't entirely his fault that he didn't see it coming—she'd fooled him with her finishing-school manners and Southern sweet talk.

Tyler seemed different. In a lot of ways. One, she'd left her house without wearing makeup—something Emma would never do. Two, she appreciated music—and good music, too! Cary loved a simple melody more than life itself, and he wanted someone who had the same passion for music that he did. In fact, he'd watched the Peter Jackson Beatles documentary on a loop the first week it came out.

When he was a young boy the radio had kept him company, like a trusted friend. He was a shy child so he struggled to make friends. Not only that, as an only child he was often lonely, not having a sibling to play with, but everything changed for him the year he turned eight and found a guitar under the Christmas tree. Music became his best friend, his escape, his solace and reason for living. He carried that guitar with him until high school, when he worked after school and on weekends to earn enough money for his next one, a brand-new Fender. He scribbled songs on napkins and the backs of receipts. He played melodies in his head and wrote songs when he was supposed to be studying.

As soon as he graduated he gigged nonstop at open mic nights until he met Sebastien, and the rest, as they say, was history. So it was no wonder that he wanted a woman, a partner in his life who shared his passion for music. He thought—he hoped—that woman just might be Tyler Robertson.

CHAPTER 2

Tyler drove back to the office with "People's Champ" by Arkells cranked to ten. Every generation had a rock 'n' roll anthem, and that song belonged to them.

Did Cary Kingston ask her out on a date? *Don't be silly.* He had checks for Sebastien.

"What do you think, Rory Bear? Do you like him?"

Rory wagged his tail, and she agreed with his assessment.

After Tyler showered, she twisted her hair into a topknot and left it. She didn't know how to apply makeup so she stuck to the basics: mascara, blush, and lipstick. Why was that other stuff necessary? Lady Gaga said that she was born this way, and she had no reason to doubt her.

She googled: *What to wear on a non-date?*

The answers weren't super helpful so she changed into jeans, a striped top, and a jean jacket. She put on mid-calf boots with a low heel since she was tall already. The rest of her family were tall, too, with the exception of her dad. Bert was a wee Scotsman; his clan was from the Highlands. The Robertson children, two daughters and two sons, came by their height on the maternal side of their family.

★　★　★

The Wine Bar was a stone's throw from Cary's building if you had a decent throwing arm, and like Tyler and Kim, he was always on time. In fact, it was so weird for a musician to be punctual that *Wikipedia* should have added it to his list of accomplishments.

Cary was sitting alone on the patio when she arrived, but this time he was easily recognizable as the famous rock star. His thick blond hair was combed to the side and he wasn't wearing glasses as a disguise.

As Tyler approached his table she giggled nervously. They'd worn the same thing, although his t-shirt was white instead of striped. From the back they could have passed for twins, the fraternal kind.

"Jean jacket weather," Cary said, tugging on his denim collar.

"Exactly."

How am I going to keep it together with him looking so adorable?

"Did you know the Canadian tuxedo was named after an incident with Bing Crosby?" he asked. "The Hotel Vancouver wouldn't let him in wearing denim."

"You should try out for *Jeopardy*."

"Funny. No Rory?" He sounded disappointed.

"No Rory." She gave him a playful grin. "I found some money in his harness. He's probably spending the ten dollars you gave him." She pointed to the heat lamps and rolled up her sleeves. "I didn't know we'd be sitting outside. It's kind of hot, actually."

His bottom lip turned into a cute frown. "Poor Rory."

"Yeah." She sank into her seat. "Poor Rory."

A young man crept up beside them. "Hey, Cary!" he said, removing a pen from the half-apron slung around his hips. "How long are you in town, man?"

"Just for tonight." Cary gestured to his guest. "This is Tyler."

Hearing her name was like angels singing.

"I'm Kevin." He smiled and turned to the rock star. "Do you want the Penfolds Grange, man?"

"2011? Is that good with you, Tyler?"

I don't care, just keep saying Tyler.

"I'm afraid I'm not much of a wine connoisseur," she said. Quite frankly, she knew nothing about wine until she'd watched a documentary about sommeliers. It looked impossible to pass the test, even with Rory's nose. "They usually serve the house red or white at music industry events, so that's kind of what I'm stuck with. I'm more of a beer person anyway, although I'll drink champagne on special occasions."

"Go for it." Cary passed her the beverage pamphlet. "Have whatever you want."

She waved the paper away, not wanting to be a bother. "No, it's okay. I'll try the wine. My dad bought a do-it-yourself kit and he can't wait to try it."

"You've come to the right place," Kevin said confidently.

"And some water, please?" Tyler said, raising her hand. "Sometimes wine gives me a headache."

Kevin nodded before going inside.

Cary placed his hand on her forearm and her skin sizzled from the heat. She checked to see if it had left a mark, but it was just her imagination. If she'd told her thirteen-year-old self that this would happen one day, she wouldn't have believed it. She was so infatuated with him back then that she'd doodled *Mrs. Cary Kingston* in her notebook.

"Thanks for saving me," he said, squeezing her arm twice. "I couldn't remember his name for the life of me."

"Really?" She arched an eyebrow in disbelief. "I thought you two were besties?"

"Besties?" He burst out laughing. "No, no, it's a road trick. If you introduce the person you know, people introduce themselves voluntarily."

"Interesting." She pulled out her phone and placed it on the table.

"Expecting a call?" he asked nonchalantly.

"Sorry, I want to make sure the band got in okay." She glanced at her watch. "They had a few stops. We booked their flights on points so they're just landing." By *we* she meant Sebastien.

A few moments later Kevin arrived with a bottle of wine and two fancy glasses. The server poured a splash into Cary's stemware, and with a nod of approval he continued.

"I forgot the stupid decanter," Kevin muttered, clearly upset with himself.

Cary shook his head. "Don't even bother."

"Are you ordering food?" the server asked, pouring a glass of wine for Tyler.

"I haven't eaten all day." Cary scanned a menu the size of a boxing-round card. "The appetizers, please."

"Anything else? Any mains?"

Cary offered the boxing-round card to Tyler but she'd already eaten, not thinking it was a date.

"No thanks." She dug in her boots and inched up her chair. "Appetizers sound great."

"Cheers." Cary raised his glass to hers.

"Cheers." She took a sip and relished the silky blend against her tongue. "I think I'm a convert." *What is the name of this wine?* She twisted the bottle around: PENFOLDS GRANGE 2011.

From the side of his seat, Cary retrieved a manila envelope. "Would you mind giving these checks to Sebastien? I've got to fly out in the morning."

Right. The checks for Sebastien.

She blinked into work mode. "Chicago, I know. Vegas was busy so I advanced your show." The Cary Kingston tour was a well-oiled machine so she only had to confirm their hotel rooms instead of liaising with production, promotion, and payment, like she did with smaller venues. She took the envelope and stretched a smile. "No problem. I'll put them on his desk first thing."

He scratched his head. "I keep my personal business private from SDM. That's why I pay my own bills and sign my checks by hand."

"The Billy Joel episode on *Behind the Music* is a good lesson for everyone." It was reported that the Piano Man's ex-brother-in-law had embezzled 90 million dollars when he was Billy's financial manager. Conversely, Tyler would've noticed if two dollars were missing from her bank account.

"I keep forgetting how much you know about the business." He gave her a lazy smile. "I've known you for what? About ten years—"

"Thirteen." It didn't surprise her that he'd forgotten; he'd probably shaken more hands and kissed more babies than any dignitary in history. "I started interning when I was eighteen, almost nineteen."

"Thirteen years." He drummed his fingers against the table to the beat of "We Will Rock You." He stopped mid-drum. "Tell me something about yourself."

Where to begin? She'd never been on a job interview, although the thought was enticing. She straightened her spine. "What do you want to know?"

"Well, what do you do in your spare time?"

Have you met Sebastien? Spare time wasn't in her job description.

"I work a lot." She paused briefly, not sure how much information to share. "And I'm really into hockey."

"The Jets?" He smirked with an angled chin. "I know you're from the Peg. That I remember."

She nodded, wiping her mouth with a napkin.

Cary continued, "I'm singing the anthem at their home opener." She tilted her head like a dog trying to understand a new command. She probably knew his schedule better than he did. "Is that why I've been playing there?" His eyes rounded, changing colors as they widened. "You're using me to watch hockey?" He folded his arms in protest. "I'm offended."

She raised her hand and lowered her head. "Guilty as charged. It's Sebastien's doing—he's been making the calls. They give us a really nice box, and it's fully stocked with booze." She figured that he wasn't much of a sports fan since she'd never seen him there. Maybe it wasn't a big deal to him, but it was to her. A big fucking deal.

He gave her a flirtatious wink. "As long as it's a really nice box."

"It is." She twisted the stem of her wine glass. "I love watching games there."

"Winnipeg . . ." He hesitated for a second. "You don't miss it, do you?"

A pang of sadness pierced her chest. "More than you can imagine."

They turned their heads as metal scraped the concrete. Kevin seemed to be using all his strength to drag a wrought-iron table toward them. Cary covered his ears and winced like he was being tortured by the Dave Matthews Band.

"You're sensitive to noise, aren't you?" Tyler asked, picking up on his reaction.

He glanced at the server. "It's a blessing and a curse."

Like being here with you.

Was she catching feelings for this guy? This rock star? The most eligible bachelor in the world? Or were they remnants from her high school crush. Either way, it wasn't like he was into her.

"Wow!" Cary's eyebrows lifted when Kevin returned with two large trays. "I didn't know there'd be this much food."

"How many are we expecting?" Tyler couldn't help being a smartass. She glanced over her shoulder. "There's no one else in the restaurant."

Cary placed his palm on his cheek. "I didn't realize the portions were this big."

Kevin unloaded the food onto both tables and topped up their glasses. "All set, man?"

"Thanks." Cary's manners were impeccable—another checkmark in her book. He passed her a side plate and a cloth napkin. "Tyler. That's usually a guy's name, isn't it?"

"What?" She folded the napkin onto her lap. "Cary's a girl's name."

"Cary Grant," he said with a grin. "My mom's favorite actor. She loves those old movies. How did you get your name?"

"My dad named me after a singer." She took a sip of wine before elaborating. "He's into seventies rock, obviously."

"I know the singer you mean."

She rolled down the sleeves of her denim jacket and smirked. "Of course, you know him. You're you."

Cary half-smiled, acknowledging her comment. "I take it he's a big music fan, your dad?"

"He's a musician. Bert Robertson."

His eyes popped open. "He's your dad?"

"Why?" A hint of suspicion crept into her voice. "Do you know him?"

"No . . . no." Cary leaned forward. "Nothing like that. But I saw Bert's—your dad's—band when I was a kid. He's a gifted guitar player." He lowered his voice. "His tone is incredible."

Although Tyler wasn't hungry she munched on truffle popcorn, one of her weaknesses. Another weakness was sappy love songs like the ones Cary used to be known for. But he hadn't written a ballad in over a decade, maybe longer.

"That's what people say," she answered finally.

"You must play?"

"Nope." She licked the oil off her fingers. "I don't know what happened to me. All my siblings play something." She gulped a mouth full of water and wiped her hands on the napkin. "What about your family? Do your parents play?"

"My folks? No, they don't play anything."

"What would you do if you didn't play music?"

"Photography," he said without skipping a beat.

"That's right." Cary Kingston was also famous for taking pictures of models and actresses—and dating them. "I forgot you did that. I've seen some of them. They're pretty good, actually." The women in his pictures looked flawless, and probably not from Photoshop.

"I'd like to take your picture sometime."

Tyler's phone vibrated. It was a text message from Kim.

Landed.

"Sorry, I have to take this." She texted back a thumbs-up emoji. "I love Kim, and she's a great TM, but she's on the road with this band from hell."

"That's why I pay people." He rubbed his chin. "It's just easier."

"What about the guys in your band?"

"It's more like an arranged marriage." He poured a glass of water. "Both sides know the deal going into it."

Her phone vibrated—Kim again.

Josh can't find his cymbals. FML.

"Oh my god." She gasped, reading her screen.

Of all the days for this to be happening. She didn't want to lose her shit in front of Cary, but Josh wasn't making it easy.

"What's wrong?" he asked, tone even.

"Just everything." Her heart pounded like the kettledrum in *2001: A Space Odyssey.* Kubrick, the GOAT of filmmaking. "The airline lost the drummer's cymbals—or he didn't bring them." She used both thumbs to text. "It's highly likely he forgot them."

"Where are they?" Cary swept a long piece of hair back into place. "The band. What city are they in?"

"Fredericton." She held her thumbs in a ready position.

"Well, today's your lucky day."

She tried to muster a grin but couldn't. She didn't have a knack for bullshitting unless it was with Sebastien. "To tell you the truth it didn't start off great."

"Sabian cymbals are an hour away from Fredericton." Cary powered on his phone. "I'll text Vegas." He placed his hand on her shoulder, a sweet and gentle gesture that didn't go unnoticed. "He'll sort it out."

"Thanks, but I think I can get a loaner." It wasn't in her nature to ask for help. Plus as a woman in the music industry you had to be tough as hell, work twice as hard, and do everything yourself. "I know the headliner's manager, but he's kind of hard to deal with."

Cary's phone lit up and he glanced at his screen. "See?" He moved his chair closer. "It's already taken care of, like I said."

"Really?" She began texting frantically. "You saved my life! And Kim's." A few seconds later she drew in a breath, then exhaled through her nostrils. "Thank you."

"No worries." He wrung his hands together. "So, will you be in Winnipeg for the home opener?"

"I'll be in Winnipeg for my family's benefit concert." She dumped the red container of truffle popcorn onto her plate and picked out the kernels. The container looked like the cups from Josh's house, but this one was made out of metal and probably not used for beer pong.

"Benefit?" His eyes seemed to soften. "What's the cause?"

"Cancer." She slid back her chair and grabbed her bag in a hurry. "Excuse me. I have to use the restroom." It probably seemed like she was going to pee her pants, but that wasn't the case at all. She hated talking about her mom and didn't want anyone to feel sorry for her. Michelle Robertson had passed away from cancer when Tyler was two, and the benefit concert they held every year was in her memory.

"Of course." Cary stood like a gentleman as she passed him.

A short while later she returned with a fresh topknot and lipstick.

Cary stood again. "Is everything okay?"

She nodded. "What's next for you, other than touring?"

"I've been writing—co-writing—trying to get another hit. You?"

"Same." She giggled, taking her seat. "I mean working, not writing. I'm mainly scouting bands on TikTok and YouTube."

"YouTube?" He sounded confused.

"I'm looking for live footage. There's nothing worse than hearing a great song, then finding out they can't play it without Pro Tools." She sighed, dropping her shoulders. "There's nothing, other than my indie band and that girl band from Toronto."

"Well, I'll let you know if I hear anything." He combed back his hair with his fingers. "So, will I see you in Winnipeg?"

"If you stay and watch the hockey game. I'll explain the rules." She was testing the waters to see where she stood. It was a little less embarrassing than asking him out and getting rejected. "It's more fun if you know them," she added.

His brow creased like an accordion. "I don't like rules."

It was just around midnight when the Wine Bar was shutting down. Kevin and the rest of the staff had come by to take selfies with Cary, but they'd promised not to post them. All they needed was a hundred screaming fans showing up at closing time.

Cary gestured to the Jenga tower of plates. "Please take the rest of this food home with you."

"I'm stuffed." Tyler waved jazz hands in his direction. "Why don't you give it to your building's concierge? I'm sure the overnight shift is boring."

Cary snapped his fingers. "Good idea." He signaled for Kevin to wrap up their plates.

"Who's working tonight?" She was more curious than anything.

"Who's working?"

"Your building's concierge . . . their name?"

He shrugged. "I've got no idea."

"That's weird." Was he too important to know their names? One checkmark erased.

Kevin broke up their conversation, arriving with a giant to-go bag. He'd packed it like carry-on luggage, not wasting a square inch of space.

"Ready?" Cary stood, holding the bag like an old lady's purse.

Tyler bit on her knuckles. "What about the bill?"

Sebastien would have fired her on the spot for not paying the check and expensing it to Cary's account. Too bad she had no intention of telling her boss anything, ever.

"I've got a tab," he said easily and slipped a few hundred-dollar bills under the empty wine bottle. "What part of town are you in?"

"The West End."

"So, you're a West End girl?"

"Ha-ha."

He smiled. "I'll call you a taxi."

"Don't." She flapped her denim sleeves against the breeze. "It's a pleasant night for a walk."

He gazed at the sky. "It's a full moon."

"Don't worry, I won't bark."

"Funny."

She followed his eyes. "You're right. I stand corrected. It's a *perfect* night for a walk. Anyway, I doubt you have the app for a taxi or an Uber."

"No, but my concierge does, and I've got his number."

With anyone else she would have argued her case, but he was their number-one client and the biggest rock star in the world.

After he instructed his building's concierge to order a taxi, he asked, "And who am I speaking with? Thanks, Arjun." He ended the call. "His name is Arjun."

Okay, point taken.

"You could've googled the number," she teased.

"Right." His face flushed from his collar, so she stopped poking fun at him.

When they crossed the street to his building, a yellow taxi pulled into the driveway and her heart sank into her boots. Being alone with him was a rare occurrence with Sebastien always lurking.

Cary gave her a serious look. "Text when you get home, okay?"

She nodded, and after a slight hesitation he wrapped his arms around her waist, and she hugged him with more familiarity than earlier that day.

You smell like heaven.

"Thanks, I had a nice time," she said.

"No, thank *you*." He smiled at her awkwardly, then leaned in and gave her a peck on the lips. *Oh my god!* Her head jerked back involuntarily. *Did he just kiss me?* She took a deep breath to steady her heart rate. Who was she kidding? That wasn't a real kiss. It was probably an LA thing. That city was lousy with touchy-feely types.

The taxi was idling so Tyler climbed into the back seat and cracked the window an inch.

"Don't forget!" she yelled. "It's your mom's birthday on Tuesday!"

Cary stood in place and waved, but she lost track of him as the taxi turned left down the street.

What the hell is even happening?

CARY

"I can't believe I did that," Cary said under his breath on the elevator ride to his penthouse. Was he *that* guy? Was it possible he'd been mistaken? Maybe he'd misread her body language. But they'd had such a great time . . . at least in *his* mind.

Tyler was smart and funny, not like those fake Hollywood types. Not that she wasn't beautiful. She was *all* kinds of beautiful. Like how she wore her hair up in an "I don't care" style. Her blue eyes reminded him of Pelican Lake, where his family had gone camping in the summer when he was a child. But the dimples on her cheeks really knocked him out. They were cute but sexy, livening up her already perfect smile . . .

And here he was, trying to impress her like some douchebag when her dad was Bert Robertson. *The* Bert Robertson. To guitar players, he was a legend. Tyler sure as hell wasn't going to be impressed by him or any musician, given her lineage. In fact, she was probably on the phone right now telling Kim what a jerk he'd been for kissing her—and for not knowing the name of his building's attendant. The truth was that he rarely came into contact with anyone who wasn't a Kinger.

Hopefully she'd send a text when she got home, and he could reply with something funny. He loved that she'd laughed at his jokes; it even seemed genuine. He could hardly wait to see her in Winnipeg, even though it meant watching hockey.

CHAPTER 3

Advanced Excel was the most useful course Tyler had taken during her Arts and Entertainment Management program. She was busy updating SDM's tour budgets and adding line items to the forecasts. That is, until she became distracted.

It had been two weeks and four days since that kiss, but who was counting? As much as she'd tried to forget it she couldn't, because SDM had plastered its walls with CARY KINGSTON: LIVE posters they'd so brilliantly marketed.

"Concentrate," she said under her breath. Rory glanced up from his bed, but it probably didn't sound enough like "cookie" so he stayed put.

Tyler needed to shake it off because musicians—other than her dad—weren't exactly trustworthy. Her ex-boyfriend, Dave, a singer in a local band, had slept with every groupie on the tour routing she'd mapped out for him. She'd also spent countless hours on logistics, merchandising, and monetizing his music—it was like interning all over again but without the chance of a promotion.

Five years wasted and she was no closer to having a baby. In the meantime, Rory was perfect company. He was loyal—unlike Dave—and she always knew his location.

"Knock, knock." Kim tapped on her office door and Rory ran in circles before greeting her with tail wags and kisses.

"Have a seat." Tyler gestured for her bestie to come in. "How was the tour?"

"Dude, it fucking sucked." Kim pulled on the roots of her faded pink hair. "They're the worst band I've ever worked with." She slumped into a plastic chair in front of the desk and crossed her legs like a yogi. "Little shits. They were late for everything, refused soundchecks . . . and fought at press appearances." She locked eyes with her friend. "Literally with fists."

"I know. You told me." Tyler leaned forward and clasped her hands on the desk. "The shows were good, weren't they?"

"Yeah." Kim paused for a second. "They were great. I can't believe they sold out of merch."

"Tell me about it. Sebastien had a conniption when we ran out of t-shirts." She tapped her pen against the desk. "Sorry, I know they're a headache, but the Westgrays are the only band we have on tour right now. Well, other than Cary's."

"You thanked him for me, right?" Tyler nodded, so she went on, "Those cymbal guys pretty much saved Josh's life." Kim massaged the back of her neck, then cracked it. "I swear I was going to kill him. Plead self-defense." She stared at Tyler and bit her bottom lip. "Why were you with him?"

"Who?"

"Cary."

Shit.

"I was going to tell you—"

"I'm here now." Kim pushed herself upright. "So tell me."

"Ugh, this is so embarrassing." She hung her head before lifting her gaze, then blurted out, "He kissed me."

"Get. The. Fuck. Out."

"I-I mean, it was a peck." Tyler rolled a pen between her fingers and shook the image out of her head. "We went for a drink. That's it."

"Yeah, I know what a drink means." Kim shrugged and gave her a shit-eating grin. "Go for it!"

"I can't go for that." She dropped her pen onto the desk. "The most eligible bachelor in the free world, Kim? Are you crazy?" She cringed at the thought of everyone knowing her business, her every move, her whereabouts. Dating was difficult enough without everyone making comments on Cary's Facebook page and Reddit.

"I thought you had a major crush on him?"

"*Had.*" Tyler emphasized the word. "I broke my own rule with Dave." She'd taken a vow to never, under any circumstances, date another musician.

"Too bad there's only one half-decent guy in the industry who isn't a jagoff."

"George," they said at the same time, then had a laughing fit.

A ding chimed from Tyler's computer, so she clicked her mouse. "It looks like Tommy has an offer for the Westgrays to play at some festival for no money."

Tommy Napolitano was Cary's agent too, tasked with booking his live performances. Sebastien and Tommy were thick as thieves, which explained a lot, because Tommy was an asshole.

"Fucking Tommy." Kim's voice became hostile. "Why did Allie pass on them? She's the best agent for new bands."

"She met them." No further explanation was necessary.

Allie Kowalski was their hot-shot booking-agent friend from Toronto. Tyler had met her at Canadian Music Week, and she knew they were going to be friends immediately. Allie hated the high school drama of the Toronto music scene. She was all business. A shark with sharper teeth.

"What about your heritage acts?" Kim asked. "Can't you dust them off? Resurrect them from their crypts or something?"

SDM's old bands were super high-maintenance and a million times worse than any new artist. Sebastien needed them on their roster to cover his expenses when Cary wasn't on tour, so Tyler spent most of her time explaining why they couldn't play Coachella and Glastonbury while trying to keep their egos intact.

"Everyone's writing or in the studio," Tyler said.

"Ew. Why?"

"Honestly? I can't explain."

"What about Afternoon Delight? They're pretty good for a local band."

"Are you joking? That singer has zero charisma, and no one wants to fuck him."

Kim bounced her hands in a steeple. "What about your band—Yestown?"

"Yeah, they're killer, but they don't have enough songs for a full set." She picked up her pen and clicked it. "And they can't afford a TM as an unsigned band."

"I know." Kim uncrossed her legs and kicked a tennis ball from underneath her chair. Rory chased after it like a ball kid at Wimbledon. "Vancouver just sucks sometimes."

That was an understatement.

"Especially your hockey team," Tyler heckled. "If I had fuck-you money I'd buy season tickets and cheer for the away team." She stared at Kim, smirking. "What a bunch of sore losers. Remember when they lost the cup and people rioted in the streets?"

"How could I forget."

"It's why we can't have nice things." Tyler's computer dinged again and she rolled her eyes dismissively. "The city shut down everything after that happened."

"'No fun city.'" Kim shook her head. "I've got a love-hate relationship with Vancouver, being born here, but I'd rather die than live in Toronto. Fuck 'We the North.'"

"'We *are* the North' is grammatically correct."

"The French are saying, 'Oui the North.'"

"Of course they are." She sighed deeply, frustrated with where her life was heading, nowhere in a hurry. She'd already stayed at SDM for ten years longer than she'd expected to. "I wish I could move back to Winnipeg."

"Oh, I caught that band you like." Kim snapped her fingers. "The chick band you found on TikTok."

"The Oh Claires?" Her voice increased an octave. "How were they?"

"Dude, straight fire."

"I haven't given up." Tyler had listened to Peter Gabriel's record too many times for that to happen. *So* was one of her dad's favorite albums and "Don't Give Up" gave her all the feels every time she listened to it. "I'm dying to work with them."

"So do it."

"I'd have to leave SDM to manage them."

"Even more of a reason, if you ask me." Kim scrolled through her Apple Watch. "What time is your flight?"

Tyler pulled up the e-ticket on her phone as it didn't hurt to check twice. "Noon."

"Sebastard's going to be there, I assume?"

Tyler shuddered, closing her eyes. A visit to the dentist's office was more fun than hanging out with her boss, but at least she was going to Winnipeg, and he knew people there. When they traveled he insisted on eating dinner together and if that wasn't bad enough, he chewed with his mouth open and didn't use a napkin.

"He wouldn't miss it," Tyler said with certainty.

Kim sat in her seat like a petulant child. "Dude, I hate that you're leaving me."

"What do you mean?" She tried to keep a straight face. "Lara's here." SDM's new receptionist was as useless as Vancouver's first-round draft pick. Lara, pronounced "Ley-rah" instead of "Laa-rah," had been with the company for three months. She was an aspiring singer from the Philippines—a country with the most vocalists per capita.

"That's not funny, dude." Kim folded her arms and looked straight ahead. "She gives Asian chicks a bad rap."

Later that day Tyler arrived at her dad's house, Rory in tow. She'd flown on points, so her out-of-pocket expenses were almost zero. Living paycheck to paycheck, she knew how to stretch a budget. None of her bands had earned a commission yet, so macaroni and cheese was her go-to dinner. *No ketchup—that's gross.*

"Hello?" Tyler yelled as the door squeaked open.

The three-bedroom bungalow had changed little since the nineties, everything was in rough shape and needed to be replaced. The yellow and orange-flowered wallpaper peeled at the seams, the braided multi-colored area rug frayed at the edges, and her dad's black leather recliner, which sat in front of the TV, was worn at the arms and the seat.

An overweight black Labrador Retriever bounded toward the door.

"Wilbur! Who's a good boy?" Tyler bent over to say hello but he greeted Rory instead, and the dogs wagged their tails into a windstorm.

"Tyler!" Dylan hollered from the kitchen. "In here."

Her sister lived across the street with her husband Joe and their sixteen-year-old daughter, Nadie, a Cree name meaning "wise." Dylan got pregnant when she was eighteen and it wasn't exactly planned, but she and Joe had welcomed Nadie with open arms.

"Dylan!" Tyler met her halfway.

Apart from Dylan's dark hair they could have passed for twins, the identical kind.

Dylan frowned. "I would've picked you up, dummy."

"Don't be silly." She embraced her big sister. "Where's Dad?"

The tapping paws of a miniature panda grabbed Dylan's attention. "Hi Rory!" She scooped up her nephew and kissed him on the head. "He's at the casino getting everything ready for tomorrow."

"Congrats on selling it out."

"It wasn't easy," she admitted. "Joe sold a lot of tickets. He says hi, by the way."

"Where's Nadie?" Tyler swiveled her head, expecting to see her.

"At practice. She's disappointed that she won't get to see you."

Nadie was preparing for the lead role of Laurey in her high school's production of *Oklahoma!* She'd told her aunt that she'd won the part over twelve other girls, and Tyler couldn't have been prouder.

"I'll see her tomorrow." Tyler checked her watch. "Come talk to me in the bathroom. I have to leave in twenty minutes."

"To see Cary?" Dylan teased.

"Shut up! Just get in here."

Dylan put down the dog and followed her into the bathroom. "What's going on with you two?" She sat on a toilet-lid cover made of high-pile fibers. "Spill the tea."

"I'm done with musicians." Tyler applied a thin coat of mascara to her top eyelashes. "I'm not falling for Cary fucking Kingston."

"Why not? You said he was a nice guy—and he kissed you."

"It was a peck," she clarified, regretting telling her sister the gory details of their encounter. "Don't get too excited."

"What's he like in person?" Not surprisingly, she'd also had a crush on him in high school. In fact, it was Dylan who had turned her onto his music.

"He's like, a person."

Dylan traced the outline of her lips with her finger. "He's got nice eyes. They're brown, right?"

"Hazel with specks of gold."

"Yeah, I thought so." Dylan grabbed an orange stick and scraped off her janky red nail polish. "You said he likes Rory, right?"

A moment later Rory dashed into the bathroom, tail wagging.

"He loves him." Tyler smiled at her dog. "Hi buddy." She turned to Dylan. "He's looking for c-o-o-k-i-e-s."

"What's the problem?" Dylan sounded frustrated.

Tyler rolled her eyes in the mirror. "Other than being the most famous rock star in the world? Anyway, it doesn't matter. I haven't heard from him."

"He asked you to text him."

"Which I did."

"Yeah, you sent a house emoji with a thumbs-up sign." Dylan spun the toilet paper roll. "Nice going."

"He sent a thumbs-up back." That damn emoji had haunted her for weeks. Why didn't she text him, *I'm home! Thanks for an amazing night!* Because she was an idiot when it came to men. Like, the worst of all-time.

"What was he supposed to do?" Dylan picked up Rory and held him on her lap. "You didn't leave an opening for him to follow up with you."

"Please. He dates models and actresses, not music managers." Tyler had done her homework. Googling *Cary Kingston + girlfriend* had nearly given her a heart attack. The list of women he'd dated was extensive. "Emma Turner? He's obviously shallow." She spoke in a drawl. "Emma's the belle of the ball."

"They broke up. Again."

"It was probably his fault."

"Cary writes love songs, Tyler."

"Correction. He used to write love songs." She raised an eyebrow, not sure where her sister was going. "What's your point?"

"He's a romantic at heart." Dylan covered Rory's ears. "He didn't make that shit up just to sell records."

She scoffed. "He's a musician, Dylan."

"Watch it. Mom married one, and he's our father."

An hour later Tyler arrived at the arena and headed straight to the private suite level. True North Sports and Entertainment, the Winnipeg Jets' organization, was providing SDM with exclusive use of their house suite, and she wasn't about to waste it. Her job came with all kinds of perks, but this was by far the greatest.

She entered the private suite, her mouth drying up like she'd eaten a bag of pretzels with saltines as a palate cleanser. Cary was somewhere in the building and it made her nervous just thinking about it.

I need a drink.

She opened the bar fridge and grabbed a beer, Blue Moon, her favorite. She twisted off the cap and chugged a few gulps, feeling slightly better.

The suite door opened and a young woman with a jaunty ponytail entered. She balanced a sizable tray of cheese and crackers on her shoulder.

"Hi, I'm Jessica. I'll be your server." She set down the tray next to a plate of cold cuts, creating a poor man's charcuterie board.

"Tyler," she said, introducing herself. "It's nice to meet you."

"I'll get you a glass and an orange for that right away."

She inspected her bottle and nodded. "Thank you."

"I . . . I heard this was Cary Kingston's suite?" the server stuttered.

She scanned Jessica from head to toe, sizing up the competition. "For tonight it is."

"Have you met him?"

"Cary? I work for his manager."

Jessica's eyes rounded into globes. "Is he nice?"

"He's the best." That kiss wasn't too shabby for a non-kiss, either. "Really. He's a great guy. Super nice."

But don't get any ideas.

Jessica straightened her skirt at the waist. "Is he coming up here?"

It was a good question, but she didn't want to get Jessica's hopes up—or her own, for that matter. "I doubt it."

"That's a bummer."

Tell me about it.

The voices in the hall gradually became louder as Sebastien and his buddies were like megaphones personified. He was always the loudest person in the room—not a shocker.

Sebastien brought his Winnipeg entourage with him: club owners, promoters, and musicians from his heyday. But they weren't his friends, not really. Sebastien had invited them so he could brag about his net worth, mostly because he was a braggart.

"Hi doll," Sebastien said, waddling into the suite. He called Tyler "doll" whenever he'd been drinking, which was regularly.

"Hi." She turned her head and cringed in anticipation. Like every French person known to mankind, he kissed her on both cheeks. *Ow! Shit!* His beard scratched her face and she recoiled, scrunching her nose from the stench of whiskey and cigarettes on his breath. In fact, it almost made her vomit.

"Fix us some drinks," he ordered.

"She's our server," Tyler pointed to Jessica. "She's a big Cary Kingston fan."

Sebastien gave her the once-over. "Cute," he grunted, adjusting his Quebec Nordiques baseball cap. Being a slob, he dressed more like a comedy writer than a music mogul—missing the sense-of-humor part.

From years of experience Tyler could tell that her boss was about to bust a move on Jessica, but he was no Mick Jagger. Or Adam Levine, for that matter.

"I'll introduce her when he gets here," Sebastien said.

Tyler cleared her throat. "Cary's coming up here?"

"He wants to watch the game."

"Why?" She hung her thumb from her belt loop, lowering one hip.

"I didn't ask," he said, voice grouchy like Oscar's.

Sebastien never questioned Cary or told him what to do, since their management contract was a handshake deal, not anything legally binding. SDM's other clients had iron-clad agreements, which meant that Sebastien owned them for life. But not Cary. He could leave whenever he wanted to, and that would mean disaster for Mr. Halitosis's bottom line.

Tyler's chest tightened and her heart pounded through her sweater. *Pull yourself together. It was just a peck on the lips, remember.* She held her palm against her eye to stop it from twitching, a tell that she was freaking out.

The house lights dimmed and the announcer introduced Cary to the sold-out arena. The crowd erupted in cheers for their hometown hero. Brandon was close enough to Winnipeg that people didn't get offended when they said he was a local.

Cary strutted down the blue carpet toward center ice and Tyler bowed her head, stretching out her white Jets jersey. *Great minds* . . . They'd worn the same thing again. Maybe they had telepathy.

Not long after the anthem ended, Vegas stood in the doorway of their hospitality suite. His 6'6" frame took up a lot of space. People assumed that he was a biker because of his neck tattoos, ponytail, and black leather jacket, but Cary's tour manager wouldn't have been caught dead riding a motorcycle. He was the voice of reason and never did anything reckless.

Tyler waved at Vegas and he stepped aside, leaving her unshielded from Cary's piercing gaze. *Oh my god, he's here.* What was she going to do? Too bad there wasn't a window to jump through.

Be cool.

She took a swig of beer as the string parts from *Requiem for a Dream* echoed in her head.

Be cooler.

One after another Sebastien's buddies posed for pictures with Cary as if he were the Second Coming. Truth be told, Jesus would have taken fewer selfies before he got annoyed.

The puck was about to drop so Tyler turned on her heel. She was there to watch the game, not Cary Kingston, even though it was a nice view.

"Is this seat taken?" a voice from behind her asked.

It's him.

She half-turned around and smiled. "Be my guest."

Cary lowered himself into the seat beside her. "We've really got to stop coordinating our outfits." She laughed, triggering a rush of blood to her head. "Where's Rory?" he asked.

"He's at my dad's."

"Are you staying there?" She nodded, holding her breath and counting to ten. It was the only way she knew how to calm herself down, a trick from her adolescence. Cary pointed to her beer and twisted around. "Where do I order?"

Jessica was already staring at him when Tyler waved her over.

"What can I-I get you, Mr. Kingston?" Jessica's voice trembled.

"Mr. Kingston is my dad. Please, call me Cary."

She giggled. "What can I get you, Cary?"

"How's the wine?"

Tyler touched the arm of his jersey. "I'm sure it's not great, not like what you're used to."

"Yeah, it's not the greatest," Jessica admitted. "Red or white?"

"Red, please." Cary placed his hand on Tyler's thigh and her pelvic muscles contracted. *Move your hand higher.* To her disappointment he removed his hand and gave her a clumsy grin just as things were starting. "It'll be fine."

Jessica giggled again. "Another beer for you, Tyler?"

"Please."

Without hesitation Jessica took off as if her life depended on it.

"I think someone wants an autograph." Tyler batted her eyelashes.

"Sure," Cary said. "Where should I sign?"

She squeezed his upper arm, not expecting to find muscle there. "Not me, Cary. Our server."

"Ow!" He smiled, holding his arm. "I've got to play tomorrow."

"In less than twenty-four hours you'll be playing down there." She pointed to the rink. "They're doing the conversion overnight."

"Thank god. It'd be kind of slippery otherwise."

She laughed. "Very funny."

"Here you go." Jessica passed him a glass of red wine filled to the brim. "And another beer for you."

"Thank you." Tyler took the bottle and smiled politely.

Jessica stood in place, swaying like a rocking horse. "How is it, Cary? I can get you something else if you don't like it? A beer? A mixed drink?"

He took a sip and his mouth puckered. "It's fine. Thank you."

Tyler could tell that it tasted like liquified shit.

"Ca—Cary?" Jessica stammered. "Can I please have your autograph?"

I called it.

"How about a picture?" Cary offered.

Tyler took a sip from her bottle, not amused by the server's interruption.

Jessica's gaze shifted to Tyler, then bounced to the rock star. "Are you serious?"

In an attempt to be the bigger person, Tyler put down her beer. "Here, hand me your phone."

Jessica did just that and Tyler took their picture.

"Are you coming to my show?" Cary asked the server.

Her gaze lowered to the ground. "I couldn't get tickets."

Cary pointed to the suite. "See that tall guy standing in the corner?"

"Yeah, he's pretty hard to miss."

Isn't Jessica a fucking comedian.

Cary laughed. "Ask him to put your name on the guest list."

"Thank you!" Jessica said, and with a skip in her step she took off to see Vegas.

"You're good with the Kingers." Tyler gave him a tight-lipped smile. "Are your parents coming tomorrow?" In all the years she'd worked at SDM, she'd never met the Kingstons.

Cary shook his head. "No."

"They're not?" She cocked her head to the side. "Brandon's less than three hours from here."

He shrugged. "They've seen me play a million times."

"Did you invite them?"

"They don't need an invitation, Tyler."

"No, but they need their names on the guest list." She kicked into work mode, making sure they'd get into the venue. "Invite them."

"Okay." He continued watching the game. For someone who didn't like hockey he seemed to be captivated by it.

She shook her phone like an Etch A Sketch. "Invite them now."

"Okay, I will." He took out his phone and she nodded, encouraging him to do it. She couldn't imagine his parents declining the invitation.

A few minutes later Cary's phone lit up and he chuckled, sharing his screen with Tyler.

We'd love to! Mom.

Cary pointed out, "She always signs her texts with 'Mom.'"

"That's cute. I'll get Vegas to add them to the guest list."

As promised, Tyler explained the rules to Cary. He was a quick study, except for grasping the concept of an offside call. It was a complicated rule so she was patient with him—not exactly a chore. They laughed and joked like it was two weeks and four days ago.

Was she obsessing over nothing? Maybe his cologne. Did he remember the kiss? She didn't think so.

"That's my favorite part." Tyler pointed to the players as they lined up to congratulate their goalie. "I like it when they pat him on the head. I do that with Rory."

"Your favorite part of the game?"

She nodded. "Yeah, and I get annoyed when the telecast cuts it out. It's kind of like when they don't show the ending of *Saturday Night Live*. I like the hugging. It's nice."

"Got your text." Vegas raised his phone. "The Kingstons are on the list." He nodded once at Cary. "Ready to roll, man? Big day tomorrow."

Cary smiled at Tyler. "So, I'll see you at the show?"

"No," she said. "I mean, it's my family's concert."

"What time does it start?"

She glanced at her watch. "Around eight, I think—"

"What's around eight?" Sebastien interrupted, eyes bloodshot and clearly intoxicated.

This asshole.

She softened her voice and said, "My family's benefit concert."

"You guys are still doing that?" Sebastien hiccupped and his turkey neck flapped, skin folding inward. "How many years now?"

She used her eyes as daggers. "Thirty, if you must know."

"You don't say?" He stroked his beard. "I want a list of producers for the Westgrays by the morning."

"I sent you a list a few weeks ago."

"Send another one." A droplet of spit stuck to his beard and she turned up her nose. "More pucks on the net."

I'm sending the same list and you'll never know.

Her boss squinted, trying to focus. "We're hitting the bar, Cary. Are you coming?"

"Big day tomorrow," Vegas said, throwing him some rope.

"Yeah, I'm kind of beat." Cary rubbed one eye with his fist, although he didn't seem tired in the slightest.

"What about you?" Sebastien raised his empty glass at Tyler. "Free booze if you're interested?"

Before she could answer, Vegas ushered him back to his cronies.

Thanks, Vegas. I owe you.

"Why don't you come by for the first set?" Cary stared at her intensely, pleading with her to go.

"Okay." She nodded, then had second thoughts. "Well . . . maybe."

I can't look too desperate.

CARY

"She hates my music," Cary told Vegas as he climbed into their chauffeured SUV.

Vegas turned his head. "What?"

"Tyler Robertson." His tone became impatient as he went on, "She hates my music, Vegas. It's kind of obvious."

He shrugged. "What the fuck do you care?"

"What did she say? Does she think I'm a has-been?" His biggest fear in life was becoming obsolete. His records weren't selling like they used to and hit singles were few and far between. He'd rather die than have his new love interesting thinking he was passé.

"She hasn't said anything." Vegas arched an eyebrow. "At least not to me. What's gotten into you, man?"

Cary slid down in his seat and scrolled through his phone. "Nothing," he said dismissively, not wanting to talk about it even though he'd been the one to bring it up in the first place. Tyler was the first woman in years, maybe ever, who'd made him feel insecure.

"It didn't look like nothing." Knowing Vegas, he'd watched the whole thing. He always kept a close eye on him. From time to time the Kingers could become unruly.

"She said maybe." Cary ran his fingers through his hair, replaying the last thing she'd said to him before they'd hugged goodbye. Their embrace was more than friendly but not quite romantic, and she pulled away first, leaving him wondering, *What the hell?*

"Maybe what?" Vegas asked.

"Maybe she'd come to my show." What was he thinking? Of course she couldn't come. It was her family's benefit concert tomorrow and that was her priority. "How well do you know her?"

"I don't know." Vegas shrugged. "I can tell you she's cool as fuck, though."

"She treats me like a regular person." Nothing killed him more than a woman he liked asking for a selfie or an autograph.

"A regular person?"

"You know what I mean." He steadied his gaze. "Has she got a boyfriend?" Until now the thought hadn't crossed his mind. Was it even a possibility?

Vegas let out a chuckle. "We don't braid each other's hair, man." He held his phone. "Want me to ask? I can do it, no problem."

"No! No." It would be too obvious if, out of nowhere, Vegas asked about her love life. They weren't in high school anymore, even though it sure felt like it.

CHAPTER 4

The next morning, Tyler woke up in her childhood bed a little later than usual. The two-hour time difference wasn't in her favor and she yawned, stretching her arms above her head.

"It's Mommy's birthday, Ror-Ror." The dog let out a sigh and went back to sleep. "I hear you, buddy. Birthdays are shitty."

She was thirty-two years old and no closer to having a baby, unless she counted the acts on SDM's roster that she was constantly bottle-feeding.

Out of habit she checked her phone, but it was too early for their artists to bother her. No doubt the heritage acts would text her later with questions they could have googled.

She smiled as she read the e-birthday cards from Marnie and Heather. She'd been friends with them since kindergarten, and they'd grown up together. But after high school Marnie and Heather moved to Toronto to attend university, and they ended up staying after graduating to be closer to their boyfriends, now husbands. Long-distance relationships were tough, even with girlfriends. Would it be easier if she was on Facebook? Sure. But at least it had spared her from random Happy Birthday wishes from people she used to know or who were just acquaintances.

What's Cary doing?

Last night was so much fun. She couldn't believe that he'd actually shown up in the hospitality suite after he'd sung the anthem. After the initial shock had worn off she was able to have a decent hang with him, but she'd fumbled the ball when he'd asked her to go to his concert. Of course, she wanted to go, but she was also starting to have feelings for him. And that was a no-no.

She scrolled through his Instagram but found nothing new. The habit of stalking his account started after their kiss—or whatever you wanted to call it. She had to admit that the photos he posted were spectacular, but the comments from his fans, mostly women, were more than suggestive. In fact, if people had said those things to his face they would have been arrested. Hopefully he'd disabled his DMs. She couldn't imagine the filth in those messages.

But enough about Cary. Today was a big day for her family. The benefit concert was meant to celebrate her mom's legacy. Her dad believed that music, not laughter, was the best medicine.

She wanted to buy something special to commemorate the benefit's anniversary. She googled *dad + gifts*, but it resulted in nothing more than corny coffee mugs and jokey t-shirts.

Cary's wine.

She searched *penfolds grange + 2011 + liquor mart* and clicked the link.

"Eight hundred and fifty dollars!" she cried, waking Rory again.

Not in this lifetime.

There wasn't a soul—or a balloon—in sight when Tyler came out of her bedroom that morning, so she walked across the street to give Dylan a chance to wish her a happy birthday.

"Hello?" Tyler opened the door and a blond Afghan Hound barked. "Samson! Shh . . . who's a good boy?" The dog galloped toward her, his hair blowing like Beyoncé's.

"In here!" Dylan hollered from the kitchen. "Samson! Shut the hell up!"

"Auntie Ty!" Nadie ran toward her.

Tyler beamed at her niece. Their bond was undeniable. Her brothers had sons, and she loved them too, but it wasn't the same thing as having a girl.

Nadie was an only child, not for a lack of trying. Dylan and Joe had always wanted another baby, but in her late twenties, her sister was diagnosed with fibroids. After several attempts at removing the tumors the doctors predicted her condition wouldn't improve, but it wasn't the end of the world. They'd always said that Nadie was a gift, and they counted their blessings.

Full stop.

"Hi honey." Tyler hugged her niece. "How are you?" She floated her hand over Nadie's head. "I think you're still growing."

"Geez." Nadie glanced at the floor and wiggled her stocking feet. "I sure hope not. I'm the tallest girl in my school." She twirled her long black hair with her fingers. "I'm stoked for tonight! I can't wait to sing in front of a live audience."

Although Dylan had assured her that Nadie was ready to perform a solo number, it was still a lot of pressure for someone so young and inexperienced.

"Tyler! Get your ass in here!" Her brother-in-law's voice bellowed from the kitchen.

Joe Grant was a stand-up guy. He was Cree, First Nations, and his family had lived on the lands for hundreds if not thousands of years. The Grants had embraced the Robertsons as if they'd belonged to their nation, and they'd reciprocated in kind.

"Looking good, Joe," Tyler said.

Joe placed his hands on his belly, exaggerating its size. "I'm down ten. Only ten more to go."

Tyler laughed and looked at her sister. "Don't get up or anything." Dylan sat at the kitchen table holding a needle and thread between her fingers. "What are you doing?"

"Sewing a hem on Nadie's dress."

Dylan was an expert seamstress, and with no formal training she'd set up a home-based alterations business when Nadie was an infant. She said that she'd rather spend time with her daughter than put her into daycare with a bunch of spoiled kids.

"May I borrow your car, please?" Tyler directed her question at her sister. "I want to check out the casino." She'd seen a lot of day-of-show disasters and mitigating damage was the only way to solve it. She didn't trust people to do their jobs, and more often than not she was right not to.

"Yeah, the keys are on the hook." Dylan seemed to be concentrating on her slip stitch, not paying any attention to her.

Did they really forget my birthday?

She crossed her fingers but saved her wish.

By mid-afternoon everyone was at the Robertsons' house for the last practice before the concert. The Family Band included Tyler's brothers, Perry and Stewart; her sisters-in-law and nephews; plus the Grants and Bert. It had been years since she'd played music with her family. She had as much rhythm as a white woman in a Southern Baptist church.

Still, no one had said anything about her birthday.

WTF?

"Watch me, Auntie Ty!" Nadie grabbed the microphone from its stand.

"One . . . two . . ." Bert counted the band in and Nadie began to sing "River" from Joni Mitchell's album, *Blue*: one of the best records ever made, according to her dad.

"Holy shit!" Tyler nodded along to the music, and when it ended she clapped. "Bravo, honey! Bravo!"

"What did you really think?" Nadie asked, hip jutting out.

"What did I really think?" Tyler shook her head, not believing what she'd heard. "I think you're the best singer in this family." Which was really saying something.

Tyler's phone vibrated. It was a text message from Vegas.

Can u come 2 the Meet & Greet at 5? Radio station screwed up. Seb made the promo girl cry.

She'd gone nearly twenty-four hours without babysitting an SDM artist, possibly setting a new world record. *Note to self: check Guinness.* It must have been important since Vegas had never asked her for a favor. Conversely, she owed him more solids than she could remember. Plus she'd been on the receiving end of Sebastien's tirades enough times to know how the promotions person felt. Her boss had made her cry . . . often.

Not long after, Tyler arrived at the arena. Vegas met her at the side entrance looking thoroughly unimpressed. As they walked down the hall he explained what was happening.

"The local radio station gave away a hundred meet-and-greet passes," he said matter-of-factly.

She scrunched her nose. "So?"

"All of them with plus-ones."

"No!" She covered her mouth with her hand. "Two hundred in total?"

"Yeah, and when Seb found out, he yelled at the radio station's promotions person, even though it was our intern's fault."

"Figures."

It was oh-so typical, like that Tegan and Sara song.

"It's a shitshow in there," he said, opening the green room door. *Fuck.* He was right. They'd squeezed two hundred people into a tiny holding area, breaking every fire code occupancy regulation in the province of Manitoba. "A hundred people have to go."

Tyler had a feeling—more than a feeling—that Cary didn't know.

"What did Cary say?" she asked.

Vegas shrugged. "No idea. He's at catering with Seb and Tommy."

"Tommy?" She turned up her nose as if his name smelled.

"Fucking Tommy," he confirmed, shaking his head. The reaction to Cary's booking agent was ubiquitous, everyone hated him.

"Cary's going to be pissed off if he catches wind of this." The back of her neck was wet to the touch from the sweltering heat, so she took off her coat. It surprised her that Sebastien wasn't marketing the green room as a sauna and charging top dollar for it.

Vegas sighed. "Do you want to tell Sebastard? Because I don't."

She shook her head, making a split-second decision. "I'm telling Cary. They're his fans, not Sebastien's."

"It's your funeral." Vegas held out his hand. "Here, I'll put your shit in our room."

Tyler handed him her coat, but she kept her bag over her shoulder because Sebastien snooped through everything that he wasn't supposed to.

She texted Cary. *Hi. Meet & Greet is now 200 people! Sebastien said to send 100 away.*

A few seconds later her phone vibrated, and her heart fluttered when she read Cary's name. It was almost impossible to wrap her head around the fact that the biggest rock star on the planet had her number. Little ol' Tyler Robertson.

Are you here? he asked.

She answered, *Green Room.*

I'll be right there. Don't send anyone away. xo

There was no doubt in her mind that she'd done the right thing, but what was the "xo" about? She would obsess about it later, but for now she needed to put this fire out.

Five minutes later Cary, Sebastien, and Tommy swaggered down the hall like they were astronauts in *Armageddon*.

"Hi doll," Sebastien said.

Drinking so early?

"How are you feeling?" she asked as they exchanged fake pleasantries.

"Bit of a rough start this morning." Her boss cleared his throat and straightened his baseball cap. "It's nothing a few drinks can't solve. Hair of the dog and all that."

It's called a drinking problem.

"Wow!" Cary clutched his chest. "We are *definitely* not wearing the same thing." He was all smiles, and she smiled back until her cheeks hurt.

"I wouldn't be so sure of that," she teased, resting her hands on her hips. "I bet you have this *exact* dress in your closet."

Cary laughed and gave her a hug. She was wearing kitten heels so she was slightly taller than him, a perfect height for hugging, and she inhaled him like a drug.

"Sorry about the meet and greet," she whispered into his ear.

"Thanks for telling me." His breath on her neck was warm, giving her tingles all over.

Tommy, fresh from a spray tan, flashed his used-car-salesman smile. He wore his hair slicked back like a greaser from the fifties and stunk up the hall with cheap cologne, masking the smell of cigarettes on his person. Twenty years earlier Sebastien had dumped an unknown artist into his lap, and a year later Cary's debut record went number one around the world. Tommy had won the booking agent lottery. *Lucky fucker.*

"Save some for me," Tommy said, cutting into their hug. He squeezed Tyler like a creepy uncle unrelated to the family.

"Tommy!" She pushed him away with one hand. "Get lost."

"Hey!" He yanked on his sleeves one at a time. "Watch the threads, will you?" Tommy wore a suit every day as if he had a permanent court date. "Can you believe this dude?" He latched his arm around Cary's shoulder. "Twenty years later and *this* fucking guy is still selling out arenas. Arenas. Tyler. Let me tell you—"

"You can tell her later." Cary saved her—and himself—from listening to an epic tale to nowhere. Tommy Napolitano was no raconteur, although he wore many shades of black.

"Ready?" Vegas asked Cary with his hand on the green room door.

"Ready." Cary nodded and they walked into the room, full of cheers and applause.

Sebastien and Tommy stayed out in the hall, loitering like teenagers outside of a convenience store.

"We're heading up to the fucking suite," Tommy said, running his tongue along his upper teeth. "And you're coming, Tyler."

"I'm leaving soon," she said. "It's my family's benefit concert."

"How's Bert?" Sebastien asked insincerely.

"Why don't you ask him yourself? You're more than welcome to come by after the show." Of course she was fucking with him. He wasn't welcome at all.

He snorted. "Tell him I said hello."

"Will do," she lied. As if she was going to tell her dad anything coming from that idiot's pie hole.

"The afterparty's going to be a fucking rager," Tommy added. "I'll finish my story."

Hard fucking pass, Tommy.

She waited until Sebastien and Tommy were in the elevator before heading to the dressing room. She had to leave at seven thirty, and not a second later.

As Tyler turned around she spotted an older man and woman walking toward her. How had they passed through security without anyone noticing?

"Hi, we're looking for Cary Kingston," the woman said, tugging on the lanyard around her neck.

Tyler examined the couple, squinting as if it would help her to place them.

"We're his parents," the gray-haired man said.

"Of course! Mr. and Mrs. Kingston." She rushed to shake their hands, going overboard to impress them. "I'm Tyler. I work at SDM."

"Please, call us John and Pamela," he said. "Mr. Kingston was my father."

Hi Mom and Dad! No. She stopped short of embarrassing herself.

"He's in a meet and greet, but I'll show you to his dressing room," Tyler said.

"We don't want to be a bother." Pamela's eyes sparkled like her son's. "We're just happy to be invited."

That was my idea, Pamela.

"Don't be silly." Tyler opened his door. "Help yourself to whatever you want. I'll let him know you're here."

Pamela smiled. "Thank you, Tyler."

"You're welcome. Happy birthday, Mrs. Kingston."

Brownie points.

A few minutes later Tyler entered the green room and pushed her way through the crowd. Cary sat at the end of a long table, signing posters and autographs.

"Sorry to bother you," she said, not really meaning it.

He looked up from signing his name with a Sharpie. "You're hardly a bother."

She bit her bottom lip, trying not to smile. "Your parents are here. I showed them to your dressing room."

"Thanks for doing that."

"Don't mention it." The line behind the table was a hundred people deep. "I know you're busy, so I guess I'll see you later?"

Cary continued signing autographs and posing for selfies. "Sounds good."

Sounds good? You practically begged me to be here.

Maybe he was just being polite last night, but why pay all that attention to her when he didn't have to? Ugh. She'd never understand men as long as she lived, and if there was an afterlife.

The house lights dimmed and the audience chanted, "Cary! Cary!"

Tyler folded her coat over her arms and watched from the backstage area.

The first song in his set was one of her favorites, and she danced to the beat until Cary turned around to the side of the stage and played his guitar right at her.

She stopped mid-dance and laughed, embarrassed. He laughed too, before turning back to the crowd, holding out the microphone, and making them sing the verse. He had a commanding stage presence, like it was second nature. The lyrics made her body yearn for him, desperate for his affection.

Was it possible that her sister was right? He'd written some of the most heart-wrenching love songs she'd ever heard. If he'd felt those things, even half of those things, she was in trouble. The biggest kind.

Dammit.

Two songs turned into five before she checked the time on her phone: 7:35.

She had to go.

When Tyler arrived at the casino she went straight to the dressing room and opened the door. She half expected it to be decorated with balloons that spelled Happy Birthday.

But it wasn't. Thank god for small miracles.

She looked around the empty room, bummed that she wouldn't be seeing Cary later. She took a deep breath and exhaled through her mouth.

Happy fucking birthday.

Several hours later, after most of the bands had played, Tyler delegated her babysitting duties to the casino's stage manager before he blew a gasket. Older guys hated taking direction, especially from women.

Besides, it was still her birthday for another hour, and it was time for a drink. Or two.

Her phone vibrated, and she held that thought. It was Vegas on text.

On r way 2 casino.

Shit. What if Sebastien was calling her bluff? Nadie was hitting the stage in ten minutes and she didn't feel like dealing with his bullshit. Or smelling his breath.

She texted back. *Who are you with?*

CK.

As in Cary Kingston.

Oh my god. She placed her hand on her chest. Why was Cary with him? Maybe Vegas was joking. But maybe he wasn't. No. That wasn't like him.

The casino was a dump compared to the venues that Cary played and the sound echoed from the metal roof, not purposely built for live music. Plus she'd have to introduce Cary to her family, explaining why the biggest rock star in the world was attending her mother's benefit.

Where was that bottle of champers?

Five minutes later her phone vibrated. It was Vegas again.

We're here.

She took a second to respond.

Meet you at the back door.

With the theme from *A Summer Place*—her grandma's favorite movie—swirling in her head, she drew in a breath and strolled down the hall as if it were a Sunday on the seawall, without the hazard of cyclists.

Tyler opened the door. *Yep, that's Cary.* He'd obviously showered, as his hair was wet, but she wasn't worried about him catching a cold, because that wasn't an actual thing.

"Where are your parents?" she asked, tilting her head.

His forehead creased, confused by the question. "They're staying at my aunt's."

Right. He had family in Winnipeg.

She pointed to his guitar case. "Are you planning on busking or something?"

"No." He scowled at Vegas. "Didn't you tell her?"

"Sorry, man." Vegas shook his head. "You didn't ask."

"Ask me what?" She cut Vegas off, ears perked.

This ought to be good.

"I thought I'd play a few songs." Cary tapped on the side of his guitar case. "Help out a good cause if I can?"

Ha! Like she was going to say no to him. She opened the door wider. "I think we can squeeze you in." The knots in her stomach tightened into a ball. Maybe this was his master plan all along. Or maybe it was an afterthought.

A few seconds later Tyler caught the stage manager's eye and he flashed his hands, holding up three fingers.

"You're on next," she told Cary. "But they only have time for three songs."

"No worries." He swept his hair away from his eyes. "Sorry for crashing your concert."

She smirked. "Don't make a habit of it."

As a precaution Tyler guided him to the side of the stage. She didn't want Nadie to see him and freak out. She was freaking out enough for both of them, and then some.

Bert, the MC and musical director for the night, lifted the microphone from its stand. "Please give a warm welcome to Winnipeg's next big star, Nadie Grant!"

The crowd followed suit and applauded.

Nadie sang the same Joni Mitchell song that she'd rehearsed earlier in the day and Tyler choked back the tears pooling in her eyes, preventing a waterfall down her face. She didn't want to cry in front of Cary Kingston, especially not on her birthday.

"She's amazing," Cary said.

"Really good," Vegas agreed.

"She's my niece."

"Your niece?" Cary's eyes shocked open.

"She's sixteen," Tyler added. "Almost seventeen."

"Wow." Cary pointed to the stage. "She's talented."

"It runs in the family. The Robertsons are backing her up, and my sister made her the dress she's wearing."

After the song ended Bert boomed, "Give it up for Nadie Grant!" The crowd cheered and whistled. "Don't forget to bid on the silent auction! It ends at midnight."

Nadie skipped down the steps and smiled at her aunt.

"You killed it," Tyler said, hugging her niece. "As Kim would say, straight fire."

Nadie stammered, "Ho-holy shit."

"Nadie!" Tyler laughed, but it was hardly offensive. The language that she'd heard on tour buses would have shocked the filthiest comedian.

"Sorry, Auntie Ty, but"—she pointed—"that's Cary Kingston."

"You were amazing," Cary said, shrugging into his guitar. "The pressure's on, superstar."

Bert jogged down the steps. "What the . . . ?"

Tyler cupped her hand over her dad's ear. "Slight change in plans."

"Nice meeting you, sir." Cary extended his hand. "I'm Cary. Big fan."

Bert stared at Tyler, eyes bulging while shaking Cary's hand. "Same, but—"

"He's playing a few songs, Dad."

"Thanks son," Bert said. "Means a lot."

Son-in-law sounds better.

"Don't mention it." Cary shook his head like it was nothing.

Bert turned back around and climbed the stairs with a pep in his step. He grabbed the microphone and shouted, "Winnipeg, we've got an extra special treat for you!" He revved up the crowd by raising his arms. "Put your hands together for Manitoba's own . . . Cary Kingston!"

The audience half-applauded, probably expecting to see a tribute artist. Cover bands were common in casinos, especially in the Prairies where it was challenging to draw headliners.

Darting up the steps with a guitar slung over his shoulder, Cary hugged Bert as if they were close friends.

Cary grabbed the microphone and yelled, "Winnipeg! It's good to be home!"

The crowd went into a frenzy and phones flashed like fireflies in the darkness.

A few moments later Dylan appeared, glaring at her sister, and mouthed, *What the fuck?*

Tyler shrugged as if she didn't understand the question, but she knew perfectly well what was up. Cary Kingston was playing at her family's benefit concert. Who woulda thunk?

"Did you know he was coming?" Dylan asked, pouring champagne into her sister's glass.

Tyler shook her head, eyes fixed on the stage. "I'm totally freaking out."

"Me too." Dylan blew out a breath. "What happened last night?"

"Nothing. We watched the game."

"I thought he didn't like hockey."

"He doesn't."

Tyler studied Cary's fingers as they moved along the neck of his guitar. She closed her eyes and imagined what his fingers could do to her in the bedroom.

It's getting hot in here. She fanned herself with her hand but it was no use.

After he played two up-tempo hits, Cary strummed the first few chords of his most popular love song and flashed his famous smile at her. She smiled back, goosebumps running down her arms.

"Yeah, I'm sure that kiss meant nothing." Dylan nudged her shoulder. "You're such a loser."

"What?" Tyler avoided her sister's gaze and continued to focus on Cary.

"Are you kidding me? He's totally into you."

"You're crazy." She finished her second glass of champagne before pouring a third. "Bottoms up!"

Dylan covered her glass. "I don't like Nickelback."

"What?"

"It's one of their songs, dummy."

"Right." She didn't understand why they were the most hated band in the world. Nickelback had great songs, an amazing live show, and were super nice guys too.

Cary's song ended and he addressed the crowd. "Thank you, Winnipeg! Don't forget to bid on the silent auction." He held his Gibson Montana by its neck. "You can bid on this one too!"

"Did he just give his guitar away?" Dylan didn't seem to trust what she'd heard.

"I think so." Tyler blinked until her eyes blurred. "Do you want to meet him?"

"No." Dylan glanced at the rock star. "I need to stay objective . . . for you."

"There's nothing going on, Dylan."

"I don't believe you."

I don't believe me, either.

Tyler clicked her kitten heels across the floor to where Cary stood. "Thank you! You didn't have to do that."

"My guitar?" He flicked his wrist dismissively. "I've got a million of them."

"It's the big finale if you want to join us, son?" Bert interrupted.

"Dad!" She couldn't believe that he'd put Cary on the spot after what he'd done for them.

Cary hung his head, disappointed. "I don't have a guitar anymore."

"Thanks for doing that." Bert shook his hand again. "Above and beyond. You can play mine if you'd like."

Pardon?

Bert didn't let anyone play his beloved Stratocaster 2-tone sunburst. The guitar was a gift from his wife on their first anniversary and he held it sacred, almost worshiped it. Michelle had worked extra shifts when Bert was on the road that winter. His wife had told Bert—and he'd told the kids—the delight on his face had been worth it.

"I'd love to," Cary said.

What kind of fresh hell is this?

Not long after the finale ended, the dressing room door opened and Tyler stumbled backward, rolling over on her kitten heels and nearly twisting her ankle.

"Happy birthday!" the Robertson family shouted as Dylan and her dad carried a slab of white cake with lit candles.

Cary frowned at his tour manager like he was in deep shit for something.

Tyler covered her face with both hands. "You guys . . ."

"You thought we forgot!" Bert chuckled from his belly. "Gotcha!"

"I couldn't even look at you this morning." Dylan bent over laughing. "It's your favorite." She stood up and pointed. "Red velvet with cream cheese frosting."

"I'm a better actor than you, Dylan." Joe hugged his sister-in-law. "Happy birthday."

Nadie hopped on the balls of her shoes. "Happy birthday, Auntie Ty!"

"Happy birthday." Perry, her eldest brother, kissed her on the cheek. "Now blow out the candles. I'm starving."

Stewart, who was two years younger than Perry, hugged her warmly. "Happy birthday, Tiger." When Stewart was a little kid he couldn't pronounce "Tyler."

"Make a wish," Bert reminded her.

What should I wish for?

She glanced at Cary but her mind flashed X-rated images—too dirty for birthday wishes. She closed her eyes and wished he'd write another love song, then blew out the candles in one breath.

"Your mom would've been proud of you, kiddo." Bert licked the icing off a candle.

"Would've?" Cary's eyes shifted in her direction.

After thirty years Bert still had trouble saying it. "My wife passed away from cancer." He twisted his wedding ring in semicircles. He'd never taken it off, not even to play slide guitar. "That's when we started this benefit concert."

"I'm sorry." Cary's voice softened. "I didn't know." He hugged Tyler gently. "Is there anything else you want to tell me?"

Like my birthday wish?

"No."

"Everyone!" Bert clapped twice. "Take a glass. There's wine, champagne, sparkling grape juice for the kids." He handed Cary a glass of red wine. "Made it myself."

"Thanks." Cary took the glass willingly.

"No!" Tyler cautioned. "You don't have to drink that."

The rock star cracked a smile from the side of his mouth. "I'm sure it's fine."

"Raise 'em up!" Bert lifted his glass over his head. "To Michelle!"

Everyone echoed, "To Michelle!"

After eating his fair share of cake, Perry grabbed Tyler in a playful headlock. Not much had changed since she was a child— he was still the clown of the family, taking after their father. Now his kids had to put up with his shenanigans and his poor wife, of course.

"Birthday noogies!" Perry rubbed her head with his knuckles but she twisted out of his grip and straightened her half-pulled-out topknot.

"Jesus, Perry. Grow up."

"I'm six four," Perry joked.

"We've got company." Tyler gestured to Cary and her brother made googly eyes. Staring at Perry, she drew a line across her neck with her finger as a warning.

Perry seemed to catch her drift and extended his hand. "Hope to see you back here, Cary. Thanks for playing our concert."

"Pleasure's mine," he said, shaking his hand. "I hope to see you, too."

You do?

Perry winked at the birthday girl. "We're heading out, Ty-Ty. It's way past the kids' bedtime." His face dropped. "We sure do miss you."

She dodged his gaze and mustered a tight-lipped smile.

Stewart whistled with two fingers. "Boys! Go hug your aunt. We're leaving now."

All four boys ran up to Tyler, nearly knocking her over again, but she was happy to see their hockey conditioning was paying off. They were all tall enough to be defensemen.

"Bye, sweetie," Perry's wife said with a pout. She loved her sister-in-law more than life itself.

"I'll be home at Christmas, Tamera. Take care of yourself."

"I love you," Stewart told his baby sister. "Be good now."

A single tear hung from her lash line, meaning an ugly cry was coming. It never got easier saying goodbye to her family. In fact, the older she got, it was harder to handle.

"I love you too." Tyler raised her voice. "But get out of here!"

★　★　★

Shortly after midnight Bert whistled, quieting the dressing room.

"The auction's officially sold out," he said. "Cary's guitar went for twenty-five grand!" As far as it concerned Tyler, he could crash their benefit anytime he wanted to. "Thanks again, son." Bert's voice cracked on the last word. "Means everything."

Tyler added, "It really does, Cary."

He nodded, humbled by their gratitude. "Can I ask you a question, sir?"

"Shoot." Bert stood up straight, fingers jammed into the front pockets of his jeans, thumbs hanging out. She couldn't imagine what he was going to ask her dad. Hopefully nothing too personal.

"What was it like playing with the Humbler? Other than you, he's my favorite guitar player."

Bert gave him a heartfelt smile. "He was a sweet guy, soft-spoken. He let his guitar do the talking."

"Did he ever," Cary said. "His fingers were like butter."

"I'm just glad I knew him." Bert stared into the distance as if he were trying to remember something. "I'd be happy to show you a few of his tricks the next time you're in town."

"I'd love that." Cary beamed.

I'll show you a few tricks, Cary Kingston.

Vegas walked over and gently rested his hand on Cary's shoulder. "Hey, man, we've got an early flight tomorrow."

Cary sighed. "No rest for the wicked."

"I'll walk you." Tyler slipped out of her kitten heels. "Ooh . . ." She wiggled her toes. "That's much better."

After Cary and Vegas said goodbye to her family, they followed her down the hall to the back-door exit. Her heart ticked like a bomb about to explode, but she didn't know how to defuse it. The countdown started in her head: 10 . . . 9 . . . 8 . . .

"Is the car here?" Cary asked impatiently.

"I'll go see." Vegas zipped up his coat. "See you, Tyler."

The door shut and a cool breeze whistled into the casino. *It's now or never.* Tyler wrapped her arms around Cary's shoulders in a more-than-friendly manner. "Thank you for everything."

"Happy birthday." He gave her waist a squeeze. "I wish I'd known. I would've brought you something."

"Are you kidding?" She balked. "You donated your guitar."

"Really, it was nothing."

With liquid courage running through her veins she leaned in and kissed him, finding their mouths fit together like Lego pieces. If only she'd worn Le-Glue on her lips instead of gloss.

Mmm . . . red velvet cake and cheap wine.

She'd dreamed about this moment a thousand times, his slow, long kiss, his full lips parting . . .

The door banged twice.

Shit.

Their lip-lock broke and she smiled shyly.

"Text and let me know you got back safe?" she asked, meeting his bewildered gaze.

"Sure. Say hi to Rory for me."

"Will do, Cary."

CARY

"Say hi to Rory for me?" Cary repeated as he climbed into the car and slammed the door shut. He had to go and ruin a perfectly good kiss with that stupid comment.

Vegas tapped on the back of the driver's seat. "Let's go."

"That's what I told her." He buckled his seat belt, shaking his head. "To say hi to her dog."

"Real smooth, Ex-Lax." Vegas pulled his hair back and laughed.

Cary shoved his tour manager's shoulder, but he barely flinched. "How come you didn't know it was her birthday?" He didn't mean to sound like a spoiled child and corrected his tone. "I mean, you two are friends, aren't you?"

"We're not Facebook friends, man." Vegas scrolled through his phone. "It's not in my calendar either. I'll fix that."

"Did you know Bert was her dad?" Cary raised an eyebrow of suspicion. Why hadn't this come up before? He'd practically spent every waking moment with Vegas. Hell, they'd even listened to some of Bert's old records together. Not a peep out of Sebastien either.

"Of course," Vegas said. "Everyone from Winnipeg knows Bert Robertson."

"The Robertsons are kind of like the Partridge Family." That described them perfectly. "I wish I were closer to my folks, but the constant touring, you know."

Over the years he'd grown apart from his family. The road was grueling and he'd put up barriers as a means of protection. Being famous was weird and he didn't think they'd understand. But seeing how happy his mom was tonight really hit home. His parents had always been supportive of his career, and all he'd ever done was buy them a Tudor-style house, some considered a mansion. Real estate was easy to come by in Brandon, so even that wasn't a big deal to him.

"Yeah, I know," Vegas said. "I make an effort, though. I call my mom every Sunday."

"I wouldn't know what to say."

"They don't care, man. Moms are good that way. So, when are you seeing Tyler again?"

He closed his eyes. *That kiss . . . her lips . . . say hi to Rory for me.* What a chump.

"I guess I'll see her next month at my show. Or now." Cary pulled out his phone and frowned at the screen. "Her Instagram's locked."

"Stalker," Vegas joked.

"Trust me." He rubbed the back of his neck. "I feel like one."

"Just send her a follow request."

"I can't do that!"

"Why not?"

What if she didn't accept? He'd be left hanging without a net. But he wanted to see her, needed to see her, if only in two dimensions. He took a deep breath and clicked on the screen. His request was now pending.

CHAPTER 5

"Fuck!" Sebastien yelled from his office, jolting Rory awake from an afternoon nap.

"Was that a regular fuck, or, like, extra aggressive?" Kim asked.

Tyler angled her head toward his door, but she couldn't see him. "That was a little much, even for Sebastard."

Kim crinkled her nose. "Dude, are you *seriously* not going tonight?"

Cary Kingston had sold out the local stadium in record time, but SDM had marketed it as a "homecoming" concert, and it pissed Tyler off. Cary was from Brandon, Manitoba, and as much as the city had tried they couldn't turn him into a Vancouverite.

Tyler leaned forward and lowered her voice. "I told you, I drunk kissed him." She'd been trying to forget what little she could remember from that night a few weeks earlier. "I'm an idiot. I kissed Cary Kingston."

"He kissed you first," Kim reminded her. "And he followed you on Insta."

The day after the benefit concert Cary had sent her a follower request. After deleting any unflattering pictures of herself, she accepted it.

Tyler let out a sigh. "Yeah, and his fans sent me a million requests." It didn't take long for the Kingers to clue in that he was following her, so she changed her picture to an avatar and shut off her notifications.

"Here." Kim wiggled her fingers. "Hand me your phone." With reluctance she did as she was told. "See? He sent you a hotel emoji, followed by a thumbs-up, then—ooh!" She winked. "X-O."

Had the ancient Egyptians been any better at deciphering hieroglyphics? Tyler didn't think so. It was her own damn fault for texting him in symbols rather than using her words.

"I sent him a thumbs-up back." Tyler doodled hearts on her notepad, but she didn't write their initials because it was a long shot.

"Yeah, everyone knows that's when the conversation ends." Kim shared the same theory as her sister. "You're not an idiot," she added.

Tyler put down her pen and crossed her arms. "I'm done with musicians."

"Dude, he's hardly wearing a CBGB t-shirt and skinny jeans."

She snorted a laugh. "Even if he were interested—which he's not—I can't date our biggest client, Kim."

"So what? You're not his day-to-day." Her bestie had an answer for everything. It was true, Sebastien and Vegas managed his daily activities while Cheryl, his superstar publicist, handled his press.

"Still, it's not professional." She reasoned her way out of it.

"You can always quit." Kim held her hands in prayer. "But please take me with you. He's sending me back out with the Westgrays, I just know it." She crossed her ankles underneath the chair. "I keep getting mistaken for one of their girlfriends. Like I'd date them and their gross diseases. No thank you."

"Allie's trying her best to get you on another tour." Tyler pursed her lips, then plumped them. "As for Cary, I can't go through that again." Her ex-boyfriend had ruined her faith in men, probably forever and then some. "Not after Dave."

"If I see him, I'll kill him," Kim said in a serious tone. "It's bad enough you bankrolled him, but cheating on you? Dude, fuck him and his stupid band."

She was right, his band was stupid. "Yet he always found money for weed and booze—go figure. He said I'd be paying the same rent whether he lived there or not. I didn't invite him to move in, remember? He showed up with a duffel bag and never left." Tyler gave her head the shake it deserved. "Duffel Bag Dave."

"Fuck Duffel Bag Dave." Kim shifted in her seat. "Have you *ever* had a nice boyfriend?"

"Born losers, every single one of them." She stared into space. "You know, he didn't even say 'bless you' when I sneezed."

"Monster!"

"He was super lazy in bed too."

"Imagine if, like, women needed to have orgasms to get pregnant?"

"Humans would be extinct by now." They nodded and Tyler went on, "Half the time he couldn't get it up because he was too hammered."

"Ew. Whiskey dick is the worst."

"Exactly. So what's going on with you? Let's get you on Tinder or something."

"Dude, I can't date a *civilian*." Kim threw her hands in the air. "Normal guys freak the fuck out when I tell them what I do for a living."

"What? Like you're giving BJs on the back of the tour bus? I'm not surprised, though. Civilians are jealous of the bands or way too eager to hang out with them."

Kim laughed. "Yeah. I know, right? I deserve hazard pay as it is."

Tyler's door flew open.

"Didn't you fucking hear me?" Sebastien shouted while Rory darted under the desk.

"How may I help you?" Tyler asked calmly, trying to de-escalate whatever situation had put him in a bad mood—or a worse mood than usual.

Sebastien crossed his eyes. "Vegas broke his leg. On show day."

"Oh no! Is he okay?"

"Okay? Who the fuck cares if he's okay? I don't have a tour manager, Tyler. Do I have to remind you that Cary's on the road until next summer?"

She did not need reminding.

"How long is he out for?" Tyler asked, voice concerned.

"Six to eight weeks," Sebastien answered, calming down slightly but not enough to make a difference to his demeanor.

Tyler raised her brow at Kim, hoping it would be of interest to her, and she nodded.

"Kim can do it," she suggested.

"I totally can." Kim sat up straight, seeming more presentable. "I've been tour managing for, like, forever."

Sebastien glared at Tyler. "A girl?" He snickered as his nostrils flared. "Tour managing Cary Kingston?" He turned the bill of his baseball cap in Kim's direction. "It's bad enough Bob Shaw hired you without my permission."

Everyone called SDM's chief operating officer by his full name. It sounded like one word, Bobshaw, when people said it. Next to Kim, Bob was Tyler's favorite person in the office.

Instead of trying to change his mind, Tyler played him. "It's just for tonight. You won't find anyone on this short notice. I'll find someone—a man—to pick up the tour. Deal?"

"Fine." Sebastien huffed, slamming the door as he left. Kim stuck out her tongue, flipping him off behind his back.

"Vegas will help you with everything," Tyler promised while texting him.

"Are you really going to find another TM?"

Tyler blinked up from her phone. "What do you think?"

For the next hour Tyler and Kim scrutinized the guest list. Three hundred people were on it, and they needed to whittle it down by half. Everyone thought they were important but they weren't, so Tyler highlighted the names of ten VIPs and gave the rest "after-show" passes.

When they were finished with the list, Tyler opened the door to her office to find Lara chatting with someone at the reception desk, loud as all get-out. Of course Detective Rory went to investigate while his mom and Kim followed him.

"Rory!" Cary picked up the dog. "Who's a good boy?"

Rory answered by wagging his tail and kissing the rock star.

I'm jealous.

"Hi Tyler," Cary said with a smile.

The receptionist interjected, "I forgot to tell you my name. I'm Lara."

"Cary," he said, keeping his gaze on Tyler.

"I know who you are." Lara gushed over him. "I can't wait for tonight."

"Cary!" Bob greeted him from down the hall. He'd recently lost a lot of weight and his suit hung from his body.

The music industry had nearly ruined Bob Shaw with its free drugs and open bars. He used to be the life of the party, but after taking twelve steps he lost his music industry friends to sobriety. He was an accountant by trade and a certified financial planner, so nowadays he kept to himself and his numbers. He cracked up every time he said, "*Those* I can count on."

Sebastien poked his big stupid head out of his office. "Cary! I didn't know you were coming by." Nothing irked him more than being surprised, like a goalie's reaction when the puck went in from friendly fire. "C'mon, take a load off."

"I was hoping to sit down with Kim." Cary scanned the office. "Vegas said she'd be around?"

"Over here." Kim raised her hand.

"I've heard great things," Cary said.

Kim nodded. "Likewise."

"Got a minute to talk about tonight?"

"Sure, we can use the conference room."

"Aren't you forgetting something?" Tyler asked, resting her hands on her hips. "My dog?"

"What dog?" Cary hid Rory under his jacket.

A tickle ran up Tyler's nose and she sneezed into her elbow. "Excuse me," she said.

"Bless you," Cary replied, and Kim winked at her with a knowing smile.

Tyler extended her arms to grab him. "May I have him back, please?"

"Sorry, finders keepers."

Cary gave her a cheeky grin and followed Kim down the hall.

A short while later Cary knocked on Tyler's half-open door as Rory came barreling around the corner.

"All done?" she asked.

"Kim knows what she's doing. Thanks for suggesting her."

"No problem. Hey, how's Vegas? I mean, he said he was fine, but I don't believe him."

"He's not good." Cary snapped his fingers. "I almost forgot. I brought Mutt Muffs for Rory."

"Mutt Muffs?" She repeated in confusion.

Cary retrieved the Mutt Muffs from his bag and placed them over Rory's ears.

"Hold still." He lined up the shot with his phone and took the dog's picture. Of course, Rory liked all forms of attention and posed willingly. "They're for the show," he added.

"Thanks, but Rory . . . I mean, I'm not going to your show." His eyes opened as if surprised, so she elaborated, "I promised Bob Shaw I'd help him with his templates." Bob had earned his accounting degree in the eighties, so she was his in-house tech support.

"Not going?" Cary dropped his head, shoulders rounding. "Let's go talk to Bob Shaw."

As soon as they left her office Rory followed them down the hall. Bob kept cookies in the bottom drawer of his desk, and the dog knew exactly where they were.

"Bob Shaw!" Cary opened his arms. "You're not going to the show? What the hell?"

Bob didn't trust himself around alcohol—or Tommy—and no one could blame him. Tommy was a bad influence.

"Sorry, Cary." Bob grimaced. "These numbers don't add themselves."

"I'll help you," Tyler said.

Kim entered Bob's office and gave her friend *the look*. Tyler shrugged one shoulder and smirked as if to say, *I'm still not going.*

"Dude, I could use your help at the venue. It sounds like Vegas's leg is really fucked up."

Tyler gestured in Bob's direction. "I promised him."

"You don't mind, do you, Bob Shaw?" Kim asked. "She can help you later."

Bob pushed his glasses along the bridge of his nose. "No." He shook his head. "Not at all. You kids go have fun."

The *Jeopardy* music looped in Tyler's head as she weighed her options. Cary wanted her to go, but he'd also said that about his Winnipeg show, practically ignoring her. Then again, he had shown up at the benefit concert. And her hair looked especially good today, so at least there was something positive. "Fine, but I'm not bringing Rory. He's staying at home."

"Poor Rory." Cary's bottom lip turned into a cute frown.

"Yes." Tyler held back a smile. "Poor Rory."

"Who wants a cookie?" Bob asked, and the dog performed his obligatory dance.

A few moments later Cary waved on his way out the door. "See you tonight."

"Bye, Cary!" Lara shouted, loud enough for the next building to close its windows. "Let me know if you need anything!" Like he would call Lara. *Pfft.*

After Cary left, Kim showed herself into Tyler's office. "In here," she said, widening the door.

"Why?" Tyler asked, going there anyway.

"I have something to tell you." Kim closed the door behind them. "Dude, are you fucking crazy?"

"No?" She meant to sound more certain of her mental state.

"He dropped your name, like, a thousand times, and he got your dog earmuffs."

"He likes my dog."

"You're missing the plot." Kim sighed, exasperated.

Tyler lowered her gaze. "There's no story here."

Where's my happily ever after?

CARY

What the hell was that about? Cary had been looking forward to seeing Tyler since they were in Winnipeg. Counting the days if he were honest with himself. Obviously she'd changed her mind about him and wasn't going to his show. Well, not until he'd sulked like a kid not getting his choice of cereal at the grocery store.

Was his past catching up with him? Or was it something more. His reputation as a ladies' man wasn't true—okay, it was a *little* true. Or it had been in his youth. Most of his ex-girlfriends had waited around like in that Adele tune, but he never got back together with them—other than Emma—and she didn't do anything differently and wasn't any better to him.

At least Rory was happy to see him. He smiled and pulled out his phone. Rory looked cute in his Mutt Muffs, so he posted the picture on Instagram.

Cary's car service was waiting outside—doors locked, of course. He half expected to find Vegas in the back seat before he remembered about his injury. What was he going to do? Vegas did *everything* for him on tour. Maybe Kim would work out. Not to mention she was Tyler's best friend and could put in a good word.

He wasn't used to chasing after women.

One more try was all he had in him.

CHAPTER 6

Tyler arrived at the stadium a few hours later, tied a lanyard around her belt loop, and shoved an all-access pass into her back pocket. She was there as a music industry professional, not as a Kinger, even though she considered herself to be an honorary member.

Cary's visit to the office was a bit of a let-down so she was determined to fix it—to save face if nothing else.

Tyler's phone vibrated, it was Kim on text.

Green Room.

She walked backstage and found her bestie directing Cary's team like a Navy SEAL commander.

"How's it going?" Tyler asked.

"So far so good," Kim said, adjusting her headset. "But they're, like, working with a skeleton crew—bare-bones. It's kind of weird for something of this magnitude."

Tyler cranked her neck. "Is Vegas around?"

"Over there." Kim pointed in his direction. He was hobbling around on elbow crutches since he was too tall for the regular ones.

"Vegas!" Tyler slow-motion jogged toward him. "How are you, buddy?"

"I'm pissed." He stood on his good leg. "I'm out for six weeks. At least. No pay."

"Not even a per diem?" She tightened her topknot. "You got hurt at work." Apparently he'd tripped over some cables that shouldn't have been there in the first place. *Fucking crew workers.*

"Sebastard refused to file an insurance claim." He shook his head, frustrated, but knowing Sebastien it wasn't entirely unexpected.

"That sucks."

"It more than sucks." Vegas turned his head and pointed at Kim. "But thanks for finding this gem. The guys are already afraid of her."

"They should be afraid." She laughed. "They need to know who's in charge."

"I'm already calling her the Boss, like Springsteen."

That made Tyler laugh even harder.

Meanwhile, the SDM team strutted down the hall like they were in an old-timey Western. Everyone wore laminates with lanyards around their necks except for Cary—not a shocker.

"Fucking Tommy," Vegas groaned. "I'm not in the mood for his long-winded stories."

Tyler turned her head, perplexed. "Why is Lara with them?"

"She's been here since five," Kim grumbled. "Fucking Tommy brought her."

"I see you got the memo!" Cary shouted.

She squinted and mouthed, *What?*

"Black . . . we're both wearing black," he said, pointing to his outfit.

She walked toward Cary and went in for a hug, but at the last second Tommy swooped in, creating a human roadblock.

Fuck off.

"We're having a bash at the casino later," Tommy said. "An after-afterparty. You should come. Bring some friends."

As if.

"Hi Tyler!" Lara gave her a toothy smile. "How are you?"

Tyler frowned at her skimpy red dress and leopard-print heels.

Jesus, put some clothes on.

When Lara started working at SDM, Tyler told her to buckle down and roll up her sleeves, but she'd unbuttoned her shirt instead of listening. That kind of attention from men always came at a price, especially in the music industry.

"We're heading up to the fucking suite," Tommy said.

"Free drinks," Sebastien added.

Tommy pointed at Tyler. "You're coming."

"I need her down here." Cary's voice was stern, demanding. "She's helping me with something."

Yeah, Tommy.

Lara raised her hand. "I can stay and help—"

"We've got it," Kim snapped at her.

"Good," Sebastien said. "Let's get out of here."

After they left, Cary turned to the women. "I take it you guys don't like Lara?"

The Price Is Right music rang in Tyler's head.

Kim fiddled with a knob on her headset. "She's annoying, dude."

"Super thirsty," Tyler chimed in, checking her back pocket to see if her pass was still intact. "I guess it's not her fault that Sebastien hired her on the spot."

With no experience or credentials, Sebastien had hired Lara after she sent him a link to her demo. He didn't listen to her music but he liked the pictures on her website.

"Are you ready?" Kim asked Cary with her hand on the green-room door.

"Ready." He winked at Tyler and followed Kim inside.

Twenty minutes later, Vegas's phone lit up and he glanced at his screen.

"Um . . . do you know how to sew?" he asked Tyler.

That's a weird question.

"As a matter of fact, I do."

Grandma Mary—Tyler's paternal grandmother—had taught the girls when they were adolescents. She'd practically moved into the Robertsons' house after her mom's untimely passing but died five years earlier, leaving Tyler without a mother figure or a shoulder to cry on.

"Cary's button fell off," Vegas explained.

"I bet he has a million black shirts."

"I didn't ask. I'll tell him you'll fix it." Vegas resumed texting. "He'll meet you in his dressing room. There's a sewing kit in his wardrobe case."

Does he need babysitting?

Tyler walked into his dressing room and opened his wardrobe case. *Aha!* There were ten shirts hanging in a row like half-window blackout curtains. Damn. She hated being right when she didn't want to be.

Seconds later the door flew open and Cary rushed in.

"Thanks for fixing this." He handed her the orphaned button. "It popped off while I was signing autographs."

She scrunched her nose, not understanding why he needed it fixed. "You have a bunch of shirts just like this."

"I know, but I sound-checked in this one."

"Are you superstitious?"

"Big time."

Rock stars and athletes—go figure.

"Okay, how do you want to do this?" she asked. Could she handle seeing him half naked? Who was she kidding. She'd dreamed about it every night since September.

"It's probably easier if I take it off." Cary shut the door and unfastened his buttons from the top. She focused on threading the needle instead of watching him disrobe. The shirt dropped onto the armchair beside her and a waft of cologne went up her nose.

Obsession.

She grabbed the shirt and the loose button. "This is the problem with these cheap shirts," she teased, fingering the expensive material. "Crappy buttons."

"Funny," he said. "Thanks again for Kim. She's a force to be reckoned with." Tyler concentrated on sewing his shirt like it was plastic surgery. He continued, "I want to keep her on. At least until Vegas gets back."

"Yeah, try convincing Sebastien." Her tone had a dusting of sarcasm.

"He works for me, not the other way around."

Try telling him that.

"Aren't you leaving tomorrow?" she asked, keeping her eyes on the garment.

"Tomorrow night," he confirmed. "Kim said that she'd be ready if she could get on a flight."

"I'm surprised you don't have your own plane."

"I'm conscious of my carbon footprint."

Right, the environment.

"All done." She handed him the shirt without making eye contact and caught his reflection in the full-length mirror. *Jesus Christ!* He was in seriously good shape, and not just for thirty-eight.

A wave of heat traveled up her spine and she wiped the back of her neck.

"Thanks for the assist," Cary said.

She snapped out of her daze and turned on her heel. "No problem."

"Wait," he said.

She stopped dead in her tracks and spun around.

Cary gave her an awkward smile. "How about a kiss for good luck?"

"Why not?" she said, playing it cool. "For good luck."

She grabbed her hands to stop them from trembling and walked toward him. She stared into his eyes and a calmness melted her body as she fell into his arms. They kissed with closed mouths until his lips parted . . .

There was a knock at the door.

Foiled again.

"Ten minutes, Cary!" Her best friend's voice came through loud and clear, then they burst out laughing.

"I've never noticed your freckles," he said. "They're cute."

She covered her nose with both hands. "I hate them."

"They're perfect." He lifted her hands away from her face. "How about meeting me for a drink later?"

"Here?" she asked, not sure what he meant.

"No, definitely not here. The Wine Bar. I'll meet you at ten-thirty?"

"Okay." She walked toward the door and turned around. "Break a leg."

"Don't say that to Vegas," he joked.

Stick to your day job, Cary.

The November air was crisp but mild, considering the time of year. Tyler strolled along Pacific Boulevard after the show, reliving the kiss like a broken record.

Is my dream finally being realized?

The Wine Bar was crowded, so she sat at *their* table on the patio to give them some privacy. He'd just performed in front of forty-thousand people and she wanted him all to herself. To hoard him like Sebastien.

"Have you decided?" a man holding a pen asked. She could tell by his vacant stare that Kevin didn't recognize her from two months earlier.

"I'm waiting for someone." She checked her watch. "He should be here any minute."

The server nodded and excused himself.

Tyler's phone vibrated. It was a text message from Cary.

Is he cancelling?

Granted, it was almost impossible for an artist to leave after a show, especially a "hometown" show. And her boss was throwing an afterparty. Groupies. They were everywhere. It wasn't lost on

Sebastien that women used him to get access to rock stars, but he used them too, mostly because he was a user.

Tyler read the message.

Sorry! En route. Some jerk's concert is holding up traffic! xo

She laughed out loud and surveyed the patio, but she knew no one there. Her phone was on the table so she scrolled through Cary's Instagram.

"Rory!" she cheered. Cary had posted a picture of her dog wearing Mutt Muffs and had captioned it: *I love this little guy!* *#goodboy*

Tyler smiled, but she was jealous again. Thank god Sebastien didn't check Instagram. He didn't use the apps on his phone because his fingers were too "wide," as he called them. To her they looked more like upholstered fabric than skin. Anyway, Sebastien preferred to use his computer to talk shit about people in the music industry behind the safety of a firewall, but little did he know, she had access to his emails because he was too cheap to hire an in-house IT person.

Moments later a shiny black SUV pulled up to the curb. Cary stepped out of the truck wearing the same beanie as before but not the glasses.

"Sorry, traffic," he said, almost out of breath.

"Why didn't you walk?" She twisted her mouth and bit her lip.

"I don't know. I forgot it was an option." He leaned over and kissed her cheek like they were an old married couple. "I'm glad our table was available."

Kismet.

Across the patio, Kevin spotted Cary and hollered, "Hey, man!"

"Kevin!" He greeted the server with a wave, winking at Tyler.

"How was the show?" Kevin asked, approaching them. "I would've gone. But it sold out so fast."

"I've got a guest list," Cary said three hours too late.

"Ah, man," Kevin groaned. "What'll it be? Penfolds Grange?"

Cary answered, "Yes, please."

"Any food?"

"I'm always hungry after a show. Can you throw a few appetizers together? Not the entire menu, though." He pushed the beanie away from his eyes. "And truffle popcorn for Tyler."

Good memory.

"It's too expensive," she whispered.

"What is? Truffle popcorn?" he joked, but she didn't laugh.

Tyler frowned. "The wine."

"I sold out the stadium," he whispered back. "I think I'll be all right."

"May I please pay for the food?"

He reached for a carafe of water on the table. "Don't be ridiculous, Tyler."

"I have money." She didn't have Penfolds Grange kind of money, but she had enough for truffle popcorn. "I can afford the food."

Cary's eyes softened and he placed her hands between his like a sandwich. "Please promise me you won't bring it up again?"

"No."

He laughed, shaking his head. "What am I going to do with you?"

Anything you want, Cary Kingston.

"So, did you like the show?" he asked.

"I loved it, and I'm not just saying that. You play every concert like it's your last."

"Well, people pay their hard-earned money, and just knowing it's *someone's* first concert makes me want to give them a great experience."

"Why don't you have an opening act?"

Cary leaned back and clasped his hands behind his beanie. "That's a good question. I haven't heard anything I like enough." He leaned forward and took a sip of water before adding, "I don't know . . . I guess I'm too old to know what the kids like."

Tyler shook her head. "There are lots of good bands out there."

"That's the problem. They're good, not great."

"Arkells are pretty great."

He laughed. "I had no idea they were so popular. You were right. Banger after banger."

"Would you ever consider changing your position?"

He shrugged. "Sure, if they were great."

"Don't look now." Tyler leaned over the table and widened her eyes. "The people behind you are wearing your merch."

Cary pulled down his beanie and smirked, embarrassed by it. She couldn't imagine people walking around with her picture on their clothes. That would have been too weird for her.

After Kevin brought over the wine—with a decanter this time—Cary raised his glass.

"Cheers," he said.

"Cheers." Tyler sipped the wine slowly and closed her eyes. It was better than she'd remembered it, and it didn't give her a headache like she'd expected it would.

Her phone vibrated.

"Anyone we know?" Cary asked casually.

She read the message. "It's Tommy," she told him. "They're at the casino."

"Fucking Tommy." Cary rolled his eyes. "I don't like the way he was talking to you."

"He talks to everyone that way."

"Not me, he doesn't. I'm afraid I've been too easy on him because he helped me when I was just starting."

Tyler texted back and dropped the phone into her bag. "I told them to meet us here."

"What?" His eyes jumped out of his head.

"Just kidding." She laughed.

He blew out a breath, relieved. "I'm not used to people messing with me, but I kind of like it."

"Shh," she whispered, raising a finger to her lips. "Listen . . ."

The people sitting behind them were raving about his concert. "Best one yet. It just gets better and better," one of the women said.

They eavesdropped for a minute, then he twisted around. "How did you like the show?"

Tyler nudged his arm. "Stop it."

"Ow!" he joked, smiling at her with a flirtatious glance.

The woman with frosted highlights spoke first. "Like the show?" she asked. "We loved it!"

"We've been going to his concerts for twenty years," the other woman bragged. "Since we were in college, in fact." She stretched out her Cary Kingston hoodie, showing them that she was a big fan. "Did you have tickets?" she asked, unsuspectingly.

Tyler shook her head. "No, we didn't."

"Well, it sold out early," Bragging Woman told them. "Better luck next time."

A little while later Kevin came by their table and hovered. "Another bottle?" he asked, like it was water or something.

"Yes, please," Cary said, emptying the decanter.

"Cary . . ." Tyler crossed her arms and lowered her chin. She prided herself on being financially responsible, and the wine was downright extravagant.

"What?" He shrugged. "It isn't a school night."

"Why don't we have a glass instead?" she suggested.

"You can't order it by the glass," Kevin said.

Cary gave her a saucy grin. "We don't have to drink it all."

She shook the container of truffle popcorn onto her plate, trying to empty the last piece. "It's your call, but I need to tell you something."

"So you're keeping secrets from me?"

"It's not exactly a secret, but I thought you should know."

Cary's eyes flashed a look of worry. "What is it?"

"It's about Vegas . . ."

"Vegas?"

She nodded. "Sebastien isn't paying his per diem. That's the industry standard."

Without hesitation he said, "I'll take care of it."

"Thanks. Vegas doesn't like to cause problems, you know." She shifted in her seat. "So, back on the road tomorrow?" It was a rhetorical question since she'd memorized his schedule. She acknowledged having that kind of access to his whereabouts probably wasn't healthy.

"I am indeed. Hey, have you seen anything good lately?" he asked. "Any documentaries you can recommend?"

"I only watch music docs," she told him. "I'm sure you've seen the good ones. I haven't seen anything new—wait. I stand corrected. The Beastie Boys Story was amazing. Adam Yauch . . ." She lowered her eyes. "What a tragedy."

"The Beatles documentary is the only one I've seen in years," he confessed. "MCA was a great rapper and an even nicer human."

She lifted an eyebrow. "You've seen the Metallica one, right?"

"Nope."

"Cary!" She grabbed his arm. "You have to see it. It's my favorite movie."

"Of all time?"

"Pretty much. After Metallica's, watch the Eagles', and Anvil's. Tom Petty's is good, too, and Rush's Beyond the Lighted Stage is my second favorite."

"Okay, okay!" He made his hand into a stop sign. "I didn't think girls liked Rush."

"They don't." She placed her hand over her heart. "But I love them. Why do you think the alarm code to the office is 2-1-1-2?"

"Rush's album! I didn't put it together." He snapped his fingers. "I bet Sarah Jane would like Rush too."

"Oh my god." She laughed. "That Dead Milkmen song is hilarious." She glanced at her watch and adjusted the band.

"Curfew?" he asked.

"No, it's Rory. He's home alone."

"So"—Cary winked—"he's my competition?"

There wasn't even a close second.

"I've got to warn you, he's very competitive," she joked.

"It's nothing a few cookies can't solve. I've seen him in action." He leaned forward and held her hand. "I'd like to see you again, if that's all right?"

"It's all right. Just complicated."

"More complicated than deciphering emojis?"

She laughed. "No. Your life . . . Sebastien."

Cary sighed. "I'll talk to him."

"Please don't." She unfolded her napkin and set it on the table. "If there's something to tell, we'll tell him." Not to mention if Sebastien found out, she'd have to go into a witness protection program.

Tyler and Cary each had a glass of wine and talked until it was last call. Despite their seven-year age difference, they had a lot in common. They both like music from Drake, Rihanna, and the Weeknd, but they couldn't understand the appeal of Ed Sheeran. Plus his fans were called "Sheerios." *Gross.*

Cary stood from the table and zipped up his jacket. "Come, walk me home."

"But the wine . . . ?"

He grabbed the bottle and turned to the people behind him. They were arguing over which Cary Kingston song the show had opened with.

He winked at Tyler. "I think I can help settle this."

You're ridiculous.

Cary passed them the bottle. "She's right." He pointed to Frosted Highlights. "I opened with that song."

Shrieks of "No! It can't be!" and "Oh my god!" ensued for several minutes, disrupting everyone on the patio and the residential high-rise buildings in the area.

Bragging Woman eyed Tyler up and down. "You're a lucky lady," she said, kind of snotty. *What, like I'm not good enough for him? I already know that.*

Cary grabbed her hand. "I'm the lucky one."

Moments later the patrons from inside the bar spilled onto the patio, and cameras flashed like runway identifier lights. Being famous looked simply exhausting, but he was great at it.

Tyler rolled her eyes and moved out of the spotlight as he posed for selfies and signed every last autograph.

When he was done being Cary Kingston, rock star, they crossed the street and walked toward his building. *Is he going to invite me in?*

There was only one way to find out.

"It's so weird that your biggest fans didn't recognize you," she said. "Especially the bragging woman wearing your shirt." Then again, she hadn't recognized him when he'd shown up at the office wearing a beanie and glasses.

He smirked. "It happens all the time. People say I sort of *look* like Cary Kingston."

"People aren't very smart."

"Yeah, I suppose."

Cary stopped at the front door of his building and cradled her face with his hands. The tips of his fingers were rough, callused, but she didn't mind. The guitar was a relentless instrument. He leaned in and kissed her slowly, with purpose, and their tongues intertwined. There was no one to interrupt them, so she arched her back and pressed her hips forward, and he kissed her deeper than Marianas Trench.

After they made out like teenagers he wrapped his arms around her shoulders, and the warmth of his body cocooned her. The metamorphosis of falling in love was happening, and if she wasn't careful she'd float away like a butterfly.

"Have breakfast with me," he whispered into her neck.

Is it too soon to sleep with him? Her head and her heart had an argument.

She glanced at her watch. "Sorry, I have to get home to Rory—"

"No!" He took a step backward and pulled down his beanie. "I meant in the *morning*. Come back and have breakfast with me in the morning."

Tyler exhaled, relieved that he wasn't trying to sleep with her but also a bit disappointed that he wasn't trying to sleep with her. It had been years since she'd felt wanted.

A taxi pulled into the driveway, presumably for her.

"Did you call this?" she asked.

He smiled proudly. "I downloaded the app."

"Look at you. Such a man of the people." She tried to diffuse the awkwardness of the situation with humor. "I'd love to have breakfast. What time?"

"Come by after nine."

"Are you cooking?" She raised her brow in suspicion. "Or ordering in."

"I'm not completely useless," he said, not answering the question. "Bring Rory. I'm up for a little friendly competition."

"I'll ask him if he's available. He's Insta-famous, you know."

"He had more likes than anything I've ever posted."

"You're just as cute."

"Funny." He gave her a kiss on the cheek. "Text when you get home, okay?"

She nodded. "I promise no emojis."

Maybe just one.

CARY

Cary waved as the taxi disappeared around the corner. How lucky was he? He'd found the world's only female Rush fan, and she'd given him documentary suggestions up the yin yang.

Why was she worried about Sebastien?

Okay, his manager didn't have the greatest bedside manner, and not paying Vegas while he was injured, that was indefensible. At least he'd found Kim. What a godsend. This upcoming tour was a big one, but the timing was rotten. The thought of not seeing her for six weeks almost killed him. But maybe she could visit.

Otherwise he'd be back in Malibu for the holidays, and he'd invite her to stay with him. Who could say no to LA in December? And by then, hopefully she'd feel comfortable about sharing a bed. He'd almost died when she'd thought that he'd meant tonight. Of course it had crossed his mind, especially with that kiss, but he had no intention of rushing things. The women he'd dated always moved too quickly. Maybe they thought the faster they slept with him, the faster they'd get a ring.

Tyler was worth it.

But waiting was the hardest part.

And he was definitely hard.

CHAPTER 7

Tyler tossed and turned all night, unsure if having breakfast with him was the wisest idea. The heart of the matter was that Cary Kingston wasn't boyfriend material, let alone husband material. She wanted a baby more than anything and going down this road was a dead end with caution lights.

There was also the problem of Sebastien: he was paranoid of anyone getting close to his rock star, because without Cary he was nothing but a regular piece of shit in a Quebec Nordiques cap.

"What's Mommy going to do?" Rory glanced at her from the foot of the bed, but he obviously didn't have a clue.

She picked up her phone to call Dylan. Her sister was honest to a fault, whether she liked it or not.

"What's up?" Dylan answered in a cheery voice.

"I'm in a bit of a pickle," Tyler said.

"Oh?" Her sister sounded confused.

"I'm not literally in a pickle, Dylan." Impatience came out in her tone. "It's Cary."

"What happened?"

"We kissed last night."

"I knew it!"

You're a know-it-all.

"He wants to keep seeing me—" Tyler pulled the phone away from her ear while her sister shrieked in excitement. "You need to calm down." she whispered. "I'm supposed to have breakfast with him this morning."

"Yeah, that sounds awful." A dog barked in the background and Dylan shouted, "Shut the hell up, Samson!"

"Aw, poor Samson."

"Yeah? Want to trade dogs? Yours doesn't bark, and mine won't stop—hold on. Goddammit, Samson! Fucking shut up already!"

She smiled at Rory, now lying on her chest, his loving eyes looking up at her. "Not in a million."

"So, what are you going to do?"

That was the sixty-four-thousand-dollar question. It was Grandma Mary's favorite saying, but it didn't seem like a lot of money in today's economy.

She closed her eyes and rubbed her left temple. "He's been on the Most Eligible Bachelors list for twenty years. I must be a fucking masochist."

"You're being an idiot," Dylan scolded her like Samson. "What if he hasn't met the right person yet?"

"Look at all the women he's dated." She shuddered at the thought: a literal catwalk of models and actresses. There wasn't one regular woman in the lot.

"Some people never find their person, Tyler."

"I suppose. Okay, what am I going to do about Sebastien?"

"Fuck that guy." Dylan didn't mince words. "You're always saying you want to quit, so pull the plug already."

"I wish I could afford it." Not that she was getting paid a king's ransom at SDM, but her base salary covered her rent. "Oh, and Cary did something weird last night."

"How weird?"

"He insisted on wearing the shirt he wore at soundcheck."

"You're making excuses."

Dylan was right. She stopped petting Rory for a second and he pawed at her hand. "I'm going to cancel."

"Don't be such a fucking baby. Have breakfast with him. I'm dying to know what his house looks like."

"Should I Stay or Should I Go" by the Clash played in her head.

A little breakfast never hurt anyone.

Tyler hung up the phone and changed into her usual weekend attire: a Skull Skates hoodie and black leggings. It was the same thing she'd worn on their coffee date, and she hadn't washed her hoodie since, kind of accidentally on purpose.

She held the sleeve against her nose and took a whiff as she closed her eyes, reliving the kiss from last night. His tongue had discovered new places, making her sex twitch with every twist. Maybe she'd regret going to his house but there was only one way to find out.

An hour later she fastened Rory's leash to his harness and headed toward Yaletown. The skies were clear—a miracle for November—so she stopped at a bakery to pick up croissants she bought on special occasions. After all, her father had taught her not to arrive empty-handed. Manners had always been stressed in her family.

She sent Cary a text of her ETA: *9:30?*

He replied, *Perfect. xo*

A friendly concierge with a thick Eastern European accent opened the door to his building. *Am I making a terrible mistake?* Would it be like dating Dave all over again? No. She was pretty sure that he wasn't going to show up with a duffel bag and move in.

She knocked on his door at exactly nine thirty.

"Welcome." Cary gave her a quick kiss on the cheek and she handed him the bakery bag as an offering. "Thanks," he said. "You didn't need to bring anything." He glanced at the floor. "Except Rory. Hi Rory! How's my boy?"

Your boy?

Rory sat and wagged his tail, not understanding the implication.

Tyler stepped out of her boots and surveyed the penthouse, left to right, up and down. The multi-million-dollar property featured clean, straight lines, wall-to-wall windows, wide-plank floors, and an over-height ceiling. But the best part about his house was that it smelled like a Calvin Klein's Obsession factory, without any equipment in sight.

"This is incredible," she said, figuring that it would be nice, but not this nice.

"Sorry." He picked up a sock from the couch. "It's a bit of a mess. I'm in the middle of doing laundry." *Why are people always "in the middle" of doing laundry and not at the beginning or the end?* Still, it impressed her that he was doing it himself. Dave had used a fluff-and-fold service to launder his clothes, but he had no money to buy groceries or pay rent.

"I'll take you on a tour," Cary said, as Tyler took mental notes for Dylan. He started out, "To the left are the guest rooms. I'm not sure why I need them." She poked her head inside. He was right. The bedding was undisturbed. "In here is my office . . ."

"Where are your awards?" she asked. "In LA?"

He'd won every award in the music industry a hundred times over, and she was sure they'd have taken up an entire room, even a gallery.

"I hate awards." He shuddered. "Award shows. All of it. Sebastien's got them, I guess?" He continued the tour while she paid close attention. "In here is my room."

Her gaze drew to his bed, and the saxophone part from "Careless Whisper" penetrated her head. Emma Turner had slept in this bed. Okay, they'd had sex. She rubbed her palms on her leggings, having no reason to be jealous other than Emma was a perfect ten.

"And this"—Cary gestured like Vanna White—"is obviously the kitchen."

A boatload of containers from Urban Fare sat on the island counter.

I knew it.

"Before you say anything," he said, unstacking the containers. "You're taking the rest of this home or I'll give it to Ivan, the concierge on duty, when I leave." Cary seemed to be proud of himself for knowing his name. "He's Russian."

She glanced at her watch. "What time are you leaving?"

"Kim got a seat on our flight, so she's picking me up at five." He gripped his hands and wrung them. "Sorry for stealing her."

"Are you kidding? Our booking-agent friend Allie has been trying to find her something for weeks. You'd like her, Allie. She's one of us. Like, no bullshit." Tyler pulled on the strings of her hoodie. "What did Sebastien say when you told him?"

"Nothing." Cary passed her a red cup with a black lid that read: ARTIGIANO. "A latte. With soy milk."

"Thanks, it's just what I needed." She took a sip.

"I love that Cars song," he said.

"Benjamin Orr was a better singer than Ric Ocasek, and it's not up for discussion."

"Fair enough."

Tyler studied the photographs hanging on the living room wall, but the subjects in the pictures weren't models or actresses. They were "civilians," as Kim called them. "These are so good," she said. "Did you take them?"

"I took them ages ago." He cleared his throat. "I'd still like to take your picture."

"I'm not a model."

"You could be."

She turned on her heel and flopped her hand on the counter. "For your information, I got straight A's in school."

"Sorry, I didn't mean to upset you. I think you're beautiful, especially without makeup."

She ignored the compliment. "I work really hard, you know."

"That's one of the many things I like about you." Cary pointed to his photos. "I've got an exhibit coming up in LA. You should come."

"When is it?"

"End of January."

"Really?" she asked, voice unsure. "It's not on your tour itinerary." *Shit.* Again, she sounded like a creeper, but this time he didn't burn her.

"I confirmed it yesterday."

She didn't get the memo.

"I'll be there anyway. In LA." She took a sip of her latte. "I have a band playing at the Troubadour."

"A band on our roster?"

"No, they're that indie band I was telling you about, Yestown." She grabbed her bag and dug out her phone. "That reminds me . . . I have to check in on the Westgrays. They need babysitting twenty-four seven."

"Babysitting?"

"That's my job. I'm a professional babysitter. It's their first day in the studio."

"The first day is always the worst."

"Get this." She rolled her eyes to the back of her head. "They're making a double album."

"Why on earth would they do that?"

"Sebastien said 'more pucks on the net.'" She shrugged. "It's ridiculous."

"It sounds like it."

Tyler walked back into the living room. "I don't see any pictures of your family." She swiveled her head to make sure she hadn't missed them. "Not even your parents."

"I should fix that. Come, have something to eat." He opened the containers. "I wasn't sure what kind of jam you liked so I got one of everything."

"Thanks but no thanks," she said politely.

"You don't eat bread?"

She sat on a high stool at the counter. "I do, but I can't eat things that aren't cut properly." She pointed to the stack of toast and wagged her finger. "It needs to be cut diagonally." *What kind of psychopath cuts it vertically?* She continued, "Croissants are safe because you have to cut them horizontally."

He laughed. "Okay, I'll keep that in mind. So, I was thinking . . . maybe you could visit me?"

"Way ahead of you." She gave him a wicked grin and he tilted his head, confused. "I'm already here."

His eyes closed for an instant. "You know what I mean, Tyler." She giggled, ripping a croissant into small pieces, and Rory performed a tap dance while she fed him. "Australia or England?" he asked. "What's your preference?"

"As a country? Australia. I think the monarchy is stupid." The whole idea of being born into privilege went against her values.

"Where do you want to visit me?" He sounded impatient.

"I haven't been to either country, but I can't go. Sebastien."
I can't afford it either.

"Okay, what about Christmas?" he asked. "Any plans for the holidays?"

"I'll be home."

His eyes flashed open. "You're staying here?"

"Home as in Winnipeg," she clarified. "I go home every year."

"Every year?" He ran his fingers through his hair. "I don't think I've been home for the holidays in twenty years." It was the craziest thing she'd ever heard. "It's cold there," he said and pretended to shiver.

She shrugged. "I'll be indoors."

"That's a lot of family time."

"It's never enough." Her eyes filled with tears. "I can't tell you how much I miss them." *Fuck.* She didn't mean to cry but she couldn't help it. Her family was everything to her and he didn't seem to understand.

He squeezed her shoulder. "Sorry. I'm really screwing up here."

"That's okay." She blinked back her tears. "Do your parents go away at Christmas?"

"My folks? No. They'll be in Brandon. They might visit my aunt. I don't know exactly."

"She lives in Winnipeg, right?"

"Yeah." He nodded. "Charleswood."

She widened her eyes. "What about your birthday?"

Me and my big mouth.

Cary smiled. "Well, it sucks when your birthday is the day after Christmas." He gave Rory a piece of toast. "I don't even bother with it."

Thank god. When did it turn into a birthday week, anyway? Or a birthday month for some people like fucking Tommy Napolitano.

"I'm guessing it would mean a lot to your parents if you came home." She gave him a serious look and added, "They won't be around forever."

"They are looking older," Cary admitted. "I noticed it in Winnipeg." He clasped his hands on the counter. "I'll consider it."

After they finished eating, Tyler cleared their plates. She hated any kind of mess but dirty dishes were at the top of her list. Dirty bathrooms were a close second, especially the skid marks that Dave used to leave in her toilet.

"You don't have to do that," Cary said, holding her arm mid-clear. "I'll do it later."

She twisted her mouth, unsure whether to tell him about her pet peeve. "It's kind of my thing. I like cleaning."

"At least let me help."

Thank you.

With the two of them working they cleaned up in no time. She zipped up her hoodie and grabbed her bag, not wanting to wear out her welcome.

"I should let you get back to your laundry," she said. "Thanks for breakfast."

"No worries." He lowered his chin and pointed to the containers. "Please take this food home. I insist."

She stepped into her boots. "I'm stuffed. Really." Her voice raised into a holler. "Come on Rory!"

The dog's collar jingled like Santa's sleigh when he ran toward her.

"When will I see you again?" he asked.

"That depends on you, Cary."

He kissed her on the lips, and she detected a hint of marmalade. "Okay, I'll see you in Winnipeg," he said after a beat.

"I thought you were *considering* it?" She narrowed her gaze, not believing a word he said. Dave used to make all kinds of promises only to break them.

"I've considered it."

She turned up the corners of her mouth. "Have a safe flight, Cary."

Is this a good idea?

CARY

Cary sorted his laundry and packed his bags for tour. Why had she left so early? He wasn't sure, but what kind of animal doesn't have pictures of his family? Or sees them over the holidays? Him, apparently. And now he was going to Winnipeg for Christmas. What the hell was he thinking? Tyler didn't seem to be impressed that he'd suddenly changed courses. Or by him in general.

He'd messed up by asking to take her picture. That was a mistake. He was used to Emma demanding he post her pictures for likes on social media. But fame didn't seem to impress Tyler. In fact, she seemed to loathe it.

He chuckled about the croissants—cut horizontally. He'd bought enough food for the Lower Mainland and yet she'd come bearing gifts. That was sweet. At least Ivan was happy.

And that dog, Rory. What a character. He'd always wanted a pooch, but his tour schedule had made it impossible—or at least that was his excuse.

He would use the next few weeks to get to know her better over texts and phone calls.

But he needed to write some new songs.

He needed a hit.

A number one.

CHAPTER 8

The next morning Sebastien yelled from his office, "Tyler! Get in here!"

What now?

She figured that his stapler was empty or the printer was out of ink or he was having a heart attack, but it didn't stop her from taking her sweet-ass time to get there.

"What is it?" She gave him a super-fake grin.

He held his phone toward her, his beady eyes squinting. "What the fuck is this?"

"I don't know. A picture?" She couldn't help being a smartass.

"Why were you with Cary?" His tone was sharp and accusatory.

Fuck. Fuck. Fuck.

She grabbed his phone and recognized herself and Cary at the Wine Bar. They were laughing at something, but she didn't know what. Thank god they weren't making out in front of his building, or worse. Not that they'd done anything worse. You had to be an idiot to make a sex tape in the age of the internet.

We look cute. No. This is bad.

"Where did you get this?" she asked.

"One of the interns saw it on social media."

Fucking interns.

"It's not a big deal." She shrugged, handing his phone back. "Cary showed up at the bar and I was already there."

True story.

Sebastien shaped the bill of his baseball cap into a perfect curve. "I want you to find another producer for the Westgrays. This one's not working out."

Tyler sighed. "It's the third one—"

"And?"

"And they're way over budget."

He laughed in her face. "I've got it all worked out. The studio owes me a favor, but I want you to invoice the label for the full amount. It's my discount, not theirs. No free rides, remember?" He groomed his beard like it mattered to his appearance. "While you're at it, find another TM. They'll be headlining a tour once this record comes out."

That's a big fucking if, buddy.

"No one will work with them," she said. "That's why Bob Shaw hired Kim in the first place." The Westgrays had gone through five TMs in the past year, each one quitting in the middle of a tour, which was simply unheard of.

"Fine," he grumbled, the red in his face rising like a thermometer. "But the second Vegas gets back, she's off that tour. I'll put her back on with the Westgrays. End of discussion."

Later that evening Tyler's phone vibrated. It was a text message from Cary.

G'day mate! How are you going?

It took her a minute to respond. She needed to catch her breath and still her racing heart.

Hi! How was your flight?

Long. Still at the airport. How are you?

Would he care about their picture being posted on social media? It could end up on TMZ or Radar. On the other hand, there was no point in drawing attention to it.

She texted, *I'm good. It's tomorrow there, right?* She'd already looked up the time in Sydney, unable to do the math in her head.

Yeah. The future's so bright :)

Cary had said no emojis, but she guessed that a smiley face didn't count.

Did you watch anything on the flight?

The 60 Minutes stopwatch ticked in her head. But it went dead on his end. Not even three flashing dots. Texting was the lowest form of communication, and a spelling mistake could cause a disaster. She used to send Dylan screenshots of Dave's texts for a second opinion, yet they both spoke perfect English. If someone were a texting interpreter they'd make serious bank. Maybe they'd work as a cryptanalyst or in the Department of National Defense.

Tyler's phone vibrated but it wasn't Cary texting back. Kim had sent her a picture of his fans waiting inside Kingsford Smith Airport as they held I LOVE YOU CARY signs and wore his face on their t-shirts. And here she thought he was in the restroom.

Not long after, her phone vibrated again. It was Cary on text.

Sorry! Some people wanted autographs. We're heading to the hotel. I'll text later. xo

Some people. She laughed and liked the message.

The next two weeks were busy at work. Tyler had asked all the name producers about working with the Westgrays but they'd flatly refused, so she settled for a producer who lived on Vancouver Island. He was full of himself, but his rates were cheaper than the studio her boss was fleecing and she needed the band away from the Lower Mainland—distractions and girlfriends. Plus the producer used to play in an eighties glam-rock band and the Westgrays thought that was cool AF.

The situation with Cary had become more intense, at least on her end. They were texting several times a day and the seventeen-hour time difference was challenging, but it didn't stop them. She'd set her alarm for six a.m. so they could text before she went to work and he went to bed.

Cary had a show that Saturday so she slept in. That was, until her phone vibrated and the screen flashed: *FedEx*.

"Hello?" she answered, not expecting a bomb or a package.

"Is this Tyler Robertson?" a woman asked, voice chipper.

"Yes?"

"Delivery."

"Come on in."

Moments later there was a knock on the door. Rory jumped off the bed and ran down the hall. She followed him and signed for the box. It was big and bulky, but it didn't weigh a lot.

"Oh my god," she said, opening the package. "Look, Rory!" Her dog stared at the gigantic stuffed koala bear, but he didn't wag his tail. He seemed apprehensive, a little scared. "What should we call him? I know . . . Aussie!" She hugged the bear. "Welcome home, Aussie."

Rory gave her a look like, *What the fuck?*

"It's okay, buddy." She pulled the note hanging from the bear's ear: WISH YOU WERE HERE, CARY. XO.

Later that afternoon Tyler answered a FaceTime call from her bestie. They hadn't talked much; Cary's tour was demanding. It was a far cry from being on the road with the Westgrays, but Kim had told her that in some ways it was easier. There were certainly fewer fights at press appearances.

"Hi!" Tyler waved at the screen.

"Dude, did you get the package?" Kim asked with a hopeful grin.

Tyler pulled Aussie into the frame and kissed the stuffed animal. "I named him Aussie." She waved the bear's paw into the phone. "Say hi to Kim!"

"Hi, Aussie!" Kim waved back. "Cary asked me to send it. Like, insisted. I hope you don't mind."

"I'm not the one who minds." She directed her phone at Rory who was lying at her feet with his head between his paws. "He's sulking like a baby who dropped his pacifier."

"Buddy!" Kim raised her voice but the dog didn't budge.

"Do you want to hear the latest with Sebastien?" Tyler was dying to tell her since she had no one to gossip with at the office.

Kim's nose scrunched. "Like I give a fuck about him."

"I know, but you'll get a kick out of this."

She tucked her pink hair behind her ears. "Okay, I'm listening."

Tyler laughed. "He got his hearing insured for a million bucks."

"Ew. Why?"

"Because he's a narcissist, that's why. That music publisher dummy talked him into it. You know, the tall guy, bald, thinks he's a genius. His wife's always drunk at music industry events. They've got that kid who's a real screw-up."

"Fuck that guy." Kim moved her phone closer. "And fuck the patriarchy. You need to leave SDM, like, tomorrow."

"I'm working on it." She blew out a breath, stressed about her future there—or anywhere. "I couldn't find another TM for the Westgrays. Sorry, but Sebastien said you'd have to do it if they get offered a New Year's gig."

"Is he pulling me from Cary's tour?" Kim's face dropped, disappointed.

"Oh, don't worry about it." She crossed her feet onto the coffee table. "Vegas is still in rehab. There's no way he'll be back before the end of the year."

"What's the weather doing out there?" Kim asked.

Tyler twisted her neck and peered out the window. "It's raining. Pouring, actually. And my umbrella broke. Piece of shit. I mean, how many umbrellas have you gone through in your lifetime?"

"None." Kim rolled her eyes. "People from Vancouver don't use them."

"Maybe not for rain, but I've seen people using umbrellas when it snows here. Anyway, things are really heating up with Yestown," Tyler said. "The headliner added another band to their tour because they didn't want to play right after them—go figure. How's your tour going?"

"I'm fucking exhausted, dude." A machine whirred in the background. "But I love it."

Tyler squinted. "Where are you?"

Kim turned her phone around. "Starbucks, getting coffee."

"Holy shit!" She pointed. "Look behind you."

"Busted," Cary said, sneaking up on his tour manager.

Tyler sucked in a breath of air at the sight of him, gorgeous as ever, and she stretched a smile across her face. "Thanks for Aussie."

"Who?" he asked, appearing larger in the frame.

She grabbed the bear to show him. "I named him Aussie."

Cary chuckled. "How about letting me in on this?" Kim blew a kiss into the screen and gave her phone to him. "It's good to see you."

"You, too. You're so tanned." She turned to her dog. "Rory! It's Cary!" He wagged his tail but didn't come.

"What's up with him?" Cary asked.

She made a pouty face. "He doesn't like Aussie."

"Sorry, little buddy!" He paused for a second. "How come we don't FaceTime?"

"I don't know, but I like it."

"Let's do this from now on."

"Okay, but I'm not wearing makeup or getting dressed on weekends."

"Me neither." He laughed and she rolled her eyes. "We're heading to London in the morning. I can't wait for Monmouth coffee and biscuits."

"Just a few more weeks until you're back." She'd been marking off the days on her calendar like a madwoman.

"So, I was thinking . . ."

"Uh-oh."

"Funny." He rested his sunglasses on his head. "As you know, I'll be in Winnipeg for Christmas. My parents are going to my aunt's anyway, so I'm booking a hotel room for the twenty-fifth."

Do all hotel rooms have beds?

"Yeah, that makes sense," she said.

"You're welcome to join me. No pressure or anything."

"My family's having an open house on Christmas, but I can stop by the hotel later. Unless you want to come? Fair warning: everyone will be there. And I do mean everyone."

His face exploded into a smile. "I'd love to."

Shit.

What would it be like to see him in person? Would it be awkward? What would she say? Sure, they'd been texting every day, but they hadn't talked about their relationship and she couldn't bring him home and say he was just a friend, like that Biz Markie song.

She squeezed the koala bear. "I'm looking forward to it."

What am I going to tell my family?

CARY

Two days before Christmas, Cary and Kim waited for their flight in a private lounge at Heathrow Airport. The tour had been a huge success—sellouts in every city—but he was ready to go home and see Tyler. In fact, he was downright giddy about it.

"Do you think she'll like the presents?" he asked.

Kim frowned at the party of gift bags beside them. "Dude, you got her too much shit."

"*You* got her too much shit." He'd sent Kim to run errands instead of shutting down the stores to shop privately. He'd felt like a jerk whenever he'd had to do that, but he understood it was for the store's safety as well as his. "Thanks for doing my shopping. I know Bond Street isn't your scene."

"It is when I've got your credit card." Her eyes sharpened. "Seriously, she, like, won't be into all this."

"I didn't get her a birthday gift so I'm making up for it." He scratched the stubble on his face. "Okay, I'll keep some of it for Valentine's Day."

"C'mon, dude. That's not very romantic."

She had a good point. "Okay, what should I get her, then. For Valentine's?"

"A new car?" Kim smirked. "Seriously, she doesn't like most things."

"Hopefully she likes me." He nudged Kim's arm. "Can you keep a secret?" She looked up from her coffee and nodded. "I'm seeing her later tonight."

Kim tilted her head. "Is she meeting you in Brandon?"

"No, no. From Toronto I'm flying straight to Winnipeg. And from there I'll drive to my parents' house."

Kim glanced at her phone and squinted. "I didn't change your ticket."

"No, Vegas did." He took a sip of coffee and surveyed the lounge. "I'm going to her family's open house on Christmas."

She sighed, annoyed with him. "Dude, that's the hundredth time you've told me."

"Hundred and first," he added. "Are you happy to be going home?"

"I kind of like being on the road." She shrugged. "At least I'm not working on New Year's."

"What happened with the Westgrays?"

"They held out for more money so the promoter rescinded their offer." Kim shook her head. "Stupid fuckers, those kids."

Cary reached inside his jacket and pulled out a card. "Here. Thanks for everything."

Kim opened the envelope. "Cary! The Scandinave Spa in Whistler?"

"You deserve it," he said. "I know this tour's been hectic. Stay at the Fairmont. I've got an account there. Please use it. I'm dead serious."

"Thank you!" She gave him a quick hug. "You deserve my bestie."

CHAPTER 9

The same day, Tyler was making plans with Marnie and Heather, and by default their husbands, to meet at the King's Head Pub in Winnipeg. When they were home for the holidays they always made time to catch up. But this year it would be different, since Marnie and Heather were both five months pregnant. They'd scheduled their due dates down to the last minute.

As usual Tyler was the first to arrive. She scanned the room and recognized a few guys from her high school's football team—once athletic, now anything but.

"Sorry we're late," Marnie said, stomping the snow from her boots. "I'm not used to driving in this weather."

"No worries. It's a blizzard out there." Tyler hugged her friend, the baby bump protruding from her jacket. It was the size of a honeydew melon and hard to the touch.

Heather popped off her knitted hat by its pom-pom, dark curls bouncing at her shoulders. "It's great to see you."

"Likewise." Tyler hugged her other friend. "I can't believe it's been a year."

"It feels like a millennium." Marnie cradled her bump. "I can't wait to get this baby out."

"We had to bring Hank and Mark with us. They need constant supervision." Heather turned to the clean-cut men beside them.

"Hi," Tyler said. "How are you?" It was easy to remember that the M's and H's were husband and wife. Tyler called them the "husbands," collectively.

"I'm putting on sympathy pounds," Mark said, rubbing his belly over his coat.

"Same," Hank agreed.

After the hostess showed them to their table, everyone hung their coats on the rack and positioned their chairs to face the TV. *Hockey Night in Canada* was a big deal to most people in the country, including them. The Winnipeg Jets were playing the Toronto Maple Leafs and that meant war—blood, if necessary.

Tyler winked at Marnie and Heather for wearing their Jets jerseys, but she stopped smiling once she realized the husbands had worn theirs, too. The husbands were from Toronto, the home of the Bay Street Bullies, a.k.a. the Leafs, and she hated them almost as much as Vancouver's hockey team. But make no mistake, if the two teams ever met in the finals she'd cheer, "Go Leafs go!" in a heartbeat.

"Tell me everything," Tyler said, holding Marnie's hand. "The last time I spoke to you, you were finding out the sex."

Marnie shook her head and tightened her lips. "We found out this week."

"She's having a boy and I'm having a girl," Heather interjected, finishing Marnie's sentence, but there wasn't a smile to be found between them.

"What's the problem?" Tyler narrowed her gaze. "One of each sounds perfect. Ideal, even."

Marnie parted her honey-blond curtain bangs with her fingers. "We wanted to have the same thing so our kids could be best friends."

"They can still be best friends," Tyler said. "Even better, they might get married one day." What the fuck was she saying? "Not that they couldn't get married if they were the same sex, is what I meant."

Their faces lit up like the Christmas tree in the corner.

"Oh my god, that *is* better," Marnie said, while the husbands shook their heads, clearly annoyed with their spouses.

"I need a drink," Tyler said to no one in particular. On the taxi ride over she'd thought about staying sober in solidarity with her friends, but it had been a fleeting consideration at best.

"On it." Mark whistled, waving down a server.

"What's new and exciting in the music business?" Heather asked, ever the optimist. But there was nothing exciting about babysitting grown-ass men with Peter Pan syndrome.

"Same old." Tyler shrugged. "Same old."

A young man in his late teens popped out of nowhere like a Phil Collins drum solo. He pinched a golf pencil between his fingers and held a mini notebook in his hand. "Do you guys know what you want?"

"Beer," Hank said curtly.

Mark raised his brow in Tyler's direction. "Are you in for a pitcher?"

"Have you met me?" she asked, not realizing it was a rhetorical question.

"We'll have a pitcher, please." Mark tapped on his gut. "Something light."

The server jotted down their order. "And for the ladies?"

"We'll have Diet Cokes, please. We're pregnant and I'm driving." Marnie had a habit of divulging too much information. "And nachos with everything."

"Can you bring a bunch of small plates, please?" Heather added.

"If you could turn up the volume on the TV, that would be great." Mark pointed to the screen. "The game's about to start."

The server scowled at Mark's jersey and stormed off in a huff. Tyler could hardly blame him. Wearing that jersey in public was asking for trouble.

Marnie rested her palm on her chin. "Tyler, are you *still* not dating anyone?" Her tone made it seem like it had been a million years but it had only been two years, now closer to three.

"Anyone special you've got your eye on?" Heather rubbed her hands together, eyes as big as her head.

What was she supposed to say, *I've been talking to Cary Kingston*? You couldn't go around telling people, especially not in Winnipeg. On the other hand, she didn't want to lie to her oldest friends, so she shrugged and took a sip of water.

"What does that mean?" *Fuck.* Marnie didn't miss a thing.

Tyler twisted her mouth from side to side, deliberating what to tell them.

"So there someone." Heather gave her a wink. "What does he do for a living?"

Tyler ignored her question.

"Is he a musician?" Marnie asked, voice judgmental.

Tyler looked at the menu. "I guess."

There wasn't any world in which Cary wasn't a musician. She should have said yes.

"Tyler!" Marnie crossed her arms over her belly. "I thought you wanted a family?"

I do, Marnie.

"Leave her alone," Heather said. "Let her be happy."

No. Marnie was right. What in the living fuck was she thinking? She'd been so caught up with his texts and FaceTimes that she'd lost sight of his single guy status. What was she going to do? Marry Cary Kingston?

Not in this lifetime.

It was the second period of the hockey game and the Leafs were up 3–2. Tyler and the husbands had polished off two pitchers of beer and were debating a third when her phone vibrated. It was Cary on text.

Are you still at the bar? he asked.

Earlier in the day she'd told him about meeting her friends at the King's Head. He'd said that he knew it well and had played there when he was starting out.

She replied, *Yes. Jets are losing :(*

Cary didn't text back. He probably had another fan encounter, someone asking for a selfie or an autograph.

A few seconds later the Jets scored on the power play.

"Goal!" Tyler yelled as the hockey fans in the room, minus the husbands, cheered loudly. Their server was nowhere in sight, so she went to the bar to order another pitcher. Not surprisingly her buzz had worn off from the light beer.

She waved at the bartender. "Another one, please." It made her think about DJ Khaled and how he didn't go down on his wife. "The light one."

A man's voice behind her asked, "Come here often?"

It can't be.

She spun around and cracked a smile. "Cary!" He wore a parka like Nanook of the North but with faux fur, naturally. "What are you doing here?"

"I flew into Winnipeg," he said. "I'm driving to Brandon later."

She snapped into work mode. *Oh no! What a terrible routing. Did Kim fuck it up?* Cary could have taken a direct flight from Toronto to Brandon and saved two hours of driving. Three, in this weather.

She adjusted the elastic on her topknot. "Why did you fly into Winnipeg?"

"I wanted to see you, babe."

Babe Robertson.

"I wanted to see you too."

He gave her a big parka hug and she buried her face into his collar. The stubble on his cheek scratched the side of her neck, but she didn't care. It had been too long since she'd been in his arms. Six weeks had felt like an eternity, like she'd been living in slow motion. When she was with Dave she could have gone six weeks without seeing him while standing on her head and not blinking.

"Are you sure I can't convince you to come home with me?" he asked.

"I can't." She rubbed the arm of his coat. "I told you, we're spending tomorrow at my sister's. Joe's family will be there, and I hardly ever get to see them."

"Cash or charge?" the bartender asked, sliding a pitcher of beer toward them.

She mimicked a scribble. "Put it on our tab, please and thank you."

Back at the table Tyler waved to her friends, but they were too focused on the screen to notice him, so she waited for a TV timeout.

"Come, sit next to me." She grabbed the pitcher by its handle. "It's not exactly Penfolds Grange, but may I pour you one?"

Cary pushed an empty glass toward her. "Just half, please. I'm driving."

"It's crappy anyway." She gestured to the husbands. "It's light beer."

Cary glanced at the TV. "What's happening here?"

"It's tied 3–3."

"Goal!" Marnie raised her arms over her head.

Mark stood from his seat and pointed at the screen. "That was offside by a mile!"

"What a bullshit goal." Hank slammed his hand on the table, causing his beer to spill. "Jesus fucking Christ."

"His skate was on the line," Tyler said and smiled at Cary. "They're saying he crossed the blue line before the puck." She thought it was a stupid rule and hoped they'd change it in the off-season. In fact, she had a list of suggestions to give to the commissioner if she ever got a chance to talk to him.

Hank blew out a breath. "They're reviewing it. Can you pass the—holy shit!" He stared at Cary, stunned, and grabbed Mark's arm.

"What the fuck?" Mark rubbed his eyes aggressively.

"This is Cary," Tyler said, voice even. "Cary, this is Marnie, Heather, Mark, and Hank."

"Nice meeting you," Cary said, shaking hands with the husbands and waving at Marnie and Heather across the table.

Her friends giggled like schoolgirls while the husbands went mute. Had they suddenly taken a vow of silence? If so, good.

"We're pregnant, not fat," Marnie said, arching her back. Cary nodded politely as Tyler shook her head, unamused.

"They're calling it back." Heather sighed, disappointed.

"Yes!" Mark fist-pumped the air.

"Shit," Tyler said, while a sad trombone *womp womped* in her head.

"What are you doing here?" Marnie asked Cary, pointedly. "In town, I mean."

"I came to see her." He winked at Tyler, squeezing her hand. "I'm heading to Brandon to spend Christmas with my family."

"That's so nice," Heather said, voice sweet like a mom-to-be.

"We're having frigging beers with Cary Kingston." Hank said. "I can't believe it."

"Fangirl." Mark punched him in the arm a little harder than necessary.

"I hardly ever drink beer," Cary said. "I'm a wine guy."

The husbands laughed uncontrollably, even though it wasn't funny in the slightest.

"I know this is super uncool, but can I have your autograph, man?" Hank's voice came out almost sheepishly.

"No problem," Cary said, not making a big deal out of it.

"Hat trick!" Tyler pointed at the TV and the Jets fans cheered. She turned to Cary. "It's when the same player scores three goals.

121

Not to be confused with a Gordie Howe hat trick which is a goal, an assist, and a fight."

Moments later Hank went to the bar and came back with a Sharpie. "Can you sign my jersey, please?" he asked politely.

"Mine too." Mark flattened a spot on his chest.

"Fangirl." Hank ribbed him back.

"Sorry, I can't sign a Leafs jersey." Cary glanced at Tyler with a closed-lip grin. "She'd kill me in my sleep."

I'd kill you wide awake.

"He's a keeper," Heather said, dimples digging into her cheeks.

Cary nudged Tyler's arm. "See? I'm a keeper."

She couldn't give up her dream of having a family. It was sweet that he'd flown into Winnipeg to see her, and had met her friends, but she needed to have a serious talk with him before it went any further.

"Will you sign our jerseys, please?" Heather asked politely.

"Absolutely." Cary uncapped the marker and personalized their sweaters.

Mark poured another beer. "Do chicks ever get you to sign their boobs, man?"

"Do they?" Tyler lowered her chin while her heart screeched to a halt. Of course she'd seen a lot of boob-signing with their heritage acts, women in their fifties with their tits hanging out of their crop tops. But Cary's fans weren't like that. Or were they? The chorus from "Foolin'" by Def Leppard played in her head.

Cary chuckled. "No, not very often, but I've got a one-hand rule." The husbands leaned in, ears perked. "I never use the other hand for support." Cary pretended to weigh an apple in his palm and the guys cracked up.

"Awesome!" Mark said.

Marnie pushed herself up from the table. "I've got to pee every five seconds."

"Same," Heather added.

Tyler held in her stomach. "Me too. In my case it's the beer."

As the restroom door closed, Marnie turned to Tyler. "Are you fucking serious?"

"I know, I know." She smacked her head like she'd forgotten to have a V8. "He's a musician."

"He's not some broke-ass guy in a punk band," Heather said. "He's Cary Kingston."

"You're right." Tyler nodded at Marnie. "He's thirty-eight and still single. I mean, he's had tons of girlfriends, but nothing's lasted."

"At least he's not thirty-eight years old and never kissed a girl." Heather sang the Tragically Hip song poorly.

"How's the sex?" Marnie raised an eyebrow. "You can at least tell us that."

I wish I knew.

Tyler shrugged. "He's been on tour, and we haven't exactly—"

"See?" Heather said. "He's serious about you. Otherwise he would've slept with you already. And he came all this way to see you, don't forget."

"A heads-up would've been nice," Marnie said.

"Are you kidding?" Heather's tone was sarcastic. "We got to meet Cary Kingston. Like, in person."

Marnie gave Heather an eye roll and shifted her gaze to the mirror where Tyler stood tying her topknot tighter. "Tyler?"

"What?" she said. "He was supposed to fly into Brandon. I didn't know he was coming. Honest, guys."

Heather's mouth twisted. "So, let me get this straight. Instead of taking a direct flight home he's driving to Brandon in a fricking blizzard tonight?"

Tyler shrugged. "I guess?"

"Apart from being famous, do you like him?" Marnie asked.

She confessed, "I like him despite it."

More than like.

CARY

"Her friends seem nice," Cary told Vegas over Bluetooth on his drive to Brandon later that night. "I really thought she'd come home with me but I got shut down. Big time."

In fact, he was so used to people saying yes to him that he hadn't considered the possibility of Tyler declining, especially since he'd never brought anyone home to Brandon. Bringing Emma home to meet his family was never an option.

"She's got her own life," Vegas said.

"Yeah." Cary turned down the volume on the radio. "I guess she does." He smiled to himself. "I think it's probably good for me."

"Do you think she was surprised?"

"I think so." He kept his eyes on the road as giant snowflakes pummeled the windshield. "I thought Kim might've told her."

"No way, man. Kim's the best."

"I think I'm going to ask Tyler to be my girlfriend."

"Seb won't like it."

"Let me worry about that. So, how's your recovery coming along?"

"Fucking rehab." Vegas sighed. "Three more weeks at least. I'm done with it."

"You have to finish your physical therapy." Cary tapped on the steering wheel to "When the Levee Breaks." Tyler had gotten him back into listening to Led Zeppelin, which was also her favorite band. She loved Jimmy Page so much that a twinge of jealousy surfaced whenever she'd mentioned him.

"I'm dying to get back on the road, man. I'm bored as shit."

"Kim's been doing a great job in your stead," Cary said. "How do you feel about keeping her on after you're back?"

"Honestly? I could use the extra help. Sebastien's budget for this tour is shit."

"I'll pay double your rate."

"No, man. I can't accept it. Seb's already pissed off that you're paying me as it is."

Cary cringed as one of his old songs came on the radio, and he pressed the off button with force.

"Wasn't that your song?" Vegas asked.

"Yeah. On a classic rock station." *Is this what it's come to?* Would he end up playing retro rock festivals and casinos in tourist towns? He went on, "Some of my early stuff is dated, and my new songs just suck."

"You should take a break after this tour."

"And do what?" He paused for a few seconds. "Did I tell you I'm going to the Robertsons' on Christmas?" He'd thought of little else since Tyler had invited him to her family's house.

Vegas chuckled. "Yeah, you've mentioned it."

"So, you're staying in Vancouver over Christmas, I take it?"

"I can't fly with my leg this fucked."

"Well, try to have a great holiday, bud."

CHAPTER 10

"Merry Christmas, Rory!" Tyler said from her childhood bed. "Cary's coming to see you, buddy." She still couldn't believe that he'd surprised her at the pub two days earlier, but it confused her more than anything since they weren't exactly an item.

Rory hopped down from the bed and searched the room, but he didn't understand that she meant later. Poor Rory.

"Tyler?" Dylan's voice boomed through her door. "Are you up?"

"Yeah, I'll be right out."

A few minutes later Tyler walked into the living room, expecting to find a house full of guests, but no one was there. "Where is everyone? Where's Wilbur?"

"My house," Dylan said, bending over to kiss her nephew. "Merry Christmas, Rory!" Her sister gave him a new bully stick with a bow on it and he wagged his tail.

At the kitchen counter Tyler poured two cups of coffee. "Here." She passed a mug to Dylan and sat at the table. "Why are you here so early?" she asked and blew on her coffee.

Dylan folded genie arms onto the table before resting her head. "I'm tired." She closed her eyes. "I love Joe's family, but it's so crowded over there."

"Some of them can stay here." A waft of coffee traveled up her nose. "There's an extra bedroom."

"I know, but they insist on being under the same roof." Dylan opened one eye. "It's how they grew up." Tyler had lived alone

126

since Dave and she could barely remember what it felt like to share her place with someone other than the miniature panda.

"We need to get ready for the open house." Tyler glanced at her watch. "Soonish."

"Just let me rest my eyes for a minute."

"Okay, but I need your advice." Dylan nodded but kept her eyes shut. "As you know, Cary's coming by later, but I think we need to have *the talk* first."

"The talk?" Dylan mumbled.

"Yeah. Before I sleep with him."

Her sister sighed through her nose. "What's the problem?"

"Well . . ." She crossed her legs. "You know I want a baby, and he's one of these eternally single guys. And a musician. Probably a cheater too, from my experience."

Dylan's shoulders rolled up like a marionette on strings. "Not all musicians are cheaters, Tyler. Look at Dad."

The front door opened and Bert walked in, pressing his hands to his head. "My ears are burning," he said. "What are you two talking about?"

Tyler stared at her sister and shook her head once.

Dylan turned toward the door. "She thinks all musicians are cheaters, Dad." Tyler kicked her under the table. "Ow! Fuck, my leg!" Dylan rubbed her shin.

Bert pulled up a chair and joined his daughters at the table. "Merry Christmas, kiddo." He smiled at his youngest child and gave her a kiss on the cheek. "What's this all about?"

"Cary," they said in unison.

"I see." Bert nodded. "He seems like a good guy. Isn't he?"

"He is," Tyler said. "But you've been around musicians your entire life, Dad. You know what they're like."

Bert clasped his hands on the top of his head. "I do, but it's not just musicians. Accountants, lawyers, doctors—depends on the man, not what he does for a living. Seen plenty of guys not cheat on their wives." He shrugged. "Seen plenty of guys that did."

Like, most of them.

"Dad, you see the good in everyone," Tyler said. "But Dave—"

"Forget Dave." Dylan stabbed the air with her finger. "You're punishing Cary for that asshole's sins. That's not really fair, is it?"

No, it isn't.

The Robertsons' open house was a Christmas tradition. It had been her mom's idea, since it was her favorite time of the year. Growing up Tyler had watched old home movies of the festivities to make sure that everything was done right. On some level she thought her mother might be looking over her.

As usual, Bert led the Christmas carols in the living room while Tyler and Dylan served drinks in the kitchen. Her brothers greeted their guests wearing Santa suits while their wives wore Mrs. Claus outfits. By the early evening the Robertsons' house was bustling with joy, and it wouldn't have seemed like Christmas otherwise.

Tyler kept a close eye on her phone, not wanting to miss Cary's text, and when it finally came through her stomach folded like origami. Would she be strong enough to have a talk with him? Or would she succumb to his sexy smile and throw caution to the wind.

Almost there. xo, he texted.

She weaved through their guests like it was last call at the bar and took a deep breath before opening the door. "Merry Christmas," she said and nuzzled her face into the faux fur of his parka.

"Merry Christmas, babe." Cary handed her an armful of gift bags and a tin holiday container in the shape of a tree. "My mom insisted. It's shortbread . . . her family's recipe." He lifted his finger. "Hold on a sec."

"What the . . ." her voice trailed off as he jogged to the car and came back lugging a guitar case into the house.

"I never leave this one unattended."

She angled her head like a goalie through traffic. "Where's your bag?"

"I've already checked in."

The Fairmont Winnipeg—sex.

Tyler took shallow breaths so that she wouldn't pass out in front of their guests. Were they about to have sex? Of course she wanted to, but not if it meant a one-night stand. She still had to work with him . . . at least until she left SDM.

"Merry Christmas, Rory!" Cary picked up her dog and kissed him while Wilbur pawed at his leg. "Who've we got here?" He put down Rory and petted the Labrador Retriever.

"That's my brother, Wilbur," Tyler said. "He's my dad's dog." Wilbur spotted food on the floor and hurried to eat it. "Obviously a Lab." She pointed to the gift bags. "What's all this?"

"Presents!" Cary handed her a festive gift bag and she tossed the tissue paper like confetti.

"Cary!" she cried. The label on the trench coat read BURBERRY.

"Kim picked it out." A smile stretched across his face. "She knew your size. Here . . ." He gave her another bag. "An umbrella to go with it. James Smith and Sons from London. I heard yours was busted."

"Thank you. You shouldn't have."

Next he passed her a green bag that read: HARRODS. "This one's for Rory."

"Really, you didn't have to." She pulled out a plush teddy bear and squished it like a marshmallow. "Rory!" The dog sat and wagged his tail. "Who's this?"

"It's their annual bear." Cary lifted the bear's foot, showing her the year. "I was hoping to make up for Aussie."

She laughed, passing him the bear. "You give it to him."

"Look, Rory!" He lowered the stuffie. "It's Teddy!" They laughed as the dog grabbed it with his mouth and ran off.

Cary passed her two wine bags. "These are for Bert and Dylan."

Tyler peeked inside. "Cary! No, they're too expensive." She handed them back but he wouldn't accept them. "I know how much Penfolds Grange is."

He shrugged. "It was on sale."

Liar.

Cary grabbed the last bag—the smallest. "This one's for Nadie."

"What is it?" Tyler rested her hands on her hips.

"A Shure microphone, and you can't get mad, because I've got an endorsement."

"All of this is too much, Cary." She set down the wine bags on the buffet table and grabbed a small, wrapped present. "This pales in comparison."

"You didn't have to get me anything. I've got everything I need and then some." He unwrapped the paper and smiled at an old, worn-out guitar capo. "Thank you."

"It was the Humbler's." She pointed out his initials on the side. "I found it kicking around in the basement."

His jaw dropped to his boots. "The Humbler's? Wow! This is the best present ever." He examined the guitar nut, turning it over. "This should be in a jazz museum. Seriously, I—"

"My man." Hank hugged him as if they were pals while Heather mouthed, *Sorry.* "How's it hanging?"

"Thanks for the other night," Mark butted in. "That was so freaking awesome, hanging out and shooting the shit."

"Yeah, thanks," Hank said.

Cary nodded once. "Don't mention it."

Not only had Cary picked up their tab but he'd quietly paid the bill for everyone at the pub. It was difficult for Tyler to wrap her head around having that kind of money, since she was proud of herself when she'd collected enough reward points to earn a free product at the supermarket. She'd even diarized her calendar for double-points days—two for one.

"Cary!" Dylan said, raising a glass of wine.

"Thanks for having me, Dylan." He gestured to the Robertsons' family band. "Aren't you playing tonight?"

Dylan raised her glass again. "I'm drinking instead."

"I can see that," he said.

"You know what?" she blabbed into his ear.

"What?" Cary lifted his brow.

She flung her arm around his shoulder. "You fit right in here."

That's enough, Dylan.

After Tyler introduced Cary to the rest of their guests, they stood in the living room and listened to Christmas carols. All standards: popular music, not religious.

"Auntie Ty!" Nadie shouted over the music. "I'm singing your favorite next."

She nodded while Cary squinted. "Silver Bells," she told him.

"It's my favorite too," Nadie added.

After the video of Nadie singing at their benefit had gone viral she'd turned into a minor local celebrity. She'd told her aunt that she wanted to be a star, but Tyler reminded her that school was first. A deal was a deal, after all.

Bert played the first few notes before counting Nadie in, and the room fell silent as her voice exploded. *Hark! The Herald. This angel can sing!* Cary took out his phone and pressed the red button to capture the moment.

When the song ended Nadie took a bow, and the room erupted with clapping and cheers.

"Come sit in, son." Bert tapped on the empty seat beside him.

"Dad!" Tyler's voice came out shrill. She hadn't invited Cary there to perform. He'd just ended a six-week stint.

"I want to sing Santa Baby!" Nadie clapped, jumping up and down. It wasn't surprising, given the amount of sugar in the vicinity.

"I know that one," Cary said, lifting his guitar out of its case. "C major I think." He clamped the Humbler's capo onto the neck of his guitar and strummed the first few chords. "Sorry, it's out of tune . . . I should've checked." Of course he was used to having people do that for him, like everything else.

Cary tuned his guitar by ear and started to play, and Dylan beamed at her daughter singing "Santa Baby" with the most famous rock star in the world.

"What do you think?" Tyler asked her sister.

"Their voices sound great together."

"Yeah, they do." It surprised her how well they harmonized.

Dylan took a gulp of wine. "You should definitely sleep with him."

"Dylan," she hissed. "Keep your voice down. I still need to talk to him."

The song ended and everyone applauded.

"Happy Merry Christmas!" Nadie called out the song like James Brown directing the Soul G's. It was her niece's second favorite Christmas song, almost tied with the first.

With a guitar pick between his fingers, Cary tapped his lips. "I don't know that one."

"Key of G." Bert played the simple chord on his guitar. "Follow my lead."

Everyone sang along except for Cary and Tyler. She couldn't carry a tune if she were in the Abbey Road Studios' echo chamber.

Again the room erupted with clapping and cheers.

"Good job," Bert said to his family.

"I think I've been on the road too long." Cary shrugged out of his guitar. "I don't know any new Christmas songs."

"It's not new," Tyler said.

"Daddy wrote it." Dylan pointed at Bert, and her wine spilled onto the floor. "Didn't you, Daddy?"

"I did." Bert covered his mouth, trying not to laugh.

Tyler shook her head. "Oh, Dylan. You really must learn how to pace yourself."

At the stroke of midnight, when Cary Kingston turned thirty-nine, Tyler sneaked him into her childhood bedroom like a juvenile delinquent. But before they did anything she had to know where she stood.

She handed him a flat box wrapped in "Happy Birthday" paper.

"You already gave me a present," Cary said, pushing the gift away. "I'll say it again. The best present ever."

"It's for your birthday." Tyler clapped in excitement. "Open it."

He peeled the wrapping paper like a Christmas orange, thumbs digging in. "Is it a onesie?" he asked, opening the box. He held the bodysuit against his chest.

"A Winnipeg Jets onesie. I have the same one. If we're going to start dressing alike—"

"Start?" He chuckled. "Thanks. We can wear them tonight. Are you ready to go?"

"No." She sat on the edge of her twin-size bed and puffed out her cheeks before exhaling. This was it. The time had come. But what if he wanted to keep it casual. Could she play along?

"What's wrong, babe?" he asked.

Her eyes became heavy, her conscience weighing in. "I think we want different things."

"What are you talking about?"

She stalled to collect her thoughts. "I'm thirty-two, and I want to settle down. Not right this minute, but I want a family, and these things can take time, years even."

Cary ran his fingers through his hair. "Okay, I'm not sure how that means we want different things. Is it because I'm on the road?"

"No, that's your job." She shrugged one shoulder. "I get it."

"Is there something I should know?"

She blinked back the tears on her lash line. "I'm not trying to change you. I don't want to change you."

"Good," he said. "I don't want to change you either."

"I know it's stupid." Her voice softened as she spoke. "But I want happily ever after. Or some version of it."

He stared at the floor, not saying a word. Had she blown it? Why couldn't she just leave well enough alone? Why wasn't it good enough to hang out with him? A million women would have killed to be in her position. And here she was, making demands on him.

"And you aren't happy, I take it?" he said after a beat.

How could she explain it without hurting his feelings or giving him an ultimatum? "Marry me or else we're done" didn't seem like the right approach It was too soon for that conversation.

She continued, "I want something more than this, and you're this eternally single guy—"

"Eternally single guy?" His eyes leaped forward, mouth gaping open. "Is that what you think?" She nodded. "Babe, I assure you, that's not the case." He held her hand and kissed it. "I promise, we want the same thing. I've always wanted a family. Look at me. I'm almost forty years old. A washed-up musician."

"You're hardly washed up." She smirked, not believing him. "Why didn't you have a family sooner—I mean, if you wanted one."

"I don't know. I guess I put my career first." He shook his head. "If I'm being honest I hadn't met the right person—until now. In fact, I wanted to know if you'd be my girlfriend."

Girlfriend. Did he just say girlfriend?

"Of course I'd love to be your girlfriend, but I promised myself I wouldn't fall for a musician."

"I'll quit music." He wiped his palms on his jeans. "Just say the word."

She rolled her eyes. "You're crazy."

"Let's go crazy together."

"I never want you to stop playing music."

"Thank god." He held his hands in prayer. "I love rock and roll."

"You and Joan Jett."

"Funny," he said. "So, is that a yes?"

Who wouldn't want to be Cary Kingston's girlfriend?

"That's a yes."

Cary leaned over and kissed her on the lips. "Are you ready to get out of here?"

"Do you mind if I meet you there?" She gave him a crooked grin. "I have to clean up since Dylan's incapacitated."

"Want me to stay and help?"

"No thank you."

"Okay, but don't keep me waiting too long." He winked. "These things can take years."

Touché.

An hour later Tyler pressed her ear against the door of the Countess of Dufferin Suite. A guitar strummed from inside the room, but it wasn't one of Cary's songs. Maybe it was something new he was working on. Hopefully it would be the hit that he'd wanted so desperately.

The song ended and she knocked on the door. This time there'd be no dog to distract them. She'd left Rory at her dad's house. He seemed happy to hang out with Wilbur and eat cookies with his grandpa.

Cary cracked open the door. "Come on in."

"What a dump," she joked, stepping out of her boots.

"Sorry." He sat on the loveseat. "The bigger room was taken."

She pointed to his acoustic guitar. "I heard you playing something?"

"Just writing," he said. "I'm not sure what it is yet."

She pulled out her topknot, shook her hair, and tilted her head. "Are you writing a song about me?"

"You're so vain, babe." He laughed and picked up the guitar. "But maybe."

"Make sure it doesn't suck, okay?"

She was obviously joking. He'd won the ASCAP—American Society of Composers, Authors, and Publishers—Songwriter of the Year award more times than anyone in its history. To songwriters it was everything.

"No promises," he said, and grabbed his phone. "I've been watching this video of Nadie singing Silver Bells. Would Dylan mind if I posted it?"

Tyler surveyed the tastefully appointed room. "Knock yourself out." She was no dummy. Any post on Cary's socials was sure to get thousands, if not millions, of views.

"The song Bert wrote." He put down his phone and strummed a few chords. "The Christmas one . . ."

"What about it?"

"Has he ever recorded it?"

"No. He's more of a musician than a songwriter." She transferred the elastic band onto her wrist. "I think he wrote it before Perry was born, if I'm not mistaken."

He got up and walked across the room. "I'm opening a bottle of red. Unless you want champagne?"

She shook her head. "No, red's great."

He lifted a bottle from the Liquor Market bag on the side table.

"What?" She sat on the loveseat. "Did you buy out the city's entire supply of Penfolds Grange?"

He poured the wine into two glasses. "You know, I probably did."

"Happy birthday!" she cheered.

"Thanks," He sat beside her and clinked her glass. "How about coming with me to LA?"

She curled her lip, not expecting an invitation. Plus she didn't exactly have clothes for warm weather, and she couldn't take Rory across the border without proper documentation. "I can't. The World Juniors start tomorrow."

"And?"

"And it's the best hockey tournament of the year."

Cary snapped his fingers. "You can watch it in LA." He picked up his phone from the coffee table. "I'll order the channel."

"We all watch it together," she said. "At my dad's house. My brothers and their families will be there. It's a holiday thing."

He sighed. "I'm back on the road next week."

He didn't have to remind her the situation was temporary. And even if she borrowed some of her sister's clothes and left Rory in Winnipeg, she couldn't swing another charge on her credit card, especially a first-class ticket.

"I know." She nodded and changed the subject before he pressed any further. "Kim told me about the gift you got her." Earlier in the day her bestie had texted a picture from a hot tub in Whistler. "You're too generous. Really."

"Did I tell you I'm keeping her on after Vegas comes back?"

"Ugh." She gritted her teeth. "How does Sebastien feel about that?"

"The last time I checked, my name was on the marquee." He leaned back on the loveseat and grabbed her hand. "Come with me, just for a few days."

"Why don't you stay here?" she asked. It was a reasonable request given he was already there. "Joe's family is leaving tomorrow and there's room at my dad's."

He took her hand and shook it. "Deal. But we're sleeping here."

After Tyler and Cary finished talking over a bottle of wine, she gave him a kiss on the lips.

"I've got another present for you," she said, gesturing to the bedroom, which seemed lightyears away.

Cary's gaze turned toward her as his eyes lowered. "We don't have to—"

"Yes, we do. I mean, I want to."

He hesitated for a second. "Are you sure?"

"One hundred percent."

I want your sex.

He kissed her neck, under her ear. "What about—"

"Protection? I have a cervical cup. After my ex, I got tested for everything. I haven't been with anyone since."

He seemed perplexed. "That was what . . . two years ago?"

"Something like that." She was too embarrassed to tell him it was closer to three.

"Well, I haven't been with anyone either since I was last tested."

She smiled. "All good then."

The bedroom was dark but for a break in the curtain where the streetlight let in an iridescent glow. Tyler sat on the edge of the freshly made bed and pulled him forcefully toward her. Cary kissed her like he needed her breath to live, and her body tingled from head to toe in anticipation of knowing him—all of him, in the biblical sense.

She kissed him deeply, hungry like the wolf, running her fingers through his hair while he caressed her bare breasts underneath her hoodie, nipples hard and sensitive to the touch. His callused fingers rubbed against her skin and her breasts plumped until they almost burst through her bra. She twitched when he traced his fingers down her stomach, reaching between her thighs. She widened her legs readily, moaning when he brushed against her sex with his thumb.

He was right—it had been too long.

Enjoying the moment, she closed her eyes as his slow, steady fingers stroked her in light circles until she swelled like a wave in the ocean and her wetness seeped through her leggings, drenching them inside and out, causing her toes to go numb.

"You're sure?" he whispered, kissing the curve of her neck.

She nodded and grabbed the back of his head, directing his mouth onto hers. Her hand traveled to his zipper, cupping a substantial bulge in his jeans, and his tongue slacked in her mouth with a grunt of pleasure when she squeezed him. But in a quick motion he gripped her wrist away from his manhood and held her hands as she lay back on the bed. Her stomach tensed when he peeled down her leggings inch by inch, breath quickening at the thought of his mouth on her sex.

Is this really happening? She dug her thumbnails into her fingers to make sure that she wasn't dreaming. *Ow!* Thank god she wasn't.

A smile painted across his face when he removed her red lace panties, slipping them off as she slinked toward the pillows. He ran his finger along the edge of her sex, teasing her until she jolted back before submitting.

"Your pussy is perfect," he whispered. The warmth of his breath on her skin sent tingles down her spine, and she bit her bottom lip when he placed kisses down her leg, using his tongue and digits in concert like anyone at that age should have been.

His fingers played her like an instrument—after all he was a professional, and she, the beneficiary of his musicianship.

The strokes of his tongue were long and firm, licking her with precision and bringing her to completion with a shudder, messing the sheets underneath. She'd been right about what he could do—he had a PhD in sex.

"Come here," she said, kissing him again, enjoying her satisfaction on his lips.

They kissed and kissed, looking longingly into each other's eyes. The presence of love in the room could not be mistaken for anything under the sun.

After an epic make-out session, he pulled her hoodie over her head and the light from outside bounced off his eyes, widening when she pushed her breasts together. She'd purposely worn her only lingerie set. He undid her bra with one hand—a tell of experience—and his other hand covered his mouth when the undergarment fell limp.

He said, "They're magnificent." He widened his mouth around her nipple while his hands massaged her breasts.

With eager hands on his zipper she undid the top button of his jeans, and the cotton of his boxer-briefs tightened like a fitted bed sheet. She cycled through a breath and turned over her wrist, shoving her hand past the waistband of his boxer-briefs.

Holy shit.

Her hand was unable to close around him, but it didn't stop her from trying harder, and it was plenty hard already. But he stopped her mid-stroke and touched himself slowly while she paid close attention. After all, she was an attentive student—as she'd said, straight A's in school.

His erection stared at her like a weapon of mass destruction. "Cary, I . . . it's really big."

"We'll go slow, okay?"

Will it even fit?

He kept his promise and kissed every inch of her body before making slow and thoughtful love to her while the theme from *Star Wars* played in her head. It was like nothing she'd ever experienced—passionate yet tender, playful yet serious. Their hands intertwined above her head as his hip thrusts made her whimper. With one last push he came inside her and crashed his head on her chest.

CARY

Laying on the hotel bed, Cary stared at the ceiling and thought about what Tyler had said. Eternally single? People had labeled him that way, but it was their take on his life, not his. What was he supposed to do? Marry the first woman he dated, then get divorced every time he went on tour. No. He needed to find the right person and now he had: the woman sleeping next to him, Tyler Robertson.

But he was afraid of ruining things like he'd done in the past. She was the closest thing he'd found to perfection and he didn't want to mess with it. What would he do about the paparazzi in Los Angeles? They were relentless. Tyler was a private person, and she hadn't signed up for this.

And what would happen if—no, when—they had kids? More things to consider when deciding where they should live. At least for now no one would bother them in Winnipeg. Maybe they'd never leave. Maybe they'd have a bed-in like John and Yoko. Except that John and Yoko didn't have to watch the World Juniors with her family.

His mind was racing and he couldn't sleep, so he quietly rolled out of bed and shut the French doors behind him. He picked up his guitar and finished the song that he'd been writing.

Words came easily. All he had to do was think of Tyler. Everything in his life up until now was in preparation for this. For this angel who'd been right underneath him. She was the one. There was no denying it.

But could she handle his life and everything that came with it?

CHAPTER 11

Over the Christmas break, Tyler and Cary had spent their days watching the World Juniors at her dad's house and their nights at the hotel doing other things. It had been the most amazing week of her life, which meant that leaving was the absolute worst thing. A piece of her heart was gone when he'd left for the US leg of his tour.

The time zone should have made things easier, but it was worse than before. There were more press appearances, interviews, and concerts in the US than anywhere else in the world. His schedule was insanely busy and she only got to talk to him in between flights and after his sets. Not to mention that she was carrying her phone around so that she wouldn't miss his calls or texts. How pathetic.

But she couldn't help the way she felt. She missed his touch, his lips, his scent on her skin. And the sex. They went from having it every day—sometimes several times a day—to cold turkey, which was a strange phrase. However, the lack of sex was nothing compared to sleeping alone and dreaming about him, only to wake up realizing her bed was empty.

The distance gave her a permanent heartache and she could barely eat. She questioned whether their relationship was sustainable and doubted her instincts. How could she possibly trust her choice in men after Dave?

To make matters worse, this upcoming trip to Los Angeles was only two days, so they'd have to pack everything into a short timeframe. It had been five months since their first coffee date at Artigiano and he still hadn't said the L-word. She'd considered telling him first, but what if he didn't say it back? Talk about being humiliated.

Yes, she was an independent woman and all that, but come the fuck on. She deserved love just like everyone else.

Tyler landed at the Los Angeles International Airport at 11:45 a.m. She'd taken the first flight out of Vancouver so that she could spend the day with Cary before Yestown's showcase at the Troubadour that night. He'd asked her to come out to Malibu, but she'd insisted on staying at the Hollywood Roosevelt Hotel with her band. Plus she'd lined up meetings for tomorrow with record labels and music publishers—all the experts in town.

The hotel she was staying at was rock-and-roll friendly, but what did it have in common with its namesake, Teddy Roosevelt? From what she'd read he was a highly educated and moral man, and the hotel's guests were the antithesis.

"Tyler Robertson," she announced to the front-desk employee, placing Rory's carrier by her feet. He'd been as good as gold on the flight, and the crew had simply adored him.

The employee's name tag read: CLIFFORD. Ironically, they— she wasn't sure of the correct pronoun—weren't a big red dog, quite the opposite. Clifford wore their blue-black hair in a tight, low ponytail, and their makeup had been fashioned out of a MAC cosmetics ad.

Isn't she/he/they lovely.

"Tyler Robertson . . . here for two nights?" they asked. She nodded and handed them a credit card, but Clifford motioned her hand away. "Everything's been taken care of." Their voice trailed off, scanning the computer screen. "You're in the Marilyn Suite."

"I booked a single room." She showed them her phone. "I have an email confirmation."

Clifford moved the computer mouse in figure eights. "Your reservation was upgraded by a . . ." They squinted "Kim Tanaka."

Cary. I should've known.

"May I have a single room, please?" She was not about to start living Cary's life and the fancy things that came with it.

"Sorry," they said flatly. "We're completely sold out. How many keys?"

"One please." She leaned on the counter and smiled. "I'll leave the other one here for my guest, if that's okay."

They nodded, typing away. "Guest's name?"

"James Kirk." She'd booked enough hotel rooms for Cary Kingston to know that his pseudonym was Captain Kirk, or "CK."

A few minutes later Tyler texted Cary from the Marilyn Suite.

At the hotel :) she said.

He texted back. *How's the bed?*

Why?

You'll see.

You're all talk!

I'm all action, babe. xo

After waiting an hour, Tyler was officially pissed off. Cary had texted that he'd be a few minutes late but this was simply ridiculous. She hadn't seen him in a month and they'd barely talked about anything other than work, his shows mainly.

The suite door beeped open and Cary walked in. "Hi, honey, I'm home!" Rory sprang up on the bed and wagged his tail. "Hi, buddy!" He pointed at the stuffie. "Is that Teddy?"

"You're late."

"Sorry babe." He flashed his famous smile. "Traffic's brutal this time of day. Well, anytime of day."

"Where's your bag?" She scowled at him, not amused by his lackadaisical attitude. "You didn't ask the bellhop to bring it up, did you?"

Holy high maintenance.

He gave her a kiss on the cheek. "About that . . . I thought we'd stay in Malibu tonight and come back for my exhibit tomorrow. Just leave your suitcase here and pack an overnight bag."

Are you fucking serious?

She folded her arms across her chest. "I told you I have meetings."

"I know, but I've got a lot going on with the gallery, and—"

"What the fuck, Cary?" They'd texted about this yesterday, agreeing to stay at the hotel rather than going all the way out there.

His brow raised, stunned by her tone. "It's not a big deal. I live an hour away."

"Are you kidding?" The hairs on her arms stood up on end.

"Calm down, Tyler."

"Calm down. Seriously? I arrange my life around your schedule—shows, flights, TV appearances. You don't know how it feels staring at the phone like some military wife. I'm tired of waiting while you're out there"—she flung her wrist—"being a rock star."

"Whoa!" He went to hug her but she stiffened her arm, locking her shoulder.

"Don't whoa me. I'm not a horse." Scorching rage rushed through her veins as *Fratres* from *There Will be Blood* screeched in her brain. "This isn't fun. At least not for me. I'm not even a consideration, much less a priority."

It was déjà vu from her relationship with Dave. All that time waiting for him while he was on tour screwing groupies. Not that she had any reason to believe that Cary was two-timing on her, but she couldn't be too sure.

"Hey," he whispered. "I'm sorry. You're always on my mind."

If that were true she would have felt more secure. No. He would have made her feel more secure by putting her needs first.

"What about this suite?" she asked. "I booked a single room."

"It was comped."

Okay, fair enough.

"What about tomorrow? My meetings?" she asked.

"My car service will drive you."

She folded her arms and tapped her foot. "And Rory?"

"He's spending the day with me." Cary scratched him behind his ears while he tried to lick his face. "Rory! Who wants to go to the beach?"

The dog zoomed around the room. Rory understood the word "beach" perfectly.

Tyler bit the insides of her cheeks because there's nothing worse than laughing when you're trying not to.

"Or we can stay here," Cary told her. "No worries, babe. I just want you in my bed at some point this weekend."

She had to admit that she was curious about where he lived, where he slept, and where he took models and actresses. Yes, that was it. That old familiar feeling. The constant doubt that came with dating a musician.

"Fine." She unfolded her arms. "We can stay in Malibu, but I have to head to the venue for soundcheck."

"We'll do whatever you want." He picked up his phone. "What time are you going?"

"Around six." Her voice had returned to normal.

"Perfect. I'll stop by the gallery while you're there."

"Are you still coming to the show?"

"Absolutely." He lowered his chin and looked at her. "Are we good?"

"Yeah, we're good," she said. "I'm sorry for overreacting, but I've barely talked to you. Oh, and by the way, you're my plus one on the guest list."

"I'll give you a plus one." He sprawled across the king-size bed and patted the mattress. "Maybe we should see who's all talk?"

She stared into his penetrating gaze. "Aye, aye, Captain."

"Kim!" Tyler hollered as she hurried inside the Troubadour's showroom. Cary Kingston had spent the past few hours proving that he wasn't all talk.

"Hey," Kim said, walking toward her.

She hugged her bestie. "There's already a line around the corner."

"I know, right?"

Tyler pointed at her bright pink hair. "Nice dye job by the way."

"Thanks." Kim shook her head. "I got it done this morning."

"You're a saint for doing this. If I could, I'd canonize you."

"Dude, I love Yestown. They're so easy to work with. And I, like, owe you my life, remember?"

"I swear I had nothing to do with it." She raised her hand like she was taking an oath. "It was Cary's idea to keep you on his tour, not mine."

"How pissed is Sebastard?"

"Pissed." Tyler rolled her eyes. "Oh my god, I forgot to tell you. The Westgrays fired their producer, that guy from the Island. Right in the middle of their session. And get this, they had the audacity to ask for time off to see their girlfriends."

Kim covered her mouth and wiggled her fingers. "What did you say?"

"I said if they were taking time off, I was too." She shook her head. "Anyway, we're scrambling to find another TM for this corporate gig, but don't worry about it. I told Sebastien I'd get someone else." Tyler inspected the room, ensuring their backline—drums, amps, and mics—was up to snuff. "So Vegas is coming into town tomorrow?"

"Yeah, tomorrow morning. I'm picking him up at the airport."

"Is everything cool with you guys?"

"Dude, he's the best!"

"He is the best." She agreed wholeheartedly.

"How's Cary?" Kim stretched a lazy grin across her face. "I'm asking for a friend."

She narrowed her eyes and pursed her lips, knowing that it was Kim's handiwork, booking the room and car service. "The Marilyn Suite was a little much, don't you think?"

"Sorry, my bad." Kim stared at her for a few seconds, but she didn't speak.

"What?" Tyler wiped the sides of her mouth with her hand. "Do I have something on my face?"

"You know he's, like, fucking in love with you, right?"

She made a pouty face, embarrassed about the fight she'd picked with him. "Yeah, we kind of had a blowout."

Kim's gaze went still. "What happened?"

"I kind of freaked out. But he deserved it." She pulled out her topknot and wrapped it up tighter. "He wants to stay in Malibu tonight but I have meetings tomorrow."

"Sounds tragic."

Tyler shrugged. "I think he's wasting my time, like Dave. Everything's about him and I'm sick of it."

"Dude, are you fucking kidding me right now? He talks about you, like, every second of the day. I literally have to stop the guy from buying you dumb shit at airports. 'Will Tyler like this? Will Tyler like that?'" She lowered her voice. "He'd kill me for telling you, but he checked your Insta every hour before I told him to turn on his notifications."

"Bitches!" a young woman's voice echoed from across the room. Her dark shaggy hair bounced as she hurried toward them. She was a dead ringer for eighties Chrissie Hynde, and not by accident. The Pretenders were her favorite band.

"Allie Kowalski," Tyler said, turning toward her friend. "Thanks for coming."

"I wouldn't miss it," Allie said and smiled at Kim. "Congrats on the CK tour. I hear you're killing it, man."

"See?" Tyler said.

"I'm stoked about seeing this band." Allie checked her phone, presumably for offers. "They sounded good on TikTok." She glanced up briefly. "I mean, who sounds good on TikTok, amirite?"

"There's a huge buzz about Yestown," Kim said. "I had to shut down the guest list. It was getting ridiculous."

Allie's thumbs were busy texting. "What are they like to work with?"

"Dude, they're so pro, easy-peasy."

Tyler gave Kim a tight-lipped smile and nodded, acknowledging the compliment.

"I'm signing them." Allie lowered her phone. "Before the vultures get here. Fucking sycophants in LA, I'm telling you."

"Don't you want to meet them first?" Tyler asked.

Back on her phone, Allie shook her head. "No, I'm good, man."

The doors opened at seven p.m. and a flood of people rushed the stage to secure their positions. The Troubadour was a general admission venue: first come, first served.

After the fans took their places it was easy for Tyler to spot the music industry executives she'd invited. They were at the bar, flashing credit cards like magicians and charging drinks to their companies—bills disappearing into their artists' recoupable expenses.

"All the experts are here," Tyler said, and Kim nodded. She couldn't believe how many VIPs were in the room. It was standard for industry people to say they were going, then pull a no-show.

"What's *he* doing here?" Allie frowned, pointing her finger.

Tyler followed her gaze. "Who?"

"Fucking Tommy." Allie faked a retch and the women laughed.

Allie and Tommy worked for the same booking agency but lived in different cities. Allie hated Tommy, and the feeling was mutual.

"I'm sure he's just here to network," Tyler said. "He passed on the band last year."

"Sebastien put him on the list." Kim frowned. "But I didn't give him a plus one, even though he asked."

"Is Sebastard coming?" Allie plugged her nose.

"You hate him too?" Kim asked.

Allie scoffed, staring at her screen. "You can't trust the French." She glanced at Tyler. "I'm surprised he's letting you work with them."

She smirked. "As long as his other acts are bringing in money, he doesn't care about my indie bands. He thinks it's laughable."

"Fucker," Kim added.

"Did you guys hear?" Allie scrolled through her phone.

"Hear what?" Tyler asked.

"The Westgrays imploded."

"No!" Tyler said. "When?"

"Today," Allie said. "It's on their socials."

Kim closed her eyes and held her hands in prayer. "Thank fucking god."

"That was Sebastien's only new act." Tyler checked her phone. *Three missed calls.*

Allie laughed. "Tommy's too. I'm not going to lie, I'm not mad at it."

There was some sort of commotion at the entrance, so Tyler assumed that Cary had arrived. She'd asked him about hiring a bodyguard in Vegas's absence but he wouldn't hear of it, so as a workaround she'd given the venue's security the heads-up that he was coming.

Tyler shot up her arm and waved. "Over here!"

Cary squeezed through the crowd, holding his beanie while people fell over themselves. "There's a line around the corner," he said.

"Hey dude." Kim nodded at her boss. "I'm going back to check on the band."

"You're cheating on me," Cary said to his tour manager, laughing.

Tyler shouted over the din in the room, "This is Allie. She's signing the band."

"Wow! That was fast." He extended his hand. "I'm Cary."

Allie plunked her phone into her crossbody bag and shook his hand. "Happy to meet you, man."

Cary smiled. "Pleasure's mine."

Allie turned to Tyler and rubbed her chin. "You know, I just had someone drop out of Coachella."

"Coachella," she repeated. "Why?"

"Why else? Their radius clause. I'm pitching Yestown for their slot."

The music festival had strict rules about their artists not playing shows near Indio, or, depending on their draw, the rest of California. By contrast Bert had imposed a reverse radius clause after her mom had died, only taking gigs within a day's drive.

Tyler clapped. "I'm so excited!"

"Whatever," Allie said. "It's a side stage during the day."

Still, Coachella.

Cary pushed up his beanie. "I'd love to play Coachella."

"You could totally headline Coachella," Allie said, voice certain.

He scowled. "Why am I not playing there?"

"You should probably ask your agent." Allie pointed to the bar. "He's over there, downing shots with industry people half his age."

"Fucking Tommy." Cary shook his head. "Some things never change."

After Yestown's set ended Tyler stood proudly. Their gig had gone just as she'd imagined it would, only better and louder.

"They're good," Cary said, rubbing his ears.

"I think so too." Tyler waved at a record company executive as she walked by him. "They're just missing that one song—a radio song."

"I might have something."

"A song?" she asked, not sure if he was offering. Cary only wrote for himself, despite his music publisher's attempts to get him to write for other artists.

"I wrote it ages ago. It's not a"—he used air quotes—"Cary Kingston song."

"I bet it's amazing."

"I don't know about that." He paused for a second. "Unless they don't want an outside writer. I completely understand. I didn't want an outside writer when I was their age either. It took me years to understand that co-writers were allies, not enemies. It's all about writing the best song possible."

"Are you kidding?" She balked. "They're huge fans. They grew up on your music."

The cords in his neck tightened. "That makes me feel old."

"Old?" She whispered into his ear, "I haven't recovered from earlier. I'm still a little sore if you want to know the truth."

"Don't look now." He stepped in front of her, using his body as a shield. "Fucking Tommy's on his way over."

"Cary, buddy!" Tommy greeted him with a bro-hug. "What are you doing here?"

"Checking out the music," he said. "What did you think of the band?"

"These fucking kids today." Tommy slung his arm around Cary's shoulder. "I just don't get it."

"Really? I thought they were good."

"Have you seen—" Tommy unlatched his arm and nodded at Tyler. "Never mind." He went on, "The afterparty's going to be

a fucking rager. It's at the Chateau and"—he pointed at Tyler—
"you're coming."

Like hell I am.

Chateau Marmont was a playground for young Hollywood.
With the Playboy Mansion closed, it was the next best option for
middle-aged creeps and borderline pedophiles.

Speaking through her teeth, she said, "We have plans with
the band."

"Next time," Tommy said, which she took as a threat. "What
about you, Cary?"

"No thanks, but I want to headline Coachella."

"I'm on it." Tommy flashed a phony grin and excused himself.

Later that evening Tyler took the band, Allie, Kim, and Cary
to her favorite Los Angeles restaurant, Subito's, to celebrate. She
had just enough room on her credit card if Penfolds Grange wasn't
on the menu.

Allie shared the news that she was signing Yestown and the
guys were ecstatic. Every local band in the country was dying to
work with her, and it gave Tyler hope for the next generation of
artists. One day women in the music industry would be valued—
and paid—as equals. But it wouldn't be today. Or tomorrow,
unfortunately.

A few years back there'd been a half-hearted attempt to elect
more women to music industry boards. Advocacy groups and
government agencies had demanded gender parity, but it wasn't
long before the men delegated the administrative duties to the
newly elected members while they'd kept positions of influence
and six-figure salaries for themselves.

The house never loses.

After dinner Tyler and Cary collected her dog from the
hotel, then headed west toward Malibu along the Pacific Coast
Highway—PCH to the locals. With the windows rolled down the
warm ocean breeze swept through the vehicle and waves crashed

along the perimeter. There were palm trees and houses and little shops along the road, and a lot of cars honking.

It was LA, after all.

Cary's beach house sat on some of the most expensive real estate in California. He'd told her that he'd purchased the five-thousand-square-foot, two-story concrete-and-glass building after the market had crashed years earlier. The previous owners had left it in such a state of disarray that he'd had to gut it. The upside was that it allowed him to design it the way he wanted it.

"What a dump," Tyler laughed, kicking off her shoes. "You should think about buying something bigger." She inhaled through her nose, swallowing salt from the air.

"I'll start saving," Cary said, turning on the lights. "What do you think? Dessert now or later?"

"Depends on what you mean by dessert."

"Funny." He waved at her to follow him. "Come, I'll show you around."

Cary guided her on a tour while Rory shadowed them, presumably looking for cookies. The décor was similar to his penthouse, contemporary and sparse, hardwood floors throughout.

"Pictures!" She clapped at the framed photographs of his parents that sat on a wooden sideboard. "Are your parents coming to your exhibit tomorrow?"

"My folks?" He shook his head. "No, they're not."

"Let me guess." She rested her hands on her hips. "You didn't invite them?"

"It didn't cross my mind, unfortunately."

She shook her head. "I'm putting myself in charge of inviting them to your events."

"Okay," he said, not putting up a fuss.

"Really? You're not just saying that."

"Do I still have to prove I'm not all talk?"

She laughed. "Always."

And forever, I hope.

CARY

Cary hated that they'd fought earlier in the day. He'd had enough fights with Emma to earn him a championship belt, not that he was proud of it. He'd spent his entire adult life thinking about himself and now it was time to prioritize someone else. He was always thinking about Tyler, but he needed to do a better job of expressing himself.

What a sweetheart she was to get excited about the pictures of his family. He didn't have the heart to tell her they were new, brand new, in fact. *Damn*. He should have invited his folks to his exhibit. At least he'd have two people in attendance. Three, including his girlfriend.

It begged the question: would anyone show up at the gallery? Would they laugh at his photographs? Anyone could point and shoot a camera. Was it too late to cancel?

The gallery's capacity was capped at three hundred, but he was more nervous than a sold-out concert at Wembley Arena. The music critics he could handle—most of them were failed musicians themselves—but art critics had gone to school to rip you a new one in several languages.

They were cultural assassins.

Having Tyler there would make a difference. She was a calming presence, except for earlier today, which was out of character. It was the first time they'd had any real disagreement. But he did change their plans without asking. He'd have to try to stop being Cary Kingston, rock star, and just be her boyfriend.

CHAPTER 12

The next morning Tyler's alarm played "Wake Me Up Before You Go-Go" by Wham!

Cary muffled a laugh under his pillow. "Are you serious?"

"Best wake-up song ever," she said, rolling out of bed. She'd seen George Michael on his last tour and was blown away by his voice and stage presence, not to mention his songwriting. But whatever happened to Andrew Ridgeley? She made a mental note to google it.

"Stay." He reached out his arms and tried to hug her.

"I can't. It was your bright idea to come all the way out here." The drive between LA and Malibu was farther than she'd planned.

"I know." He shocked one eye open. "Did I hear you get up in the middle of the night?"

"We forgot to clean our plates after dessert." She rummaged through her bag and pulled out a pair of fresh underwear. "I can't sleep if there are dirty dishes in the sink."

After stepping out of the shower, Tyler slipped into a floral cotton dress. She didn't particularly like what she was wearing but planned on changing into something fancier for Cary's exhibit later.

"You're dropping Rory off at the Roosevelt on your way to the gallery, right?" she asked.

Rory's ears twitched when she said his name, but like a child avoiding his mother's call for dinner he didn't stir a bit.

157

"Cary?" She raised her voice a smidge.

"I'll drop him off around six," he mumbled, burying his face into the pillow.

She kissed his bare shoulder. "Remember, no touching in front of Sebastien."

"Who cares?" He turned over and shielded his face from the light.

"I care," she said. "I might get fired."

"If he fires you, I'll fire him." He lowered his hand from his face and squinted. "Don't worry about it."

If Cary fired Sebastien he'd be out for revenge, an honor killing for bringing shame upon the SDM family.

"Please?" She kissed the nape of his neck, trying to stress the importance of keeping their relationship a secret.

"Fine." He pointed toward the kitchen. "Croissants are beside the fridge." She stretched a smile across her face. "Have a great day, babe." His voice trailed off as he closed his eyes.

"You too," she said, and blew him a kiss.

The car service picked up Tyler at seven thirty, and the driver explained that traffic was heavier than usual along PCH because of road work and general maintenance. Her chest tightened and her heart pounded at the thought of being late, even though music industry meetings were often delayed. Being on time was more of a guideline than a rule in LA. She'd scheduled meetings with record labels, music publishers, and streaming platforms during the day, and had purposely booked her last appointment with ASCAP outside of regular business hours so they could have drinks at their usual hangout. When she was an intern, Sebastien had told her that Canadian songwriters could join ASCAP to collect their performance royalties. In fact, it was the only advice he'd given her other than saying that she should smile.

He could go fuck himself.

At two minutes to nine she arrived at Warner Music Group and flew through the doors of the old Ford automobile factory. *Fuck, I'm late.* She ran to the reception desk where a young blond woman sat, filing her long acrylic nails.

"I'm Tyler Robertson," she said, catching her breath.

The blond motioned toward the chairs. "Please, take a seat."

I killed myself trying to get here.

The dampness in her armpits trickled down her sides, so she flapped her elbows and took a seat. She pulled out her phone and almost dropped it from the heat. There were dozens of messages waiting to be read and she needed to reply in her standard one-hour timeframe.

A notification flashed across her screen, and she checked Cary's Instagram.

"Rory!" It was a selfie of Cary with her dog, barely recognizable underneath the sheets, and he'd captioned it with a heart emoji.

Lucky dog.

She smiled and liked the picture.

The rest of Tyler's day was busy since everyone was interested in signing her band, but she knew better than to believe them—LA was a fickle town. Although the meetings were easy to get, the follow-through was non-existent, so she learned not to get her hopes up. She'd been disappointed enough by Dave.

The ASCAP people were different. They worked for a non-profit organization so they had no agenda. Plus their CEO was a highly educated woman, along with many of their top executives.

Straight from beers with the ASCAP people, Tyler jumped into an Uber and zipped across town. She arrived a little tipsy at Cary's art exhibit just before seven.

The gallery was smaller than it looked on their website but it was well-suited for a photography exhibit, as far as she could tell. She smiled at the life-size poster of her boyfriend on the front of the building. It read: CARY KINGSTON, CANDID.

"Tyler Robertson," she said to the tall, burly security guard who stood at the entrance like Saint Peter at the gates of heaven. She flashed him a toothy smile but he didn't reciprocate, probably because he had a serious job to do, like checking names off the guest list.

"I don't see your name?" he questioned, judgy as hell. His gaze traveled from her head to her shoes and he smirked. *Fuck.* She'd planned on changing out of her floral cotton dress, but one beer had led to another . . .

"I'm on Cary Kingston's list." She dropped his name like a rap record.

The security guard flipped over the page and traced his finger down the list of names. "Got any ID?"

"Yes sir." She reached inside her bag and pulled out her passport.

"Canadian?" he asked rhetorically, crossing her name off the list. She nodded and he stamped her wrist, returning her passport without saying anything.

Inside the gallery Tyler scanned the room, but it was hopeless to find anyone in the crowd so she sent Cary a text: *Here.* She hid in the corner to answer her messages. It was out of character for her not to reply right away, but she found it impossible to work in the City of Angels and understood why Mötley Crüe had shouted at the devil.

"Tyler!" Tommy crept up behind her before she could escape. "I've changed my mind." He lifted two shrimp rolls from a plate of passing canapés. "I'll take that band off your hands."

Go fuck yourself.

"Yestown?" She waved away a tray of champagne. "Allie signed them."

"When?"

"Last night."

"Fucking bitch," he said under his breath.

Fucking dick.

"You passed on them," she reminded him. "Twice."

He scoffed. "Yeah? We'll see what Sebastien has to say about that. Speaking of . . ."

"Hi doll," Sebastien said, whiskey in hand. His face was extra splotchy and his beard unkempt, but thank god his baseball cap covered the rest of his head.

"Sorry about the Westgrays." She scrunched her nose and shook her head like she'd meant it. "I know you sunk a lot of money into them."

"I never liked them," Tommy added.

You're full of shit.

Sebastien's face turned crimson. "I'm suing them."

"They're broke," she told him. "They blew their advance money on partying." Booze and drugs, she figured.

"It's the principle." Her boss gulped down the rest of his drink. "I heard the show went well last night."

"It did," she said. "Yestown killed it."

"Good," Sebastien snorted. "Sign them to SDM. We need more pucks on the net."

What the fuck?

"I thought you didn't like them." She distinctly remembered him saying they "sucked shit."

"I don't," he said. "But as long as they're making money"

"You should've come last night," Tommy said, interrupting their conversation. "We threw an epic afterparty at the Chateau . . . tons of hot chicks."

Sebastien frowned. "I don't do amateur night."

Tyler stopped herself from saying, *That's what she said.*

Tommy straightened his tie at the knot. "Cary thought they were good, but I wasn't sold. I'll let Allie take them . . . throw her a bone."

Sebastien's eyes crossed. "Why was Cary there?"

Jesus fucking Christ.

"I don't know, but he wants to headline Coachella next year." Tommy's laugh turned into a cackle. "Fucking Coachella. Can you f—"

"I can't wait to play Coachella next year," a man behind them said.

"Cary!" Tommy spun around and shook his hand. He pointed to the photographs. "Nice fucking snaps."

Cary scowled at him, insulted.

"I'm going out for a smoke," Sebastien said. Her boss hated schmoozing with artsy-fartsy people, and they, obviously, with him.

"I'll join you," Tommy said, brown-nosing like a piece of shit.

After they left Tyler straightened her dress at the hips. "Sorry," she said. "My meetings ran late and I didn't have time to change."

"You look beautiful, babe." Cary kissed her on the cheek.

Liar.

"Not here." She peered out the window, but Sebastien had more than likely booked it out of there. "How's Rory?" she asked.

"Tuckered out," Cary said. "He played on the beach all day. I dropped him off at the hotel a couple hours ago and he was already asleep. Hey, how's my ASCAP family?"

"They loved the band!"

"Of course they did." Cary squinted at the entrance. "Have you seen Vegas?"

She shook her head. "Kim picked him up this morning. But I haven't seen her either, now that you mention it."

"I'm sure he's on his—"

"Cary darling!" a woman's voice drawled, pleasant and sugary like sweet tea. She was from somewhere in the South. Maybe Texas or Oklahoma. Tyler couldn't tell the difference between them.

"Uh . . . hi," he said, voice shaky as hell.

The petite blond woman wore a tight fuchsia dress with a push-up bra, tits hanging out. Her thick foundation had been plastered on, presumably with a finishing trowel, noticeably different shades of skin showing where her foundation ended.

"Darling!" Her duck lips puckered and she kissed Cary's cheek, branding him with an imprint so perfect it could have been a tattoo stencil.

Tyler raised her brow and glared at him. *What the fuck?*

"Tyler, this is Emma." His voice was cold and clinical.

No shit, Dr. Kingston.

"Emma Turner." She said her full name, no doubt, making a point.

Tyler stared at her with a pang of jealousy so acute that she could have turned into the Hulk. "Hi," she spit out, lifting a glass of champagne from a passing tray.

The actress's pale blue eyes zeroed in on her floral cotton dress. "Hello." She extended her hand and Tyler squeezed it firmly. "What is it you do, Tyler?"

"She works at SDM," Cary said as if she were mute. "She works for Sebastien."

And I fuck you, remember.

A photographer interrupted them, asking for Emma's picture with Cary while Tyler's heart shattered like a thin sheet of ice. She turned away and gulped the champagne like it was water, then closed her eyes and willed the earth to vaporize six billion years ahead of schedule. She cursed herself for wearing a stupid cotton dress, wedges on her feet, and no makeup on top of it.

How could Cary like both of them? Emma was her complete opposite. And she was a fucking movie star. Okay, she was a B-list actress, but her ego couldn't get past it.

"Cary!" a well-dressed older gentleman with salt and pepper hair called him over.

With a grimace, Cary looked at Tyler and said, "I'll be right back."

"Take your time, darling." Emma batted her fake eyelashes and wiped the lipstick stain from his cheek with her thumb before he left.

Oh, fuck off already.

Tyler's beer buzz was wearing off so she grabbed another glass of champagne. The more she drank, the less she'd have to say to Cary's ex-girlfriend. A win-win if there ever was one.

"I had too much sun today," Emma mused, swooping her hand across her forehead in a dramatic fashion. The actress stepped closer as a waft of Chanel No. 5 followed her. "Cary's house doesn't have any shade," she added.

"Excuse me," Tyler choked out, turning on her heel.

The voice in her head looped: *Cary's house doesn't have any shade.*

She half-walked, half-ran across the room balancing her champagne glasses like hockey players fighting.

Oh my god! Did Emma meet Rory?

She chugged both glasses in quick succession before pulling up Emma's Instagram.

"Fuck!" Emma had posted a picture of Rory on the beach and she'd captioned it: *Love this little guy! #whosagoodboy*

Using both hands she grabbed onto the high-top table beside her, knees buckling inward like a fawn trying to stand. She didn't know whether to cry or yell or commit murder. It was like discovering those emails on Dave's computer. A complete blindside, no left tackle to protect her.

Her head pounded to the beat of *The Tell-Tale Heart*. *Lub dub. Lub dub.*

After she steadied herself and caught her breath, her heart crashed into her ribs like waves against a steamship.

I can't believe this is happening.

A server came by with another tray and she snatched a glass of champagne and dumped it into her gullet. The bubbles froze her brain and she clenched her teeth while her eye twitched uncontrollably.

Meanwhile, across the room, Emma glommed onto Cary and smiled for the cameras. And once again the actress kissed his cheek like they were a couple.

I've had enough of this shit.

With alcohol now taking over her body and the *Chariots of Fire* music keeping her pace, she ran toward the entrance in her sturdy wedges, but bumped into someone walking into the gallery.

"Sorry," she said.

"Dude?"

She spun around and cried, "Kim!"

"Hey Tyler!" a man's voice boomed above her head.

"Hi Vegas." She tried to smile but couldn't muster a grin.

"Where are you going?" Kim asked, and Tyler started to cry. "Fuck, what is it?" She gave Tyler a hug and shooed Vegas inside the gallery. "What happened?"

Tyler could barely enunciate the words through her sniffles. "Em-Emma's in there."

"Fuck that skanky bitch."

"Wait." She showed Kim the picture of Rory on her phone.

"She's fucking dead."

"While I appreciate that, it's more Cary's fault than hers." Tyler glanced at her watch. "If I hurry I can catch the last flight home. Please don't tell him I'm leaving."

Kim nodded and stormed inside, visibly pissed off.

On her way to the hotel Tyler booked the last seat on the last flight back to Vancouver. Time would be tight but she had Nexus, so she could bypass the line at the airport.

After she fetched Rory and her bags, the bellhop waved down a taxi.

"L-A-X," she instructed the driver. "Take La Brea, please. I'm in a hurry."

She'd been to Los Angeles enough times to know better than to leave the routing up to the driver. They always took the long way around, driving slower than any grandma.

Where was Sammy Hagar when you needed him? Probably in Cabo drinking tequila.

As the car bumped down the road she leaned back and held on to Rory.

"Sorry, buddy," she cooed. *What* is *that?* She sniffed his head and widened her eyes. Chanel No. 5. *Holy fucking hell.*

The thought of Emma touching her dog gave her the heebie-jeebies. Poor Rory. She'd make it up to him with cookies and a bath and more cookies to reward him.

At that moment Cary's most popular love song blared through the radio like torture music, making her stomach churn.

She leaned forward and implored, "Please turn it off."

Of all the songs in the world.

A few minutes later her phone vibrated. It was a text message from Cary.

Where are you?

She sent him a screenshot of Emma's post and shut off her phone.

Good riddance.

CARY

"What the hell is this?" Cary asked, dazed by the picture on his screen.

Vegas angled the phone closer to his face. "Looks like Rory, doesn't it?"

Cary pinched his eyebrows together. "Of course it's Rory. This is Emma's Instagram, and Tyler just sent it." He cranked his neck. "Where is she?"

"I saw her outside, man," Vegas admitted.

"What?"

He elaborated, "She was crying."

Cary closed his eyes and took a deep breath. "Why didn't you tell me?"

"It's none of my business." Vegas shrugged, not one to get involved in drama. "Why does Emma have a picture of Tyler's dog?"

"To mess with her, obviously. I told Emma it was Tyler's dog. I wasn't even thinking."

Vegas rolled his eyes. "Emma's a b—"

"She dropped by my place earlier unannounced, saying she'd left some necklace there. Like months ago. I told her to wait outside while I asked my housekeeper if she'd found it. And of course she said no." He clenched his jaw as he breathed through his nose. "That's when she took the picture. I'm sure of it."

Vegas shook his head. "Doesn't look good, man."

"You think?" A rare tone of sarcasm rolled off his tongue.

"Just explain what happened," Vegas said. "She'll understand."

"I'm calling the hotel." A man answered on the other end. "Tyler Robertson's room, please?" There was a lengthy pause. "The Marilyn Suite."

"Sorry sir," the man said. "She's already checked out."

"What do you mean she's checked out?"

Was this all because of Emma? Had she ruined everything? For once in his life he was genuinely happy, and now his girlfriend was upset. He had to make some changes in his life and truly commit. If that meant moving for Tyler to be happy, so be it.

CHAPTER 13

Tyler gave herself exactly one day to stay in bed and listen to "Landslide" on repeat. It was her mother's favorite song, and Stevie Nicks made her cry every time she listened to it. But she wasn't angry with Stevie or Cary—she was furious with herself because she'd let it happen. Again.

She turned off her phone and didn't touch her computer. She didn't even call Dylan to make herself feel better or to talk shit about Emma. She needed to feel this pain and remember it for the next time. But most of all she needed to learn her lesson and not fall for a musician.

The cycle between devastation and rage continued throughout the day as her blood ran hot then cold, like a drug addict kicking a habit. But that's what he was: a hard habit to break.

At least Rory was beside her and he smelled better after his bath. The cookies were hardly adequate after what he'd gone through. He probably needed a dog therapist.

Maybe it was time to have a baby? If Yestown signed a record deal she'd have enough money to freeze her eggs. Of course she'd use a sperm donor, because the idea of another man touching her made her queasy and she almost puked trying to imagine it.

Admittedly the next two weeks weren't her best, but she soldiered on and dealt with Cary's music publisher for the rights to record his song. There wasn't any reason to communicate with him directly so she ignored his texts, emails, and phone calls; a big fuck you from someone who always answered her messages. In fact, she almost blocked his number but thought better of it. As long as he was still allowing Yestown to record his song, she didn't have much choice in the matter. It would be for the best in the long run.

Tyler woke up earlier than usual in a pool of sweat. Her dreams about Cary had become more frequent, not less, and it pissed her off to the fullest extent. She rolled over and checked her phone. It read: FEBRUARY 14.

Ugh.

Valentine's Day was bullshit. And not just because she was single. When she was with Dave it was even worse. He'd forgotten four out of the five years they were together, and the one year he'd remembered he used a coupon at an inexpensive restaurant. But seriously, with everyone being so sensitive these days it surprised her that some trigger warning advocates weren't calling for its abolishment.

Her phone vibrated a few minutes later. It was Kim calling from the East Coast. She probably wanted to commiserate about this stupid-ass day that people made up to sell flowers and candy to hopeless romantics.

"What's going on?" Tyler answered.

Kim paused on the other end. "Cary's, like, going to kill me if he finds out I told you—"

"What? I bet he's sending roses. That's lame as fuck." She'd have to compost them in her building's green bin. What a fucking hassle.

"Dude, he blew off his interview and he's on his way there." Kim's tone was short. "Oh, and the segment producer had a fucking conniption on my head, so thanks for that."

"What?" Tyler hyperventilated, leaving her breathless. "Why's he coming out here?"

"Because you won't take his calls or answer his texts."

"Boo fucking hoo."

"Don't be like that." Unfortunately the fiasco had put Kim in an awkward spot, and Tyler wasn't helping the matter by not responding. "He said something about going to the office."

"I'll work from home."

"You're not supposed to know!"

"Fine." Tyler sighed in frustration. "But I'm not talking to him."

"What are you going to do? Avoid him forever?"

"Works for me."

"Dude, he said nothing happened and I believe him."

"Yeah right." She couldn't help being sarcastic. Dave had also denied that he'd cheated on her before she'd found hundreds of incriminating emails. Of course Dave didn't have money to buy his own laptop so he used hers but forgot to log out of his account. "Kim, I know he's your boss but I need you to be on my side, not his."

"I'm on Team Tyler. Why do you think I'm calling? Do you honestly think I'd, like, try to fix this if he was some asshole?"

"I guess," she said, and changed the subject before Kim could fire back. "How's everything with Vegas?"

"So good! I thought he'd be pissed. You know, with me staying on, but he's, like, the nicest person ever invented." Her voice flipped back into work mode. "Look, Sebastien doesn't know yet but I rescheduled Cary's interview for tomorrow afternoon. If he doesn't get on that flight I'm getting fired for sure."

"What time is his flight?"

"Eleven twenty-five."

"Okay, I'll make sure he's on it," she conceded. "But *only* for you. We still don't have any bands on tour. Did I tell you? I'm trying to get Yestown on the awards show broadcast?"

"Ew. Why?"

"They asked me to."

An hour later Tyler arrived at the office and called her contacts in Toronto to ask if Yestown could perform at the upcoming music awards. Normally she didn't care about what music industry people called the "Mickey Mouse Awards," but they were being held in the band's hometown of Saskatoon so she felt obligated to put forth her best effort. No offense to Mickey Mouse, of course.

She'd struck out with her first few calls so Allie was next on her list.

Allie picked up her phone on the first ring. "I was just about to call you!" she shouted over a commotion in the background.

"Where are you?" Tyler asked.

"Winnipeg. Hold on, I'll go somewhere quieter." Her boots stomped away from the bustle in the room. "There," she said, out of breath. "I'm at the Voyager Festival."

"The Festival du Voyageur?"

"Yeah, that. I've got a band playing here."

"How is it?"

"I like it here, man. Lots of cool shit, nice people."

Tyler pulled up their artists' calendar on her computer. "Sebastien has one of his heritage acts there. Brad's band, in fact."

Jamespoke had garnered some notoriety in the nineties, but they didn't become a festival draw until a popular American act had covered one of their songs. After that, Brad, the lead singer and Captain Jerk of the band, changed the song splits in favor of himself so that he'd earn more in royalties than his co-writers, a dick move by anyone's standards.

Allie chuckled. "I'm well aware Brad's here."

"What do you mean?"

Tyler couldn't imagine that Allie was a fan of Jamespoke, or the guys in the band. Their hospitality rider listed two things: whiskey and coke. And not the cola in the can.

"Are you ready for this?" Allie's voice became giddy. "They played all new material last night."

"No!" Tyler shrieked.

As a heritage act, the festival had hired the band to perform their back catalog, which meant their old songs, the hits. Not the new songs that people didn't know or care about.

"Fuck yes." Allie laughed. "Not one popular tune in their set."

"Not even—"

"Nope. Not even their number one song. I'm not going to lie, man, it pissed people off."

"Jamespoke," Tyler said in a heavy breath. "Is Tommy still their agent?"

"Totally." A thud came from the other end and a faint curse word followed. "I dropped my phone. Just hearing his name ruins my day. You called for a reason?"

Tyler had almost forgotten the purpose of her call. "Any chance you can get Yestown on the awards' live broadcast?"

"Are you punishing them for something?"

"No, it's their hometown. They're from Saskatoon."

"Saskatoon, that's right," she repeated. "Sorry, man. Fucking Tommy has it on lockdown with that dipshit from the awards."

"That guy sucks."

"Yeah, he really does."

"Thanks anyway," she said, defeated. "I'm going to tell Sebastien about Jamespoke. He can't stand that band."

"Can't stand them?" Allie sounded confused. "He manages them."

"It's just a cash grab, like all of his heritage acts."

"Would you ever sign a band just for the money?"

"Never."

"Me neither," Allie said with certainty.

"I'd rather have one artist I'm in love with than ten mediocre acts."

"Same," she said. "See you in Toon Town."

Tyler was about to give up on the awards when she received an email from Yestown's producer. The subject line read: Banger.

They'd finished recording Cary's song.

Fuck my life up the butt.

She clicked on the track and played it again. And again. "Banger" was an understatement. Yestown had to play this song at the awards, but she would need Sebastien's help.

Dammit.

A few minutes later Tyler knocked on her boss's door. "Hello?"

"What?" he barked at the disturbance. "Do I look like Lionel Richie?"

You're definitely not as handsome . . . or talented.

She poked her head inside his office. "Have you got a minute?"

"What is it?" Sebastien grumbled, though he didn't appear to be busy.

Tyler sat in the chair across from his desk, knowing that it was a risk. People didn't sit down in his office unless he'd invited them in, like comedians on the old *Tonight Show*.

"I need a favor, please?" she asked him politely. Being nice almost killed her, but it was a necessity. He loved it when people kissed his ass.

He raised the bill of his baseball cap. "I'm listening."

"I want Yestown to play on the awards' live broadcast." She leaned forward and clasped her hands on her lap. "I know there's a slot left."

Sebastien reclined in his chair and put his feet on the desk.

"I'll tell you what," he said, voice lingering. "I'll help you if you help me." A pending negotiation came out of his nicotine-ridden breath.

"What is it?" she dared to ask.

He adjusted his baseball cap to its original position. "You and Cary are chummy, right?"

"I wouldn't say chummy." She drew her eyebrows inward. "But we're friends, I guess?"

Were *friends, no apostrophe.*

"Friends, whatever. If you can persuade him to accept his lifetime achievement award, I'll see to it that your little band plays on the idiot box."

You're an idiot box.

"He's not accepting it?" she asked, shocked. The awards were for the fans and she couldn't imagine him disappointing them by not showing up.

"He's accepting it by video," Sebastien said before clearing his throat. "I need him there in person, you know."

In other words, Sebastien wanted the recognition for himself. She shook her head. "Cary hates that kind of thing."

"What do I hate?" The voice behind her sent needles down her spine. She instinctively turned her head toward him but didn't smile.

"Cary!" Sebastien cried. "What are you doing here? I thought you had an interview this afternoon?"

"It got pushed to tomorrow," he lied. "I had some things to take care of. Anyway, what do I hate?"

"Award shows," Tyler said bluntly. He stepped into the office and his cologne hit her smack in the face. It reminded her to start a petition to boycott Calvin Klein's Obsession under a human rights violation.

Sebastien snorted. "I told her if you accept your award in person I'd get her band on the live broadcast."

Cary stared at her, eyes intense. "What do you think, Tyler?"

I think you should go back the way you came in.

"Maybe take a little time to think it over," she said, voice unsure.

"What am I, in Foreigner?" he joked. "Fine, I'll do it."

"Wait, are you serious?" Sebastien asked, almost falling over.

"Saskatoon, right?" Cary asked.

"Right." Sebastien nodded. "They're offering to pay us an exorbitant amount."

"Tell them I'll do it for free," he said. "But it's on the condition that Yestown plays solo."

"Why?" Sebastien asked.

"The awards pair artists together like supergroups, but nothing will ever top the Traveling Wilburys, so why bother?"

Tyler held back a laugh.

"Got a minute to help me with my speech?" Cary asked her, gold eyes sparkling in the light.

I can't say no in front of Sebastien.

She nodded once.

"It's settled then," Sebastien said, no doubt cooking up ways he could still earn a commission.

Tyler stood from her chair. "I heard Jamespoke only played new songs at their gig last night." She loved tattling on them. "None of their hits."

"What the fuck do I care?" Sebastien shrugged. "They've already paid us."

Moments later Tyler and Cary left Sebastien's office and walked down the hall in silence.

"Hi Cary!" Lara shouted from the reception desk.

He waved but said nothing.

She opened the door to her office and Rory whizzed by them, circling back once he recognized Cary, wagging his tail like a metronome.

"Rory!" Cary picked up her dog and closed the door behind them.

Tyler sat at her desk and stared at his vacant *what did I do?* face while her dog sat on his lap like a traitor and licked his face. *Aw, that's cute.* No. She shook her head and peered out the window. *Would he fit through it?*

With every passing second her temperature rose until she broke out in a sweat.

Cary leaned forward in his seat. "I'm sorry, babe."

Don't you fucking "babe" me.

She shrugged. "You don't have to explain."

"Explain? I've been trying to explain for two weeks. I get it. I'm sorry you're upset." He apologized as if he'd stepped on her foot by accident, not slept with his ex.

Her voice came out shakier than expected, "You-you don't owe me anything."

"Wait. Do you think something happened between Emma and me? Are you serious?"

How dare you say her name in front of me! Do you really want to hurt me? If so, mission accomplished.

All he needed was a banner on a naval ship.

"It's none of my business," she said, breath smoldering. She doodled a knife on her notebook; the shower scene from *Psycho* serving as her soundtrack.

"Nothing happened," he professed. "I swear on Rory's life."

The dog perked his ears and tilted his head.

Bite him, Rory.

The blood in her veins bubbled underneath her skin. She'd heard enough lies from musicians to last her this life and the next.

"Emma dropped by unannounced and said she'd left a necklace at my place. Which, by the way, she hasn't been in for months. I told her to wait outside while I asked my housekeeper, and that's when she took the picture of Rory."

"Sounds like you owe him an apology," she said coldly, pointing at her dog.

Cary scratched him behind his ears. "Sorry, buddy."

Rory licked his hand as if to say, *That's okay,* and she glared at the little Benedict Arnold.

No more cookies.

"At the gallery you introduced me as someone who works at SDM," she snipped.

"You told me not to tell anyone!" He seemed to catch his voice rising and lowered it. "I mean, obviously Kim knows." He clasped his hands on his lap. "I wanted to introduce you as my girlfriend."

His eyes leaped open. "Not that I invited her—I didn't. Emma must've figured it out, seeing as your dog was at my house."

Had she been mistaken? She'd shown up to his exhibit a few beers in and ended up in a foul mood after running into Tommy. That fucking idiot. Kim was convinced that he hadn't done anything wrong. Maybe it was all in her head.

"I haven't told anyone here," she whispered, although the door was shut.

"Let's tell everyone!" He extended his arms across her desk and touched her hand. "Tyler, it's hard being in love with you and keeping it quiet."

Her voice came out softly, "You're in love with me?"

"Absolutely. I'm sorry I didn't say it sooner, but I had to be sure. And now I am."

"I love you too." Her heart skipped a beat. "I'm sorry I ever doubted you. Trust is something I have to work on. But now I feel bad that you came all this way to see me."

"I didn't. I came to see Rory. I wanted to ask if he'd be my Valentine."

She laughed. "Really? Is that a fact?"

"I got you something."

"Yeah, my band on the awards. Thank you." She shook her head. "You didn't have to do that."

"I wanted to help," he said with a smile. "I love that band, and they're recording my song."

"Record*ed*," she clarified. "Do you want to hear it?"

"Of course I do."

She turned her computer speakers toward him and clicked on the track. He closed his eyes and rocked to the beat, smiling from the beginning to the end.

"Incredible." He straightened his spine, squaring his shoulders. "Really. I'm impressed."

"I want them to play it on the live broadcast."

"See, it all worked out." Cary winked. "Come downstairs and bring your bag." He checked his phone. "I've only got seven hours left."

"What about Sebastien? I can't just leave—"

"Let's tell him right now."

She hesitated for a moment. "Is it okay if we wait until after the awards? I don't want him screwing with Yestown."

"You promise?"

"Only if you promise me something."

"Name it."

"Please stop following me on Instagram," she said. "I had to turn off my notifications because of your fans."

"Oh, shit." He covered his mouth, letting a grin slip. "I'll set up a private account," he said. "I love seeing pictures of you and my Valentine."

After Cary told Sebastien that he needed Tyler's help to pick out a new suit—which wasn't a total lie because he didn't say when—they walked down two flights of stairs to SDM's parking garage.

"Surprise!" Cary said, more excited than a rich kid on Christmas. They stood in front of a brand-new car with a red bow wrapped around it. "It's blue, but we can have them paint it black if you don't like it. This is all they had on hand."

He passed her a key card. It read: TESLA.

"You bought me a car?" she asked in disbelief.

"A Tesla," he clarified. "You said you wanted something electric, and let's face it, your truck has seen better days."

She handed back the key card. "I can't accept a fifty-thousand-dollar gift from you, Cary." She guessed the amount, but it could have been more.

"I made that in merch last night, babe." His attempt to put things into perspective didn't help his cause.

She rephrased her statement. "I can't accept a car from you."

"I told you, it's not a car, it's a Tesla." He gave her a cheeky grin. "I didn't buy it for you. I bought it for Rory. For Valentine's Day."

The dog's ears twitched when he said "Rory" and "car."

Cary reached into the front pocket of his jeans and pulled out a single key attached to a fob. "Here, keys to my place."

"Why?" She tightened her topknot.

"Isn't that what couples do?"

She grabbed his keys. "Okay, what about the car? The Tesla. What's Sebastien going to think?"

"Are you kidding? Who do you think bought his car? I gave Tommy and Bob Shaw their cars too."

That made sense. Her boss was too cheap to buy a Porsche himself. "Did you buy him his boat too?" Cary shrugged. "He called it *Relentless*."

"Well, I didn't know he was going to name it that." He picked up Rory and cradled him like a baby. "I can't have my Valentine driving around in an unsafe vehicle."

Tyler gripped her hands in front of her chest. "Please take it back."

"I can't." He turned his bottom lip into a cute frown. "The owner did me a solid."

"The owner of the dealership?"

He laughed. "Someone a little higher up."

She sighed, but he was right. Her truck *had* seen better days. "Thank you but I'm paying you back, every last cent."

"I already told you." He handed her the key card again. "I bought it for Rory."

"No more gifts, you promise?"

He nodded. "We have reservations at Provence, beside the Wine Bar."

It was a thoughtful gesture but it was also Valentine's Day, and the restaurant would be too crowded for him to go unnoticed.

She gave him a closed-mouth smile. "Thanks, but do you mind if we stay in and watch the hockey game? The Jets are playing."

"A win puts them first in their division, right?"

She furrowed her brow. "You've been watching?"

"I said I would."

"I'm used to you being all talk."

Cary laughed, shaking his head. "What am I going to do with you?"

Where's the suggestion box?

CARY

Cary had meant to tell Tyler in a more romantic way that he was in love with her. He'd even practiced what he might say. To think that he'd cheat on her with Emma—with anyone—made his heart ache with regret that he hadn't said it earlier.

But what was the problem with telling Sebastien? And why would he screw over Yestown?

He had to get to the bottom of it.

Then there was the lifetime achievement award. God help him. He didn't feel old enough to accept it. In fact, he was trying to write another hit. Sure, he loved playing his old stuff—most of it—but those songs were for his fans, not him. He wasn't the type of person to look back and reminisce. There was too much ahead of him. He was grateful for his career but the best was yet to come. And he'd proved it by finding Tyler Robertson.

Now he had to make sure to not fuck it up.

He'd barely slept over the past two weeks and his shows had suffered the consequences. Truth be told, he should have given his fans their money back, but Vegas had assured him that the reviews were good, even great, and he remembered why he had so little faith in music journalism.

CHAPTER 14

Ten minutes later Tyler and Cary arrived at his building, stopping briefly to say hello to the concierge on duty. Rory seemed to like Arjun, even though he didn't have any cookies. They rode up to his penthouse while "Love in an Elevator" played in her head.

This song is silly.

He opened the door, spun her around, and kissed the curve of her neck as his jaw drew up to her mouth, her body pulsing with lust, longing for him. He crushed his full lips onto hers, parting them with a heavy breath, and she melted into his warmth, chin lifting.

"Cary," she whispered in between breaths. He ignored her while his tongue circled her mouth and her nipples hardened with ache. She'd missed everything about this and savored the moment. "Cary . . ." She pulled away an inch from his lips.

"Yeah babe?"

"Do you mind if we talk?"

"You said I was all talk, so I'm showing action," he teased, swiping his hand between her thighs and pushing her panties against her sex.

She rolled her eyes into the back of her head and moaned, "Fuck."

"I want you." He scratched the crotch of her jeans with his fingers. "Badly."

She blew out a breath "Can we maybe talk first?"

"What's wrong?"

"Come sit." She motioned toward the couch where Rory was already sleeping like the dead. "I want to explain why I acted like that. I owe you more than an apology."

He shook his head, adjusting the bulge in his jeans. "I should've known better."

"It's my ex." She sat on the couch and unlaced her old, worn-out Dayton boots. "He cheated on me the whole time we were together and now I have major trust issues." She hated Dave for making her feel like this. When she found out about his cheating she was more angry than upset. She hated how he'd taken advantage of her kindness and free rent.

He sat beside her and held her hand. "How long were you together?"

She met his gaze and cringed. "Five years—just over."

His eyes turned dark. "What an asshole. I'm sorry to hear that, babe."

"There's more." She blinked away the moisture in her eyes. "He strung me along and promised we'd have a baby, and like an idiot I waited. I have to tell you, Cary, I'm batting zero with musicians."

"Well, I'm glad you're not with him. I can't speak for all musicians, just this one. I love you." He gave her hand a squeeze. "My tour ends in August."

"I know when your tour ends."

He laughed. "I guess you do. How about we try then?"

She flashed open her eyes. "Seriously?"

"I'm not getting any younger." He smiled, nudging his head toward the bedroom. "Want to practice?"

"I *am* a perfectionist."

Still holding his hand, she followed him into his bedroom and shut the door. *Privacy please, Rory.* Who was she kidding? That dog wasn't waking up for anything.

She lay on top of the duvet and started to unbutton her jeans, but his hand clamped on top of hers and he said, "Let me." She lifted her hips and he pulled down her pants, wiggling them off at the ankles. After removing her socks he slid his hand up her thigh until it reached the triangle of cotton between her legs. The tips of his fingers were rough, of course, and the calluses rubbed against her sex. "You're so wet," he said, which only exacerbated the situation. She needed to issue a flood warning. Maybe an evacuation.

"Get these off of me!"

He laughed and tugged on the elastic of her panties until they were by her feet. Her bottom lip quivered when his tongue pressed against her sex and she gripped the duvet, squeezing her toes as the tension progressed like the guitar riff in "Kashmir." His tongue slid along her flesh until . . .

"Fuck." Her hips convulsed on the bed.

An earthquake warning was now in effect.

"I love how you taste," he said, climbing on top of her, his hair hanging in her face. "I could do that all day." He unsnapped the buttons on her shirt one by one until her bra was the only thing left. She unhooked the front closure—a trap for any man—and her breasts fell to the sides, nipples erect. He stretched his hands over her breasts and kneaded them before his mouth enveloped one, then the other, sucking on her nipples until they turned a purplish red.

"My turn," she said, cupping her hand between his legs. She used her finger to trace the outline of his erection through his jeans and he closed his eyes, moaning several curse words strung together like George Carlin. She loved watching old stand-up specials—the filthier the better.

"Really?" she asked, eyebrows raised, using both hands to unbutton his jeans.

He laughed. "Button fly—go figure."

A clunky jingle reverberated when his jeans hit the floor and she slid her hands inside his boxer-briefs, massaging underneath. His already impressive member swelled to twice its size when she wrapped her mouth around him, and opening wide she gorged on him like a feast. He let out a yelp. "I'm going to come."

She stopped for a second. "That's kind of the point."

"No way, not yet." He flipped her onto her back and pulled the loose elastic from her topknot, then combed her hair with his fingers. His gaze penetrated her soul as she widened her legs, and he grabbed his girth, slowly entering the wetlands.

"I love you," he said.

"I love you too." She gasped, drawing in a breath with every inch of his hardness, and there were many breaths. With a final thrust he pushed inside her. "Holy fuck!" She balled her fists on the bed so she wouldn't lose consciousness.

"There's nothing holy about this." He breathed into her ear and sucked on her neck before biting it.

They rocked every corner of his bed, and the sheets became soaked with sweat until he pulled out his thickness and blew out a breath. He stroked himself slowly as it dripped like candle wax.

"I don't want to come yet," he said. She nodded as he entered her again, and she pushed her breasts together and squeezed them, biting her bottom lip. "Fuck!" A warm liquid blasted inside of her and he collapsed on the bed.

She giggled. "I thought you didn't want to come yet?"

He opened one eye. "That was just practice, remember?"

After Tyler and Cary took a shower they ordered Indian food from Vij's and turned on the hockey game. The Winnipeg Jets had scored early in the game and were leading 1–0.

"They waved off icing." Tyler pointed to the screen. "See, he could've played the puck." She continued to watch the game while she ate. "This food is delicious!"

"You've lived here for how long and never had Vij's?" He shook his head. "How's that even possible?"

"I don't eat out much unless I'm with Sebastien. He hates Indian food. Indian anything, really." She darted her gaze back to the game. "Goal! That dummy scored on his own net. I wish they'd make it two points like a safety in football."

He laughed. "Any other suggestions?"

"Oh, this is spicy." She took a gulp of water. "I think if you score a shorty—when the other team has a power play—your guy should get out of the penalty box."

Her phone vibrated. It was an email from Sebastien. She laughed as she read the message.

Your band is in. You're welcome.

"What's so funny?" he asked.

"Nothing, really. I'm laughing at Sebastien's deal. You for my band. It's like a prisoner exchange."

"I suppose it is."

"Why do you hate awards so much?" She put down her plate on the coffee table and crossed her legs over his lap.

He paused. "I don't have a problem with awards based on merit. Record sales or number of streams—"

"Or tickets sold."

"Exactly." He nodded. "I've got a problem with voting on best song or best artist. It turns into a popularity contest, and the person with the most likes wins."

"How do you feel about your lifetime achievement award?"

He rolled his eyes. "I'm not even forty."

"What am I missing here?"

"They're for old people." His shoulders rounded as he cringed. "I don't want to be a heritage act like Jamespoke. I play a lot of new songs in my set."

"You've had twenty years of hits," she reminded him. "Jamespoke had one hit, and another group made it famous. Plus, Brad's a colossal idiot."

He tilted his head. "My last number one was five years ago." Had it really been that long? His tours had always sold out, so she'd never kept track of his chart positions.

"The song Yestown recorded is a banger."

"I was talking about a new song." He sighed. "As much as I hate to say it, a Cary Kingston song."

What had she done? She'd practically forced him to accept his award in person.

"Forget it," she said. "I'm pulling Yestown and then you won't have to do it."

"I'm not backing out, babe. I committed."

Why did he think he had something to prove? He'd been a best-selling artist for two decades. Maybe he was just like Prince's mother: never satisfied.

"High stick!" she shouted at the TV. "His stick was higher than the crossbar."

"You sure know a lot about hockey."

"I'm surprised you don't know more, being a Manitoban." She tapped her lips. "You're on the road too much." She scooched behind him and rubbed his shoulders. "You don't have enough downtime to write."

"I've got plenty of downtime," he said over his shoulder. "It's called hurry up and wait."

"I don't push my artists to write on the road. Writing and performing are two different things."

"You know, you really understand musicians. And I'm not just saying that. I think we both know I'm not all talk by now."

"I can't help it." She shrugged. "I was raised by one." She'd told her family that Cary had cheated on her with his ex but they didn't seem to believe it. Of course Dylan thought she was overreacting, which pissed her off more than anything.

"Maybe you should go out on your own? I know you're not happy at SDM, or at least with Sebastien."

She stopped mid-rub and rested her chin on his shoulder. "If I went out on my own I'd want to work with Kim and Allie—make it a full-service operation."

"So do it!"

"Have you met Sebastien?"

"I know he's a little rough around the edges." *Rough around the edges?* A hand saw was smoother than Sebastien. "Don't worry, I'll talk to him."

"No, you won't," she said firmly. "I'm not ready to leave yet." He twisted his neck and stared at her. "Cary?"

"I promise." He crossed his heart.

She stared at the ceiling. "I could sign that girl band I was telling you about. And Nadie when she's done school. But I'd want to take Yestown with me. I found them myself."

"You should talk to Bob Shaw about setting up your business," he suggested.

She burst out laughing. "Yeah, right. And Bob Shaw won't tell Sebastien?"

"Trust me." His look turned dead serious. "He won't."

"What makes you so sure?"

"He manages my finances outside of SDM. I hired him after he got sober."

"I didn't know that."

"Well, he's keeping it on the downlow from SDM."

Interesting . . .

It was the first intermission when Tyler's phone vibrated. Dylan called on FaceTime, knowing they were in between periods. Her sister was a die-hard Jets fan, like the rest of the Robertsons.

Cary glanced at her screen. "Is your sister upset with me?"

"No, she's cool," Tyler said. "She didn't think you were cheating—I mean, with someone else. She's doing her Valentine's Day check-in."

Tyler answered the call. "Happy Valentine's Day! Rory says happy Valentine's Day too." She waved Rory's paw into the phone.

"Happy Valentine's Day!" Cary said, moving his face into view.

"Cary?" Dylan's eyes rounded.

"Are you surprised?" he asked.

"Yeah, I guess, but I'm glad you're there." Dylan sounded sincere but it surprised Tyler there wasn't an "I told you so" in there.

"Best Valentine's ever," Tyler said. "Indian food and a hockey game."

"I think I can make it better." Dylan thinned her lips into a smirk. "I'm pregnant!"

Tyler covered her mouth. "Shut the fuck up!"

"You shut the fuck up," Dylan laughed.

"Oh my god!" she cried. "Congratulations! When are you due?"

Dylan could hardly spit out the words. "September. I'm only six weeks along. I got pregnant around New Year's. Good thing I quit drinking on Christmas."

"You didn't quit drinking, you had an extended hangover, if memory serves." Her voice became concerned. "How do you feel?"

"I'm nervous, naturally, but I feel pretty great." Dylan paused. "Any chance you can be here for the birth?"

"I can guarantee it," she confirmed.

As soon as the game ended—of course Winnipeg won—Cary zipped up his jacket. Tyler insisted on driving him to the airport because she'd promised Kim that she would.

"Ready to go?" he asked, waving her key card.

"Sure," she said, barely able to make a sound from the couch.

"Babe?" He walked toward her and she dropped her head into her hands. "What is it?" he asked.

"I'm sorry." She wiped her cheeks with the cuff of her shirt.

Cary handed her a tissue. "Are those happy tears for Dylan or . . . ?"

"They are." She heaved, drying her eyes as she strained to focus. "But I've missed so much of Nadie's life, and my nephews' lives, too. I want to go home."

"For good?"

"Eventually." She nodded, blowing her nose. "I don't have any work there, but—"

"We'll figure it out," he promised, wrapping his arms around her like a security blanket.

She buried her face into his jacket. "I won't see you for a whole month."

Who was she turning into? Some needy chick? *Gross.*

"It's less than a month," he said. "And if it's too much I'll fly back for a day, or I'll fly you to wherever. I'll do anything to make this work."

"I feel silly." She dabbed her eyes with the crumpled tissue.

"I'm a phone call away." His voice sounded reassuring. "If you can't reach me, text Vegas. He'll know where to find me."

She sat up straight. "Vegas knows?"

Cary stretched a smile across his face. "He figured it out at the hockey game."

"I had no idea." She paused. "You probably shouldn't play poker with him."

Maybe that's how Vegas got his nickname.

CARY

After Cary checked into the airport he called Kim from Air Canada's Maple Leaf Lounge.

"I got her back!" he said while signing an autograph. "And my flight's on time. See, no worries." It was a miracle for an Air Canada flight to be on time, but there was still half an hour until it boarded.

"Dude, I won't be happy until you land." Kim's voice came out thin. "But you sound like your old self again."

"Sorry for bailing today." He smiled at the fan and returned his pen. "I had to come out here. It's Valentine's Day."

Kim sighed. "Okay, what did you end up getting her?"

"A Tesla."

"You bought her a car?" Kim sucked in a breath. "Cary, what the fuck?"

"Her truck's not safe," he said. "Besides, you told me to."

"I was fucking kidding, dude. Haven't you heard of, like, flowers or chocolates? How did she take it?"

"Not great at first, but I told her I couldn't return it." He smiled at a middle-aged woman who'd snapped his picture. "She accepted it on the condition I let her pay me back."

"That sounds like her. She'll fucking do it too."

He scoffed. "Yeah, I'd like to see her try."

"She'll find a way."

"That's pretty unlikely, considering I'd never take money from her." He chuckled. "Hey, can you sort out my travel arrangements for the awards weekend in Saskatoon, please?"

"Ew. Why?"

"I'm accepting the lifetime achievement award . . . long story."

"Do you want me to book Vegas's flight while I'm at it?"

"Yes please. And I want you there too."

"Lucky me, I guess."

CHAPTER 15

Two weeks later Tyler's phone vibrated on her desk. It was Cary on FaceTime, which didn't surprise her because they'd been on the phone nonstop since he'd left. She answered, keeping the door open because Sebastien was away and Lara wasn't at her post where she should have been.

"Hi!" Tyler said. "How are you?"

"Pack your bags!" Cary sounded like a game show host giving away a free vacation.

"Why?" She tilted her head. "What's happening?"

"I booked you a flight, babe. You're meeting me in Austin."

"You booked it?" She raised an eyebrow, not believing him.

"Okay, Kim booked it." He rolled his eyes, copping to it. "Your flight leaves on Friday afternoon and gets in around midnight. Kim will send you the details. She checked your calendar, so don't worry about Sebastien finding out."

She scanned his tour itinerary on her computer, not remembering a break in his schedule. "Aren't you playing a show the next night?"

"It's being rescheduled as we speak," he said. "Tommy's taking care of it."

"Fucking Tommy." She pressed her tongue against her teeth.

"Yeah, I know, but there's a problem with the venue and I'd rather reschedule than cancel."

"Why Austin?" She shrugged. "Can't you come home instead? I mean, don't get me wrong. I'm excited to see you."

"Austin's one of my favorite cities. They have an incredible music scene and the best Mexican food north of the border."

"I've been," she assured him. "I've been to South by."

South by Southwest—SXSW—was one of the largest showcasing music festivals in the United States. She'd attended a few years ago but found it as useless as Vancouver's hockey team playing in a game seven. Everyone went there to party, not to listen to music.

"South by?" he repeated. "No, no, it's nothing like that. You need to experience Austin outside of the festival."

"Okay, I'll take your word for it."

Two Saturdays later Tyler and Cary awoke in the Governor's Suite of the Four Seasons Hotel in Austin. The night before, his tour bus had driven from San Antonio to Austin, making it in time to pick Tyler up from the airport. The band and crew were thankful to have a day off in the live music capital of the world. They'd be doing their part to keep Austin weird.

"What's the plan?" she asked, hoping to spend the day in bed, or at least the morning. Their suite was luxury at its finest, having a magnificent view of Lady Bird Lake. "We have a Rory-free day since Kim insisted on keeping him."

"I'm sure she gets lonely on the road." He swept back the hair from his face. "I thought we'd visit a few museums then check out some music later. But first I'd like to pay my respects."

She used a pillow to prop up her head. "Your respects?"

He nodded. "Stevie Ray Vaughan."

"His grave?" she asked.

"No, he's buried in Dallas, but there's a statue here." He closed his eyes before he went on, "I was just a kid but it hit me really hard, his death. I know I'm more of a rock guy but everything comes from the blues."

"I know how to take your mind off the blues." She traced her finger down the middle of his bare chest, teasing him until she reached his boxer briefs.

"You're in trouble." He wrapped the sheet around them like a burrito.

She rolled over and straddled him. "Double trouble."

Tyler and Cary had dinner at Manuel's that evening, then strolled around the Red River District, ending up on 5th Street outside of Antone's Nightclub.

"Cary goddamn Kingston, as I live and breathe." A doorman greeted him with a smile, extending his hand. "Reggie. Big fan."

Cary obviously needed a better disguise than wearing his glasses.

"Nice meeting you, Reggie," Cary said. "This is Tyler." She waved and Reggie nodded. "What's it like in there tonight?"

Reggie turned toward the entrance and lowered his head. "Indie music. Mostly college kids." He shook his head and frowned, seemingly embarrassed by their patrons. "A lot of kids with beards and flannel."

"Well, that doesn't sound too promising," Cary said. "But since we're already here . . ."

"Follow me." Reggie waved, leading them inside.

They followed Reggie as he parted the crowd, seating them at a reserved table at the side of the stage. Reggie was right, they could have easily been in Portland or Seattle and not known the difference.

Fucking hipsters.

Reggie asked, "What'll it be?"

"I'll go to the bar." Tyler stood from her seat. "You've done enough. Thank you. Really."

"It's no bother." Reggie pointed to the line at the bar, fifty people deep. "You'll be waiting a goddamn hour otherwise, Mrs. Kingston."

She grabbed her chest and sucked in a breath. "I'm not . . . we're not . . . I'm . . ." She fanned her sundress to diffuse the heat. "I'm his girlfriend," she clarified while Cary cracked up like it was the funniest thing.

Shut up, Cary.

"You'd better put a ring on it," Reggie said.

"I'm planning on it, Reggie." Cary winked at the doorman.

Really?

Reggie mustered a chuckle. "What'll it be?"

"Beer?" She shrugged at Cary. "We'll have two beers, please. And we're paying full price."

"It's on the house," Reggie said. "Your money's no good here."

"I insist, Reggie." Cary pulled out his wallet and flashed a twenty-dollar bill.

"Cary goddamn Kingston," Reggie said and walked away, not taking his money.

The room was at capacity, but luckily the hipsters hadn't spotted Cary—or if they had they were too cool to acknowledge him. Even their server ignored them when she dropped off their beers. For once they were enjoying themselves like a regular couple until she glanced at the stage.

Chris? No. It can't be.

Chris was the drummer in her ex-boyfriend's band, and she hadn't seen him in two years, at least. He was tolerable—as far as drummers went—but what were the chances of him being there? Apparently 100 percent.

Fuck! The rest of the band, including Dave, walked across the stage. Was this some kind of joke? She scanned the room for hidden cameras, convinced that she was being punked.

The house lights flashed on Dave's olive-green eyes and he squinted, holding his hand above his chiseled face. Loose black curls hung past his shoulders and he tousled his locks while a few girls screamed. *Ugh, spare me.* He wore a tight black t-shirt that hugged his lean muscles, although he never worked out or lifted a finger.

Dave adjusted the microphone stand to reach his 6'2" frame and peered over the crowd, focusing on the tables near the stage. When he met Tyler's gaze he stretched a sexy grin until he glanced at the person sitting beside her, jaw hanging like a picture frame.

That's right, asshole. I've upgraded.

With an aggressive grab of the microphone, Dave counted his band in. The song was the fourth track from their second record, one of their self-proclaimed hits.

She closed her eyes and shook her head, disgusted with herself for remembering the album sequence. During their set a wave of bile inched up her chest, quickening her pulse with every word he sang. Was she going to puke or have a heart attack?

"They're not that good," Cary said, casually drinking his beer.

She nodded, not letting on that she knew them. "Yeah, it's pretty bad."

After Dave's band finished their set, Cary flashed his wallet at their server.

"It's been taken care of by some fans," she said, setting down two bottles of beer.

"Here." He took out a twenty-dollar bill. "This is for you." He turned his head and leaned back in his chair. "I'm happy to say hi to them or sign an autograph."

She plucked the bill from Cary's hand. "It's from those guys over there."

Oh shit.

Tyler spied Dave heading over in that annoying strut of his while the first four notes of Beethoven's 5th Symphony droned in her head. Was it too late to trade in her birthday wish?

"Tyler," Dave said smirking, like he knew he was her dirty little secret.

Cary narrowed his eyes, looking suspicious. "How do you know each other?"

"I'm Dave."

Cary gave him a blank stare, then looked at Tyler.

"He's somebody that I used to know—an old friend," Tyler explained, omitting the five years they'd known each other intimately. She hated how much she'd let him get away with and it was difficult to accept how naive she'd been.

"I'm not old," Dave said staring at Cary, trying to get a rise out of him.

"I mean, we used to be friends," she clarified, ignoring the insinuation that her boyfriend was older than him.

"With benefits," Dave added for good measure.

When you weren't too drunk, that is.

"What are you doing here?" she asked. "In Austin?" She could have cared less about his answer but she needed to change the subject before he started to talk about their relationship.

"We're touring before South by . . . Chris needs the practice. You know, it was kind of a train wreck." It was always someone else's fault—not a shocker. "What are *you* doing here?" he asked.

She gulped down a swig of beer. "Cary's show . . . I mean, his show got canceled, so we're hanging out down here."

"That's right, you work at SDM." Dave faked a laugh as if he'd forgotten. She made a fist under the table but didn't believe in violence.

"She's not here on business." Cary grabbed her hand and put it on the table. "She's here with me."

"What?" Dave threw his head back and laughed maniacally. "Are you guys together or something?"

"It's none of your business." She owed him nothing—less than nothing, actually.

"She's my girlfriend." Cary interlaced his fingers with hers and squeezed them. "I don't cheat on her either, in case you were wondering."

Nice one. She stretched out her hand to loosen his grip while Cary's eyes turned dark and cold behind his glasses. He guzzled his beer with his free hand and slammed the bottle on the table, causing a racket. Was he jealous of this piece of shit? He was the better man, obviously.

Towering over her, Dave rested his hand on the back of her chair. "I guess you won't be having that baby, after all. Them's the breaks, Tyler."

Dave had thought of the meanest thing to say and said it. He knew how much she'd wanted a baby. Relationships had an ethical duty of confidentiality, and he'd broken it.

She glared into his olive-green eyes. "Fuck off, Dave."

Cary chose that moment to weigh in. "We're waiting until my tour's over, but believe me, buddy, we're practicing. And not for nothing, the problem with your band isn't the drummer. Your songs are shit."

A short while later Tyler and Cary left the bar and walked south on San Jacinto Boulevard toward the Four Seasons in silence. Was he upset about Dave? She had no idea he was going to be there. She would have stayed in Vancouver if that were the case.

"Are you mad at me?" she asked as the hotel elevator doors closed.

"Wait until we're in our room, please." His gaze locked onto the call buttons and didn't move an inch.

This silent treatment is bullshit. Then again, she'd ignored him for two weeks straight when she was mad at him.

Cary beeped them into their room, closed the door, and removed his glasses. "Have a seat."

"I swear, I didn't know he was here!" she said. The last thing she wanted was for them to meet.

"Why didn't you say something?" He sat on the desk chair and kicked off his shoes. "I looked like an idiot."

"*He* looked like an idiot." She grabbed a beer from the minibar and sat on the couch. "I don't know why I didn't tell you when I saw him. I kind of freaked out."

He stood from the desk chair, opened a bottle of red wine, and poured a hefty glass before sitting back down. "Would you have told me?"

She shrugged, not sure of the answer. "I'd like to think yes, but I'd just as soon forget it—and him. Are you seriously mad at me right now? Because I can stay with Kim."

"No, not mad." He took a sip of wine avoiding her eyes. "I don't even know what I'm feeling, to be honest."

"Are you jealous of my loser ex-boyfriend?"

"Yeah, maybe." He sank into the chair. "I kind of feel like punching him in the head." *Join the club.* "And, for your information, his band sucks."

"I love you, Cary." She stood from the couch and walked over to the desk. "Not him."

"I know, babe." He squeezed his eyes and grimaced.

Swiveling the chair, he pulled her onto his lap. She laughed, and he parted his lips and kissed her on the mouth. There was a hint of something fruity on his tongue, not Penfolds Grange but something similar.

"I want to fuck you," he whispered, sliding down her bra strap. He fondled her bare breast with one hand while the other hand skirted up her sundress. She stopped him mid-thigh and shook her head. "What's wrong, babe? I know I acted like a jerk, but please let me make it up to you."

"I got my period a few hours ago." She scrunched her nose, almost apologizing for it. "But we can do other stuff."

"I'm sorry. Are you not feeling well?"

"No, I feel fine." She brushed her hand over the front of his jeans and his zipper almost busted open. "Let me take care of you."

"I want you." He sucked on her neck and glided his hand up her thigh until his fingers rubbed against her cotton underwear. "You might want to consider wearing dresses more often. I almost fucked you in the restroom."

"Lousy timing," she said.

He lifted her head until their eyes met. "I still want you."

"What about . . . you know?"

"Your period?" He shook his head. "I don't care if you don't."

"Really?" she asked. "I've never—"

"You've never had period sex?"

She bit her bottom lip, embarrassed. "I mean, I've wanted to."

"Didn't you live with that piece of shit for five years?"

Don't remind me.

"Yes, I did."

"Well, let's see if we can fix that." He lifted her from the chair and carried her into the bedroom. "I love the idea of being your first."

"I have to, um, freshen up," she said, kicking her way onto the hardwood floor.

"You mean, take out your tampon?"

"If you must know, I have a menstrual cup."

"You and your cups." He shrugged one shoulder. "Just take it out."

"Cary!" She laughed. "Take it easy on me. I'm a period-sex virgin."

A few minutes later she came out of the bathroom wearing a hotel robe and nothing else. She held a towel in front of her body. "Is this good?" she asked. He nodded, lying on the bed. "What if it gets messy?"

"I'll buy the hotel," he quipped. "Get over here."

She flattened the towel across the bed and shrugged out of her robe, pulling the covers over them. He caressed the back of her neck and pulled her mouth onto his while his hand reached between her legs, and she twitched.

"Relax, babe." He teased her sex with light strokes before his middle finger penetrated her until it was no longer visible. She rolled her eyes into her head and kissed him deeper every time his knuckles bent. With the covers now off the bed she glanced at his hardness, standing like the Washington Monument, and she moved her hand down his chest before he grabbed her wrist. "You first—always," he said.

A far cry from her ex-boyfriend who was selfish in bed.

As the pressure mounted she spasmed, then he slipped his finger out and licked it.

"I fucking love you," he said, fastening his teeth onto her nipple while her abdominal muscles flexed. He touched and kissed every inch of her stomach before he spread out her legs.

She lifted her head. "Cary! No . . ."

He looked up and nodded. "I want to."

With a sigh she flopped her head onto the pillow and didn't argue when his tongue stroked her like a paintbrush, even and slow, not missing an inch. She arched her back and he closed his mouth around her sex until she irrupted like a water dam breaking, letting the tension release.

Oh god.

"I love how you taste, especially now."

"Fuck me." She opened her legs and he smiled, wiping his mouth with the back of his hand. He stroked his length over her before doing what she asked of him. She didn't want it sweet or tender, none of that bullshit, and with pleading eyes she said, "Fuck me harder." He happily obliged, rocking her with thrusts, making the bed jump and the headboard bang like gunshots.

"Mrs. Kingston" sounds perfect.

CARY

"You should've seen this guy," Cary told Vegas the next morning while they stood in front of their tour bus. Tyler's ex-boyfriend had made him hot under the collar, unlike anyone he'd met. "What an idiot."

"Yeah, I met him when they were dating. A real tool, that guy. I used to call him Stanley, but he didn't get it." Vegas laughed as they climbed aboard the bus.

"His band sucks." Cary ducked into the sofa bench. "Don't you think?"

"Can't say." Vegas sat next to him. "I've never seen him play."

"Trust me." They were the worst band he'd seen in a decade— not that he frequented small venues, but he knew music.

"Are you okay?" Vegas asked, pulling out a deck of cards from the inside pocket of his leather jacket.

"He said that I was old, in front of Tyler." Cary folded his arms and huffed. "Screw that indie rocker."

"You sound jealous, man." Vegas smirked, shuffling the cards like a casino dealer.

Cary rolled his eyes but didn't answer. "The doorman at the bar called her Mrs. Kingston."

"He obviously doesn't know you." Vegas dealt a hand to each of them.

"What?" He lengthened his spine, not sure what Vegas had meant.

"Come on, man. You, married?"

"Why not? I want a family and so does Tyler. Despite what that asshole said." He peered out the window but the bus wasn't moving. "We're waiting until my tour's over, but I hate waiting."

"I'm aware." Vegas scratched his face. "Don't take this the wrong way. You know I don't get involved in your personal shit."

"What?"

"Think about it. Tyler alone with some kid in Vancouver while you're out here doing"—he flashed the ace of spades on the table—"this."

"They can come on the road." Cary shrugged. "We've got our own bus."

"Yeah, that sounds like fun for everyone."

Vegas was right. The road was no place to raise a family, and he couldn't ask Tyler to quit her job or to become a stay-at-home mom.

"On second thought, maybe I'll take some time off."

"I've been telling you that for years, man."

"Well, I didn't have a reason to, did I?"

But now he had one.

CHAPTER 16

The awards show weekend was Tyler's least favorite time of the year. Sebastien brought the SDM team with him to show everyone in the music industry that he was successful and still relevant. He'd even sprung for business-class seats—using points, of course. This year he was going all out because Cary Kingston was receiving the lifetime achievement award and being inducted into the hall of fame. Sebastien, being an opportunist, was aware of the optics.

Tyler had some time to kill when she arrived at the hotel in Saskatoon. Cary's flight wasn't arriving until later that afternoon, so she called Dylan on FaceTime.

"What's up?" her sister asked, lowering the phone to her belly.

"Oh! I can see the bump! How do you feel?"

"A little tired but pretty good, in general." Dylan brought the phone up to her face. "Where are you? Where's the little panda?"

"I'm in Saskatoon. I dropped Rory off at the Rex Dog Hotel. The little stinker didn't even look back when I left."

Dylan inched the phone closer. "Is everything okay?"

"Yeah, I haven't talked to you since Austin," she said. "I'm just waiting for Cary."

"How was it, Austin?"

She twisted her mouth, not sure what to say. "I didn't want to tell you."

"What did you do?" Dylan asked.

"Nothing." She shook her head and rolled her eyes. "We ran into Dave."

Dylan's eyes flashed open. "What the fuck?"

"I know. His band was playing at the bar we went to, and I nearly died, Dylan."

"And he saw you?"

"Oh fuck, yeah. And Cary too."

"No!" Dylan covered her mouth with her hand. "What did you say?"

"I told him to fuck off."

"That was a long time coming," her sister said. "How did Cary react?"

"Kind of jealous." She giggled, still not understanding how her ex-boyfriend could pose a threat to the most eligible bachelor in the country. "If you want to know the truth, he took me back to the hotel and nearly ripped my clothes off."

"Men." Dylan sighed. "It's always some pissing contest, isn't it?"

"We had period sex."

"Well, it happens every month, Tyler. Although right now I don't miss having it."

"I'd never had period sex."

"You're kidding? Even with Dave?"

"He wouldn't touch me that week," she said. "It was like I was hexed."

"Fucking Dave." Dylan breathed audibly. "I never liked him."

"That makes two of us, three counting Dad."

Later that afternoon Tyler's phone vibrated. It was a text message from Cary.

Here. Club Level. Where are you? xo

She replied, *Room 909. Come :)*

After Cary had agreed to accept his award she'd told Lara to book a block of rooms for the SDM team on the same floor. But of course Sebastien wanted to stay in the room beside his number one client. The problem was that he didn't want to pay for a suite.

And he didn't have to. The hotel upgraded him at no extra charge when he said that it was for the rock star. He was always dropping Cary's name to get free stuff.

Moments later Tyler opened the door and stuck out her head, looking both ways like she was crossing the street. The music industry rivaled any gossip column and she couldn't let anyone find out about her and Cary before the awards show on Sunday. It was still possible for Sebastien to pull the plug on her band, and she couldn't let that happen. Millions of people were going to see Yestown's TV appearance, if it was the last thing she did.

"Hi babe." Cary planted a kiss on her cheek. "God, you look beautiful."

"Shh!" she cautioned, closing the door after him. "We've got to be careful."

"It's nuts we aren't sharing a room," he said. "We're sneaking around like criminals."

"Smooth criminals." Michael Jackson's song was one of her favorite dance jams and she didn't give a fuck who knew it. She had no problem separating an artist from whatever bad things they allegedly did. It wasn't her job to judge them. "It's just until Sunday, I promise." She kissed him quickly. "After your rehearsal I thought we'd grab dinner with Kim and Vegas before the show."

"I'd rather stay here and grab you." He wrapped his arms around her waist. "Are you trying to babysit me?"

She lowered her head onto his shoulder and gave him a hug. "Maybe a little. Sorry. You don't have to go."

"Like hell." He straightened his arms and looked at her. "You've only been raving about the Oh Claires for how many months?"

"I know! I had to pull some strings to get them on the showcase." She popped off his beanie and tousled his hair. "I even played the chick card."

"Yeah, I don't blame you," he said. "I'd imagine being a girl band is a hard sell around here."

The truth was a girl band was a hard sell everywhere.

She gave him a lazy smile and edged her fingers down his zipper. "I don't mind that it's hard. In fact, I prefer it."

"How much time do we have?"

Tyler had scheduled his awards show rehearsal for five p.m. It was the same time as the world's lamest event, the President's Reception. Her plan was ingenious. She'd have him all to herself without any distractions. Sebastien loved hobnobbing with music industry executives more than life itself.

"Two hours," she told him. "It's plenty of time for what I have in mind."

"I'm afraid we're not on the same page."

"Oh yeah?" She sat on the bed. "Why's that?"

"A hundred years isn't enough time for what I had in mind."

She glanced at her watch. "You'd better get to it, then."

Kim and Vegas had bailed on going to the showcase in favor of catching up on their sleep. Tyler couldn't blame them. They'd been working nonstop for weeks, except for that day in Austin, which now seemed like a vague memory.

Tyler and Cary arrived at the venue with their all-access passes in hand and flashed them at the bouncer, bypassing the line. On their way in a few people gave him a second glance, but he was wearing his beanie and dark-rimmed glasses so no one bothered him.

Their timing was perfect. A local band from Vancouver had just finished their set. She'd seen them play a million times but they hadn't gotten any better. Why hadn't they given up yet? Free drinks and groupies were all that she could come up with.

Tyler surveyed the room, but as she'd suspected the only music industry person there was Allie Kowalski. Everyone else was out partying like it was SXSW.

"I'm stoked to see this band," Allie said, standing on her tiptoes and peering over Cary's head. "No fucking Tommy?"

"No fucking Tommy." Tyler hugged her friend. "I wasn't about to invite him."

Allie wiped her brow and blew out a breath. "Fucking asshole."

"I know," she concurred. "Him and Sebastien."

"Is Porter coming?" Cary asked.

Porter Reynolds was the president of Allie and Tommy's booking agency. He'd made the "30 Under 30 List" when he was twenty-one for selling his first business. Sebastien and the old guard hated him for it, and the fact that he negotiated deals in the millions.

"Totally not his scene, man." Allie's thumbs tapped on her screen. "He thinks everyone's a moron, especially in the music business."

"He's not far off." Tyler shook her head and rested her hands on her hips. "Look around. Nobody we know is here watching bands."

"Good," Allie said.

"Can I get you ladies a drink?" Cary offered.

"Who are you calling a lady?" Allie laughed at her joke. "Sure, I'll have a beer. Thanks."

"Beer, please," Tyler said. *What if someone recognizes him?* Then again, Cary Kingston in a shitty bar in Saskatoon? Not likely.

After he was out of earshot Allie gave her a sideways glance. "What's that about?"

"It's exactly what you think it is." She wasn't about to lie to her. "He's my boyfriend."

"Nice!" Her eyes drew inward. "Does Sebastard know?"

"Not yet."

"Don't worry, man." She angled her head toward the bar. "My lips are sealed. So, how's the sex?"

Tyler closed her eyes and bit her bottom lip. "God, I can't even."

A few minutes later the Oh Claires plugged in their guitars and cranked their volume knobs to eleven. Their Marshall amplifiers looked like *Hollywood Squares*, stacked 3 x 3.

"It's loud!" Allie shouted, twisting foam plugs into her ears.

"What?" Tyler said.

"It's loud!"

"Loud like AC/DC." Tyler's dad had taken her to see their Stiff Upper Lip Tour when she was nine years old, and it surprised her that she didn't have permanent hearing damage.

Allie laughed. "It's weird they're Australian."

"I think of them as British," Tyler said, agreeing.

"I'm going up," Allie beamed, heading toward the stage.

"Wow!" Cary yelled over the music. "It's a little loud, don't you think?"

"Rock and roll ain't noise pollution."

Cary smirked and continued to watch the band. "They can really play!"

"Do you mean for girls?"

"No." He shook his head. "For anyone. They play better than me."

She gave him a *don't bullshit me* look and drank her beer.

After their set, Allie found Tyler and clinked her bottle. "I'm signing them."

"I'm not managing them," Tyler reminded her. "I mean, officially, but they're perfect for my non-existent roster."

"So manage them unofficially." Allie shrugged one shoulder.

Tyler wrinkled her nose. "Behind Sebastien's back?"

"Who cares, man? This band is breaking regardless."

She shifted her gaze in Cary's direction. "What do you think?"

"Just quit," he said.

"I'm not ready."

"I'm ready." He winked and grabbed her hand. "Let's get out of here."

"I'll call an Uber," she said. "You can't get a taxi around here."

A minute later her phone vibrated. "The car's here." She grabbed his hand. "Follow me."

"I'd follow you anywhere."

As she stepped outside, the blustery Saskatchewan wind made her eyes tear until she blinked. She touched her face but felt nothing, like that song by the Weeknd.

"Over there!" she said as a gray minivan pulled up to the curb.

"Cary Kingston!" a man's voice bellowed in the distance.

Their heads jerked back and a series of flashes temporarily blinded them.

"Is that the paparazzi?" she asked, running toward the van.

"I don't think so. Maybe a reporter for a local paper or something." Cary helped her get into the van as more flashes followed. "The James Hotel, please," he told the driver. "And hurry."

"Are they following you?" she asked, voice shaky.

"I don't think so." He kissed her forehead. "Are you okay?"

She nodded, breathing heavily. "What if they post the pictures?"

"I don't care. I'm more concerned about your safety than anything. I hate waking him, but I'm calling Vegas to meet us in the lobby." He hit a button on his phone. "Weird. It went to voicemail."

"Call his room," she suggested.

He snapped his fingers. "Good idea."

"I texted you the number."

He nodded and put the phone to his ear. "Yes, this is Cary Kingston." The driver glanced over his shoulder. "I need my tour manager's room, please. Vegas—yes, that's right. Thank you." He placed his hand over his phone. "They're connecting me." After a lengthy pause he said, "No answer there either."

Luckily no one had followed them to their hotel but their driver had asked for an autograph—not a shocker. It was the first time that she'd feared for her safety, and it rattled her more than she'd imagined it would. How did Cary do it? Or any famous person, for that matter. It was one thing for people to take his picture when he was on tour, but tonight was an invasion of privacy, pure and simple.

As a precaution Cary went to his room first while she took the next elevator up to the suite. The host hotel of the award's show, where everyone was partying, was down the street, but they couldn't be too careful about being spotted.

She beeped open his door and went in. "I didn't see anyone on my way up."

"That's strange," Cary said. "I wonder where Vegas is?"

"Maybe he just needed a good night's sleep."

"Yeah, maybe."

She refreshed her phone every few seconds. "I haven't seen anything online yet."

"People will know after Sunday, babe."

"I know, but Sebastien could still fuck over Yestown."

"I'm telling you, you're worrying for nothing." Her phone vibrated. "Who is it?" he asked bluntly.

"It's just a Google alert." She sucked in a breath and stared at her phone. "Oh, there's a picture!" She zoomed out her screen. "Fuck me."

"Is that an offer?" he joked.

"I'm serious, Cary. There's a picture of us on the internet, for god's sake." She angled her phone toward him. "Maybe you should call Cheryl to do some damage control."

He tilted his head. "Babe, your face is totally blocked."

"But my jacket . . ." She pointed to the screen. "You can see it."

He laughed. "I wouldn't be able to pick it out of a lineup, and I know you intimately."

She moistened her lips. "How intimately?"

"Why don't I show you?" He parted his lips to kiss her, then stopped abruptly. "Wait . . ." His pupils dilated. "You've got a Google alert on me?"

Obviously.

CARY

Later that night Cary was wide awake so he walked to the window and gazed over the flat Saskatchewan landscape. How could Tyler get used to his life and everything that came with it? She could never live in LA with the paparazzi tracking his every move. But Vancouver? She didn't seem too happy about living there either.

There was no reason he couldn't move. He could be happy anywhere as long as they were together. Vegas was right about taking some time off from touring. Having a baby would change everything, and it *should* change everything. He wanted to be a hands-on dad, and he couldn't do that if he was focused on performing. Hell, it took him an hour every day just to write his set list. His catalogue was so extensive that he could play an entirely different set for three nights straight.

But he was also concerned about keeping his band and crew employed. They'd given up so much of their lives so that he could live his dream. However, there was no reason why he couldn't keep paying them while he took some time for himself. Knowing Vegas, he'd still want to work; he hated being idle.

And where was Vegas anyway?

CHAPTER 17

Early the next morning Tyler sneaked back to her floor wearing a robe and slippers from Cary's suite. She walked quickly to her room without being seen by any music industry people coming back to the hotel from a night of partying.

"Dammit!" she said as the key card reader blinked red. What was she supposed to do? Go to the lobby looking like this? She practically had "sex" written on her forehead.

Two voices—one low, one high—laughed down the hall. Who was up so early on a Saturday morning?

The Pink Panther music crept into her head as she shuffled her slippers down the hall until she reached the end.

"Holy shit!" she said. Kim and Vegas stopped dead in their tracks. He was more than two heads taller than her bestie and twice her body width. "Are you two—"

"Dude." Kim grabbed Vegas's hand "He's the best."

How long had this been going on? And why were they keeping it a secret? She had a long list of questions, but first things first.

"Cary's been looking for you," she told Vegas.

"Is everything okay?" he asked, voice concerned.

Tyler held out her phone and Kim grabbed it. "What's this?" She squinted at the screen.

"Last night a photographer, reporter, whatever, took pictures of us at the bar."

"Dude . . ." Kim zoomed in. "You can barely see your face."

"That's not the point," Vegas said.

"Exactly." Tyler nodded, taking back her phone. "It could've been the paparazzi."

"In Saskatoon?" Kim arched an eyebrow. "Hardly."

"Sorry, Tyler. It won't happen again," Vegas promised. "Is he in his room?"

She nodded, then Vegas kissed Kim on the cheek and left.

"It's not his fault." Kim beeped open her door. "We deserve a night off—just like you and Cary. Vegas is his TM, not his bodyguard, for your information."

After a pause, Tyler said, "You're right. I'm sorry. I'm being overprotective." She followed Kim into her room. "How long have you and Vegas been—"

"Just last night."

"Tell me everything!"

After Yestown's awards' show rehearsal Tyler raced back to the hotel for her hair and makeup appointment. She wanted to look her best for Cary, even though the gala wasn't being televised. The non-broadcast awards were for genres that people didn't listen to and for accolades they didn't deserve. An artist could win for selling five records, while they feted music industry people with hardware for collecting their paychecks.

She changed into a black fitted dress and slipped on three-inch stilettos. She had warned Cary about the height of her footwear, but he didn't give a shit as long as she was happy.

She wobbled her way into the bathroom for one last inspection. "Yuck," she said into the mirror and wiped off her clown makeup with a tissue. This always happened when she had her makeup done professionally, but there was no time to wash it off. The SDM team was meeting in the hotel bar and she didn't want to be tardy for the party.

A few minutes later she arrived at the bar and spotted Cary, Sebastien, Tommy, and Bob sitting at a table having drinks. Then again, they didn't have to spend an hour getting ready and a hundred dollars on their hair and makeup.

"Wow!" Cary stood from his seat as she approached them. He wore a black suit with a black shirt and looked like a million bucks—or however much money he had. Her smile faded and she stared him down as if to say, *Be quiet.* "You're so fucking hot," he whispered into her ear. "I want to fuck you right here."

"Likewise," she whispered back as her lady muscles contracted against her underwear. Fanny flutters, the English called it. "Hi guys." She nodded to the stunned table. They weren't used to seeing her in high heels, or with her hair down, or wearing makeup.

"Hi doll." Sebastien raised a flute of champagne and took a sip. He wore a black suit jacket, two sizes too small, jeans, and that goddamn Quebec Nordiques baseball cap. At least he'd trimmed his beard, although it made his jowls seem more prominent.

"Baby," Tommy said, almost drooling down his tux. "Give ol' Tommy a hug!"

Who let the dogs out?

He tried to hug her but she batted his arm away. "That's enough, Tommaso." She used his full name like his Italian mother to get his attention. "Sit down. I just had my hair and makeup done."

"Don't bother her," Cary said, scowling at Tommy while Sebastien casually sipped champagne from his flute. Her boss was oblivious to any form of sexual harassment since he was often the culprit.

"Hi Bob Shaw." Tyler sat beside him as he lifted his mocktail to acknowledge her. She felt bad for him and his terrible sober time. If he'd listened to Doug Stanhope he wouldn't have been in this predicament.

"Can I get you a drink?" Sebastien asked, inspecting his empty glass. "It's time to switch to whiskey anyway." He held up a cocktail glass of amber liquid from the table, presumably Tommy's drink, and signaled to a server.

Tyler pointed to the magnum sitting in a bucket of half-melted ice. "I'll have champagne, thanks."

"I'll do it," Cary said, pouring her a glass.

"Cary, my man!" Tommy slung his arm around his shoulder. "Who's this little minx?" He took out his phone and shared his screen. "Did you get into trouble last night?" He laughed. "I'm sorry I missed it."

Shit.

"How was the fan event?" Tyler asked, changing the subject. "I saw the socials." She scrolled through his Instagram. "You were there all afternoon, weren't you?"

"I was." He nodded. "I must've signed a thousand autographs."

"It was cold." Sebastien took a glass of whiskey from their server without saying thank you. "And they didn't even pay us."

"It was a charity event," Tyler reminded him.

"It looked fucking awful," Tommy said. "Tyler, let me tell you—"

"Where's your wife, Tommy?" she asked point-blank. He'd never brought her to any music industry events. In fact, Tyler had never met her or seen a picture of Mrs. Napolitano. She couldn't imagine what kind of woman would put up with him.

"Not fucking here, thank god." He slapped his knee and laughed at her expense before Sebastien joined him.

Fucking idiots.

A few minutes later Lara showed up wearing a strapless leopard-print dress and matching heels. Leopard print was her trademark. If she were in the jungle a lion would have eaten her.

Tommy whistled with two fingers while Tyler rolled her eyes.

Dirty old bastard. Not to be confused with Old Dirty Bastard from the Wu-Tang Clan, her favorite member next to Method Man.

"Hi Cary." Lara clasped her hands below her waist, squishing her boobs together.

Cary nodded politely. "Maybe you could move down my way a bit, Tyler?"

At least he didn't say "babe."

"That's okay." Lara pulled up a chair beside him "I'll scoot around."

Get away from my boyfriend.

"Where the fuck is Vegas and what's-her-name?" Sebastien glanced at his watch, annoyed.

"Kim," Cary said. "Her name is Kim, once and for all."

Tyler texted Kim: *ETA?*

She wrote back. *Sorry. 2 seconds.*

"There they are." Tyler gestured toward the lobby. Kim wore a simple blue dress and Vegas wore a black suit with a white shirt that he must have bought at the big & tall shop.

You guys look cute together!

They arrived at the convention center and Cary walked the red carpet with Sebastien not far behind him. The cameras flashed and the rock star posed like they'd nominated him for new artist of the year, not like someone who was about to receive a lifetime achievement award. A music journalist had once called him a national treasure, and his bandmates still teased him about it.

By the time the SDM team found their seats, Cary's bandmates had already devoured the bread on their table, leaving a few pieces of pumpernickel, everyone's least favorite. The musicians weren't about to turn down a three-course meal. Saying no to free food was practically a violation of the American Federation of Musicians' rules and regulations.

Cary pulled out the chair next to Tyler, but before he took a seat Sebastien cleared his throat. "Sit here," he said, patting the seat beside him. "Next to me." Tyler held her face steady and didn't react as Cary moved to the other side of the table. Not surprisingly Lara raced to grab the empty chair beside her boyfriend.

Meanwhile Tommy plopped himself down next to Tyler while Kim sat on her other side, and Vegas next to her, so it wasn't a total disaster.

"Dude, what's Lara even doing right now?" Kim stared across the table. "She shouldn't be sitting with the talent."

"I'll talk to her," Tyler said. "Maybe Vegas shouldn't sit next to you. Sebastien keeps looking over here."

Kim bit her bottom lip and glanced at their boss. "Do you think he'd, like, fire me?"

"On the spot. He'd take pleasure in doing it too."

Sebastien had been trying to kick Kim off the tour ever since Vegas had returned to work. He'd said that it was "money coming out of my pocket," but having another TM on the payroll wouldn't break the bank or put a dent into it. Plus, Vegas needed the extra help and Kim was great to work with. She knew her shit better than any tour manager, man or woman.

When everyone was finally seated, Cary picked up the bottle of red wine on the table and examined its label.

"Don't do it," Tyler warned him. She'd been to enough industry galas to know why the wine sponsor had donated its product. The vineyard was from the Niagara region in Ontario, and year after year their shitty wine had given her a terrible headache.

Cary nodded and put down the bottle. "I'm ordering wine for the table."

"It's red or white"—she shrugged—"or nothing." She picked up her glass. "I'm drinking water."

Cary flagged down a server and whispered something into his ear. A few minutes later the server returned with six bottles of 2011 Mission Hill Oculus. Knowing Cary, it was probably the most expensive wine they'd had on the menu.

She scrunched her nose in confusion. "How did you do that?"

Cary stretched a grin and handed his credit card to the server. "If you don't ask, you don't get."

"Fucking right," Tommy said, pouring himself a glass instead of waiting to be served like everyone else.

"Let me pay for that." Sebastien reached into the breast pocket of his jacket. But Tyler was onto him—she'd seen it before. Her boss waited until someone threw down their plastic before he offered to pony up.

"I've got it," Cary said, and Sebastien put his wallet away without protesting.

After the meal, a choice between rubber chicken or slimy mushroom-stuffed peppers, Cary's bandmates said their goodbyes and left. Tyler was jealous. She was ready to go herself but the gala would be another two hours. Maybe three if people couldn't stop congratulating themselves.

By nine p.m. she was a goner. With every stupid story Tommy told she edged the butter knife closer to her wrist. *Is it sharp enough?* Sure the gala was punishment, but this was cruel and unusual. And potentially dangerous.

She held her phone underneath the table and texted Cary. *Want to get out of here? Jets are playing. Game just started.*

He replied, *Please! Be right back. xo*

How was she going to ditch her colleagues without being found out?

Cary stood from the table and Vegas said, "I'll come with you."

"Thanks, I've got it."

A few minutes later her phone vibrated. It was a text message from Cary.

Play along.

At that point she was game for anything.

A few minutes later Cary arrived back at their table. "It came off," he said, opening his fist and revealing a black button in his palm.

"Again?" Vegas asked. "Tyler, you know how to sew, right?"

"I do," she said nonchalantly.

"I don't want to walk around like this." Cary opened the middle of his shirt.

"Tyler!" Sebastien yelled and she jolted back in her seat. "Go help him."

"Fine," she muttered, squeezing Kim's hand.

She wasn't the only person to have devised an ingenious plan. Little did she know that Cary was as crafty as that girl on the Beastie Boys record.

"You're still coming to the party, right Cary?" Tommy asked while stealing his seat. "There'll be tons of hot chicks! Bring that little minx."

Cary's jaw tightened. "I'll try, but I've got a speech to write."

"I thought Tyler was helping with that." Sebastien gave her the stare of death.

"It's my fault for procrastinating." He placed his hand on his chest. "I should've done it before I got here."

Sebastien pointed at Tyler. "Help him with his speech while you're at it."

Vegas had arranged a car service to bring Tyler and Cary back to their hotel. Truth be told, she'd never been so happy to see an Uber in her life. She would have even settled for a rickshaw, pulled by Dave, of course.

"I'm assuming you took the button off your shirt?" Tyler asked.

"It wasn't the first time." Cary laughed.

"Cary! Did you—"

"Sorry, but I had to get you alone." He held her hand and kissed it. "I'm not even superstitious, babe. I could've easily worn another shirt that night."

She closed her eyes and smiled. "I'm not superstitious either, except for the Jets and birthday wishes. How did you know I could sew?"

"Dylan. I figured it ran in the family."

She squeezed his arm. "You're keeping secrets from me."

"Ouch!" Cary said jokingly, rubbing his arm. "Just this one." He crossed his heart.

"Really?" She tilted her head, doubting him. "Vegas didn't tell you—"

"About Kim?"

She nodded. "What do you think?"

"I'm happy for them."

"Me too," she said. "My bestie and Vegas."

Back at the hotel they changed into their Winnipeg Jets onesies, crawled into bed, and turned on the TV.

"What about your speech?" Tyler asked during a commercial break.

Cary smirked. "I haven't written a speech in my life. I'm not about to start now."

"What?" She sat up. "You're just going to wing it?" She would have been on her umpteenth draft by now, practicing in front of a mirror.

He rubbed her shoulder. "I've got some idea of what I'll say."

"It's back on." She swiveled her head and pointed to the TV. "That's goalie interference!" she said. "He was in the crease." She turned to Cary. "Aren't you nervous?"

"Why would I be nervous?" He ran his fingers through his hair.

She widened her eyes. "All of those people?"

"Babe, I do this regularly."

Right, you're Cary Kingston.

She grabbed the remote control. "Want to watch SNL after this?"

"I haven't seen it in years," he said. "Probably since I was on it. Who's the musical guest?"

She pulled up the schedule on the TV. "I love them!"

"I'm officially old." He sighed. "I like the host, but I've never heard of this band."

"That's okay, I've never heard of the host," she admitted. "We make a great pair, don't we?"

"The best pair." He laughed, although he seemed to mean it.

She rested her head on a pile of pillows. "I wish John Mulaney or Dave Chappelle hosted every week."

He laughed. "Like a residency?"

"Yeah, or at least get a comedian to guest write or something, not some stupid actor who isn't even funny." She continued to watch the hockey game, rubbing her thumb against his. "Make sure to thank your parents tomorrow."

"Okay." He squeezed her hand. "I'm sure they'll be watching it on TV."

She giggled and covered her mouth. "They're sitting with us, Cary."

"My folks are coming?" His eyes flew out of his head. "Here? To Saskatoon?" She nodded, biting her bottom lip. "You invited them?"

"Of course I did," she said. "I put myself in charge of your events, remember?"

"Ah, but you're usually all talk."

She grabbed the remote and shut off the TV. "You're going to pay for that, Cary Kingston."

He flashed a sexy smile at her. "I knew I had money for some reason."

She straddled him and grinded her hips, then slowly undid the buttons on her onesie, letting the middle fall open to expose her midsection. He reached for her but she motioned his hand away and arched her back, letting her hair touch the bed. *Is this turning you on, Cary?* With both hands she massaged her breasts, feeling the mound between his legs change shape beneath her wetness.

Once he was fully erect she leaned forward and hung her hair in his face, and with his breath on her skin, she said, "You're right, I'm all talk."

"No . . . no! I was joking!" He begged her to keep going.

She gave him a cheeky grin and buttoned up her onesie, then grabbed the remote and turned on the TV. "As if, Cary. The Jets are playing."

That'll teach you not to mess with me.

CARY

I deserved that, Cary said to himself after several rounds of making love—*no, fucking. It was definitely fucking.* Tyler had made him watch the hockey game and SNL before giving in. In fact, he'd enjoyed waiting for it.

What the hell had happened with Tommy? He'd practically accosted his girlfriend while Sebastien sipped on champagne. He should have said something, but she'd told him not to fight her battles, and stupidly he'd listened. How could he get her to leave SDM? It was time for them to move. Toronto was close to Winnipeg and central enough for him to travel, so that was an option. He'd be closer to his family, and she to the Robertsons.

And she'd invited his folks! It blew him away, really. She was the most thoughtful woman he'd ever dated. But *girlfriend* sounded stupid, considering the way he felt. No. He needed, not wanted, *needed* her to be his wife. Hell, she already talked to his mother more than he did.

A baby. He could hardly wait. But maybe he didn't have to. The thought of her pregnant made him hard again. Was that sick? No, it was a natural reaction. He swept her hair away from her neck and hugged her from behind, cupping her soft, naked breasts. To his surprise she was awake. She reached back and angled his hardness into her and he gently rocked her before they fell asleep.

CHAPTER 18

At the awards that evening, Cary walked the red carpet wearing a local designer's suit. He always supported Canadians and their creative endeavors—fashion, art, or music. One picture of him on social media meant catapulting their career into the stratosphere. People everywhere wanted to be like him, and Tyler could hardly blame them.

Once inside the arena, Tyler ushered Cary's parents to their seats in the music industry section of the venue, close enough to the stage but not on the floor where the fans were standing.

"Sebastien will sit here, then Cary," Tyler told the Kingstons. "And you can sit on the other side of him."

His mother smiled. "Why don't you sit beside Cary, dear? We'll just be one seat over."

"That's okay, Mrs. Kingston," she said, not wanting to be a bother.

"It's Pamela." She shook her head sternly. "And I won't hear of it."

A few minutes later Cary and Sebastien climbed the steps. Her boss lagged behind the rock star, huffing and puffing, dripping with sweat.

Tyler gave Cary a crooked smile and he winked, raising his eyebrows. He sat beside her while a gust of cologne swirled up her nose, playing the synthesizer notes from Animotion's "Obsession."

The lights dimmed and she closed her eyes, cycling through a breath. Yestown was up first and the broadcast was televised, a permanent record if they fucked up.

"I'm nervous," she whispered to Cary as Yestown walked across the stage.

"I can help with those nerves," he whispered back. He slid his hand between their seats, his fingers inching up her thigh. She crossed her legs, pulling her A-line skirt over her knees and placing her coat over their laps like a blanket.

"Your parents are right there," she hissed. He shrugged and kept teasing her until the band was done playing and she was ready to burst.

With his eyes on the stage he removed his hand. "Are you still nervous?"

She couldn't speak and shook her head.

After she gained composure she turned to Pamela. "Cary wrote that song."

His mother gave her a toothy grin. "Isn't he talented?"

You've got no idea, Mrs. Kingston.

Cary leaned over the armrest. "I'm bringing them on tour."

"You don't have an opening act," she reminded him.

"I do now. You were right. They're great."

Halfway through the awards a young man with a clipboard came by to collect Cary from his seat. The time had come for his lifetime achievement award and induction into the hall of fame.

The tribute started with a video montage showing highlights from his career. The impossible task of compressing twenty years into ten minutes had been challenging, but she'd pulled it off. Luckily everyone had jumped at the chance to congratulate Cary. Unlike Sebastien, people liked him.

As the video was ending, Cary stepped up to the microphone and held his chest. "Hello Saskatoon! It feels good to be back in the Prairies . . . the Paris of the Prairies!" The audience erupted in cheers. "I'd like to thank my fans. I couldn't do this without you." There were more cheers. "I'd also like to thank Sebastien, Bob Shaw, and everyone at SDM. Tommy, my agent . . ."

The music industry section yelled, "Fucking Tommy!"

And everyone laughed.

Cary continued, "My band and crew. Vegas and Kim . . . you somehow make it look easy." Tyler turned and nodded at her bestie. "My label and publisher. My ASCAP family. Thank you for being here. My parents, John and Pamela, for my first guitar. Oh, sorry, that was from Santa." The audience laughed and Pamela squeezed Tyler's hand. "And last but not least . . . my girlfriend. You're the love of my life, babe." Tears fell down Tyler's face as the flute solo from *Titanic* whistled in her head. "Thank you for everything."

The audience gave him a standing ovation and Cary took a bow. Sebastien shook his head when his gaze met Tyler's tear-soaked face.

"You and Cary?" he asked with a grunt at the end. She nodded without making eye contact. "You could've saved me the cost of an extra hotel room."

Fuck off, Sebastien.

After the awards Tyler and Cary met up with Kim and Vegas, and a limousine took them to the Warner Music party. Sebastien, Tommy, and Lara—Bob had opted out—said that they'd meet them there later, going to the Universal party first, but it was a fool's errand. Like every year, the Warner party would be at capacity within an hour.

The foursome arrived at the party and the rock star posed for pictures along the step and repeat before they went inside. An open bar was waiting for them, and live music too. And no Sebastien, Tommy, or Lara to ruin the mood.

The Warner Music party had a 'no phones' policy. If you had to make a call or send a text you had to go outside. Surprisingly it wasn't too difficult to self-police, and it should have been the industry standard, not those phone pouches.

With a little help from her friends at Warner Music in Los Angeles, Tyler had arranged for Yestown to play a set at the party. There was no better way to get the music industry's attention than to play at a private event with free alcohol.

There was only one problem: Rick "the Dick" Harding.

Back in the day Rick had played in a mildly successful rock band, and now he was a mildly successful entertainment lawyer. Anything to stay in the music business. Like a lot of men who worked in the industry, he'd had aspirations of making it as an artist, but he ended up settling for plan B: a desk job, and fewer women who wanted to sleep with him.

Less than zero, actually.

As he did every year, Rick parked himself on the drum throne and held court as the most famous musicians in the country played cover tunes. It was a chance for the rock stars to let their hair down and for Rick to relive his youth.

"What are they waiting for?" Cary asked Tyler, waving to the guys in Yestown.

"Rick the Dick's on drums," she complained. "I'm surprised he's not playing 'Glory Days.'"

"The guys can join in, can't they?" Cary asked.

"No, I want the whole band up there and Rick off that goddamn stage."

"I'm going up!" he shouted over the music.

She grabbed his arm. "You don't have to do that."

"I know, but I love playing." Cary kissed her on the cheek, walked over to Yestown, and said something as they nodded.

The crowd quietened when Cary lifted the microphone from its stand. It was a well-known fact that he didn't play covers unless it was "O Canada."

"How 'bout a little 'La Villa Strangiato?'" he asked the crowd.

Everyone cheered and Rick exited the stage. The song was the most complex in Rush's catalog and Rick sucked on drums—worse than the drummer from KISS.

"Boys?" Cary waved the band over, and to Tyler's pride they played the song with the precision of Lee, Lifeson, and Peart (RIP).

"I love this fucking band, man," Allie said, hugging Tyler. "This is one of my favorite Rush tunes."

"Mine too!"

"What do you make of Cary bringing Yestown on tour?" Allie's eyes darkened as she frowned. "Was he serious?"

Tyler shrugged. "He sounded serious."

"I'll get their contracts ready. I don't give a shit that it's Sunday or about this stupid rule." She pulled out her phone and hid it under her jacket. "Fuck me."

"What?" Tyler asked.

"Fucking Tommy." She scrolled through her phone. "He's with Sebastien. They're here, waiting in line."

Tyler grabbed her phone from her purse: five missed calls from Sebastien.

Fuck.

Kim ran toward them with her phone in full view. "Dude, they're outside." She showed them her screen. "What should we do?"

"Sebastien's such a buzzkill, man." Allie stuck out her tongue in disgust. "So help me god, I'll kill fucking Tommy if I see him, just for fun."

"Remember this party last year?" Tyler asked. "When everyone sang 'Sweet Caroline' and Sebastien didn't sing the *ba-ba-ba* part? I mean, really?"

"Who doesn't sing the *ba-ba-ba* part?" Kim asked.

"Exactly." Tyler arched an eyebrow. "We're at the Warner party, right?" Allie and Kim nodded. "No phones allowed."

The night was one for the books. Cary and Yestown played for an hour as people shouted out song requests like they were at a wedding reception. Tyler had asked them to play the "Hockey Song" by Stompin' Tom Connors, not thinking that Cary knew it, but he sang every word. Even some of the Universal Music artists had shown up later. The singer from Arkells arrived toward the end of the night and Cary sang with him while the women nearly died of hotness overload, including Tyler.

When they arrived back at their hotel Tyler flopped on Cary's bed.

"I'm exhausted," she said, unzipping her boots.

Cary beamed. "I can't remember when I've had more fun."

"Really?" she teased.

He smirked. "You know what I mean."

"I do." She smiled wryly. "Aren't you glad you did this?"

"Thank you."

"Don't thank me. It was all you." She tied up her hair with the elastic band on her wrist. "I can't thank you enough for getting Yestown on that show . . . and playing with them."

"I can think of several ways you can thank me."

Her elbows straightened, pushing forward on the bed. "Another three weeks until I see you again."

"I know, but you can come visit."

"I can't, Cary. I'm busy at work."

"Maybe it's time for a move?"

"Where were you thinking?" She furrowed her brow. "LA? I can't live there, and I certainly can't work there. They make it impossible for Canadians unless you're an athlete or an actor."

"Toronto," he said. "The Canadian music industry is based there. You'd be closer to your family, and I'd be—"

"No way." She shook her head. "If I'm moving anywhere, I'm going back to Winnipeg."

"Toronto is central to everything," he said, as if she didn't know that.

"For your information, Winnipeg is the actual center of Canada." She thinned her lips, then plumped them. "You're gone all the time anyway, so it shouldn't matter where you live."

"Okay, babe. Wherever you want. How about that thank you?"

Twist my arm, Cary.

CARY

"Tyler wants to move home," Cary told Vegas on their flight to Denver the next day. There was no reason that he couldn't live there and keep his place in Malibu.

"Like, as in Winnipeg?" Vegas asked, turning toward him.

"Yeah." He plugged his phone into the back of the seat. "I'm thinking about it, just thinking. Don't get any crazy ideas."

Vegas reclined his seat. "That's not really your scene, man."

"I know, but she said I'm hardly ever home, which is true."

"Real estate's cheap," he said. "That's why I bought a house and rented it."

"That's the least of my worries."

Vegas chuckled and pulled back his hair. "I'd give up my place in Vancouver in a heartbeat to move back there."

"What about Kim?" Cary checked over his shoulder to see if she was listening. "Would she move?"

"She's ready for a change." Vegas took out a deck of cards from his bag. "Vancouver's nice, but not exactly convenient. And those fucking bike lanes."

"Tell me about it," he said. "I'm ready for a change too. A big one."

CHAPTER 19

"Tyler!" Sebastien yelled from his office the following afternoon.

"I knew this was coming," she told Rory. "Stay here, buddy."

She walked to the reception desk and stopped in front of Lara. "I've been meaning to talk to you."

"What did I do?" Lara asked, wide-eyed.

"If you could tone down the flirting with Cary, I'd appreciate it."

Lara covered her mouth. "Oh, I'm sorry! I'm such a big fan. I didn't know you two were dating. Like, OMG. You're so lucky. He's lucky too. I mean, I didn't know women managed bands before I worked here. If you ever have any advice—"

"Actually . . ." She stared at the receptionist's open blouse. "People might take you more seriously if you dressed professionally."

Lara covered her chest. "Of course! I've never worked in an office before and I wanted to look nice for the clients."

"It's the music industry." Tyler rolled her eyes. "As long as what you're wearing is clean, it's fine."

"Thanks for the tip."

Tyler nodded and continued walking toward Sebastien's office. She poked her head inside. "I'm here."

"What the fuck was that about?" Sebastien folded his arms on top of his belly.

She picked at her fingernails. "What?"

"The Warner party. I called you."

"Oh, that. Sorry. You know the rule at Warner—no phones allowed."

"You need to check your phone no matter what, Tyler." He unfolded his arms and adjusted his stupid baseball cap. "Yestown—"

"What about them?" she asked flatly.

"I've had some interest."

"Yeah, people are losing their shit over them." She glanced at her watch. "Warner's putting an offer together. I should have it by the end of the week if not sooner."

"Hold off." He stroked his beard and crumbs dropped on his desk. "I'm heading to Toronto tomorrow."

"Why?" she asked, trying to keep a straight face instead of jumping up and down.

"To get competing offers. More pucks on the net."

"They're my band."

"Signed to SDM," he said. "After that stunt you pulled at the awards you need to get them ready for Cary's tour ASAP."

"They're ready. And I didn't pull any stunts. I had no idea Cary was going to do that."

"Don't bullshit a bullshitter." He seemed proud of it.

She shrugged one shoulder. "Think whatever you want."

"Well, thanks to you the press is having a field day looking for dirt on Cary's new girlfriend. I have Cheryl troubleshooting this mess. And don't think you're getting any special treatment around here because of"—he cleared his throat in a smoker's cough—"your boyfriend." He emphasized the word *boyfriend* like it was a joke or something.

Don't worry, I wouldn't dream of it.

Tyler stormed out of Sebastien's office and slammed her door shut. Rory jumped up on all fours and ran under her desk.

"Sorry buddy," she said. "I forgot you were here. Who wants a cookie?" Rory wagged his tail from under the desk and she gave him a treat as a peace offering.

Her phone vibrated. It was Cary on FaceTime.

"Hi!" she said, not expecting his call. She lowered her phone to show Rory the screen.

"Rory!" he said. "Is that a cookie I see?"

"Why are you calling?" she asked, nose scrunched.

"Can't I just call to say I love you?"

She laughed. "Okay, Stevie Wonder."

"Funny." He gave her a goofy smile. "I've got an idea."

"Uh-oh," she teased.

He rolled his eyes. "As you know, I'm singing the anthem at the Jets' last game."

"It's the last game of the regular season. They made the playoffs."

"Like you haven't told me a thousand times." He paused for a second. "What do you think about Nadie singing with me?"

She smiled. "Thanks for asking, but my sister wants her to finish school first."

"She'll be done in June," he said, making a good point. "That's in a few months."

"It's Dylan's rule, not mine."

"If you don't ask, you don't get." He shrugged and rubbed his chin. "The worst she can say is no."

"What about Sebastien?" she asked. "He's already given me shit about this weekend."

"I won't tell if you don't."

"Okay, I'll ask."

After Tyler ended the call she FaceTimed her sister. Dylan was in high spirits since she'd been healthy throughout her first trimester.

"What's up?" Dylan asked with a needle and thread between her fingers.

"What are you doing?"

"Making overalls, gender-neutral, but I still think it's a boy. And by the way, Cary's speech was sweet. Dad almost cried."

"I'm in deep shit with Sebastien."

"Fuck that guy."

"Yeah, he's the worst." She pursed her lips. "Don't say no until you hear me out."

Dylan glanced up from her stitch. "This doesn't sound good."

"Cary just called. He wants Nadie to sing the anthem at the Jets' last game."

"The last game of the regular season," Dylan corrected her.

"That's what I meant." She laughed. "The last game of the regular season."

"That's in what—three weeks?"

"I know. I'm coming out there, remember? It's Marnie and Heather's baby shower. I told you."

"Sorry. Pregnancy brain. It's in my calendar." Dylan's eyes narrowed. "Did you already ask Joe about this?"

"No, but I probably should've, come to think of it," she said. "He's the easiest-going guy on the planet."

"Okay, Nadie can do it if she wants."

"Really?"

"Yeah, she'll be done school soon enough. I think she feels a little left out with all the baby stuff. She's been an only child for seventeen years. I'm sure it's a shock to the system."

"You'll let me manage her, right?"

"I wouldn't trust her with anyone else. But hey, I don't want you shopping her to labels until after school's out."

"That's fair. Thank you."

"No, thank you. And thank Cary for me. He's a good guy."

On the day of the hockey game she caught a late-morning flight and arrived in Winnipeg mid-afternoon, Rory in tow. She headed straight to the arena so that she could visit her niece during their rehearsal. Nadie had been practicing with Cary via FaceTime for the past three weeks. Nadie Grant was just like her aunt: over-prepared for everything.

Luckily Sebastien had been in Toronto for most of that time so Tyler didn't have to hide them singing behind his back. Her boss knew the owners of the Jets, and she was certain he'd put the kibosh on their anthem plans. Plus he'd been icing her out of Yestown's label negotiations, and she really felt like sticking it to him.

"Auntie Ty!" Nadie yelled, running toward her like a 100-meter-dash participant.

"Hi honey." Tyler hugged her tightly.

"Thank you so much!"

"Don't thank me, thank Cary. I had nothing to do with it."

Cary grinned, approaching them. "Did I hear my name?"

"Thank you, Uncle Cary!" Nadie said.

"Are you kidding me?" He picked up the dog. "You're doing me a favor."

Tyler raised an eyebrow at her niece, not sure if her boyfriend was ready for that kind of commitment. "Uncle Cary?"

"Well, you're my aunt, so Cary's my uncle, right?"

"I don't know about that," she said. "But come to think of it, you don't have to call me Auntie Ty anymore. You're old enough to call me Tyler."

Nadie's jaw hung open like a door to the attic. "I'll never stop calling you Auntie Ty, but can I call him Uncle Cary? Please?"

"Absolutely," he said. "And Rory can call me Dad."

Aw, sweet.

After their rehearsal Nadie took Rory home so that he could play with Samson while Tyler and Cary checked into the Fairmont Winnipeg to get ready for that evening. They asked for the same suite that they'd had over Christmas. Maybe it would bring back those memories. To think she'd gone almost three years without having sex to wanting it like chocolate.

"I'm hopping in the shower, babe," Cary told her from the bathroom.

"I'll be there in a minute."

Tyler's phone vibrated—a text message from Kim.

Where are you?

She replied, *Fairmont.*

Kim responded with a video attached. *CK is going viral.*

A vise-like grip tightened in Tyler's chest and her heart thumped audibly as she sat on the bed. Expecting the worst she drew in a breath, bracing herself before tapping on the screen. *What if it's a sex tape with Emma?*

She dropped her head in relief and smiled. It was footage from last night's show. Cary was onstage with Yestown, and it sounded incredible. It also had over a million hits and had only been up for an hour.

The water turned off and Cary poked his head out the door. "What are you watching?" he asked, wrapping a towel around his hips.

"You." She turned her phone to show him. "You didn't have to do that."

"I know, but it's my song and I love those guys."

"So they're behaving?"

"Are you kidding? They tried to help with the load-in."

"No!" She walked toward him. "What about IATSE?" The International Alliance of Theatrical Stage Employees was a labor union for venue technicians. They didn't allow anyone to lift a finger unless you paid your dues. She added, "I didn't think to tell them."

"I told them." He tousled his wet hair and it dripped on the floor. "It's a good thing we kept Kim on. We would've needed another TM sooner or later."

"I'm glad it worked out." He grabbed her by the waist and planted kisses along her neck. "Cary! I need a shower."

"I like you dirty," he said. "Too bad you're not on your period."

"You're sick."

"You love it."

You're right.

Cary dropped his towel and she stared at him with a hard swallow. *Did it get bigger?* She moistened her lips and went to touch him but he stopped her, inching down her leggings and panties in concert while she grabbed the curtain rod for support, hanging like a trapeze artist. She stood above him and stared at his tongue while his fingers plunged inside her, palm facing out.

With delicate strokes he circled her sex, and she moaned when his fingers slipped out, inserting his tongue instead. A few minutes later her sex tensed before it released, swollen with pleasure.

"Stay there," she said, lowering herself to straddle him.

She took off her hoodie and bra, reached between her legs, and wiped her wetness onto his manhood, stroking it up and down with a squeeze at the tip.

"Fuck," he whispered.

She smirked. "I'm getting to that."

He lowered his head, biting her nipple and cupping her breasts. When he was fully erect she angled her hips and sat on his length, taking shallow breaths. He closed his eyes, wincing with every inch, gliding her up and down faster and faster until she contracted around him.

"I love riding you," she said.

"I can't take it." He held her waist tightly. "Slow down a minute." But she didn't stop and he wrapped his arms around her back and jerked his pelvis. "Fuck. Sorry."

"No apologies." She giggled. "Just make it up to me. I mean, when you've recovered." He lifted her from the floor and carried her to bed. "I'm fine, really. I was just teasing."

"I need to see you come again," he begged.

He inserted his index and middle fingers, finding her G-spot. The tension mounted as he worked his fingers against her upper walls, and she let out a yelp and sprayed the bed.

"That's my girl." He shook his dripping hand.

She sat up and covered her mouth. "Cary! The bed's soaked."

He laughed. "You're welcome."

After they showered Tyler wrapped a towel around her chest and leaned against the doorframe as Cary combed product into his hair. He was whistling a tune she recognized but couldn't quite put a finger on. It wasn't one of his hits.

"You know, you can't keep Kim forever," she said. "I'll want her back for my girl band."

"How's that going?" He lathered shaving cream over his stubble.

Has he ever grown a beard?

She googled *Cary Kingston + beard*, and a few images popped up, but she preferred him clean-shaven.

"The Oh Claires?" she asked. "It's going great." We have some real interest from the States. Allie's working on setting up their showcase."

"You're a force to be reckoned with."

She widened her eyes. "Wait until I start managing Nadie."

"I take it you're not telling Sebastien?"

"No, but it wouldn't matter anyway. He said he'd never manage a woman."

"Shit!" He nicked himself with the razor. "He said what?"

"Are you okay?" He nodded so she continued. "He said he doesn't want to manage"—she used air quotes—"catfights and mood swings."

"It's worse than I thought."

"People in the industry call him Sebastard."

"Really?" He walked out of the bathroom, pressing a tissue against his chin. "That's pretty funny."

"Funny? It's hilarious." She wrinkled her brow. "What's that song you were whistling?"

"It's Bert's song." He twisted a towel into his ear. "It's been in my head."

"It's called 'Happy Merry Christmas.'"

"Do you think he'd let me record it?"

"I don't know." She shrugged. "Ask him."

The arena was only a few blocks away but walking there was out of the question, for Cary at least. Being famous came with some minor drawbacks, like not getting your steps in.

When they arrived at the venue the taxi pulled around to the back where a dozen fans were waiting.

"What are these people doing here?" she asked. "The players are already inside the arena."

Cary gave her a shy smile. "I think they're here to see me."

She knocked on the side of her head with her fist. "Right. I keep forgetting you're Cary Kingston."

He laughed. "When I'm with you, I forget I'm me."

Tyler said goodbye to her boyfriend, ducked into the VIP entrance, and headed up to the suite. No doubt Sebastien would be lurking somewhere in the building and she needed to avoid him, at least for the time being.

"Hi Tyler!" Jessica greeted her excitedly. "I asked to be your server tonight."

"It's nice to see you."

"I saw Cary's speech on TV." Jessica frowned and kicked the ground. "It—it seems like he's got someone special, huh? Bummer."

Tyler shrugged with a tight-lipped smile. "Yeah, bummer."

"How many people are you expecting?" The server passed her a Blue Moon beer.

"Let's see . . ." She counted on her fingers. "Four from my family. Pamela, John, Sebastien, Kim, Vegas, and Cary. So . . . ten."

Tyler's brothers couldn't make it because her nephews were playing in a hockey tournament the next morning. All four boys were on the top-seeded teams, and she chalked their achievements up to the extra conditioning they did in the off-season.

The Kingstons entered the suite and waved at Tyler.

"Thanks for inviting us, dear," Pamela said, grinning from ear to ear.

"We're too early," John added, scanning the empty room.

"Don't be silly," Tyler said. "I'll take your coats. Your son won't be up here for a while, so please make yourselves comfortable."

Pamela's eyes twinkled. "I have to tell you, we've seen more of him in the last four months than in the past ten years."

Tyler nodded and smiled. She'd suspected as much and was glad they'd reconnected with their only child.

"This is Jessica," Tyler said, introducing their server. "She'll take your order. There's an open bar, food. Have whatever you want."

"How lovely!" Pamela shook Jessica's hand. "I'm Pamela, and this is my husband John."

"Hello," John said politely.

"The Kingstons," Tyler said. "As in Cary's parents."

Jessica's eyes lit up like a pinball machine. "You're Cary's parents?"

"We are." Pamela tightened the bow on her blouse.

"Wow!" Jessica gushed. "Thank you for having him."

That's enough, Jessica.

The Kingstons laughed, embarrassed, but they were probably used to it, given their son was a celebrity.

"Cary said your family's coming?" John asked.

Tyler nodded. "My dad, my sister, her husband, and my niece. She's singing the anthem with Cary. My brothers couldn't make it. My nephews are playing in a hockey tournament."

"I remember those days," Pamela said, gazing at the ceiling.

"It seems like yesterday," John added. "Those morning practices almost killed us, didn't they Pammy?"

Tyler wrinkled her brow. "Who played hockey?"

"Cary did," John told her. "Junior hockey." He scooped a handful of peanuts from the snack tray. "Man, that kid could skate."

"Cary played hockey?" She was certain she'd misheard him.

John nodded. "It was a tough decision between music and hockey, but I think he made the right choice."

"Once he commits, he commits," Pamela chimed in. "He did both for a while but something had to give. I'm sure you know with Cary it's perfection or nothing. Why do you think he's been single for so long?" She twitched a smile. "Or *was* single, I should say."

I'm going to get you for this, Cary Kingston.

The suite door opened and Tyler's family walked in. They'd never been in a private suite, so it was something special for them.

"Look at this spread!" Bert whistled as he cased the place. "I'm not sure where to start."

"Knock yourself out, Dad," Tyler said. "There's an open bar."

"I'm going to puke," her sister cautioned, rubbing her temples.

"Are you not feeling well?" Tyler placed her hand over Dylan's midsection. "Do you want a cold compress or something?"

"It's not the baby!" Dylan slapped her hand away. "I'm nervous about Nadie."

"Me too," Tyler said. "Let me take your coats." She helped her family one sleeve at a time. Dylan, Bert, and Joe wore their old-school jerseys. They were fans before Winnipeg sold the team to Phoenix in 1996—the biggest mistake in franchise history.

"Hi," the Kingstons said in unison.

"These are Cary's parents." Tyler performed introductions between the two families.

Inspecting his brown cardigan, John said, "We need to get some jerseys, Pammy."

Pamela nodded and extended her arm to shake Bert's hand.

"We're practically family!" Bert shooed her hand away, hugging her warmly.

"Dad!" Tyler said while her father let out a hearty laugh.

"We're hoping so too." Pamela winked at her.

This is embarrassing.

A few minutes later the house lights dimmed and the announcer introduced Nadie and Cary.

"Oh my god." Dylan paced like an expectant father. "Joe, aren't you supposed to be doing this?"

"There they are!" Tyler pointed out as Nadie and Cary marched along the blue carpet step by step beside each other.

After a beat Cary strummed his guitar, and they took turns singing the verses of the Star-Spangled Banner. It was a difficult anthem but they performed it as simply as a nursery rhyme while the crowd listened intently.

The Canadian anthem was next. This time Nadie and Cary sang in perfect harmony while the crowd sang along, a little out of the pocket and forgetting the new lyrics—not a shocker. Tyler was all for changing the words to be more inclusive, but why leave in the "God" part when so many people worshiped other deities, and others none.

"She's a star," Tyler whispered into her sister's ear. "I can't wait to manage her properly."

"She's so talented," Pamela said, nodding at Dylan. "I hear it runs in the family."

"It was your son's idea for Nadie to sing with him," Dylan said, holding her belly.

Pamela stretched a smile across her face. "That's nice to know, Dylan. Thank you for telling me."

I could tell you a few things, Pamela.

"I'll be right back," Tyler promised, leaving the suite.

When she returned she was holding a bag from the pro shop.

"Here," she said, passing the bag to Cary's dad. He opened it and pulled out two Jets jerseys. The lettering on the backs read: MR. KINGSTON AND MRS. KINGSTON.

"Thank you!" John said, slipping the jersey over his brown cardigan. He reached into his back pocket and pulled out his wallet.

"No!" She pushed his wallet aside. "They're from Cary."

"We want to pay for them," John insisted.

"Take it up with him."

Pamela shrugged her jersey over her blouse. "Thank you, dear. You'll be able to wear this one soon." She pointed to the lettering on her back and Tyler's face practically burst into flames. Of course she'd fantasized about one day becoming Mrs. Cary Kingston . . .

With a loud bang the door flew open and Sebastien and Tommy barged into the suite. *Why is Tommy here?* She glanced at the bar and answered her own question.

Free booze.

"Tyler," Sebastien seethed slowly. The days of "Hi doll" were long gone, and that was just fine—no, preferred.

"Sebastien," she said, returning his tone. "What's going on with the contract?" He'd been fucking around with Yestown's deal and she'd had it. "It's been weeks."

"It'll take as long as it takes." He turned his head. "Why is Bert here?"

"Cary invited my family."

He grunted, stroking his beard. "Who was that singing with Cary?"

"A local girl." She told him the truth without revealing her relationship to Nadie. "You might want to say hi to Pamela and John." She pointed at them, diverting his attention. "They're over there."

"Yeah, I think I will." He waved at Cary's parents and wobbled toward them, presumably with puckered lips to kiss their asses.

"Tyler," Tommy said, and her neck muscles tightened. "I didn't realize you were such a fucking groupie." He straightened his tie and gave her a smart-ass grin.

"Fuck off, Tommy."

And he did.

The next people to arrive were Kim and Vegas but they peeled off in opposite directions, neither of them wanting to risk Sebastien seeing them together.

"What's with this?" Tyler yanked on the hem of Kim's Jets jersey.

"Fuck it," Kim said. "I'm giving up on Vancouver."

"It's about time," she told her as Kim grabbed a beer. "Where's Cary?"

"Oh, he's still signing autographs."

"Nadie too?"

"Dude, it's super cute." Kim laughed. "A bunch of little girls are lined up to take pictures with her."

Tyler turned her head to make sure that Sebastien and Tommy weren't in earshot and whispered, "My sister gave me the go-ahead to manage her."

"I'll be her TM, right?" Kim asked. "When the time comes."

"Of course." She turned up the corners of her mouth. "Allie and I are making headway with the Oh Claires too."

"Dude, you have to leave SDM, like, soon."

"I know, but it's not that easy going out on your own."

"So what?" Kim shrugged. "If it were easy everyone would do it."

"That's true," she agreed. "Do you want to head back to the hotel with us after the game?"

"We're not staying there."

"You're not?"

"No, Vegas's renters moved out of his house, so we're staying there."

"I didn't know that."

"Yeah, he's getting rid of his rental in Vancouver." She took a gulp of beer. "We're moving here after the tour."

"Here? As in Winnipeg?"

Kim nodded. "It makes the most sense financially. We'd never be able to afford a place in Vancouver. And it's not like Sebastard will hire me after this tour. Not that I'd want him to."

"Up top!" she said, high-fiving her bestie. "You're going to love it here."

A few minutes later Sebastien and Tommy left the suite without saying anything. If it was that easy to get rid of them she would have tried to date Cary sooner.

"Sorry we're late, babe." Cary walked into the suite and pointed at Nadie. "We had to wait for this superstar to finish signing autographs."

"Auntie Ty!" Nadie was simply beaming. "Hi Kim!"

"You killed it!" Tyler said.

"You did, dude," Kim added. "Straight fire!"

"I'm going to say hi to Mom and Dad," Nadie told them. "They probably want my autograph."

"I'll get you a beer," Kim said, bringing Nadie over to see her parents.

"I heard that, Kim!" Tyler shook her finger.

"My folks seem to be getting along with everyone," Cary said, rubbing her back and making her toes curl.

Tyler gestured in Pamela and John's direction. "If they ask, their jerseys are from you."

"Mr. and Mrs. Kingston." He laughed. "Was that your idea?" She nodded. "My mom's jersey would look better on you."

"You made us proud out there, son," Bert interrupted.

Your timing is impeccable, Dad.

"It was all Nadie, sir." Cary shook his hand. "She comes by it honestly."

Bert smiled. "Nice of you to say, but she's more talented than all of us put together. I wish I could take the credit."

"Did you have something to ask my dad, Cary?" she prompted.

Bert lifted his brow. "Oh, I see . . ."

"No, Dad, not that." She covered her mouth, embarrassed. Cary wasn't about to ask for her hand in marriage. At least not in front of her.

After an awkward pause, Cary said, "The song you wrote . . . the Christmas one?"

"'Happy Merry Christmas?'" Bert asked. "What about it?"

"How would you feel if I recorded it? No pressure or anything."

Bert placed his hand over his heart. "Son, it'd be a great honor."

I love you, Dad.

CARY

"So, I hear you're moving?" Cary said to Vegas as the others chatted and watched the hockey game.

Vegas took a swig of beer. "Yeah, I got to thinking after we talked, and my renters were moving anyway, so . . ."

"No, no. I think it's great."

"Are you still thinking about moving?"

"Tyler really wants to." Cary pointed at the Grants who were posing for pictures with Cary's parents. "Her family's here."

"So move."

"To Winnipeg?" he scoffed, running his fingers through his hair.

"Sure, why not? Your family's here, too—a few hours away." Vegas nodded at Pamela and John, raising his beer. "Look how happy your mom is, man." His parents were laughing with Bert. "You'd have total privacy from the press here," Vegas added.

"I know she'd be happy."

"What's stopping you?"

"Nothing, I guess."

CHAPTER 20

The next morning Tyler and Cary went to her nephews' hockey tournament, and they cheered as each boy's team won in their division. Of course the hockey moms lost their shit when they saw Cary, and he posed for selfies and signed autographs, much to the chagrin of the dads.

After the hockey tournament they went to Polo Park shopping center to pick out gifts for Marnie and Heather's shower. Their due dates were coming up soon and she couldn't wait to see her friends become mothers.

At the baby store Cary insisted on buying everything left on the registry, and a few things he said were cute. She tried to put a few items back but he'd flatly refused.

When they were done they hailed a taxi and stuffed the presents into the minivan.

"You don't have to do this," Tyler said. "You scored enough bonus points at the rink this morning."

"It was fun." Cary climbed into the minivan. "Your nephews are really good. I wouldn't be surprised if they made it to the big leagues."

"As long as they play for the Jets."

She would disown them if they played for Vancouver's hockey team—blood only runs so deep.

"I've never been to a baby shower," he admitted. "You're sure it's mixed, right?"

She picked up her phone. "It says, 'Marnie and Heather's Co-Ed Baby Shower.' I don't know why they're doing it so close to their due dates."

"How could they fly, being so pregnant?"

"They didn't. They drove. They wanted their babies born in Winnipeg." She scooched forward in her seat and asked the driver, "Can you take Wellington Crescent, please?" She turned to Cary. "It's scenic."

He reached across the presents and held her hand. "I wish I wasn't leaving tomorrow. I hate missing you."

"I don't want to leave either." She sighed through her nose. "Sebastien's on my flight home."

"I can't believe he's not happy for us." He shook his head and rubbed his chin. "I thought we were better friends."

"He doesn't have any friends," she quipped.

"What about Tommy?"

"Fucking Tommy? They're not friends. They have circle jerks with money instead of dicks."

"Bob Shaw doesn't like him either," he said.

"Really?" She scrunched her nose, not understanding what he meant. "Since when?"

"Since he got sober. Bob Shaw's being professional, but he can't stand his shenanigans. And neither can I, quite frankly."

"Interesting," she said. "Do you know why he's like this?"

"It's a combination of things," Cary said. "He never made it as a musician and his first wife left him for a singer in the band he was touring with."

"Really?"

"Yeah, Bob Shaw said the singer packed up her stuff and moved her in, then fired him."

"He probably deserved it," she said as a ding chimed from her bag.

"Is that your phone again?"

"Yeah. I don't know how I'm going to keep Nadie from Sebastien. My phone's been blowing up since last night." She showed him the unread messages on her screen. "The Jets have already asked about her availability."

"She's stealing my gig," he teased. "And my fans."

When they were at the rink a few of the hockey sisters had asked Nadie for selfies, and her niece couldn't have been more accommodating.

"I can't believe she got recognized!" Tyler said, answering a message.

"It happens fast." He paused. "At least it did for me. I went from obscurity to stardom overnight. But I'm lucky I didn't grow up with social media. I love my fans but I don't appreciate people tracking me down like I'm on the FBI's most-wanted list."

"I can't imagine," she said. "I know you love your fans but you deserve a life too, don't you think? Actually, your fans would want that for you. Wouldn't they?"

"Maybe." He turned his head toward the window. "I feel lucky to live this life."

"It's the only one you're going to get." She stared out Cary's window. "Look at these houses." She pointed to a for sale sign on the front gate across the street. "The Lounts own that one. I guess they're selling it."

Cary swiveled his head. "Vegas's house is around here somewhere."

"Really? This is the rich part of town."

"I pay him well."

"I'm glad they're moving here." She mustered a smile. "Kim loves working for you, but she's not happy at SDM."

"You're unhappy too, babe." He squeezed her hand gently. "I want you to leave."

She stared into his bright hazel eyes. "I told you, he'll ruin my career."

"What if I leave? You can manage me."

"What, so he can ruin both of us? No, thank you. And don't think he won't try."

"I'm serious."

"I love you, Cary, but I don't want to manage you." The idea of spouses managing their partners grossed her out, but nothing was worse than joining their bands. She couldn't get the isolated recording of Linda McCartney's voice squawking like a seagull out of her head.

"You don't?" he asked, surprised.

"I have no interest in being your babysitter."

The taxi pulled up to Marnie's parents' house and Tyler smiled at her old neighborhood while the score from *E.T.* traveled in her head. The original owners still occupied most of the houses in the area, and the Robertsons and Marnie's parents were no exception.

"I'll grab the rest of the presents," Cary offered. "You go on ahead."

She lugged two handfuls of gift bags up the steps and rang the doorbell. She couldn't remember the last time she'd been there. It was probably back in high school, senior year.

Little Lesley, Marnie's younger sister, answered the door.

Tyler widened her eyes. "God, I haven't seen you fully grown!"

Little Lesley rolled her eyes. "Marnie's only three years older," she said, taking the gift bags. "Come in! I have to ask—are you seriously banging Cary Kingston?"

"She is," Cary said, hauling in the rest of the presents.

Little Lesley's face flushed. "Oh my god. I'm sorry."

"Don't be." He laughed. "I'm not."

"Hey Tyler, remember your locker in high school?" Little Lesley gave her a cheeky grin. "All those posters you had of him?"

Tyler shot her a *shut up* look as Cary's eyes bounced between them.

"Tell me more," Cary said.

"That's enough information for one day," Tyler said, grabbing his arm. "Besides, they were Dylan's first."

Little Lesley smiled and motioned toward the living room where a dozen women sat with their children in the company of her very pregnant friends. "Everyone's in there."

The room fell silent, jaws open, when they walked in.

"Hi," Cary said, and the women practically swooned.

Okay, calm down.

"This is Cary, everyone," Tyler introduced him. "Cary, these are my friends from high school."

"I thought it was mixed?" he whispered to Tyler.

"The guys are downstairs shooting pool," Marnie said, letting him off the hook. "My brother and his friends."

"Hank and Mark are down there too," Heather added.

"Sorry," Tyler whispered back. "I thought we'd be together. You don't have to stay if you don't want to."

"Nice meeting you," Cary said to the women before he escorted Tyler back into the hall. "I'll stay." He shrugged. "I don't mind shooting pool."

"What?" She laughed. "You know how to play pool?"

"Of course I do. Want to chalk up my cue?"

"Later." She bit her bottom lip at the thought of it. "I'm sure Mark and Hank will entertain you, but text if you need me to save you."

"Are you babysitting me?" He gave her a bratty grin.

I'll babysit the shit out of you.

Tyler didn't realize how much she'd missed her friends, but she was missing something else even more. She was the only unmarried person in the room, and as much as her friends had "oohed" and "aahed" about Cary, it was obvious that she wasn't any closer to having a family of her own. She didn't want to wait until the end of the tour. She was in love with him and desperately wanted a baby, preferably with hazel eyes and an ear for music.

Two hours later she checked her phone, but there were no messages from Cary. As long as the husbands weren't dusting off Marnie's old beer bong, she'd try not to worry.

"Please tell the guys to come up here," Marnie asked her sister, unwrapping the last present with as much enthusiasm as the first. "Mark and Hank can help cut the cake."

Little Lesley kicked the blue and pink tissue paper scattered across the living room floor, making a path to the basement door. "It's time for cake!"

A few seconds later the men trampled up the stairs like a human stampede.

"I'll cut the cake," Hank slurred, unable to hold the edge of the knife straight.

"I'll help," Mark said in no better shape.

"I've got it." Heather gently took the knife away from her husband. "We'll be at the hospital soon enough." Just like that Charlie Sexton song, Marnie and Heather were not impressed.

While her friends took over the cake-cutting, Tyler held her boyfriend's hand. She could tell that he'd been drinking, even before he whispered, "I want to fuck you right now."

"Let's wait until we're back at the hotel." She turned to meet his gaze. "It wouldn't be polite in front of everyone."

"We have an announcement!" Marnie clapped, quieting the room. "We're moving home! Heather and I are moving back here," she clarified. "With Mark and Hank, if they're lucky."

Everyone hugged and cheered while Tyler reined in her tears, trying to be happy for her friends. If only she could trade places with them.

After Tyler and Cary said their goodbyes, they walked down the street toward her dad's house. Rory had spent the weekend with his Uncle Wilbur, mostly sleeping, according to Bert.

"Did you have an okay time?" she asked, snow crunching underneath her boots.

"They're a great bunch of guys," he said. "I won at foosball!"

"Foosball?" She shook her head. "You never cease to amaze me with your talents. Did they ask for a lot of selfies?"

"No, not one. They were too busy with the beer bong." They continued to walk down the street. "Mark and Hank are coming to my show in Ottawa. Remind me to tell Kim to get them backstage passes."

She raised an eyebrow. "Mark and Hank aren't going anywhere. They're having babies any day now."

"Right." He nodded. "It's such good news about your friends moving home."

She wiped away a tear with the sleeve of her coat. "I'm happy for them."

"What's wrong, babe?" He stopped in his tracks.

"I want a baby," she said matter-of-factly. "I don't want to wait."

"I'm so glad you said that." He cracked a smile. "I don't want to wait either."

She shoved her hands into her coat pockets. "Is that the beer talking, or . . . ?"

He winked. "I was drinking wine."

Smartass.

"Why don't we get Rory in the morning?" he suggested.

"Do you mean . . . start trying tonight?"

His smile grew a foot. "No cup, though."

"Just like Vancouver's team."

God, I'm funny.

CARY

What if she's pregnant? Cary googled on his phone. *Six days!* It could take up to six days to get pregnant and another four weeks to find out. Too bad impatience was the quality he disliked the most about himself. What was he supposed to do? Sit around and wait?

No, that wouldn't work.

Cary slid out of bed and grabbed the laptop from his bag. He searched for real estate listings on Wellington Crescent, but there must have been a mistake. The price of the Lounts' house was less than his penthouse, yet it was twenty-thousand square feet with acreage and two coach houses. It had been on the market for more than a year, so he emailed his realtor and put in a lowball offer, just to see if they were serious about selling it.

"Cary?" Tyler called out in a groggy voice from the bed.

He turned off the desk light. "Sorry babe. I didn't mean to wake you."

She pulled back the covers, completely naked, and he blew out a breath. "Come back to bed and get me pregnant."

"What if you're already pregnant?"

"Then we'll have twins."

He smiled as a twitch in his boxers rubbed against his leg and he crawled back into bed. She rolled over and closed her eyes when he kissed her neck, her stomach, her sex, greedily working his tongue in circles as her stomach tensed.

After she climaxed he grabbed himself and stroked his erection. The look on her face sent chills down his spine and he bit his bottom lip.

"Make me pregnant," she said, and he almost came in his hand.

"I need a second." He smiled, inhaling a deep breath. "I'm trying to decompress."

"Why?" She pressed her full breasts together. "I thought you wanted to get me pregnant?"

"I'm going to get these sheets pregnant if you don't watch it." She laughed and he slid himself inside her. She was so tight and warm and wet that he had to take it slowly or he'd lose it in an instant. "Oh my god," he said, thrusting carefully as she arched her back into him. "Don't move." He stopped and exhaled, then started again. "Just knowing you're not on birth control is making me crazy."

"Oh, I can tell." She tightened her Kegel muscles around him.

"What am I going to do with you?"

"Fuck me."

"You got it." She scraped her fingernails down his back and he couldn't hold off any longer before collapsing onto the bed. "I'm going to need a minute."

"Stay inside me," she said. "It might help get me pregnant."

"Babe, I'll stay here forever if need be. I love you. And holy fucking shit."

CHAPTER 21

Tyler was sure that she was pregnant. Her back ached, her breasts were tender, and she'd gained five pounds—okay, six. She'd promised herself that she'd wait three weeks before checking, but it didn't stop her from obsessing about it. She googled *Foods to avoid + pregnancy* and eliminated caffeine and dairy from her diet. Raw fish was also on the list but she didn't like sushi, so it didn't concern her one bit.

A few days from the three-week mark a familiar pain jolted her awake.

"No!" she cried, holding her hand below her waist. Her period had arrived like an uninvited guest, but at least she was at home in her bed. Rory snuggled her as she sobbed on his head. "Mommy's not pregnant, buddy."

He gave her a kiss.

After an ugly cry she dragged herself to the bathroom and sat on the floor, then texted Cary. *No baby :(*

Her phone vibrated right away. It was Cary on FaceTime.

"Cary . . ." She started to cry again.

"I'm sorry, babe," he said. "We'll keep trying."

She pulled Rory against her chest while she lay in the fetal position. "I had so many symptoms, but it was just wishful thinking, I guess." She wiped her nose with a few sheets of tissue paper. "It took Dylan seventeen years, Cary."

"We'll keep trying," he said again.

"We could do IVF . . . or adopt a baby?"

"We've only tried once." He smirked. "Well, one night, that is." The corners of his mouth turned down. "I can come out there if you want. I'd have to fly back tomorrow but I could be there for a few hours, at least."

"That's okay." She sniffled, holding the tissue paper against her nose. "You'll be here soon."

"The end of next week," he confirmed. "We'll get to spend two weeks together, but I have to work a little. I hope you don't mind. The pictures for my art show are due soon, and I'd like your input."

The Winnipeg Art Gallery—the WAG—had asked Cary to showcase his photographs beside the professional shots from his career. The exhibit was called: "Cary Kingston: In Front and Behind the Lens."

"I love the WAG." She blotted her eyes with a new sheet of tissue paper. "It's so much better than the galleries here."

"It's an embarrassment to the art world," he said. "It's a good thing Vancouver has those mountains to look at."

"The public art is embarrassing too, except for A-maze-ing Laughter."

The 2009–2011 Vancouver Biennale had curated a bronze sculpture of fourteen laughing men as part of its exhibition. Every time she walked past it, she marveled at its creativity.

"You'd think the city would have a better arts program with all the money I pay in empty homes taxes," he complained.

She wrinkled her brow. "What's an empty homes tax?"

"It's a vacancy tax. The City of Vancouver calculates the penalty as a percentage of the property's assessed value, which in my case is expensive."

"But you live here." She scratched her head, not understanding what he'd meant.

"Not long enough for the city's liking."

"That's ridiculous," she said. "How long are you supposed to live here?"

"Six months." He paused before saying, "They invented the tax to penalize rich people, so we should get a say in how the money's spent."

"I bet they're going to use it for bike lanes."

"No kidding," he said.

"Maybe the new mayor and city council will be better?"

"They couldn't be any worse, really."

In a city where it rained six months out of the year, Vancouver had turned into Amsterdam, or a version of it. The failure was apparent, but city council had doubled down on its efforts, citing their Greenest City action plan. Not super helpful when people were experiencing homelessness and dying from fentanyl.

"Hey, are you sure you'll be okay?" Cary's voice sounded strained.

She nodded. "There's a game tonight."

"The Jets are going to win the cup," he predicted.

"Shh," she hissed. "Don't jinx it."

Later that morning Sebastien yelled from his office. "Tyler! Get in here!"

Could her day get any worse? She wasn't in the mood to deal with his bullshit, not that she ever was.

"What?" She stood in his doorway and leaned on the frame.

"Sit," he ordered, gesturing to the empty chairs in front of his desk.

"I'll stand." She narrowed her eyes. "What is it?"

"Your niece . . . Nada?"

"Nadie." She folded her arms. "What about her?"

"Nada, Nadie, who gives a shit? She's the anthem singer?"

"Yes," she admitted. "She is."

"Why the fuck didn't anyone tell me?" His jowls jiggled like Jell-O when he yelled, "I asked you—"

"And I said that she was local, which she is."

"You should've told me who she was." Sebastien hated looking like a fool more than anything in the world, although he did it every time he passed by a mirror.

She shrugged. "Take it up with Cary."

"Nada . . . she's Native?" he asked.

"She's Cree," Tyler corrected him. "Indigenous, and her name is Nadie."

"Whatever." He rolled his soulless eyes at her. "It seems like she'd qualify for *that* kind of funding."

The Canadian music industry relied on government funding for its survival and they'd recently opened several granting streams—free money—for Indigenous artists like her niece.

"We don't manage female acts," she sassed him back.

Sebastien stroked his beard like a pet. "I might consider revising my policy for that amount of cash."

"My sister won't let me manage her until she's eighteen." She'd lied so well that she could have passed a polygraph test. It wasn't up for discussion. There was no way she'd let him anywhere near Nadie. Not in this lifetime.

He squinted until his eyes disappeared. "You've asked?" She nodded and he huffed like a toddler, then pointed to the garment bag hanging on the coat rack. "Take that on your way out."

"What is it?" she asked.

"It's Cary's suit from the awards. The designer sent it over." He shot her a dirty look. "You're probably living there, anyway."

"I'm not living there . . ." Her voice trailed off. "Yet."

He laughed in her face. "Like you're any different from all the rest."

Fuck off already.

Tyler lifted the hanger from the rack and carried it back to her office.

"That's it," she said, slamming the door. "I can't take it anymore, Rory."

The dog shook his body from head to tail, seeming to understand.

Tyler called Allie on FaceTime to hatch an exit plan.

"I was just about to call you," Allie said. "I booked the girls a tour down the coast. They'll be in LA at the end of next month."

"That's amazing! Hey, ASCAP is giving us a slot on their showcase, so why don't you add it to the end of their tour?"

"The ASCAP showcase at the Hotel Cafe?" Allie whistled. "That's a coveted gig, man."

"I know," she said. "All the experts will be there."

"I'm on it." Allie tilted her head. "You called for a reason?" Tyler closed her eyes and let out a sigh, emphasizing her frustration. "You okay?" Allie asked, moving her face closer to the screen.

"I hate it here, Allie. I'm thinking about quitting, but Yestown's deal hasn't gone through yet."

"They're still not signed?" Allie asked in disbelief. "What the fuck?"

"Sebastien's sniffing around about Nadie too. I won't be able to shop her without him knowing about it. At least not in Canada."

Allie shook her head. "It was a good idea taking those Cowtown chicks Stateside and hiding them from SDM. Sebastien and fucking Tommy are vultures, man."

"Cowtown?" She scrunched her nose. "I thought they were from Toronto."

"They live here but they're from Calgary. The Oh Claires, as in the Eau Claire District in Calgary."

"Oh!" She laughed. "I'm an idiot. Hey, do you ever think about leaving there?"

"I'm not going to lie," Allie said, "I think about it a lot, but Porter's a decent enough guy."

"He looks like a nerdier version of Clark Kent, don't you think?"

"Totally," Allie agreed. "I don't know how you do it. There's no way I'd work for Sebastard. I'd sooner leave . . . or die. No, I'd kill him first. And Tommy. A double homicide."

"I mean, I'm going to quit."

"Just do it, man."

"What do you think about us working together? Management and agency? I've already talked to Kim."

"If I can keep my bands, I'm all in."

"There's just one thing . . ." She paused, unsure of Allie's reaction. "I'm moving back to Winnipeg. But you can stay in Toronto. It's not a problem."

"I like Winnipeg." Allie shrugged.

"You'd consider moving?"

"Why not? It's too fucking expensive here." Allie's eyes became wide. "Did Kim show you the pictures of Vegas's house? It's fucking insane what you can buy there."

Tyler nodded. "You're going to love it, Allie."

In defiance Tyler worked on setting up the Oh Claires' showcase for the rest of the day. She no longer considered her employment in terms of the separation between church and state. She'd paid for her laptop and her phone, so she wasn't using SDM's resources except for the office itself and its terrible no-name coffee.

They owed her that much and more.

When the clock struck five, the steam whistle from *The Flintstones* sounded in her head. She almost yelled, "Yabba Dabba Doo!" but thought better of it.

"A quick detour, then home," she told Rory while searching for Cary's keys in the console of her car where she'd left them. She loved driving her Tesla, but she was more determined than ever to pay him back. She hated owing anything to anyone and refused to be in his debt.

A few minutes later she pulled into a spot in front of Cary's building.

"We're here," she said.

Rory smudged the window with his nose and thumped his tail against the seat. There was only one problem: Cary wasn't home, and she didn't want to disappoint the miniature panda.

"You stay here," she said, cracking the window an inch. She grabbed Cary's suit bag and closed the door while Rory looked at her, bewildered. "Sorry, buddy. I'll just be a minute!"

A plexiglass sign sat on the concierge's desk. It read: BACK IN 20 MINUTES.

Not super helpful.

Tyler pressed the elevator button, squinting to read the numbers above the steel doors. *That's strange.* One of the elevators was on the twenty-sixth floor—Cary's floor. She stared at the number, willing it to change as her chest tightened, and her heart pounded until her entire body ached. Was it possible that Cary was at home? Was he cheating on her right under her nose? Was he like Dave after all?

The floor numbers began to descend at a rapid clip, so she ducked around the corner and held her breath. A few seconds later the door slid open and she shook her head, trying to stop the internal *Jaws* music from scaring her to death.

"Tommy?" she said under her breath.

Did Cary let him into his place? It didn't seem likely since he trusted Tommy as much as NWA trusted the police.

A woman's voice came from the elevator. *Lara? No. It can't be.* But there was no mistake. Lara wore the same leopard-print coat she'd had on earlier in the day, and her hair, slightly disheveled now, was curled in its usual way.

As soon as they were out of sight she stepped into the elevator, swiped her fob against the key reader and pushed 26.

Am I in the Twilight Zone?

"No!" She shook her head before the theme song started to play. "Not today."

The elevator stopped on the twenty-sixth floor and she unlocked his door.

"Cary?" she called out.

No answer, thank god.

She entered his penthouse and the stench of cigarettes stopped her cold. Tommy had been there, it was obvious by the haze of smoke alone. She hung the garment bag in his front closet before inspecting the living room for clues, but everything seemed to be in its usual place, so she went into his bedroom. Normally she could stop the music in her head, but the *Mission Impossible* theme seemed perfect for this quest.

She scanned the room and . . . *bingo*. A half-smoked cigarette sat on the edge of a makeshift ashtray, looking more like a murder victim than a cancer stick.

She turned on the bathroom light and found a damning piece of evidence, confirming her suspicions: a condom wrapper in the garbage can.

Animals.

Lara and Tommy should have used one of the guest rooms if they were going to act like pigs.

She grabbed her phone and called Cary to break the news, sighing in relief when his phone clicked to voicemail. "Call me back when you get this, please." She stripped the sheets from his bed and threw them into the washing machine, then pressed the hottest setting and the extra rinse.

At least Cary wasn't cheating on her, but it was bad enough that she'd doubted him. Could she ever trust someone again? She didn't think so. And it wasn't fair to him. But one thing was for sure: she needed to leave Vancouver. Too many bad memories, too many broken promises, and too many bike lanes. Plus this morning she was alone when she'd discovered that she wasn't pregnant. Of course Rory was there, but he'd slept through most of it. And sure, she'd said that she didn't want him to fly out there, but come the fuck on . . .

She absolutely did.

Since Tyler was going to be at Cary's for a while she took the elevator down to grab Rory. The dog probably thought he'd been left in the car for good. They both had abandonment issues.

Arjun had finally returned to his post so she approached his desk with purpose, resting her hands on her hips.

"Hi, Arjun, I'm Tyler. Cary's girlfriend." He raised his brow and nodded. "Do you know anything about the people in his penthouse?"

"Tommy?" he asked, swiveling his chair like a little kid.

"How do you know Tommy?" Her tone came out more accusatory than planned.

"Oh, Tommy?" Arjun waved dismissively. "He's up there all the time. That guy has a lot of stories."

No fucking shit.

She lowered her chin. "Does Cary know about this?"

"He has keys. I don't ask." Arjun shrugged. "It's none of my business."

It was a reasonable way for him to keep his job, but was Cary cool with it?

"This sign." She pointed to the notice. "It says you'll be gone for twenty minutes but it doesn't say when you left." He shrugged again, so she didn't make a federal case out of it. "Do me a favor." She scribbled on a pad of paper sitting on the desk. "If Tommy comes back, please call me immediately."

"Sure thing, ma'am."

"I'm not a ma'am, I'm a miss."

Tyler returned to the penthouse and opened the door. The lingering smoke sat still in the air so she opened the windows to let in a breeze, but it wasn't strong enough to make any difference and the balcony was the only relief. She stood outside to get some fresh air and gazed over False Creek.

White boats—some were yachts like Sebastien's—traveled through the water as the tiny False Creek ferries to Granville Island zipped between them, rippling the waves. A few kayakers bobbed up and down, using their paddles to steady themselves in the wake. Along the seawall people walked their dogs, others ate ice cream—although it wasn't warm yet—without a care in the world. She smiled at an older couple wearing matching outfits and holding hands like teenagers—she wanted that, without the coordinating clothing. Cyclists raced along the path, which was poorly marked out, and there were a few near misses with pedestrians—not a shocker.

Vancouver was beautiful, no doubt about it, and it wasn't the city's fault for Dave being a cheater and an asshole; he was originally from Kelowna.

"Come here, buddy!" Rory ran onto the deck and looked through the glass barrier, tail wagging.

She took out her phone and snapped a picture. "Look at this photograph," she said to Rory. Unlike Dylan, she was a fan of Nickelback.

The hockey game was about to start so she went inside with the miniature panda and sank into Cary's deep comfy couch, stretching out her legs until she was horizontal.

A little while later the washing machine buzzed and Rory jumped to his feet, waking him from whichever number of naps he was taking. He followed her into the laundry room, presumably looking for cookies.

"This is some serious bullshit," she said, transferring the wet sheets into the dryer. To Rory's disappointment there weren't any cookies in the laundry room, and he gave her a look that said, *This is total bullshit.*

Her phone vibrated. It was Cary on FaceTime so she answered the call without video. "You're never going to believe what happened," she said, turning down the volume on the TV.

"You can tell me in a minute," he said. "I've got some news myself."

"Where are you?"

"I'm almost at your place."

"What? I'm at your place." She elaborated, "I was dropping off your suit, not moving in."

He laughed. "Thanks, babe. I'll see you in five."

Sure enough, five minutes later Rory hopped down from the couch. The sound of keys scraping in the lock was enough to set him off.

"Rory! How's my boy?" Cary kissed him and turned his head. "It smells like smoke in here."

"I know," she said, not standing to greet him. This was more "sitting" news. "It smells like a bingo hall, but believe me, that's not the worst of it."

"What's wrong?" He dropped his bag on the floor. "Other than the obvious."

She twisted her mouth to the side. "Does Tommy have keys to your place?"

"Fucking Tommy?" His eyes flashed open and he laughed. "Are you kidding? Why would you ask?"

"Please stay calm."

"What's going on?"

She paused for a moment, not sure how to break it. "I saw Tommy coming out of your elevator earlier today. Tommy and Lara, that is."

"What?" He furrowed his brow. "What the hell?"

"I know," she said. "When I came up here I smelled the smoke. There was a cigarette butt in your bedroom."

"What the f—"

"There's more," she said, cutting him off and scrunching her nose. "Your sheets had been, um, slept in. I found a condom wrapper in the garbage can. But don't worry, your sheets are in the dryer."

"Forget about my sheets. I'm burning them." *Burn, motherfucker, burn.* "Is he still married?" he asked.

"He is, but he doesn't wear a ring." She shook her head. "Classic fucking Tommy."

"How old is Lara?"

"Nineteen, I think? Tommy should've known better. He's more than twice her age."

"Jesus." He rubbed his chin, pacing the room with a blank expression on his face. When he finally stopped he glanced at the TV. "What's happening here?"

"We're losing. I swear to god if I hear 'Chelsea Dagger' one more time . . ." The Chicago Blackhawks' goal song was her least favorite piece of music.

"How'd he get in?"

"I'm guessing your spare key at SDM." She shrugged. "Arjun made it sound like he's here all the time."

"All the time? Are you fucking serious?" Cary folded his arms on the counter and hung his head. "Maybe the building has security footage?"

"They probably do," she said. "They've got cameras everywhere."

"I'm getting an alarm installed and a drink," he said, opening a bottle of Penfolds Grange. "Are you up for one?"

She shrugged. "I'm not pregnant."

"I'm sorry, babe."

"Please don't fire Tommy . . . just yet."

"Why the hell not?"

"I can't do this," she said, voice shaking. "Sorry, I'm just bad at this."

"Bad at what?" He poured the wine into two stemless glasses.

She covered her face, not wanting him to see her. "I'm quitting SDM on Friday and—"

"That's terrific!"

She glared at him through blurry eyes. "Please let me finish." He thinned his lips and nodded. "I'm moving back to Winnipeg, and I—"

"But that's what—"

"Fuck, Cary! Will you just listen for once?"

"Sorry."

He walked over to the couch and held her hand, but she pulled it away and went on, "I thought you were up here with someone else." His eyes widened and he shook his head. "I've done the long-distance thing, and it never works. This morning, going through that alone, Cary. It fucking sucked. Not to mention, I'm the one sneaking around because of this stupid media attention. I could never, ever, live in LA, and I need to be with my family." She wiped her nose with her sleeve and hugged Rory. "I need time to think."

His eyes welled up. "Can I tell you my news?"

"No. I've made up my mind, and I need to leave. I'm sorry you came all this way for nothing. The only thing I ask is that you don't say anything to Sebastien or Tommy. I have some things to sort out before Friday."

"But I—"

"Cary. Please don't speak."

No one is to blame.

CARY

How could she just leave like that? They were trying to have a baby, for god's sake. In fact, he'd thought she was pregnant until this morning. Hell, he broke down the second their call ended and cried for an hour. Maybe he should have told her how upset he was, but he didn't want her to feel any worse than she already did.

Of course he wanted her to leave Vancouver, but not like this. Not without him.

Cary picked up his phone and called Vegas. "I need you to do something for me," he said, pouring a glass of whiskey over ice. Penfolds Grange was no match for his pain.

"Sure, what?" Vegas asked.

"Cancel my shows for the next few weeks."

"But—"

"I don't care how much it costs. I'll pay for everything. Send Yestown wherever they want. And have Tommy reschedule my shows, please."

"Fucking Tommy," Vegas said. "Are you okay, man?"

"No." He stood in the kitchen with heavy feet. "I mean, physically, yes."

"Does Sebastien know about this?" Vegas's voice was softer now. "He's going to have questions. What do I say when he asks? And what about the press?"

"Just say I've got family issues." He gulped a mouthful of whiskey and shook his head. "It's the truth, Vegas."

After all, he considered Tyler part of his family. The closest person to him in the world, in fact.

"Are your parents okay?" Vegas asked.

"Yes." The ice cracked in his drink. "It's personal. I can't get into it."

"Okay, man. Whatever you need."

"Thanks, Vegas."

CHAPTER 22

When Tyler arrived home that night she was in rough shape. For the first time in a long time she wished that she could talk to her mother or just sit by her grave. But since she couldn't do that she played "Landslide" on repeat. She closed her eyes and imagined Stevie's voice was her mother's and cried like a baby.

A little while later she went to get her moving boxes from the storage locker downstairs. Over the past decade she'd moved so many times that she'd kept them, because looking for boxes was without question the worst part about changing locations.

To get out of her head she blared Led Zeppelin on shuffle. She liked the surprise of the algorithm, and it played songs that she'd forgotten about.

She stayed up for most of the night, taping boxes together and writing labels on the sides, not the top. She'd learned that lesson the hard way. She organized the kitchen into piles of keep, gross, and donate. The kitchen always took longer than she'd planned.

How many mugs does one person need?

Tyler's phone vibrated early the next morning, even before her alarm went off. It was Kim on FaceTime calling instead of texting like a normal human being.

"What's wrong?" she answered, not bothering to get up.

"Dude, what's wrong with you?" Kim tweaked her earbuds.

"Nothing." She held her screen closer and frowned. "Why are you calling so early?"

"Cary . . ." Kim's eyes shot open. "He blew out the tour."

"What?" She sat up. "What do you mean he blew out the tour?"

Kim sighed. "For three weeks, but he's paying everyone double for their time and inconvenience."

"Why?" She rubbed her eyes, not convinced that Cary would do such a thing.

"Some family issue." Kim shrugged, a coffee cup in her hand. "I don't know. Vegas was pretty tight-lipped about it."

"Are his parents okay?" she asked, a tone of worry in her voice. "Family issue" was vague, but it was the only reason he'd cancel.

"Vegas said it was personal, but we're all wondering what's up."

"I swear I know nothing." She crossed her heart and clutched her chest. "Honest. Is he still in Vancouver?"

"It doesn't sound like it." Kim took a sip from her cup. "Oh, I booked Yestown on flights home, so you don't have to worry about it."

"Thanks for doing that."

"No problem," she said. "What happened last night? If you don't mind me asking."

Tyler peered out the window, her gaze following a squirrel as it ran up a tree. "I needed some space, you know, to think." She shifted her attention back to her bestie. "I'm not sure if I can do this, Kim."

"With Cary?" Kim asked. "Dude, are you fucking kidding me right now? He couldn't wait to see you." Her expression went blank. "What happened?"

"Long story." She closed her eyes and shook her head, reliving last night and the angry words she'd said.

"I've got time." Kim rolled her eyes. "A lot of it, apparently."

"I'm sorry about the tour," she said, not that it was her fault or anything. "But get this—I caught fucking Tommy and Lara at Cary's place last night."

Kim covered her mouth and gasped. "Get. The. Fuck. Out."

She nodded, straight-faced. "They had sex in Cary's bed."

"Are you fucking with me?"

"I swear on Rory's life."

"Does Cary know?"

"Yeah, he's livid, and rightly so. I would be too. Fucking Tommy is married and twice her age. He knows better."

"What did you say?" Kim's eyes rounded. "When you saw them?"

"Oh, they didn't see me," she said, stacking her pillows like Pringles before resting her head. "I found a condom wrapper in the garbage can."

"She's such a dimwit," Kim said.

"She's just young."

"That's no excuse." Kim was right. "Did Cary fire him? Fucking Tommy?"

"No, not yet. I asked him not to do anything until Friday."

"What's Friday?"

"I'm quitting SDM."

"Fuck SDM."

"I'm moving home, Kim."

Her dark brown eyes brightened a few shades when she smiled. "I'm so fucking happy to hear that."

"That's what we fought about. Not really *fought*."

"What? You lost me."

"God, this is so embarrassing." She closed her eyes. "I didn't know it was Tommy and Lara in his penthouse and I thought Cary was cheating on me."

"He'd never!" Kim almost jumped through the phone. "He doesn't even look at other women. Fuck, dude, I look at girls more than he does." Tyler chuckled. "I'm not even joking."

"I'm not doing another long-distance thing, and it's not like Cary's moving to Winnipeg, so—"

"You never know. He might surprise you."

"That'll be the day."

"Tyler"—she jerked back when Kim said her name—"he's not Duffel Bag Dave. You really need to get over it."

"Like the Eagles' song?"

Kim laughed. "Exactly." She took another sip from her cup. "He's done nothing to deserve this. Is he away a lot? Yes. He's Cary fucking Kingston. Besides, our tour ends in August and he's taking the next year off.

"Really?" She raised an eyebrow. "I didn't know that."

"Vegas told us."

"Does this mean we can work together? I talked to Allie and she's into it. She just has to figure out how to leave with her bands."

"What about Yestown?" Kim had asked a very good question. "Over Sebastien's dead body he'd let you take them."

"That sounds like a plan. So, what do you say?"

"Fuck yeah."

Tyler had too much on her mind to go back to sleep so she took a quick shower and drove into work. The first few hours in the office were her most productive. Toronto was three hours ahead, and she was always playing catch up with people.

When she arrived at the office the alarm didn't sound; someone was up early, probably Bob counting something.

"Tyler!" Sebastien screamed from his office. "Get in here!"

With no sense of urgency, she opened the door to her office and let Rory in before going to see Uncle Scrooge.

"What do you want?" she asked, voice measured.

"You know fucking what. Cary—his tour?" Sebastien's face flashed bright red. Maybe he was having a heart attack. Not that she would have called an ambulance.

"I found out this morning from Kim." She tightened her topknot. "I know nothing about it."

"I don't believe you." he said. "I think you knew about it."

She laughed. "Like I give a shit."

"I'm still your boss, Tyler." He stood because that's what tall people do when they can't win an argument. "I'd fire you in a second if you weren't fucking our biggest client. You're lucky I don't take this loss out of your commissions."

"What commissions?" She raised her voice. "You haven't signed Yestown to a deal."

"Future commissions." He sat back down. "Where is he?"

"I don't know."

Before coming into the office, she'd phoned Cary, but it had gone straight to voicemail. She didn't leave a message, not exactly sure what to say after she'd dismissed him without listening to his side of things. Regret is an awful thing.

"Vegas said there was some sort of family issue," Sebastien probed.

"I'm telling you, I don't know where he is."

"Tyler, I'm warning you . . ."

"Or what?" His threat almost made her day. "Go ahead, fire me. I do the work of three people around here and get paid, barely, for one. Plus you owe me a million weeks' vacation time. Don't get me started." Rory's tags clanked in the distance and she turned her head.

"Hello?" Bob called out into the cavernous space.

She pointed in his direction. "Why don't you ask Bob Shaw how much work I do around here? He'll tell you."

"Is everything okay?" Bob asked, walking into Sebastien's office, holding the miniature panda.

Sebastien nodded at Bob. "I was just saying that we needed more bands on our roster. More pucks on the net."

"No you weren't." She turned her head. "He threatened to fire me because of Cary's canceled dates. He doesn't think I do any work around here."

Bob's eyes turned icy blue. "She works harder than I do." He smiled at Tyler before adding, "I ran the numbers on Cary's tour. We're still good, even with the canceled dates."

"Get the fuck out of my office. Both of you," Sebastien huffed. "And that stupid dog too."

Rory says fuck you.

Bob gave the dog to Tyler and they walked down the hall in silence. No doubt Sebastien would be listening, ear pressed against his door with a cup, trying to eavesdrop.

"Do you have a minute, Bob Shaw?" she whispered, following him into his office.

"For you?" He nodded. "Always."

She closed the door and spilled her guts, telling him everything and then some.

The next two days weren't much better. In fact, they were almost worse. Cary hadn't called her back, and he wasn't posting on Instagram either. Had she just made the biggest mistake of her life? Or would she look back, years from now, like Sheryl Crow and her favorite mistake?

Having time to think wasn't always a good thing, unless you were a philosopher or something. Plus there were pregnant women everywhere she turned. Some of the expectant mothers seemed too young and others too old, and some the same age as her were perfect, like Goldilocks. She was human after all and finally understood that Level 42 song.

On Friday, Tyler got to the office early, which she'd been doing for years. But today would be different: it was her last day and she was going to make it a good one.

She walked into SDM with a latte from Artigiano—no more shitty office coffee—then waited in Sebastien's office with the lights off and the door closed.

An hour later Sebastien's voice boomed from the reception desk before he opened his office door.

"What are you doing in here?" he barked and turned on the light.

"Have a seat," she said calmly, motioning her hand toward his chair.

"I'm busy, Tyler."

"No, you're not."

He grumbled something under his breath and sat in his chair.

She handed him a piece of paper. "My two weeks' notice," she told him, sliding back in her seat. "But since you owe me so much vacation time, I'm leaving today."

"Don't be such a girl." He mocked her like the misogynist he was. "Is this about the other day?"

"It's about *all* the days, Sebastien. You treat me like shit and I'm over it."

"What do you want?" He took out his checkbook and grabbed a pen from the holder. "How much is this going to cost me?"

"Not your money." She waited until their eyes met. "Yestown."

He snorted a laugh. "You're not taking that band."

"Want to bet?" She handed him another piece of paper. "They're exercising their key person clause. I'm taking them with me."

It took him a long time to read the document. "This is an addendum to their management contract," he said finally.

"I know what it is."

"How did this happen?" he asked, lip snarled like Elvis's.

"I asked the band to sign it," she said, voice steady. When she'd told Bob that Sebastien wanted to sign her band to SDM he'd suggested adding the clause: it would breach their contract if she left for any reason or none at all.

"Where's Bob Shaw?" He pounded his fist on the desk.

She shrugged. "Bob Shaw knows about it."

"What?" He picked up the phone on his desk and covered the receiver. "We'll see about this." A few seconds later he yelled into the handset, "Lara!" He mispronounced her name. "Get me Bob Shaw on the phone, pronto!"

They sat in silence for a few minutes, waiting for Bob to call back.

The past fourteen years flickered in her mind like a lighter running out of fluid. Had she ever been happy there? She didn't think so. A job shouldn't be a death sentence, and she wouldn't allow him to become her executioner.

"Bob Shaw's on line one," Lara said through the speaker.

Sebastien hit the line and picked up the receiver, glaring at Tyler like she'd murdered his entire family.

"What the fuck is this key man clause?" he shouted into the phone. There was a pause. "Yes, I fucking know it means the band can leave with Tyler. But how did it happen?" An even longer pause ensued. "What do you mean you approved it? I swear to fucking god, Bob Shaw, I'm going to fire you!" He slammed the phone, missing its cradle, and slammed it again while she held back her laughter.

"All good then?" she asked.

"This isn't over." He stabbed the air with his finger. "You may have them contractually"—he ripped the document in half—"but good fucking luck getting them shows. I'll have Tommy ruin your little snot-nosed friend, Allie." *Snot-nosed?* He went on, "And the rest of your bands, if you've got any."

"If that's the case, I'm sure Tommy's boss will be interested in hearing what you guys have been saying about him."

Sebastien balked, resting his hands on his belly. "You've got nothing on me."

"Only every email from the past fourteen years," she said. "Who do you think controls the passwords? Our IT person? Oh, right, that's my job too." She stood from the chair. "And another thing—"

"Sebastien!" a man's voice belted and they jerked their heads. *Thank god you're okay! But you look like hell.*

"Cary! Where have you been?" Sebastien asked. He to Tyler. "We're done here."

"Forever," she said. "You can take this job and shove it." Johnny Paycheck's song would have been the perfect music placement.

"I knew you had it in you," Cary said to Tyler, closing Sebastien's door behind him. "Do you mind sitting in on this?"

Where's the popcorn?

"I'd be happy to." She sat across from Sebastien, squaring her shoulders as Cary sat in the seat next to her.

"Is something wrong?" Sebastien asked, perplexed.

"To put it mildly." Cary's eyes narrowed. "Where are my keys?"

"Keys?" Sebastien asked. "What keys?"

"The spare keys to my house," he clarified, running his fingers through his disheveled hair.

Sebastien pushed back his chair to make room for his belly before opening the top drawer of his desk. "They must be around here somewhere . . ." He rummaged through the drawer, office supplies flying everywhere. "I'm sure they're here."

"They're not," Cary said. "Tommy's got them. She"—he pointed at Tyler—"saw Tommy and Lara coming out of my place the other night." Sebastien raised an eyebrow and she nodded twice. He continued, "My building security pulled the footage—"

"What footage?" Sebastien interrupted.

"He's been using my place as a common bawdy house," Cary said. "There was a condom wrapper in my garbage, Sebastien."

"Fucking Tommy," Sebastien seethed slowly, fixing his baseball cap. "Sorry, did you say Lara was there?" He gestured to his door while they both nodded. "Lara!" he shouted, mispronouncing her name again.

Two seconds later Lara cracked open the door. "Can I help you?"

"Get in here!" he demanded, and the receptionist slinked into his office like a dog with a lowered tail. "What the fuck were you doing at Cary's?" he asked.

"Nothing." She pursed her lips. "I mean, I wasn't at Cary's."

"I saw you the other day coming out of the elevator," Tyler said. "But it's not your fault entirely."

Lara lowered her head. "I was at Tommy's."

"That's my place," Cary said, and Lara's eyes went dead.

"He said it was his house."

"No, that's Cary's penthouse," Tyler confirmed. "Tommy lives in West Vancouver with his family. His wife and kids."

Lara's eyes teared up. "I'm sorry!" she cried. "I didn't know! He said he'd help me with my singing career and—"

"You don't have a singing career. Or any career," Sebastien told her. "Just pack your shit and go." If only Tyler had a copy of the *Employment Standards Act* on her person to show him that was illegal.

"Don't talk to her like that," Cary said. "Or anyone, for that matter."

"C'mon, do you think she's that stupid?" Sebastien asked, laughing.

"It's not her fault," Tyler chimed in. "It's Tommy's."

"I'm going to fucking kill him," Sebastien said.

"No you're not." Cary rubbed his chin. "I've been on the phone with Porter all week—"

"Fucking asshole," Sebastien added.

"I've got you saying that in an email." Tyler grinned at her former boss.

"Tommy's being fired as we speak," Cary said. "But we agreed to keep it quiet for the sake of the agency. Porter will manage me going forward."

"He's not a manager," Sebastien said.

"The last time I checked, you didn't need a certification." Cary sounded serious, like when he gave her ex-boyfriend shit at the bar in Austin.

"Please. I'll do anything," Sebastien begged.

Cary shook his head. "It's a done deal, but just so you won't fuck with anyone, I'm letting you keep your commissions on everything from the past twenty years." He raised a finger. "If I hear you're fucking around, Porter gets my back catalog and you'll be cut out of everything."

"Be nicer to the interns," Tyler added. "Or I'll find them placements before I leave here." She stood from her seat. "As I was saying . . ." She locked eyes with Sebastien and he stared at her blankly. "Fuck you and fuck the Quebec Nordiques. I hope they never get another team."

Yeah, that's right, I said it.

After Tyler stormed out of Sebastien's office she packed up a few last things. She couldn't believe the amount of junk—mostly CDs, lanyards, and laminates—she'd accumulated over the years. What was she going to do? Display her delegate passes like a collection of conquests?

A few minutes later there was a knock at her door.

"What?" she snapped.

The door inched open and Cary asked, "Have you got a minute?"

"Rory's at home," she told him. "In case you were wondering."

"I was." He took a seat. "I—"

"Are you okay? I've been worried, and you didn't call me back."

He nodded. "Sorry, I didn't mean to worry you. I had some business to take care of in Winnipeg, and you said you needed space. I should've texted, but you hurt my feelings."

"I know." She hung her head. "I'm sorry about that. I was upset about the baby, and I didn't want to do the long-distance thing." She drew her gaze up to his eyes. "What business did you have in Winnipeg?"

"That's why I flew out here the other day. I mean, other than to see you. You know that house we passed by on Wellington? The Lounts' old house?"

"Yeah. I love that place."

"Well, I put in a lowball offer and they accepted it, so I wanted to see if we should close on the deal."

"Why did you put in an offer?"

"So, we could live there." He leaned forward in his seat. "But if you don't want to, or if you've changed your mind, that's okay. I bought it anyway, and I'll use it as an investment property."

She rolled her eyes. "You can't buy me a house, Cary."

"I didn't." He smirked. "I bought it for Rory."

"Funny," she said, shaking her head.

"You can't be mad at me for giving you what you want." He'd made a good point, but what about what *he* wanted? He was used to living a spectacular life in LA.

"Do you want to live in Winnipeg?" she asked, voice skeptical.

"I'd live in this office if it meant being with you."

"As you can see, I'm packing my shit." She pointed to the boxes. "Besides, Sebastien would charge us market rent or higher to live here."

He laughed. "I'm proud of you for leaving."

"Thanks. I'm proud of me, too."

"Babe—"

"Can I say something first?" He nodded, so she continued, "I'm sorry I have trust issues, but I really do love you."

"I love you too." He stood to hug her. "You know, I'm not perfect either, but I'd never cheat on you."

"You may not be perfect, but you're perfect for me." She met his gaze. "Are you sure you'll be happy in Winnipeg?"

"I know I'm not Mr. Manitoba, but if you're happy, I'm happy. And assuming you still want kids—"

"I do!"

He went on, "I want him to grow up with his family around, not on a tour bus."

"Or her family," she added. "Or those twins we talked about . . . oh, gross, I just remembered Tommy has a twin. I can't believe there are two of them."

"That's the last you'll see of him."

She flipped her middle finger. "Good riddance."

"Good riddance is right," Cary said. "I want Allie to be my new agent, but Porter doesn't want a conflict of interest with him being my manager."

"Today's your lucky day." She gave him a toothy grin. "She wants to leave the agency and come work with me and Kim."

"In Winnipeg?"

She nodded and resumed packing. "Did I mention my dad has season tickets to the Blue Bombers?"

"Football, right?" he asked, stacking boxes on her desk.

"Fifth row, center field," she confirmed.

"Speaking of Bert, does he know you're moving?"

"No." She shook her head. "I wanted to quit first."

"Maybe you should call him."

"I'll call Dylan. She's always on that pregnancy app that tells you how big your baby is in terms of fruit."

A few seconds later Dylan answered on FaceTime.

"What's up?" she asked, dunking a tea bag into a mug like a Yo-Yo.

Tyler stared at her sister, trying not to smile. "Are you able to run over to Dad's? I have some news."

Dylan turned her phone around. "No need. He's right here."

"Hi honey!" Bert waved with vigor.

"Cary's here too." She moved him into the frame. "We're coming home."

"Ugh," Dylan grunted with an eyeroll. "This weekend isn't great, Tyler. Nadie has rehearsal, Dad has a gig, and—"

"I mean for good."

Dylan's eyes jumped forward like a cue ball on a hard break. "What? When? How?"

"You forgot where and why," Tyler said.

"You can stay with me," Bert offered. "I've got tons of room."

Tyler tilted her head and smiled sweetly. "Thanks Dad, but we're moving into the Lounts' old house on Wellington."

"Yeah, that's not a house," her sister countered. "It's a mansion." She took a sip from her mug. "Why do you need a place that big?"

"It's my fault," Cary said. "I put in a lowball offer and they accepted it. I wanted somewhere she could have an office and my folks could visit."

Bert chuckled. "Sounds like I might be staying with you, then."

"Anytime, sir," he said. "Joe's family is more than welcome. I know your place gets crowded over Christmas."

Dylan's face lit up. "Welcome home, sis!"

After Tyler hung up the phone she asked Cary, "Are you sure about the office?"

"Sure I'm sure," he said. "The property's got a separate coach house. Two of them, actually."

"I insist on leasing the office space." She rested her hands on her hips. "I won't take no for an answer." But before he could argue Tyler's phone vibrated. It was Allie on FaceTime.

"Are you ready for this?" Allie asked, and she nodded. "Fucking Tommy got fired, man. They just told us in the boardroom."

"Really?" Tyler asked, not letting on that she knew. "I guess that means Cary needs a new agent."

Cary waved at Allie on the screen. "You want the gig?"

"Fuck yeah I do!" she said.

"I'm excited about this," Cary said. "Tommy's been my agent since I was a kid."

Tyler pointed her phone at the boxes on her desk. "I'm packing my shit."

Allie wrinkled her nose. "Where are you going?"

"We have an office in Winnipeg, and we're keeping our bands." She held up her phone. "So, are you in?"

"I'm all the fuck in."

We are the champions.

CARY

It took another hour to pack up Tyler's office, but they'd thrown away most of her stuff. She wanted to start her new company with a clean slate, nothing SDM-related, except for her stapler. Apparently it was the old kind, good and sturdy.

Tyler stared at Cary with her pupils dilated. "It's your turn," she said.

"My turn for what?" he asked.

"To tell your parents we're moving home." She picked up a banker's box by its slits. "I'm going down to the garage. Be back in a minute."

He phoned his mom instead of texting.

"Hi, Cary," Pamela said. "What a nice surprise! How are you, dear?"

"I'm fine, thanks. How are you guys?"

"Same old around here. The Burnsides next door put up a new shed, and it's taller than what the by-law allows so your father's down at city hall trying to fight it." She sighed. "Some people."

"Well, Mom, I've got some news—"

"Is everything okay, Cary?" She sounded concerned.

"Better than okay." He paused. "Tyler and I are moving to Winnipeg." The phone went dead on the other end. "Mom?"

Pamela sobbed like he was coming home from the war, and her voice trembled when she finally spoke. "That's the best news I've ever heard."

Cary had no doubt that he'd made the right decision. Tyler was happy and his mom was even happier—the two most important women in the world. His dad would be pleased to hear the news, but he wouldn't say anything, being an Englishman.

CHAPTER 23

Over the next three weeks, Tyler, Allie, and Kim were busy setting up their new company, and with Bob Shaw's help they'd filed for KAT Management's articles of incorporation with the Province of Manitoba. The women organized the structure of their company according to everyone's strengths. Tyler handled the day-to-day management, Allie took care of the live performance end, and Kim pulled her weight by tour-managing Yestown. Cary's shows were ending in two months, and Kim said that she was looking forward to joining her colleagues in Winnipeg and moving in with her boyfriend.

They'd also signed Yestown to a major deal with Warner Records Canada. The record label's new president was a woman. It only made sense.

And Tyler had finally earned a commission.

Cary's hands were full with curating the photographs for his WAG exhibit. He'd told Tyler that he'd barely recognized himself in some of the old pictures, but that was nonsense. He hadn't aged a day. Maybe when they moved in together she'd find a picture like Dorian Gray's.

And if that wasn't enough they were trying to have a baby again. Little pangs of uncertainty had surfaced from time to time but she'd managed to squash them. Cary may have once been her fantasy, but now he was her reality. And the fact that he'd bought their place in Winnipeg solidified his commitment, even though a smaller, less expensive place would have been more prudent.

After Tyler packed up most of her apartment she assembled a wardrobe box in the middle of her bedroom. She and Cary had been staying at his penthouse because her place was full of boxes and was much shittier.

"Let me help you with that," Cary offered, grabbing one end of the cardboard.

"I've got it, thanks." She shooed him away.

"What can I pack?" he asked, rubbing his hands together.

"I think you should leave it to me."

He smirked. "I know how to pack, babe."

"It's not the same as packing a suitcase," she said, folding the box according to the instructions. "How many times have you done this?" He rubbed his chin, pausing for a bit, and she gave him a lopsided grin. "Exactly. I've moved six times since I've been here."

"Please let me hire movers."

She shook her head. "If you want something done right, you have to do it yourself. Besides, Vegas is coming by later to help with the heavy stuff."

"Can't you leave the furniture here?"

"I'm using some of it in the new office." She folded the flaps of the cardboard inward. "The rest I'm giving to charity."

"I'm not really comfortable with you driving alone."

She glanced at her dog. "Ror-Ror will keep me company, won't you, buddy?" His tail wagged ever so slightly. "When I drove out here it only took two days."

He sighed. "I wish I could help but I've got that show tomorrow."

"I know. I'll just see you in Winnipeg. Don't worry about it." She finished assembling the wardrobe box by securing a metal bar on each end. "Besides, if you really want to help you can take you know who to the b-e-a-c-h. I think he's depressed."

Rory hadn't been to the office in three weeks, and he was sulking around the apartment.

"Who wants to go to the beach?" Cary asked, holding the dog's leash.

Rory sprinted to the door with a look like, *What are you waiting for?*

A ding chimed from Tyler's phone. It was an email from Yestown's record label.

"Oh my god!" she cried.

"What?" Cary's eyes popped out like a cartoon character.

"Yestown's song was the most added at radio this week."

"Really?"

"Yeah, and it looks like you might have that number one after all." She started texting. "I have to tell Kim and Allie."

"I'm happy for them," he said. "But—"

"There's a but?" She glanced up from her phone and frowned.

"I want my own number one," he said. "I'm recording Bert's song, the Christmas one. I want it ready in time for the holidays."

"I didn't realize you were releasing it as a single. I know how you feel about playing other people's music."

"It's not a cover, babe. It's never been released."

She blinked into work mode. "My dad doesn't have a publishing deal to collect his royalties. God, I don't even think that song is registered." She got back on her phone. "I'll get him set up with ASCAP, and I'll ask your publisher for a single song deal, okay?"

"What would I do without you?"

She shrugged. "Hopefully you'll never find out."

Reggie told you to put a ring on it.

By the time Cary and Rory had returned from the beach, Tyler's bedroom was packed. Her life seemed so small stacked in cardboard boxes, but the lack of space and budget had forced her to downsize with every move. Truth be told, it was fine by her since she hated clutter and tchotchkes and non-functional items. The only stuff she kept, other than her clothes and toiletries, were the photos of her family, an impressive vinyl collection, and a signed edition of *All You Need to Know About the Music Business* by Donald S. Passman.

"Good job," Cary said, admiring the boxed-up room.

"How was your walk?" she asked.

"Great. Sorry we took so long but Rory had to say hi to everyone. It's funny . . . when I'm walking him no one looks up." The light shone through the window at a perfect angle, catching the gold specks in his eyes. "I feel well-rested, like a normal person," he added.

"Just think how you'll feel after August," she said. "Are you sure you won't get bored?"

He shook his head. "I'm going to write and get back into taking pictures. Putting this exhibit together has really piqued my interest. But I haven't asked . . . will you miss it here? I mean, I know you won't miss Vancouver's hockey team."

"Only the weather and truffle popcorn," she said. "Oh, and Vij's, I suppose."

"We can get Indian food in Winnipeg." She flashed open her eyes and smiled. "And we'll find you some truffle popcorn," he said. "Any regrets about moving here?"

"None," she said. "If I didn't come here I wouldn't have you . . . or Rory, for that matter."

Vegas came by later with Kim and loaded the U-Haul while Tyler checked her apartment to make sure that she hadn't forgotten anything. She stood in the middle of the empty living room and took one last gander.

"So long Vancouver." She air-kissed her apartment and waved. *Bye, bye, bye.*

CARY

"Thanks for helping," Cary said to Vegas as they stood in front of Tyler's apartment building. "Sorry again for having to reschedule everything."

"No problem, man," Vegas said. "It was worth it—fucking Tommy getting fired." Vegas pointed at the women laughing about something. "Just look at them." He turned to Cary and hung his head. "I owe you an apology."

"For what?"

Vegas scratched his face. "For saying you weren't cut out for this with Tyler. I've known you for a long time and this is the happiest I've seen you."

Cary took a few steps backward, motioning for his friend to follow him.

"What's up?" Vegas asked.

"I'm going to ask her to marry me. And I want you to be my best man."

Vegas turned his head and wiped his eyes. "Fuck, man, give a guy a little warning the next time."

"That's the thing, Vegas. There won't be a next time." Cary patted his friend on the back. "Is that a yes?"

"Of course it is, man."

CHAPTER 24

Two days later and a little worse for wear, Tyler pulled up to the gate on Wellington Crescent and pressed the intercom button. The Lounts had equipped their property with CCTV cameras around the perimeter, which was an excellent selling feature, according to Cary's realtor.

"Hi, babe," Cary greeted her over the speaker.

"We're here," she announced.

The gate buzzed open and she drove down the winding road with the *Downton Abbey* theme playing in her head. Did she deserve to live here? She didn't think so. Bragging Woman had been right about her being a lucky lady, that was for sure.

"It's a big driveway to shovel, isn't it, buddy?" she joked with Rory. After two days in the car she was talking to her dog more than usual. And unlike her family, Rory seemed to like the sound of her singing voice or at least that's what she'd told herself.

She parked in front of the limestone house—okay, mansion— and stepped out of her Tesla while Rory jumped down on the passenger's side. She stretched out her legs one at a time, taking in the panoramic view with deep breaths through her nostrils. The lawn was perfectly manicured with hedges along the sides and a variety of shrubbery she didn't know the names of. The coach houses were at the back, and an outdoor pool, tennis courts, and what looked like a putting green in front of tall trees backing onto the Assiniboine River.

Rich people things.

"What a dump," she said as Cary cut across the lawn from the main house.

"Rory!" he hollered, and the dog ran over to greet him. "How's my boy?"

"What about me?" She laughed. "Is this how it's going to be?"

He put down the miniature panda and hugged her. "I'm so glad you're here."

God, you smell good.

"How am I going to keep this house clean, Cary?" She could barely take it all in. It didn't seem real to her, like she was living in a dream.

"We have a cleaning service."

"We do?" She tilted her head and he smirked.

"How was your drive, by the way?"

"It cost me nothing to get here."

She unfastened Rory's harness and he zoomed around the property.

"He's really motoring," Cary said, throwing a tennis ball across the lawn.

"He's never had a yard, and now he's got a football pitch. So much for 'poor Rory.'"

Cary kissed her on the cheek. "Come inside."

"My stuff . . ." She pointed to the trailer.

"We'll get it later."

"Yeah, I need a shower."

"You look beautiful." He winked at her and raised an eyebrow. "And you know I like you dirty."

"Cary!" She tried to keep a straight face but couldn't.

She called Rory and he came instantly. The dog had the worst case of FOMO she'd ever seen, and that was saying something from someone who worked in the music industry.

"Welcome home." Cary lifted her off the ground.

"Put. Me. Down!" She kicked like an infant as he carried her over the threshold.

"Surprise!" he said, and she gasped. Her entire family stood in the foyer and Cary's too, plus Allie, Kim, and Vegas.

"Oh my god!" She tightened her topknot. "I look like shit."

"Yeah, join the club," Dylan said, holding her pregnant belly.

"I'd like everyone's attention, please." Cary said, passing glasses of champagne around like a rented Santa with gifts. He handed one to Tyler but she politely refused. She wasn't drinking while they were trying again, so she poured herself a glass of sparkling grape juice. He continued, "Thank you all for coming. We've officially moved to Winnipeg!"

Everyone cheered, clinking their glasses.

Cary grabbed her hand and steadied his gaze. "Babe, my favorite part of every day is when I learn something new about you. Like how you can't fall asleep if there are dirty dishes in the sink. And how your toast needs to be cut diagonally. And your favorite movie is the Metallica documentary. Which I'll admit is entertaining, but maybe not the best movie ever made. And I want to spend the rest of my life learning everything about you."

"Everything?" she asked. "Are you sure?"

Their guests laughed at her question and Cary chuckled, too, and then he presented a small velvet box perched on his palm before lowering to one knee. "It's already a yes from Bert and Rory, so what about making it—"

"A hat trick?" she asked, and another big laugh ensued. Maybe she'd missed her calling as a stand-up comedian, but probably not. It seemed like a lot of work.

Cary rolled his eyes as he opened the box, displaying an emerald-cut diamond ring. "Will you marry me?"

"Yes!" she cried, and he slipped the ring onto her shaking finger. It was a culmination of everything: her high school crush, her love of music, and being reunited with her family. It seemed like everything she'd been through was in preparation to become Mrs. Cary Kingston.

Again the room erupted with clapping and cheers.

Cary glanced at his fiancée's father. "I'd like to acknowledge Tyler's mother, Michelle. I hope she would've approved, sir."

"More than approved," Bert said, and her siblings nodded. "Raise 'em up!" He lifted his glass toward the sky and smiled. "To Michelle!"

The room echoed, "To Michelle!"

Everyone saluted.

"One more thing . . ." Cary handed her a brand-new Jets jersey.

"Thank you." She kissed him on the cheek. "I've always wanted one in blue."

"Look at the back."

She turned it around. It read: MRS. KINGSTON.

Pamela laughed and said, "Samesies!"

A few weeks later Tyler was simply exhausted, but it was understandable given the move, the new office, and setting up the Oh Claires' showcase in LA. The guest list was already at capacity and they still had to invite the press. The KAT Management team had discussed moving the girls' gig to a bigger venue, but they decided against it since creating a buzz was their primary objective.

When Tyler woke up that morning she could barely move; however, it was the grand opening of Cary's WAG exhibit later that evening so she couldn't very well stay in bed. She touched her forehead with the back of her hand, but her temperature seemed normal enough, as far as she could tell. Was it her period? She picked up her phone where she'd diarized her cycle.

No. It can't be true.

A little while later Cary arrived home from the WAG where he'd been working since the crack of dawn. He was adamant about putting the finishing touches on his exhibit. Everything had to be perfect.

"I'm home!" he said, and Rory sprinted down the hall.

"Cary?" Tyler hollered. "I need a plus one for tonight."

He walked into the kitchen and kissed her on the cheek. "It's been sold out for weeks." He grabbed an apple from the bowl on the island counter. "We're over capacity as it is."

She rephrased her statement. "I can't go without a plus one."

"What do you mean you can't go?"

"It will be physically impossible for me to go without a plus one."

"Well, who is it?" he asked, voice unsure.

"I don't know." She shrugged. "I haven't met him yet."

He held her hand and looked at her inquisitively. "You're not making any sense."

"My plus one's in here." She took his hand and placed it below her stomach.

He widened his eyes and straightened his back. "You're . . . ?"

"We're having a baby." She showed him the pregnancy test and laughed.

"We are?"

"I like this kid already," she said. "He's stealing your thunder."

"He?"

She nodded, rubbing her midsection. "It feels like a he. And you thought your biggest competition was Rory."

"Let's move up the wedding," he suggested.

She shook her head. "I don't want a wedding."

His eyes lowered to his feet. "Have you changed your mind about getting married?"

"No, not at all, but I don't want a circus wedding. I want to have a party instead." She smiled. "A surprise wedding."

"Sure, let's go for it."

"When?" She twisted her dazzling engagement ring, admiring the diamond. "According to your schedule, the only window open is July first weekend."

"Then, July first it is."

She raised her brow. "Canada Day?"

"What's more Canadian than getting married on July first?"

"It's two weeks away," she reminded him. "We won't be able to pull it off in time."

"Not with that attitude," he teased. "Babe, you've put tours together in less time, and we'll hire people."

"Okay. Let's do it." She tapped her lips. "Do you know what I was thinking?"

"Uh-oh . . ."

"Stop." She stilled her gaze. "I'm being serious."

"Okay, what?"

"You don't have to wear a ring. It will inhibit your guitar playing."

"Who am I? Fucking Tommy?" He shook his head. "I'd like to think I'm a little more skilled than that. Once it's on, it's on for good."

Later that evening at the WAG, Cary walked across the red carpet while Tyler beamed from the entrance. A story had leaked to the press about him buying a house in the area, but Winnipeggers generally minded their own business.

"Over here!" Allie whistled. She wore a white pantsuit with black Chuck Taylors. It was the most dressed up she'd ever been.

"You look great." Tyler gave her a hug.

"Thanks, man." Allie lifted the lapels on her jacket. "You don't look too shabby yourself."

"What? This old thing?" she said with a twirl. She wore a Jason Matlo black gown and candy-apple-red heels. She believed in supporting Canadian designers, just like her fiancé.

A few moments later Cary joined them and they walked into the WAG together.

"How are you settling in?" Cary asked Allie, waving at someone who shamelessly took his picture.

"I love it! My place is spacious, and everyone's nice here."

"Friendly Manitoba," Tyler added.

Allie stopped in her tracks and turned to Cary. "Hey man, I know you said you're not touring next year, but are you still open to doing one-offs and festivals?"

Cary glanced at the mother of his child. "Yeah, sure, if the timing's right."

"Good, because you're headlining Coachella." Allie grinned.

"Are you serious?" He hugged his agent. "Thanks Allie!"

"Just doing my job, man."

After Tyler and Cary said hello to the WAG board of directors, they stepped away from the crowd.

"Can you believe I'm hungry already?" she whispered.

"I've got you covered." He flagged down a server who was carrying a tray of miniature cardboard boxes.

"I don't feel like noodles," she said, holding her stomach. "Nothing spicy."

Cary lifted two boxes from the tray. "Open it."

"Truffle popcorn!" She picked up a piece and ate it. "How did you?"

He shrugged one shoulder. "I might know a guy."

A little while later Cary instructed the Robertsons, his parents, Allie, Kim, and Vegas to meet them in the lecture room of the WAG. He'd asked Tyler if she wanted to make the announcement, but she'd told him that she couldn't do it without breaking down.

"Thank you all for coming," Cary said, holding Tyler's hand. "This has been the best day of my life." Dylan's gaze darted to

Tyler, to Cary, then bounced between them. "We're having a baby!"

The room erupted with clapping and cheers.

"Get the fuck out of here!" Dylan said, pushing her sister. "Our kids are going to be like siblings."

She nodded. "Yeah, it's great timing."

"The not drinking part gets easier. It's good to give your liver a break once in a while. You know, it's your biggest organ."

Tyler looked at Cary across the room and lifted her eyebrows. "Well, it's not everyone's biggest organ." She gave her sister a cheeky grin.

"Really?" Dylan turned her head in Cary's direction. "Some guys have all the luck, don't they?" They burst out laughing, and Bert walked over.

"What's so funny, you two?" he asked.

"Nothing, Dad," they said.

"Liars." He shook his head as Cary joined them. "Thanks, son." Bert clenched a red paisley handkerchief in his hand, wiping the corners of his eyes with it. "Thanks for bringing my kid home."

"My pleasure, sir." He shook his hand. "I've got a favor to ask."

"Anything, son."

"I'm recording 'Happy Merry Christmas,' and I was wondering if you'd play on the track?"

Bert nodded emphatically. "I'd be honored."

After the baby announcement Tyler and Cary strolled around the exhibit. The photographs hung against the stark white walls: action shots, portraits, and her favorite—candid moments of her future husband. This was a side of Cary that she didn't know, and she smiled as they turned every corner.

"Why do they have red dots?" she asked. "Are you selling them?" It's not like he needed the money.

"I'm donating the proceeds to Bert's charity. It's just a small token of my appreciation." He squeezed her hand. "I still want to take your picture."

"Not now." She rubbed her non-existent belly. "I'm going to balloon." She pointed across the room. "Look at Dylan."

"*Especially* now that you're pregnant."

"It might be cool for him to see later, I guess." She lifted another box of truffle popcorn from the passing tray, grateful that her pregnancy hadn't turned her off truffle oil. She'd read that some pregnancies came with adverse reactions to all kinds of delicacies.

They continued walking around the exhibit while he explained each photograph in greater detail than what could fit onto the title cards. The past twenty years had been documented by some of the best photographers in the world, and the pictures Cary took stood up beside them.

"What's this?" he asked, staring at the back corner of the room.

"I don't know," she said, walking closer to the picture. It was a blown-up replica of his Junior hockey card, professionally framed and mounted.

His eyes narrowed. "Was this you?"

"Who's been keeping secrets?" she asked, squeezing his arm and trying to contain her laughter.

"Ow!" he said jokingly. "Sorry babe, but it's so cute when you explain the rules."

"I'll give you cute."

"Wait." His brow creased and he blinked. "How long have you known?"

"Quite a while," she admitted.

"Why didn't you say something?"

"I was waiting for the right moment." She gestured to his picture. "When this opportunity came along I couldn't resist."

"How did you . . . ?"

She waved at Cary's mother. "If you don't ask, you don't get."

Thanks, Pamela.

CARY

Cary lifted a glass of red wine from the high-top table. "Can you believe I'm going to be a dad?" he asked Vegas who held a beer in his hand.

"Congrats!" Vegas said, clinking his glass. "Are you nervous?"

"Hell yeah. I've never held a baby or changed a diaper."

Vegas chuckled. "I think you can afford a nanny, man."

"I don't think we're going to get one. I mean, I say that now." He laughed, nodding at a WAG board member who walked by. "That's part of the reason I'm taking some time off. Of course, I didn't know she was pregnant, but the timing is perfect. Tyler was born to be a mother and I couldn't be happier. As for you, Allie knows of a dozen tours you can jump on, and I'm keeping you on the payroll as insurance so you don't run off and join the circus."

Vegas took a sip of beer. "I have a couple offers."

Cary held his chest and gasped. "My body isn't even cold yet."

"Don't worry." Vegas put his hand on Cary's shoulder. "I wouldn't let anyone else be your TM, except for Kim." He pulled back his hair. "Hey, should I get a suit for your wedding?"

Cary stepped closer to his best man. "You can wear whatever you want, but I'm swearing you to secrecy. Not even Kim knows. We're getting married on July first."

"That's in two weeks!" Vegas said, eyes bugging out.

Cary clinked his glass. "I'm not a patient man."

CHAPTER 25

The next day Tyler went over to her sister's house and told her about their wedding plans.

"You're getting married, when?" Dylan asked, stunned.

"July first," Tyler repeated. "But we're not telling anyone. The invitations will say it's a barbecue or something—evites, since we're in a time crunch."

"What about the gifts?" Dylan opened her sewing kit. "You aren't even registered."

She shook her head. "We don't want anything."

"Turn around." Dylan wrapped a tape measure around Tyler's waist.

"If you don't have time to make my dress I can buy something off the rack."

"Don't be silly," she said. "Slip dresses are easy. It'll be done by the time you're back from LA."

The Oh Claire's showcase was next week, and Tyler and Allie were heading south. Unfortunately Kim couldn't make it because Cary had a show, but they'd promised her that they'd record the girls' set so she wouldn't feel left out.

"Thanks, I really appreciate it," Tyler said. "I've got something new, something borrowed, and something blue. I just need something old." She pursed her lips and stared at the ceiling.

"Here." Dylan twisted the silver ring from her pinky finger. "It's Mom's wedding band. I took it off my ring finger when my hand started to swell."

She gasped and clutched her chest. "I couldn't."

"It's tradition." Dylan slipped the ring onto her sister's finger. "It goes back generations on Mom's side of the family. They wear it on their right hand in the Netherlands."

"But it's yours."

"It's yours now." Dylan rubbed her bare finger. "I've worn it long enough. Dad told me everyone who wears this ring has a happy marriage. I know I sure have."

"Thank you." She wiped the tears on her cheeks and hugged her sister.

"Of course." Dylan flared out the fabric on her skirt. "Should I wear a dress, or a tent, in my case?"

"Just wear your normal clothes. I'm changing right after the ceremony."

"What ceremony?" Joe asked, entering the room.

"Cary and I are getting married before I blimp out," she said, then looked at Dylan. "No offense."

"None taken." Dylan scribbled notes on a scrap piece of paper.

Tyler turned to Joe and smiled. "I was wondering if you might want to officiate the wedding?"

Joe's eyes softened. "I'd love to," he said, choking up. "It would mean the world to me."

The following Thursday Tyler and Allie checked into the Hollywood Roosevelt Hotel. The Oh Claires' showcase was later that evening and their meetings weren't until the next day, so they put on their bathing suits and headed out to the Tropicana pool area, where they found two lounge chairs side by side without towels, the universal sign they weren't taken.

"My phone's blowing up," Allie said, squinting from the sun.

"Just turn it off." Tyler pulled down the brim of her floppy hat. "The guest list is already full."

"I'm not even sure how this happened." Allie held her phone to show her, but there was too much of a glare on her screen to see. "I know they're good but this is unprecedented."

"People in LA love gossiping," she said. "Plus the ASCAP people know everyone, and—"

"Hey!" a woman's voice shouted from across the pool. Tyler and Allie sat up and shielded their eyes.

"Kim! Oh my god. What are you doing here?" Tyler asked, surprised at seeing her bestie.

"Fuck me, it's hot as balls out here." Kim lifted her sunglasses and smiled. "Cary insisted, so I took the first flight I could find out of Branson."

"You were in Branson?" Allie asked. "You should've gone to the Titanic museum."

"Dude, I've never even seen that movie." Tyler and Allie stared at each other through their sunglasses. "And that song is awful." Kim sat beside Tyler on her lounge chair. "I thought we'd have some girl time, like, before you get married and shit."

"Do you have a wedding date?" Allie asked, thumbs busy on her phone.

Tyler shook her head instead of lying outright, and asked, "Are you guys coming to our Canada Day party?"

"Fuck yes," Allie said and Kim nodded. "I wouldn't miss it." She took a sip of water from her Klean Kanteen. "Do you think you'll change your name when you get married?"

Tyler sighed. "I've always wanted to be Mrs. Cary Kingston, but then I'd be his wife instead of him being my husband, so I don't think I will."

"I'd fucking never, dude."

"You're anti-marriage," Tyler reminded her.

"Yeah, I wouldn't either," Allie agreed. "It seems so antiquated. Like some sort of ownership. And hyphenating is pretentious."

Tyler uncrossed her legs and applied sunscreen to her stomach. "I wonder if the baby knows it's hot outside. I keep thinking this cream is going to seep into his eyes. I mean, it's weird to think I might have a dick growing inside me."

"I wish I had a dick inside me," Allie said, and they burst out laughing while a few older people in the pool area shook their heads.

Mind your own business.

"You won't even go on a date, dude."

Tyler snorted. "Like you should talk." Kim put her shades back on. "Before Vegas and Cary we both took extended dick vacations." She turned to Allie. "What are you looking for? I know some nice guys in Winnipeg. Mostly divorced but not too damaged."

Allie removed her sunglasses and tousled her shaggy hair. "Smart and independent. We do enough babysitting. That's why the music industry chicks in Toronto are in love with—"

"George!" Tyler and Kim said, and they burst out laughing.

"I have an idea," Tyler said.

"Like we aren't busy enough," Kim replied.

"That's just it." Tyler paused. "We need some help in the office."

"Who were you thinking?" Allie asked, thumbs back on her phone.

"Lara."

"What the fuck?" Kim rubbed her ears. "Are you joking?"

"I'm not." Tyler lowered her head. "I feel responsible. I should've warned her about fucking Tommy. I want to mentor her, and she can stay in Vancouver and work remotely."

"We can't let that happen, man." Allie said to Kim. "We can't let Sebastard ruin her career."

"Fine," Kim said.

Allie picked up her phone. "I know, I know. It's a sickness." She put on her sunglasses. "We have a lot of press coming tonight."

Tyler removed her hat. "I can hear the comparisons right now . . . L7, The Runaways . . ."

"Hole," Kim added.

"Exactly," Tyler said. "All girl bands, even though they don't sound like any of them. Why don't we do it ourselves—the comparisons—tell people they're like Jane's Addiction meets Foo Fighters?"

"I'm down with that," Allie said, texting away. "I'm still bummed about that drummer, man."

"So am I, dude." Kim pursed her lips. "Taylor Hawkins was the fucking best."

After the women ate dinner at the hotel, they walked down Hollywood Boulevard toward the Hotel Cafe as the *Sex and the City* music played in Tyler's head. They'd done it. They were officially KAT Management, and they even had business cards with QR codes to prove it.

At seven p.m. sharp, and with a full house in attendance, the Oh Claires plugged in their instruments.

"Isn't that Porter?" Tyler shouted over the music.

Porter Reynolds wasn't on their guest list, but as the president of a global booking agency he could easily get into any venue.

Allie smirked. "At the Hotel Cafe? I doubt it."

The Clark Kent lookalike approached them and smiled. "Hi Allie, Tyler."

"Hi!" Tyler shook Porter's hand, winking at Allie. "I thought that was you."

"Porter!" Allie hugged him until his throat cleared. "Oh, sorry." She let go and straightened his tie. Porter wore the same thing every day like a uniform: black pants, black shirt, black tie. "What are you doing here?"

Porter adjusted his glasses. "I came to see the band, figuring you'd be here."

"Hey dude!" Kim raised her bottle of water, clueing in he was there.

"Hi Kim." Porter gave her a half smile, then turned to Allie. "I've been talking to the labels. There's a lot of interest now that Sebastien's out of the picture. Americans don't have time for his nonsense."

"Nonsense," Tyler repeated, laughing at the euphemism. She took a sip of club soda through a paper straw that was quickly disintegrating. "Are you coming to our Canada Day party?"

"As Cary's new manager, I should probably be there," Porter said. "I guess I'll have to wear something"—he grabbed his tie—"more festive."

"Did you do this?" Allie asked, gesturing to the packed room.

"You found them," Porter said. "I might've made a few calls."

"Why are you helping us?" Allie asked point blank.

"I'd like to partner with KAT Management. To represent your bands outside of Canada."

The women smiled at each other, knowing the offer was good—okay, *great.*

"Cary's off the table," Allie said, negotiating the terms. "We'll discuss the US on a case-by-case basis."

"Do you want the Oh Claires for the States?" Tyler asked.

"I want them for the world, but I'll take what I can get." Porter shook Allie's hand. "I should never have let you go."

Allie held the handshake. "Then don't."

"Can I get you ladies a drink?" Porter asked, tightening his tie, cheeks flushed.

Tyler and Kim shook their heads.

"I could use a drink," Allie said, dragging him to the bar.

"Dude, did you see that?"

Tyler lifted the soggy straw from her glass and crumpled it into her hand. "She was looking for someone smart—"

"And she got Superman."

"He's totally Clark Kent!"

Kim laughed, and they listened to the Oh Claires blow the roof off the place.

"Hey, I need to tell you something." Tyler said. "But you have to swear on Rory's life you won't say anything."

"Dude, I know. You're pregnant."

"Funny. I wasn't going to say anything, but since Vegas knows—"

"Knows what?" Kim asked, leaning in.

"That's why I'm asking if people are coming on Canada Day. We're getting married, Kim, but we're not having a bridal party or anything."

"Get. The. Fuck. Out!" Kim hugged her bestie. "I'm so happy for you!"

"It's a surprise." She lifted a finger to her lips. "We're only telling Dylan, Joe, and Vegas—and now you."

"What about Bert?"

She rolled her eyes. "My dad hasn't met a microphone he didn't like."

"True," Kim said. "Vegas . . . fuck, that guy can keep a secret, can't he? It's no wonder he's so good at poker. That's how he got his nickname."

I knew it.

CARY

"Kim knows about the wedding," Cary told Vegas as they were having drinks at the Hilton hotel. Vegas had rented the lounge for the musicians and crew because everything closed early in Branson. And without Sebastien pinching every penny, Vegas finally had the means to keep everyone happy.

"That's good, man." Vegas said. "I hate keeping secrets from her. Did Tyler say how the showcase went?"

Cary looked at his phone. "Straight fire. I'm assuming that's good."

Vegas laughed. "It's weird not having Kim around."

"She'll be back tomorrow," Cary assured him.

Vegas glanced over his shoulder. "I can't believe you're getting married next week, man. Any wedding jitters?"

Cary took a sip of wine and shook his head. "None."

"What do your parents think about you getting married?"

"My folks? Well, my dad said it's about time"—he snickered—"and my mom can't stop crying. That's why I can't tell them about the wedding. I don't trust my mom with her bridge group and unlimited bottles of white wine."

CHAPTER 26

A professional knows when to call a professional, so Tyler hired an army of event planners to help with their Canada Day party. The biggest challenge was finding a framed tent large enough to accommodate three hundred guests. Fifty from Joe's side alone had RSVP'd yes.

Cary didn't want to spare any expense on their wedding day, so he'd told her that their budget was nonexistent; however, she'd been trying to reimburse him for her Tesla, so she used her record advance and merchandise commissions to pay for the wedding. She always made good on her promises, and he should have known better.

A few minutes before six p.m. on Canada Day, Cary knocked on their bedroom door.

"Ready?" he asked, voice hopeful.

"Ready," Tyler said before opening the door.

"Wow." Cary clutched his chest, jaw hanging open. "I'm a lucky guy."

"I'm the lucky one, remember?" She winked at her soon-to-be husband. "You don't look too bad yourself." He wore a white shirt and a new navy suit that he'd commissioned from the awards show designer.

Tyler inhaled a few shallow breaths, adjusting the straps on her slip dress.

"Are we good?" Cary asked, raising his eyebrows.

"We're good." She rubbed her stomach. "I'm glad the baby gets to join us."

"The whole family," Cary laughed.

She turned around and whistled for Rory, but he barely lifted his head from the bed. They'd made him the ring bearer but it didn't look like he gave a shit. "Rory Robertson!"

Cary held up a finger. "I know you're not changing your name, but our dog is." He walked into their bedroom and addressed him as "Rory Kingston."

Rory jumped down from the bed.

"There," she said, snapping his harness together. Dylan had sewn a pocket into the lining of Rory's harness where their wedding rings were kept.

"All set?" Cary asked.

She smiled, waving her white and navy bouquet. "Let's do this."

Cary nodded and tapped on his phone. "I'll cue the music."

They laughed as the *Hockey Night in Canada* theme played throughout the house and into the backyard. It was hardly Wagner's "Bridal Chorus," but they couldn't think of a more appropriate tune for their wedding march.

Cary held his fiancée's hand as they stepped down the stairs, Rory heeling by their feet, but a whiff of barbecue hit them, and the dog darted down the steps in a flash of black and white. FOMO had overtaken him.

"Rory!" Tyler shouted, but it was a lost cause, so they continued.

Nadie stood in the kitchen, jaw unhinged. "Holy shit, Auntie Ty!"

Tyler smiled. "Holy shit is right, Nadie."

As Tyler and Cary walked arm in arm into the tent, they smiled at each other. Everything was just as she'd planned it.

The white linen drapes cascaded to the ground and the matching chair coverings and napkins tied the room together, although they would need to be laundered from sticky fingers and hot sauce. An assortment of white flowers—roses, peonies, and lilies—filled the air like a botanical garden. No. The garden was more magical than botanical.

A fairy tale if there ever was one.

Tyler nodded as she made her way down the makeshift aisle, taking note of people's reactions.

Bert wiped his eyes with his handkerchief.

Pamela cried into John's shoulder while he handed her a napkin.

Perry, Stewart, and their wives shushed her nephews.

Kim jumped up and down, her pink hair bouncing.

Allie and Porter held hands. He wore black shorts and a black polo shirt—not a shocker.

Marnie and Heather cheered like the Jets had won game seven.

Bob Shaw raised a glass of non-alcoholic whatever.

And Rory ran around the tent greeting everyone like he was the master of ceremonies.

Once Dylan and Vegas took their places on either side of the bride and groom, Joe stepped forward and raised his arms. "Surprise!" he bellowed in his deep, baritone voice. "Please take your seats. He looked at Vegas. "Do you have the rings?"

Cary's best man tried to grab Rory but the dog thought it was a game and dashed outside.

"Fuck." Vegas shook his head. "Cookie!" he called out, and everyone laughed at his predicament.

A few seconds later Rory zipped back into the tent and sat by Vegas's feet, waiting for his treat.

"I'll hook you up later, buddy," Vegas promised him, removing the wedding rings from his harness without honoring his word.

Rory barked in a loud, "*Woof!*"

"Rory!" Tyler said laughing. "I didn't know you could bark!"

Of course, on my wedding day. Show off.

"Please take your seats," Joe said again. "Cary, your vows are first."

Cary held Tyler's hand and flashed his famous smile. "Well, babe, I promise to cheer for the Jets and the Blue Bombers." Everyone laughed as the husbands booed. "But seriously, I promise to be the best dad to our baby. And to Rory. And I promise to put us first. Always. You're my everything."

Vegas passed the rings.

"Do you take Tyler Robertson to be your wife?" Joe asked.

Cary smiled. "I do."

"Tyler?" Joe probed.

She held Cary's hand and took a deep breath. "I promise to listen, even though you're all talk. And I promise to tell you when I don't like your songs." Everyone laughed while Dylan sobbed beside her. "I promise to be the best mom to our baby. And to Rory. And I promise to put us first. Always. You're a national treasure, after all."

Cary laughed, shaking his head. "What am I going to do with you?"

Marry me!

"Do you take Cary Kingston to be your husband—"

"I do!" she cried.

Joe blessed the couple with burning white sage—a tradition from the Cree First Nations used for positive energy—and declared, "I now pronounce you husband and wife. You may kiss the bride."

And Cary did as he was told.

After an hour of wedding pictures the bride and groom headed upstairs to change into more comfortable clothes.

"We did it!" Cary said, walking into their bedroom. "I've got an idea."

"Uh-oh," she teased.

"Maybe I should take your picture?"

"We just had a million pictures taken, Cary."

"You were holding your bouquet." He mimicked her, clasping his hands in front of his waist.

"I was trying to hide my bump." She pulled her dress taut against her belly. "I started showing a few days ago."

"I'm aware." He held onto her hips. "I thought you were beautiful before, but I'm talking about pictures of your bare belly."

"Are you trying to get me naked?"

"Always." He slipped off the strap of her dress from her shoulder.

"Cary!" She moved his hand away. "We have guests."

"We haven't consummated our marriage yet." He circled her nipples through her silk dress. "But we can wait."

"No we can't." She pressed her mouth onto his and sucked Penfolds Grange from his tongue. If this was the only way she could drink for the next few months, she'd gladly deal with it.

"I know they're tender." He cupped her breasts. "I'll be gentle."

"Don't even think about it." She helped him pull the dress over her head and unfastened her strapless bra.

"I can't believe they're going to get bigger," he said, gazing at her breasts.

"Believe it." He wrapped his mouth around her right breast and lightly stroked the left. With both nipples fully erect, he placed soft kisses down her chest and stopped at her stomach. "Are you weirded out?" she asked.

Laughing, he glanced up at her. "Babe . . ." He moistened his lips. "Nothing could keep me away from this." He undressed to his boxer-briefs and inched down her satin thong, throwing it across the room. "I love you, Mrs. Kingston."

"I love you too, Mr. Robertson."

Their guests might have been waiting outside, but he took his time, sweeping light strokes along her sex. "See, I can do this with my ring on," he said, slipping his finger inside her wetness.

"Aren't you talented."

"You ain't seen nothin' yet." He removed his boxer briefs. "I'm going to fuck you until you beg me to stop."

"Maybe we shouldn't . . ." She rubbed her belly. "The baby?"

"What?" He laughed. "Do you think he's going to see my dick?"

"It's pretty hard to miss."

When Tyler and Cary arrived back at the tent the Robertsons and KAT Management's artists were playing a cover song while everyone danced.

She gave her husband a toothy smile. "What could be better than this?"

"Just wait and see." Cary picked up a guitar and clamped on the Humbler's capo.

"What the . . ." Her voice broke off as he walked across the stage.

Cary grabbed the microphone from its stand. "This one's for you, Tyler Robertson. It's called 'Everything,' and I wrote it for you last Christmas."

Through the opening in the tent she gazed at the stars and smiled. This song would be his next hit. Her birthday wish had come true.

This is it.

EPILOGUE

Later that year Cary reached the top of the charts with two number one songs. "Happy Merry Christmas" had all but guaranteed its place as a holiday standard, and Bert would never have to work again. But like Cary he loved playing music, so that's what he did.

Leonard "Lenny" Kingston was born on Valentine's Day. They named him after the Humbler. Lenny had his dad's bright hazel eyes and his mom's dimples, and it was everything Tyler had hoped for, but she still couldn't believe it.

Cary's parents had practically moved into their guest house, and there was more than enough room for Bert and the Grants. Dylan and Joe had named their son Hassun, "Hass" for short, a Cree name meaning "stone." Tyler and Cary had refused to hire a nanny, so they were grateful for the extra help. Dylan had to admit that buying the property was a good idea and she gladly ate her words.

Rory was just as happy as his parents. Not only did he have a yard to play in but he had a brother to share nap time with. But little did the miniature panda know what would be in store when Lenny started walking. Playing chase was Rory's favorite.

Except for Coachella—which was a smashing success—and a few corporate gigs, Cary took a full year off from touring to spend time with Lenny. He relished being a father, and it ignited a fire inside him. Tyler loved hearing her husband singing around the house. Sometimes she thought it was the radio, then remembered they didn't own one.

KAT Management Inc. had all its artists signed, including Nadie, a double threat. She was starring in an upcoming feature film, and her album debuted at number one with a bullet. Allie and Kim couldn't have been better business partners, or better friends. The women worked hard and laughed even harder, and Tyler was having fun again.

Living in the middle of the country had also made Vegas's life easier. He'd joined another tour, but his schedule had allowed him to fly home between gigs to hang out with his girlfriend. Kim and Vegas would eventually have children, but for now babysitting Lenny took care of their itch.

Allie and Porter had a long-distance relationship, which suited them just fine. They'd become a power couple in the music industry, and conferences from around the world paid thousands of dollars for their keynote addresses. Allie, of course, insisted on top billing.

Tommy was still an agent, but now he sold real estate in West Vancouver. It had been a relatively easy transition for him since he already owned the suits. He was in his element, showing rich divorcées houses and telling them stories ad nauseam. At least he wasn't creeping on girls half his age. His clients were middle-aged or older.

Bob Shaw had finally retired to Salt Spring Island, but he worked for Cary and KAT Management a few days a week providing financial services. He'd met a wonderful woman at one of his support group meetings, and she'd been sober for longer than him.

Sebastien was the only person left at his management company. He still had his heritage acts, but without Cary he had trouble keeping the lights on at SDM.

Cary Kingston had done the impossible: he'd failed to make the Most Eligible Bachelors list for the first time in two decades.

And nothing made him happier.

Printed in Great Britain
by Amazon

47775104R00189